ALTERED

CREWEL WORLD: BOOK TWO

ALTERED

GENNIFER ALBIN

SQUARE
FISH

FARRAR STRAUS GIROUX
NEW YORK

SQUARE
FISH

An Imprint of Macmillan
175 Fifth Avenue
New York, NY 10010
macteenbooks.com

Square Fish and the Square Fish logo are trademarks of Macmillan and are used
by Farrar Straus Giroux under license from Macmillan.

Square Fish books may be purchased for business or promotional use. For
information on bulk purchases, please contact the Macmillan Corporate and
Premium Sales Department at (800) 221-7945 x5442 or by e-mail at
specialmarkets@macmillan.com.

Library of Congress Cataloging-in-Publication Data
Albin, Gennifer.
        Altered / Gennifer Albin.
            pages cm. — (Crewel world ; book 2)
        Summary: Sixteen-year-old Adelice Lewys is called upon to harness her
    power in a battle for control of Earth, but as she uncovers the truth about her
    own history she learns that everyone holds secrets, some of which may drive
    her from her love, Jost, into his brother Erik's arms.
        ISBN 978-1-250-05073-1 (paperback) / ISBN 978-0-374-31645-7 (e-book)
        [1. Science fiction.]   I. Title.

PZ7.A3224Alt 2013   [Fic]—dc23   2013011140

Originally published in the United States by Farrar Straus Giroux
First Square Fish Edition: 2014
Book designed by Elizabeth Clark
Square Fish logo designed by Filomena Tuosto

10 9 8 7 6 5 4 3 2 1

AR: 5.2 / LEXILE: 740L

To Kalen,
who always keeps the light on

"For know there are two worlds of life and death . . ."
—Percy Bysshe Shelley, *Prometheus Unbound*

ALTERED

PROLOGUE

THEY ABANDONED EARTH. MEN LEFT THEIR HOMES and their shops. They deserted the streets to crack and scatter into the soil, renouncing dominion over the world and rejecting their own progress for the promise of the new and the next. And so Earth sits in splendid ruin.

On the horizon a metro rises in grotesque majesty, and behind us the ocean roars with life. Above us the sky twists and turns to watch us—an evolution of stars and light. I know little of this world, but hope gathers in my chest. This is our first chance. Maybe our only one.

Life.

Possibility.

Choice.

I'd been taught there was one reality: a reality guided and overseen and created by others. But standing on the edge of the past, I feel potential coursing through me. The natural strands of life are free here, glorious and unrestrained. Time slides around and wraps me in its protection. Anything can happen, and I feel the pulsing vitality of this truth in my arms and in my aching hands. Loricel was wrong about Earth and what it represents. She told me it was dead, a half-remembered relic of a different time, but this world isn't doomed.

It's waiting for me.

ONE

A SHIP'S BEACON SWEEPS OVERHEAD, BATHING US in light. My hand stretches out as though to beckon the ship toward us, but I draw my hand back to shield my eyes, fear supplanting the brief thrill of knowing we are not alone on this planet. Fear the Guild has cultivated in me since they took me from my family. It is more powerful than the hope growing roots within me.

The hull of the ship is bloated and torpid, making its flight a reluctant crawl across the sky. It doesn't change course when it coasts over us, and although the brilliance of the watchlight fades past us, blood pounds through me, reminding me of one thing: even a world away from Arras, where no one has reason to harm me, I'm not safe. But I understand now what I couldn't before. My parents were wrong about me. They taught me to hide my gift.

But my hands are my salvation, not my curse.

I watch the ship ride low along the skyline, skimming across the glittering night sky. If it stays on its current trajectory, it will collide with the mountain range nestled against the metro I spy on the horizon.

"Did it see us?" Jost whispers as though the pilot might be able to hear us. His usually bright blue eyes are dark, nearly matching his curly, shoulder-length hair, and I can see the fear in them.

"It couldn't have. Where's it going?"

Jost squints in concentration and he cocks his head, trying to see it more clearly. "I think it's on patrol."

Then it hits me. The ship isn't soaring birdlike, it's hanging from a patchwork of rough strands like a puppet dangling from a master's strings. The sky is *wrong*. I thought it was stars sparkling overhead, like the ones that peppered the evening sky in Arras. But these stars are long, and they seem to fade into a tangle of light that twinkles erratically over us. I stare for a long moment while the truth sinks in. These aren't stars nestled into a night sky.

They're *strands*.

It's the same strange, raw weave that we came through when I ripped us out. Loricel, the Creweler who trained me and the most powerful woman in Arras, showed it to me in her studio, explaining that it was a buffer between Arras and another world. She revealed the truth to me that day: that Arras was built on the ruins of Earth.

"It has to be the Guild," I say. I already knew the Guild had a presence on Earth. If I had stayed in Arras, it would have become my job to help them drill for elements here. Of course they would have security forces guarding the buffer between the worlds. The hope building in my chest evaporates, giving way to complete panic. I spot Erik to my left. He's too far away from us for me to protect him, but I can't sit by and do nothing, and before I can plan my next move, the watchlight washes over us again. I respond instinctively; my left hand lashes out and rends the air around us, looking for something to latch onto and warp into a shield of protection. There is no delicate, precisely knit weave on this planet. It's not constructed like Arras, which means I'm useless here.

And yet, I can feel the strands of Earth. They snake against my skin, and if I could calm my racing heart, I think I could even hear them because the space around me crackles with vitality. These aren't the uniform strands of Arras, but they're composed of the same material. They're loosely connected and flexible. Their vibrancy shivers across my damaged fingertips, the threads more alive than any I felt in Arras. There the weave pricked dully at my touch after my hands were scarred during Maela's torture session. But these threads aren't neatly woven into a pattern and they are full of unexpected life. During my time at the Coventry, I could warp time strands into a separate moment, protecting Jost's and my conversations and giving us time alone. Those moments were easy to construct because of the uniformity of the Coventry's weave. However, the Earth strand doesn't warp into the bubble of protection I expect. Instead the thick golden strand coils into my fingers, pulling farther and farther into the sky until it snags across the hull. The ship groans loudly, changing from tarnished steel to bloody rust, bits flaking and falling off. It crumbles more with each second until it plummets to the surface in a flood of sparks and debris.

Jost yanks me along as he runs toward the metro that lies miles away, farther under the hood of the strange raw weave of

Arras. The other direction would take us toward the ocean and there will be nowhere to hide there. I stumble behind him, tripping against rocks in our path. Fragments of the wreckage drift by us as we run. The small sparkles of fiery debris are lovely against the black air but the clattering maelstrom behind us scrapes at my ears, and I reach up to cover them. I can't attach what's happened to me. How could I have done *that*?

"In here!" Erik's cry stops our flight toward the metro. He waits against the rotting door frame of a shack that blends like a smudge into the shadowed landscape. The shack isn't sturdy or large enough to have been a home. It's hard to tell what purpose it once served—one lone building isolated miles from any other, withering and forgotten.

"You probably shouldn't lean on that," I point out as I near him.

He knocks the wooden frame with his fist and some dust sprinkles down as I duck inside the shack. "It's sound enough."

I think that is supposed to reassure me.

Erik steps outside. He's keeping watch, waiting, like me, to see what will happen now. The downing of the ship won't go unnoticed.

The air is heavy here. The chill of it and the lack of light remind me of the cell I was kept in at the Coventry—and of the cells I visited only hours ago with Jost before we made our escape. It feels like years have passed already.

Someone flips on a handlight and I wonder what treasures we've brought from Arras in our pockets. I'm suddenly aware of weight in my own—the digifile. It will be useless here, I realize.

The battered structure and the somber darkness outside

remind me how lost I am, and so I wait for something to change. Something to indicate I haven't made a terrible mistake, but not even a breeze disturbs us here. We can't hide for long now that I've attacked the ship. The Guild will find us whether we stay here or head back toward the metro. I can almost see the gloating look that will be on Cormac's too-perfect face when his officers catch us. By then they will have patched up the hole I ripped in the Coventry's weave to get to Earth. He won't waste any time sending me to be altered once he has me back. It will be straight to the clinic for me, to be made into an obedient Creweler and wife. Dread locks me to the spot, and I wait for the Guild to come and drag me away again. Erik, Jost, and I sit in silence for a long time before I start to relax. We're hidden for now. Sheltered and safe, but most important, no one has come after us yet.

I want to go outside and search for the ship—to see what I've done. I want to study the strange raw weave that floats above us here. Instead I scrape through a layer of dust on the window to peek out. Jost stands beside me and brushes ash from my hair. He frowns, examining one of my arms. I look down. Small burns speckle my pale skin, some have even blistered. I'd been too terrified to feel it.

"Does it hurt?" Jost asks.

I shake my head and a bobby pin tumbles to the floor.

"Here," he says, reaching behind me. He tugs at the remaining pins until my hair swirls down across my shoulders in a cascade of scarlet. I shake it, trying to get any remaining debris out.

"Better?" I ask. We're so close that my green eyes reflect back from his blue ones.

Jost swallows, but we're interrupted before he can respond.

"What happened back there?" Erik demands.

"I caught the ship, but—"

"Nothing," Jost cuts me off. "It was an accident."

"Looked more like suicide to me. They'll know exactly where we are now," Erik says, taking a step toward his brother.

"What if it was looking for us?" I ask, balling my fists. "At least I bought us some time."

"You destroyed it," Erik says in a soft voice. Our eyes meet and I turn away. It was an accident, and he knows that. He isn't accusing me of doing it *on purpose*. No, the accusation in his words is far more cutting. He's accusing me of not being in control.

He's right.

"I want to go check things out," I say.

"We should wait until morning," Jost suggests.

I take a slow, steadying breath. "I don't think morning is coming."

"They don't have daylight here?" he asks.

"No." Erik steps in. "Didn't you see the sky? They don't have a sun. It's that weave we fell through when she ripped us from Arras."

So Erik noticed the raw weave suspended above Earth, too. But how much did he notice? Did he see the ship was attached to the sky?

"I want to get a better look at it," I say, and start toward the door.

"If there are any survivors on that ship, they could be out there," Jost argues.

The splitting hull flashes through my mind and the memory

of ripping metal scratches in my ears. No one could live through that.

"There are no survivors," I say.

"She's right," Erik says. It's not a friendly agreement, but it isn't hostile. He's cool and distant.

"I won't be long," I assure Jost.

"Do you think you're going alone?" he asks.

"I can take care of myself. I'm not some helpless girl."

"She's right again," Erik calls from the dark recess he's crouched in. "Look what she's gotten us into."

I bite my lip. *That* was hostile. Definitely not his usual friendly banter.

"I know that," Jost says loudly. "But none of us should be wandering around on our own."

I study his face for a moment, wondering if he would be so eager to escort his brother to check out the landscape. I decide not to ask.

But Jost continues. "Of course you're welcome to wander off anytime."

I guess that answers that.

"Clearly the fact that we are in some type of forsaken alternate reality is much less important than your grudge against me, so can we get this over with and move on?" Erik asks. He moves out of the shadows to face his brother. Standing there, they mirror each other, and for the first time I study them as brothers. I'd only just figured out the real reason they were cold to each other at the Coventry: they were both hiding that secret. They're exactly the same height, something I'd not noticed before, but Jost is bulkier from his work at the Coventry. He's dressed in casual work clothes, unlike Erik, whose suit, while wrinkly, is still smart. Erik's hair brushes his shoulders and Jost's is longer, but although they share the same unruly waves, Erik's silvery hair is smoothly slicked into place. Jost's wild dark locks look like you'd expect after as much action as we've seen. The one thing that's exactly the same is their piercing blue eyes.

"Grudge?" Jost laughs, but there's a hollowness to it. "You think watching my wife, our sister, *our mother* get wiped from Arras resulted in a grudge?"

"Then why are you here? What purpose does it serve to run to the Guild if you hate them so much for what they did to Rozenn?" Erik demands.

"That's our problem." Jost steps closer to him. "You've never understood. Even I knew why Rozenn's brother and his friends were discontent. I know what the Guild is capable of, and so do you. How can you turn a blind eye? You've become one of them."

"Jost, you were at the Coventry for two years, and I never once let it slip you were from Saxun."

"It would have given away your own secret. You wouldn't want those officials knowing you were a fisherman's son," Jost accuses.

Erik's jaw tightens. "I never once gave them a reason to suspect your motives, but I'll be honest with you, I don't understand what you were waiting for. I expected you to attack them, maybe even kill the Spinster who did it. Anything," Erik says. "I wouldn't have blamed you. I stood back, and you did nothing. I actually thought maybe you'd formed some type of twisted dependency on them."

"That's not it." Jost sighs, and the lightest of lines remain on his forehead and around his eyes. "If you understood, then you'd know I wasn't looking for some quick, simple payback. I want to understand how the system operates."

"How will that help you heal?" Erik demands. "What can you possibly gain?"

"*Myself*? Not much. But understanding the system and getting the information into the right hands could do more damage."

"So that's it," Erik says in a quiet voice. "You were plotting treason."

"And killing Spinsters wouldn't have been that?" Jost asks, responding to the allegation in his brother's voice.

"Killing the one responsible would be reasonable," Erik says. "But destroying the system would undermine the peace the Guild has established."

"Peace?" Jost echoes with a laugh.

I think of the people who have been ripped, the neatly organized proof in storage at the Coventry, the look of defeat on my father's face as he tried to shove me into the tunnel the night the Guild came to claim me. No part of me wants to laugh.

Jost grabs my arm. "Ask Adelice. Ask her what it's like to rip someone from Arras. Ask *her* if it's peaceful for them."

I open my mouth to protest being dragged into the middle of this, but Jost doesn't wait for me to respond to his point.

"Or better yet, ask me, Erik. Ask me what it was like to see it happen." Jost's voice drops down and trails off. None of us speak. "I watched it. I saw her slip away piece by piece. I watched as they took her away from me."

"I'm sorry," Erik offers. He sounds sincere, but even I know his words are far from enough.

Jost shakes his head slightly as if to clear his thoughts and looks out into the dark. "Rozenn was better than any of us. You or me. So was our mother." He pauses. "And my daughter."

Erik's shock registers like a slap across the face. "Daughter?" he mouths. No actual sound comes, but the heaviness of the word presses on my chest, and judging from their expressions, they feel it, too.

"You missed out on a lot when you took off." Jost's words are dismissive, but he doesn't look away from Erik.

"You could have telebounded me," Erik insists. Now he's the one who sounds accusatory.

"And what?" Jost asks. "You would have come to visit? You didn't come when Dad got sick or I got married. I knew where we stood with you when you left to serve the Guild. Your family couldn't help you move forward politically, so we were of no use to you.

"You wouldn't have cared," Jost continues. "You were busy cozying up to Maela, following her orders like the perfect Spinster's errand boy. Just like you've been busy weaseling your way into Adelice's heart."

I should put a stop to these accusations before they kill each other, but part of me wants to see how Erik reacts. I know how Erik feels about Maela, the power-hungry Spinster he worked for at the Coventry. Erik and I both counted her as an enemy. Jost's charge sends a thrill through me, because deep down I always suspected Erik's reasons for getting close to me were about more than friendship.

"But that backfired when Ad brought you here. All that work you did to get to the top is gone. You'll never convince them that you're loyal again. You're through with the Guild," Jost says.

Erik's face contorts into a mask of rage. "You barely know me or why I came to the Coventry, but don't let that stop you from making unfair accusations. It's rather entertaining, and it doesn't look like there's much else to do around here," he spits back.

"There *is* a lot to do around here and fighting isn't on the list," I intercede, before things get more out of control. "Save your personal problems for later, we have work to do."

"What do you have in mind? Rebuild the city?" Erik asks. "Or should we skip to the repopulating part?"

"Shut up," Jost commands. "You aren't funny."

"Why? That's the nice part of getting stuck on a completely forsaken piece of dirt."

"You better hope that you find someone to help you do it then, because she's taken. I'm sure there's a nice dog around here somewhere. Maybe you should stick to your own species," Jost says.

I'm between them before Erik releases his fist, and I barely cringe when I see it moving toward my face.

Jost catches Erik's fist, and Erik freezes. But his surprise at my near-disastrous intervention is quickly replaced by a glare, leveled directly at his brother.

"We're going to check things out," Jost says through gritted teeth.

"Suit yourself," Erik says. "I certainly don't need you here, moping about the joint."

Jost grabs my arm, a bit more roughly than usual, and drags

me from the shack. I pull out of his grasp, my hand flying to rub my throbbing skin.

"That hurt," I inform him.

He stares at me for a moment and then his eyes soften. "I'm sorry. I wasn't thinking. Erik just—"

"I know," I say quietly, "but I'm not Erik. Don't take it out on me."

He nods his apology and I take his hand to let him know we can drop it. We have more important things to worry about right now.

The metro is still several miles away if I can trust my generally poor sense of direction. The ocean now lies far enough behind us that although I can make out its glassy surface, I no longer hear the beat of its waves. We stand between this world and the one we left. Between the danger that lies ahead of us in the metro and the abyss behind us that will swallow us whole. Every choice we make now will have a consequence I can't foresee, because I don't understand this world yet.

The quick crunch of approaching footsteps makes it seem as if someone has made a choice for us. We've been caught. A handlight blinds us to our approaching captor.

"Who's there?" Jost calls. He pushes me behind him, but I step back out. He doesn't try again.

"I should be asking you that." The voice is rough, but feminine. The light fades away, and I blink against spots of phosphorescence left in my vision. A girl blurs into view. She wears no cosmetics but is still quite beautiful. Not in a Spinster way though. Her features are angular, sharp and chiseled, and her dark hair cascades down her back. There is nothing artificial or stylized about her. Her clothes are practical—leather pants that lace up the side, a belt slung low on her hips, and a thick silk tunic. This is a girl who doesn't belong in Arras.

"We saw the ship go down. We came out to see what happened," I lie, hoping against everything I've been led to believe about Earth that the metro ahead of us is populated.

"And you had nothing to do with bringing the ship down from the Interface?" She gestures up to the raw weave that covers the sky.

The girl's eyes sweep over us. Jost might pass her inspection. His clothes are as utilitarian as hers, but there's no denying that I look out of place in comparison, in my lavender suit, stockings, and pumps. Nothing about me, down to the emeralds clipped to my ears, correlates to what I've seen of Earth.

"Let me see your necks," she says.

"Why?" I ask.

"Credentials."

I hesitate for a moment but then acquiesce. I don't know what she's looking for, but I know she's not going to find it. I pull my hair up, Jost does the same, and when we turn back around to face her, a rifle is leveled at us.

She utters one word: "Fail."

Time seems to slow as her finger presses against the trigger, and I scream, "Wait!" It surprises even me, and the girl takes a step back. She's checking for a mark, and I have one—a techprint burned into my wrist by my father, who was hoping I would escape the retrieval squad.

Shoving my sleeve up, I thrust my arm out to her and point to the pale hourglass imprinted on my skin like a scar.

The rifle slips in her hand, the barrel now pointing at the ground.

"Your left hand?" she whispers.

"Yes."

She's shocked, but as quickly as the rifle appeared, it disappears across her back. She pushes my sleeve down to cover the techprint.

"Go to the Icebox," she says, "and lie low. We'll find you. You aren't safe here."

"What's the Icebox?" Jost demands.

"The Icebox is the city ahead of you," she says. "It's Sunrunner territory and outside Guild control."

"Where are we?" I ask.

"The remains of the state of California," she says. "The Icebox is the only inhabited city in this territory. You'll be safe from the Guild there—for now. Stay put and stay hidden. Don't go out after hours and don't let anyone see that techprint."

"Sure," I mutter, and the girl's hand seizes my arm.

"Your life depends on it," she says.

I nod to show that I understand, even though none of this makes sense. What does my father's techprint have to do with Earth? What's a Sunrunner? But I know she's right about one thing: the Guild is coming for me, and we aren't safe here.

She strides away without giving us her name. Her warning hangs in the air. I don't watch her, even though she's not headed to the metro but back toward the ocean.

"Why would she care about your techprint?" Jost asks, but I ignore him as we start to jog back to where we left Erik. We need to get out of here, and if there are people in this Icebox, we can blend in and hide until I figure out how my techprint is linked to this girl.

Nothing tied to the night of my retrieval can be ignored, especially when that thing is a mark left before my father showed me that he and my mother were more than dissenters.

They were traitors—like me.

TWO

THE SCENTS OF THE METRO MINGLE, PERFUMING it with the aromas of sewage, baking bread, rotting fruit, and the sweat of its bustling inhabitants. It is pleasant one moment and stomach-turning the next. We've been here for a week, but it doesn't feel like home and no one's come looking for us yet.

But bit by bit I'm growing more accustomed to the strange world I've found myself in. We stumbled into the Icebox not knowing what to expect and found people, shops, and solar-powered lights. Erik discovered quickly that the small items we had on us could be pawned for currency, which bought us access to a cheap hotel room. Today Erik and Jost let me come with them to the grey market, the seedy part of the metro, where illicit trade takes place, on the condition that I don't speak to anyone. I agreed but only to get out of the rat trap masquerading as a hotel I've been stuck in during their other trips, trips that produced stale food and little else. But I'm not looking for a meal; I want information. Erik has learned a lot on his trips to the market, and we're starting to understand how things work here. But we still haven't found the mysterious girl who sent us to the Icebox.

The Icebox is a conglomeration of buildings from before the war and ones constructed by the syndicate that runs the entire metro—the Sunrunners, the powerful group that controls the Icebox by monopolizing solar trade. Our hotel's manager patiently explained the lighting systems to us our first night. He does a fair business off new refugees coming into the Icebox, and he assures us the Sunrunners are not friends of the Guild. Apparently, Sunrunners keep control of solar energy because they are the only ones brave enough to venture outside the borders of the Interface, where the Guild mining zones begin. I think I saw a Sunrunner out on patrol one day, but so far we've steered clear of them. Even if we share a mutual enemy, it doesn't mean the Sunrunners are looking for allies.

There are rules here—rules reinforced by large, threatening posters pasted to poles and buildings. As we pass through the streets, moving toward the grey market, the notices warn us:

SOLAR HOURS FROM
8 RESOLVED DAYLIGHT HOURS
TO
7 RESOLVED DAYLIGHT HOURS

PATROLS CEASE AT
7:15 RESOLVED DAYLIGHT HOURS

HEAVY CURTAINS, SALLY PORTS, AND REINFORCED FRAMING REQUIRED FOR ALL SHELTERS AND PLACES OF BUSINESS

The posters disappear as the road narrows, the pavement cracks and shatters, and the street-side food stalls are replaced with dimly lit storefronts—the kind that don't have signs. We're nearing the grey market. The rules aren't enforced here, but it's as strictly controlled by the Sunrunners as the rest of the Icebox.

We pass a man begging on the sidewalk with a sign that reads: REFUGEE. NO FAMILY. PLEASE HELP. Jost navigates me around him before I can react.

There are refugees every few feet in the main blocks of the Icebox. I haven't gotten used to seeing them yet. Even the poor in Arras had meager rations. I want to stop and ask these people what they were running from that was worse than being cold and hungry on the street.

But I already know the answer.

The thing that bothers me is that I can't help them—and Jost and Erik won't even let me try.

Erik is ahead of us, not bothering to slow his pace, but a block later he stops and turns to face us. "Look, I've got a good thing going with this guy. But he's a bit paranoid. He's already commented on my Guild paraphernalia, so—"

"You want us to stay outside," I finish for him. Most of our funds thus far have come from pawning the watches, tech, and even some of the clothes we had on us when we escaped from Arras, but I'm still clinging to my digifile, although it's run out of power. I pull it from my pocket and offer it to him. "Here, take this. It's probably worth something."

"No," Erik says quickly. "We should hold on to it."

"Why? It doesn't work down here," I say as I slide it back into my pocket.

"You never know. Besides, we wouldn't want to pawn that without wiping its memory," he explains.

"Okay. Are you sure you don't want us to tag along?" I ask.

"I don't want the guy to feel overwhelmed," he says, sounding apologetic.

I ignore the sorry tone. It's growing thin: both boys avoiding each other, speaking through me, Jost's anger, and Erik's shame. I thought it had come to a head when I ripped us from Arras, choosing to take both of them with me, but the argument that ensued revealed how large a rift exists between the brothers. Erik's shock at learning Jost has a daughter hasn't dissipated yet.

But none of this is getting us anywhere, and separating the two of them might be the opportunity I need to finally get a real conversation going with Jost. He clams up in Erik's presence. We need a plan. We can't tread water forever, waiting for the girl to find us.

"Maybe Jost and I can duck into the fine-looking establishment back there." I hitch my thumb toward the bar we've passed. I want to keep the mood light so he knows it's okay to go.

Beside me Jost takes a step back. It's good to know I still have the ability to surprise him—or maybe *horrify* is the right word. Erik shakes his head, but for a moment his grim demeanor slips and he nearly smiles. He leans over, grabs my shoulder, and whispers, "Keep your eyes open. This is not a *nice* place."

As though the claustrophobic, anonymous corridor we're in didn't give that away.

"You should smile more," I whisper back. "Or you'll lose your reputation."

"My reputation?"

"As a charmer."

This does make him smile, and the icy anger in my chest thaws a little at the sight. "I can be anything I want here, Ad. Perhaps I'll be serious."

"It doesn't suit you," I warn him.

Jost's arm circles around my shoulder, interrupting Erik's and my repartee and indicating he's ready to go.

Or rather, he's ready to take me away. From Erik.

Erik stiffens a bit, stepping back from me. "Promise me you'll stay with him."

"I'll stay close," Jost tells Erik. This is the most they've communicated since their argument on the day we arrived here.

"*We'll* stay close," I add.

"No, explore." Erik waves us off. "There's not much time before curfew."

"So we shouldn't get separated," I say.

"I can find my way back to the hotel if it takes too long. You two have . . . fun."

That's the last thing we'll be having.

"Do you want to find something to eat?" Jost asks as we circle back in the direction we came from, leaving Erik to his business.

I raise an eyebrow, as though challenging him to make that happen. If he can find a place with food—the kind that might be safe to *actually* eat—around here, I'll be impressed.

"Fair enough," he says.

"Let's walk," I offer. "Talk. See what's around."

Jost agrees, but the conversation never gets going. Instead he is silent and seems lost in another place and time. He's been this way since I told him about his daughter, Sebrina. I'd discovered she hadn't been killed along with the rest of Jost's family. She is alive, her information, which reveals exactly where she is in Arras, tucked safely in storage at the Western Coventry. Now we have to figure out a way to get to her, but it isn't possible as long as we're stuck on Earth.

In a way I understand what he's going through. My own sister, Amie, is still in Arras, and she is in more danger than ever before. Jost and I both feel the pressing desperation of each moment that has passed since we left our loved ones to the devices of the Guild, especially now that we've chosen treason instead of continuing to be complicit in the Guild's great deception. I couldn't resign myself to accepting the reality they create on their looms, not when I knew how they misused their power, and not after learning of the existence of Earth. But now that we're actually on Earth, it's becoming increasingly obvious that I can't count on either Jost or Erik to help me figure out what to do next.

I brush back the tangle of dark curls that has fallen over Jost's cheek, but he doesn't seem to notice, except to take my hand in his. The movement is automatic, but I hold his hand anyway.

We hang a left, leaving the narrow alley and heading into a

row of shops. The street lamps cast shadows against the stone, and I move closer to Jost. Even after a week here, I haven't gotten used to the perpetual darkness covering the metro. The sun that never rises. The strange twists of light that flicker and spark across the sky—the Interface. I can see it now, lingering overhead. The strands might twist and sparkle, implying movement, but the Interface is always there—a permanent buffer between Earth and Arras. It blocks the sun and separates the worlds. It's the boundary between the world we've left behind and the one we've discovered.

Some of the stores in the grey market are boarded up, others crumble toward the sidewalk, but lights burn faintly in a few. I have no interest in going inside any of them. I'm eager to explore the shops in the heart of the Icebox, not these back-alley establishments on the metro's outskirts. I want to visit the stores with real customers. I want to know more about Earth, but right now we have so little money we stay away. I'm not sure what we're waiting for though, since we're not getting any answers in the grey market.

These streets are deserted. A few hulking, old-fashioned motos chug along the streets near the main marketplace, but not here. The pedestrians we spot keep their heads low, ducking into shops and not making eye contact with us when we pass by them. Despite the constant darkness, my body tells me evening is near. Actually the airy rumble of my stomach does. Business transactions begin in huddles on street corners, and more and more customers trickle into the grey market to conduct their affairs after hours despite the curfew imposed throughout the Icebox. They don't seem concerned about the rumors of snatchers roaming the streets after the lamps go out. In the nicer sections of the Icebox, food stalls are packed up and people rush their children indoors promptly at 7:00. Not here though.

The solar lamps are already growing dim. In less than an hour, they'll be extinguished completely. On a corner, a young man inspects one of the lamps. His bag lies open, revealing a variety of wrenches and screwdrivers, but his clothing doesn't suggest he's a laborer. His pants are well cut, and his long coat is leather, which seems like a luxury given the absence of animals I've noted in the Icebox. He's not a simple worker. He must be a Sunrunner.

"Will Erik be able to find us?" I ask Jost. He drops my hand at the mention of his brother's name but stays close to me.

"We're only a street away. Trust me, Erik can take care of himself," Jost replies.

"Look, I understand—"

"No, you don't." He stops me. "You trust him. I don't. He'll take off the first chance he gets."

"And where will he go?" I ask. It's a logical question, so I'm not likely to get a straight response.

"You don't know him like I do," he says, giving me an answer as crooked as they come.

"Maybe not." I stop and face him, planning to remind him that a lot has changed in the last two years. Erik may have left Saxun to pursue a political career, turning his back on his family and friends, but it was Erik who helped me the night Jost and I were discovered sneaking around the Coventry. I've been preparing my give-him-a-chance-before-I-stab-you-both lecture for the past few days. But something I see over his shoulder stops me.

A woman. She's short, tottering in heels down the street. I catch glimpses of her face in the flicker of dying lamplight. The slope of her eyes. Her diminutive, slender form. The thick, straight hair swaying around her shoulders.

"Valery," I breathe.

"What?" Jost asks, confused by the change in conversation.

"It's Valery," I say, grabbing his arm to turn his attention to the other side of the street. The woman has passed before he can catch more than her fading shape. She's moving quickly and with purpose.

"Valery is dead," Jost reminds me in a gentle voice.

I know that. At least, she should be dead. A victim of retribution for the suicide of Enora, my mentor at the Coventry and Valery's lover. Loricel told me Valery had been ripped the night Loricel warned me of Cormac's plans to remap me, and yet I'm positive of what I've seen. "It's her."

I don't wait for him to argue with me. Valery is growing smaller in my vision, her figure blurring with each step she takes away from us, and I follow her. I don't run. That seems a sure way to draw unwanted attention to yourself in a place like the grey market, but I move quickly enough that I keep her in my sight until she turns a corner.

Skidding around the building she disappeared past, I realize I'm on the edge of the grey market. The buildings stretching before me are better maintained. Most have signs, and many are already closed. But Valery is nowhere in sight, which means she's gone into one that's still open. Doors are locked, lights turned off, and then I stumble upon a door that creaks open when I touch it. The lights are on in the store, revealing a cluttered room full of books and knick-knacks strewn in piles along the floor and filling tables. It will be a miracle if I can even walk around. But someone could hide here. I have no reason to suspect Valery saw me, but if she did, I wouldn't blame her for wanting to avoid me.

That doesn't mean I am going to let her.

THREE

I GLANCE AT THE SIGN HANGING ON a post by the door: THE OLD CURIOSITY SHOP. Curious indeed. After a few moments navigating the store, I see no signs of life, but what I do find holds my attention: relics from a forgotten world, particularly an old radio. I forget my quest and stare at it, tentatively reaching out to touch its buttons, but it's as dead as the one hidden in the secret cubby in my parents' home. A product of yesterday, and nothing more.

I'll have lost Valery completely by now, if it was even her at all, so I linger in the store and riffle through the books, knocking years of dust off them. A copy of Shakespeare's sonnets catches my eye. I read it over and over as a child, stealing it from the stash of contraband in my parents' room. We had a few books, and if my parents minded my reading them, they certainly never said anything. I understand now how precious they were, and more than anything I want to take this volume with me. I couldn't protect those books. I couldn't protect my parents, but I can have a piece of them again.

"Not many young people are interested in books these days," a raspy voice says. A face, lined and gaunt, follows the words, appearing in the doorway. The woman limps over, resting against a cane, and I notice that one of her feet is made of steel and wood.

"My parents had it," I tell her. "I read it as a child."

"Quite the luxury," she says. "Books *and* having the time to teach your child to read."

I pause, not sure how to respond. This conversation is heading in a dangerous direction. Many of the Icebox's inhabitants are refugees, but that doesn't make it any safer to admit I am one myself.

"Keep it," she offers.

"I couldn't," I say. "Not without paying."

The shop owner seems to grow an inch at the mention of payment. She can't do much business selling radios that don't work and books that can't be read.

"I don't have any money though," I admit.

"Well," she mutters, shaking her head, "at least you can read."

"I have this," I say, unlatching an earring. I only offer her one, because I know the emeralds in the pair are real and because I know the boys will be furious if I come back missing both. We've been hawking our possessions strategically and we've been saving the earrings until we have a plan for getting back to Arras and need real money.

"You're either proud or an idiot," she says, but she accepts the earring. "Look around, take some more of this junk off my hands. An emerald for a book isn't a fair trade, child."

I pocket the sonnets and consider asking for the radio, but

purely out of nostalgia. It will do us no good, and I'll be forced to abandon it as soon as we are on the move again. Instead I trail my fingers along the dusty spines of books. The books my parents kept were full of stories and poetry, but many of the books on these shelves recall the history of Earth. It's the information I've been seeking. This woman has been collecting it for me, safeguarding the information against the entropy that envelops so much of this world. I wonder how many generations of owners stacked these shelves and traded the past before her.

The tinkle of a bell interrupts my thoughts, and I turn quickly to the door to see who has entered. In my haste, I knock a few books off the shelf, but the old woman has vanished into the recesses of the shop, so I retrieve them quickly before she notices. Jost appears at my side, looking decidedly displeased.

"What was that about?" he demands, not bothering to bend down and help me.

"Valery. I couldn't let her disappear," I say, stacking the books neatly. "But I lost her, and this was the only shop open—"

He stops me. "Your earring." My hand flies to my naked earlobe, but it's too late to cover it up.

"I traded it," I admit in a low voice, but inwardly I gather up strength and stand to face him.

"For what?" he says. His voice is soft, but it isn't kind.

"A book," I say. "More than one actually. Who knows what we might find out."

Jost grabs the books and slams them down on the shelf, and as he does he knocks a stack of papers to the floor. "Have some respect," I hiss as I snatch the brittle pages, but they aren't just paper. They're *Bulletins* full of old news.

He starts in on *respect* and *scaring him to death* and *throwing away resources*, but I only hear snatches of what he says because I'm reading the headline neatly printed in block letters on faded, yellow paper:

HOPE AGAINST TYRANNY:
SCIENCE OFFERS AN END TO WAR

May 1, 1943—Preliminary studies termed the Cypress Project indicate the end of World War II is in sight. According to sources within the project, investors visited the laboratories for a presentation on the viability of the looms, which have been funded by twelve allied nations in cooperation with generous contributions from individuals in the private sector. The visit was necessary to secure permission to proceed to human trials of the project.

The war departments of all twelve nations involved with the Cypress Project have issued a call for healthy young women between the ages of sixteen and thirty years to serve as test pilots on the looms. For the first time in American history, chosen women will be considered as enlisted troops in the U.S. Army.

But it's the photograph that I can't process: a scientist demonstrating on a loom for a group of men who wear ties and horn-rimmed glasses. Hardly anyone in Arras wears glasses these days, thanks to renewal tech, but aside from the spectacles, most of the men in the clipping could pass as current officials in Arras. One in particular. Maybe Jost is right, and I've lost my mind. Maybe I'm seeing ghosts.

Jost shakes me, abandoning his rant to get my attention. "Ad!"

I don't know what to say, so I hold the paper out to him. He takes it and the color drains from his face.

I'm not the only one seeing ghosts.

"How can that be possible?" he asks me.

"A coincidence?" I offer, but no part of me believes it.

"A family member?"

I nod, because even if I can't accept these explanations, I can't *comprehend* what Cormac Patton's picture is doing in a *Bulletin* clipping from Earth that has to be almost two hundred years old. The man looks like him though, right down to his smooth jaw and dark eyes.

"Find anything?" the shop owner asks, hobbling toward us. She bobs her head in greeting at Jost but doesn't seem excited to see another poor young person.

"Can you tell us about this?" Jost asks, passing her the paper to inspect. Her eyes slit in concentration but then familiarity dawns in her expression and she leans back on her cane.

"The Cypress Project," she says with a sigh. "That's all."

"That's all?" I repeat. The Cypress Project. I've never heard of it, although I know of Cypress, Arras's capital metro. The name sends a tingle slithering through my skin.

"Your parents taught you to read," she says, annoyance seeping into her gravelly voice, "but they didn't bother to tell you how it happened?"

"You remember it, though?" I ask. "The Cypress Project?"

"Of course," she says. "You don't forget that. You don't forget being left behind."

"Tell us," I say, taking her hand gently. "I want to know too."

Her eyes soften, but then they fall to our hands, clasped tenuously together.

"Get out!" she howls, wrenching her hand from mine like I've bitten her.

I fall back against Jost in surprise and his arm circles protectively around me.

"Please!" I beg. "What do you mean 'left behind'?"

"What the Guild of Twelve Nations did was reprehensible," she seethes, raising her cane and pointing it at us. "But your kind, what you do, that's worse. Rebellion and violence—an endless cycle. The Kairos Agenda is unwelcome here. I want no part of it. I've lost enough already. Get out!"

Jost pulls me to the door, but I can't tear my eyes from the accusation blazing on her face. It is as though she knows who I am, what I can do, but how is that possible? Bringing my hand up to push Jost's arm off mine, ready to turn and flee, I see what she saw. The same mark that caught the girl's attention last week. A mark so I'll remember who I am. A mark that told her who I was. I raise the hourglass techprint to her as Jost drags me to the exit.

"This?" I ask. "Is this it?"

"You've been marked, girl," she snarls. "And I'll have no part of it." We're out the door now, and as she clutches the entrance's frame, her shouts echo against the buildings around us. "Give me that paper back."

Jost shoves it into his pocket, and we dart away. I don't feel guilty for taking it. She got fair payment. She only wants to keep it from *me*, but she doesn't know who I am.

No more than I do apparently.

The shop owner limps onto the sidewalk hurling obscenities at us as we go, and calling, "Thief!" But no one this close to the grey market cares. Not at this hour. Until someone does—a figure appearing from the fog cast about us.

"Hold up there," he says. "What's old Greta screeching about?"

FOUR

STEPPING CLOSER TO THE STRANGER, I REALIZE it's the same Sunrunner I saw examining the solar lamp before Valery appeared. He's young, not much older than I am. Even though I know he can't be Guild—not here in the Icebox—his presence, the dominant way he stands, blocking our path, makes me anxious. There's something familiar in his stance—maybe his self-assuredness reminds me of Erik—but it feels like more than that. His hair is cropped close to his head, and even though I can't see them in the dark, I know his eyes are brown.

I'm not sure how I know that.

Greta continues her hysterical ravings behind us, and Jost attempts to step around the Sunrunner, but he holds up his hand.

"What's this about, Greta?" the Sunrunner calls out to her.

Jost could probably take him, but he doesn't move. I could use my own considerable skills to get away, but I'm rooted to the spot by the familiarity I feel. The Sunrunners patrol the nicer blocks of the Icebox during the designated commerce hours, but even they're indoors once darkness arrives.

"They're thieves and hooligans," she rants.

"Is this true?" he asks us.

Jost squares his shoulders and takes a step closer to him. "No, we paid her more than what an old book is worth."

Greta hobbles closer to us, and when she hears this, she shakes her cane again. "No amount is enough when dealing with your type."

"Hey now." The stranger stops her. "I've never seen these two before, so I know they can't be too much trouble."

The only reason he thinks this is *because* he hasn't seen us before. I know differently.

Greta screws up her face and gives a large huff. "I didn't ask for your help, Sunrunner. You're as bad as they are, so maybe you don't mind keeping company with thieves."

"Some of my best friends are thieves," he says, his lip tugging up. The movement, though slight, flashes through my mind. One side curves more than the other, but his lips never give way to a smile. I've never seen him before but something about him is so *familiar*. "You should get inside. It's after hours, and there are scarier things than an old crippled woman creeping about."

I dislike how he speaks to Greta. But there's no time to call him out on it. Lockdown is imminent, which means the makeshift lighting system will power down for the evening, extinguishing the solar street lamps completely and casting the whole crumbling metro into blackness. The rumors of snatchers and cannibals replay in my mind. We have to get out of here.

"We need to go," I say to Jost.

"Good riddance," Greta calls from her shop's door frame. "Remember, thief, you reap what you sow!"

"Thank you for your assistance," I tell the Sunrunner. Despite the necessity of moving on, I'm reluctant to see him go. I wish I could unravel his mystery, or, at least, the tangle of knots he's made of my nerves. "We have a friend to find so we can take shelter."

"Better to let your friend find you at this hour," he advises, but I shake my head.

"Not how it works."

"Ad, he's probably already back at the hotel. We can't waste time looking for him when we have ten blocks to travel to get there ourselves," Jost reminds me. His tone is practical, and it almost convinces me, but I'm skeptical enough of his motives to insist once more that we look for Erik.

"I'm headed back west," the stranger says. "If you don't mind falling in with a Sunrunner, we can check for your friend along the way and then you're welcome to come inside our safe house near the grey market. Ten blocks is too far to safely travel at this point. The Rems will be out soon."

"Thanks, but—"

"Sounds like a plan," I interrupt Jost, whose jaw tenses at my rudeness. He doesn't disagree with me though.

"Excellent. Now I know you're thieves, but I don't know your names," the stranger remarks as we head back toward the narrowing alleys where we left Erik.

"I'm Adelice, and this is Jost." It occurs to me too late that I should have lied. If the Guild is looking for us, they'll advertise our names. Even if they're anti-Guild, the Sunrunners might see us as something of value.

"Dante." He holds out a hand, which Jost shakes awkwardly as we hustle toward safety. Dante takes mine next, raising it to his lips. It's possibly even more awkward than his handshake with Jost.

"Thank you again," I say, trying to sound sincere, "for stepping in back there, and for helping us now."

Dante's helpful demeanor seems out of place in the Icebox. Normally I'd wonder if we were walking into a trap, but I feel inexplicable trust in Dante. I try to shake the warm tendrils of it from my head and heart, but they refuse to budge. It is this more than anything else that pushes me into following him.

"My motives aren't entirely pure," Dante says. "Greta's a cynical old crone, but something about you spooked her, and I'm eager to find out what."

"I have no idea," I lie. "We were looking at books, talking with her, and she lost it. I didn't understand half of what she was saying. I thought she must be crazy."

"Greta's angry, but she's still firing on all cylinders. One of the few left who remembers the Exodus," Dante says. "She said something about *your type*. You have no idea why?"

"No." I keep my eyes on the shops and sidewalks, searching for Erik. I wonder what Dante means by her remembering the Exodus.

"No matter," he says. "I'll sort you out yet."

The statement leaves me uneasy. We might not be walking into a trap, but we aren't going home with a friend either. The street lamps have faded completely, and only the faintest afterglow remains. The roads are empty, but every now and then I glimpse a moving shadow.

"We won't find your friend this late," Dante says, a note of apology in his voice. He flips on a handlight, which is only bright enough for us to see one another.

"He was near here when we left him," I say, squinting to no avail. We'd have to walk right into Erik to find him now that the lamps are powered off for lockdown.

"We're close to the house." Dante directs us a few doors down. His hand skims my back to guide me in the right direction and he removes it quickly, but not before my body reacts to its presence. For a fleeting second, I feel calm. Safe.

Jost leans in to me and whispers, "He's probably at the hotel. It's what we agreed on if we got separated, remember? Besides he wouldn't want you out on the street after dark."

He's right, but the decision to abandon Erik doesn't sit well with me. I trust Erik in ways that his brother can't, but I don't trust him to follow a plan, especially while he's still feeling so bad about not being there for Jost before. Sooner or later, he'll do something stupid and heroic to prove himself to his brother. I only hope it's not tonight.

Dante stops at a thick, dark door illuminated on either side by thin spiral bulbs that glow red. He enters a code and waits until there's an audible *click* before he ushers us inside. The entry deposits us into a holding area, the concrete walls surrounding us broken only by two parallel doors.

"Sally port," he explains. "It holds us while the laser scanners approve us to enter."

"Approve us?" I ask. My eyes sweep the small space, looking for the technology that is analyzing us as a green beam of light sweeps down my body.

"Don't worry," he assures us, before adding, "unless you're on a Sunrunner 'Wanted' list."

I bite my lip, not wanting to say that being on a wanted list is a definite possibility. Concrete walls. Laser scanners. This is a place built to keep attackers out. It's a lot of security clearance, but I guess when you're running a dangerous operation like solar trafficking, it's necessary, especially if there are creatures roaming the streets after hours.

The hall on the other side of the holding area is surprisingly warm. Long solar torches hang overhead, and the walls are lacquered in a deep gray. A few broad leather chairs rest in an alcove, but Dante passes them and we follow quickly behind. We enter a lounge area with overstuffed sofas and gleaming walnut tables. On the far wall, a carved mantel arches elegantly toward the ceiling and a fire licks in a cavernous hearth. Small solar lamps with green glass shades light the windowless room.

"I'm famished," Dante announces. "I'll have the cook scrounge something together. No promises that it will be edible though." He gives a sweeping bow followed by a wink as he exits the room. I still don't know what to make of him.

Considering the canned goods we've survived on during the last week, I'm guessing the Sunrunners' cuisine will be an improvement. One of the perks of controlling the Icebox's light supply is bound to be better food. Jost and I wander to the fire and settle on the brick hearth to warm ourselves. I'm getting used to the daily chill of Earth, but it's nice to feel heat on my skin.

Jost doesn't break the silence; instead he pulls me into his arms and I dissolve against him. In the heat of the fire, I don't need his warmth, but I long for it. I bury my face under his chin and inhale his scent. He pulls back ever so slightly, but only to bring his lips to mine. I don't expect it, but I welcome it after the awkwardness between us.

The kiss is slow. On Earth there's no need to rush. No risk of being caught by the Guild. Realizing that pushes everything else out of my mind, and I focus on the crush of his lips, parting my own to deepen the kiss. He responds by drawing me closer, his hands firmly on my waist.

I push into him and let my own hands drop slowly down his shoulders across his chest, trailing along the waistband of his pants until I bring them to rest on his back. My fingertips are numb as usual but touching Jost sends shivers up my arms. They come to rest deep in my core until every part of me aches. He ends the kiss first, but neither of us breaks from the embrace. Instead his lips linger at my ear.

I want to lock the moment in place and erase the outside world.

Forget my past.

Ignore my future.

Lose myself in him.

But even I don't have that much time.

When Dante reenters the room, we break apart as he hesitates. I can see him questioning if he should leave us alone, so I motion for him to join us.

"Cook's on it," he says. "Now back to Greta."

He's not giving up on what happened at the shop, and I don't blame him. Her frantic accusations have been bouncing around in my head since we left there. They didn't mean anything to me, but it's possible they'll mean something to Dante. There was a time when I would have guarded the hourglass techprint my father placed on me the night the Guild came to retrieve me because I thought it was a secret code between him and me. A simple reminder to me of who I was. But Greta's reaction to it rattled me even more than the girl's recognition of it on the night we arrived here. Do I know who I am? My parents' actions that night had raised more and more questions in my time at the Coventry. How much had they known? Where were we going? I'd learned nothing is as it seems in Arras. Not even a simple techprint, it turns out.

So I hold out my wrist and show it to Dante. He takes a step forward to examine my offering and shock flits across his face, quickly replaced by a mask of calm. If I hadn't been watching him, I would have missed it entirely.

"That explains it," he says, his voice so low it sends goose bumps popping across my flesh.

"It means something to you then?" Jost asks.

"You don't know what this is?" Dante asks.

"No," I admit. Part of me wants to tell him the whole story. That we're refugees from Arras, about my parents and the tunnels under our house, that we're running from the Guild. But I keep quiet, waiting to see how he responds, wondering exactly what I've revealed to him about myself.

"It's the sign of Kairos," he tells us. "It seems I haven't been very polite. Welcome to Earth."

FIVE

SOMEONE HAS LAID OUT A FEAST ON a polished black table. The setting is utilitarian. No time wasted on decorations or fancy utensils, but the food is another story. The first course is a salty soup with chunks of white fish and leeks simmered slowly so they melt on my tongue. The soup scorches my throat, and I savor how it floods and stings my mouth, coming to rest hot in my belly. Next a crisp salad smothered in heavy dressing and bits of buttery toast. And then meat. I never knew how much I could miss meat until it sits in front of me. My portion is very small. The large cuts are given to the men, so I cut mine up into tiny bites, watching the red juice seep from my incisions and chewing each bite for minutes.

This is what Dante calls scrounging something up.

There was a time when I would have pushed my plate away, too anxious to eat, but even though I need answers as to what's happening around me, I'm not passing up a meal after a week with so little food.

"Tell me more about Sunrunning," I say. "I think I'm interested in joining up."

"You're an easy sale," Dante says.

"The way to my heart is through my stomach," I admit.

Jost eats slowly beside me, not saying much. He looks even more thoughtful now that our secret is out and Dante knows we're refugees, but for me, it feels as though a boulder has been lifted from my chest. Dante hasn't said anything more about the techprint, although I'm sure we'll get back to it. It's probably hard to discuss something serious with someone who's stuffing her face.

"One of the perks of the job is food, obviously. We take a quota of goods from the various hydroponic farms in the area and we trade meat and fish with the hunters. There are a few farms on the outskirts of the Interface, but it's a rough business keeping livestock there. Meat's fallen from favor in most of the Icebox since it's so hard to get. Although there's still some canned meat about," he says.

"Lucky for us," Jost says, but his face is dark.

"It's a dangerous job. Most of the area outside of the Icebox is uninhabitable."

"Uninhabitable?" I ask.

"From the mining operations and the bombings during the war."

Loricel had told me another story about Earth. She had assumed the people left on Earth annihilated one another. It seems they only succeeded in destroying most of the planet.

"I'm talented," I say, although I'm not actually interested in the occupation. I'm looking for information.

Dante hesitates, running his hand over his short hair. He

drops it down and pushes his empty plate away. "You lack certain necessary qualities."

"How would you know that?" I demand.

"Because you're a girl."

"A girl?" I repeat.

Beside me Jost trembles with held-back laughter, and I smack his shoulder.

"You don't want to underestimate this girl," he warns Dante.

"I've been gathering that much," Dante says. "It's more of a policy. Kincaid, my boss, only employs men. Very particular kinds of men."

It's implicit in his words that Jost doesn't qualify, which begs the question of why we are still here. Dante gains nothing from helping us. We have no value in his line of work.

"Kincaid only has interest in women for one reason, and something tells me you, Adelice, might object to the position," Dante adds. "Trust me, you wouldn't want to get tangled up in Kincaid's business. It's better if you steer clear of him."

"So you capture sunlight from outside the Interface and sell it as power," I say, changing the topic before Jost gets upset. If Dante is still talking, I might as well keep him at it.

"We have containment units that turn it into a form of electricity, and then we ration it out to shops and homes."

Or the highest bidder, I think. "Is that why there is a curfew?"

"Yes," he says. "We couldn't supply enough energy to keep the Icebox lit at all times. Here in the Icebox, we're close enough to the border of the Interface that the city has longer daylight hours. It's easier for us to replenish the solar panels on the city's power grid."

"Is that why you chose this place?" I ask.

"That," Dante says, "and because Kincaid liked San Simeon. He claims it's because the mountains near his estate prevent Guild interference."

"But you don't think that's it?" I guess.

"When you see his estate, you'll understand what I mean."

"So the people are left in darkness because Kincaid wanted an estate," I remark.

"They have candles. Many ration their supply for private use after hours, but the streets are dark," he says. "It's not possible to set up a community outside the cover of the Interface. There're too many Guild mining operations. We do the best we can."

"We've heard rumors of predators that roam after hours," Jost tells him.

"An unfortunate side effect of turning off the lights. It's why the curfew is necessary."

"But no one is around to enforce the curfew," I point out.

"The curfew isn't enforced so much as understood. If you're out after hours, the Rems could get you. Most don't chance it. There's always a suicidal few though. Rems like the darkness," Dante says.

"Rems?" Jost asks. We've heard the term before but we're no closer to understanding it now.

"Remnants—nasty lot," Dante says.

"Why do they take people?"

"Food mostly."

I'm suddenly glad my own meal is gone and that I haven't asked for seconds.

"Food?" Jost echoes, not quite following him.

"I'm sure you've noticed there's not a lot to go around. They don't discriminate when they hunt and the livestock we do keep is heavily guarded. Wild animals don't make it out of the mining zones. Who knows what the Guild does with them. Anyway, you can cook a human, too," Dante says with a wicked grin, and the contents of my stomach churn a little.

"So they're cannibals?" I don't bother hiding my disgust.

"They don't have the same moral code we do." He shrugs. "They don't have souls."

"I guess not," Jost mutters, setting his fork down.

"No, literally, they have no souls," Dante clarifies. "The Guild sends them here, and they're different from us. They're smart, capable. They keep to packs. But they've been hollowed out, stripped of what makes you and me human."

Jost's face pales, and I know what he's thinking. Rozenn, his wife, who the Guild ripped from the docks of his hometown— has she met a similar fate? I've been haunted by the violent death of my father at the barrel of a Guild gun during our escape attempt, but knowing what would have happened if he'd been caught changes things. Although nothing can erase from my mind the image of blood seeping from a black body bag. My mother could have been turned into a Rem, but she was terminated, according to Cormac. Amie, my sister, was safely rewoven to another family. It eases some of the guilt that's weighed me down since we got here to know that my family was spared from the worst. But how long will Amie be safe?

"Don't worry, Rems don't make it long around here," Dante tells us, responding to Jost's expression. "The conditions are too uncontrollable, the food too scarce, and sooner or later, the packs turn on each other."

I remember the storage units housed at the Coventry. I stumbled onto them while searching for information on Amie. Thin strands in crystal boxes. Personal identifying sequences marked ACTIVE. Something clicks into place, leaving a sickening realization in my mind. When I'd ripped people in Arras, their remains had been sent away, and yet I'd known the first time I saw those strands in the depository that they couldn't possibly be people's remains. The strands were what was left of them after the Guild had created these monsters. Their souls.

"Why though?" I ask. "Why would the Guild send them here?"

"How do you wage a war without an army? Do you think Guild officials would willingly volunteer? And they can't send citizens without revealing that Earth exists," Dante says in an even tone, but there is a fervor simmering below the surface of his words. "The area under the Interface is totally controlled by Kincaid, but that doesn't mean the Guild is willing to let it go."

War. The inhabitants of the Icebox struggle enough day to day, barely surviving in the conditions caused by the Interface blocking the sun. The Remnants can't merely be to keep them out of the mines, and somehow I know everything is related to the paper we took from Greta's shop. It all comes back to the looms.

"If Kincaid controls the Icebox—" I begin.

"He controls all the territory under the Interface," Dante corrects.

"Okay," I say, "but outside the Interface?"

"That's Guild territory," Dante says. "Their mines occupy a large portion of the uncovered area on Earth."

"But how do you collect the solar energy then?" Jost asks.

"Kincaid doesn't care much about Guild boundaries, but it makes Sunrunning dangerous. If you get caught, you don't come back."

"How do you manage it?" I ask.

Dante leans in and grins. "I don't get caught."

Neither side respects the other's territory. That much is clear. Sunrunners might be dangerous, but they're also the only people with the courage to stand up to the Guild.

"Why did you run from Arras?" Dante asks us.

"We've lost people to the Guild," Jost answers for us. "We saw through the Guild's lies, and the truth brought us here."

Jost is telling the truth without giving anything away.

Dante isn't appeased by this answer. "Strange things have been happening around here. More Guild presence. A ship was downed from the sky. I can't help thinking that your typical refugee doesn't show up with the sign of Kairos printed on her arm."

This is why he's interested in us. "My father did it before the Guild killed him," I admit. "Before I ran."

"And he never explained to you what it was?" Dante presses.

"There wasn't time. The Guild was onto us, so I had to go before I could ask. I assumed it was another Lewys family secret."

"What did you say?" Dante asks.

His face is ashen, and I replay my last words, trying to determine which triggered such an intense reaction. Before I land on an answer, a red light pulses through the room in sync with a shrieking alarm.

"That's not possible," Dante says, jumping up and knocking his chair over in the process.

"What's wrong?" I ask, unease creeping, unwanted, into my chest.

"It's a perimeter alert. We've had a breech in one of the entrances." He's already starting down the hall, and we have to race to catch up.

"Remnants?" I ask.

Dante doesn't respond. He's busy sliding through screens on a companel. It's Guild tech, much more advanced than anything we've seen on Earth so far.

How flexible are the Sunrunners in their alliances?

He lands on the security stream that shows the point of access. The feed glows green and white, so we can see the movement in the darkness outside. A handful of humans are tearing at Dumpsters in an alley.

"Is that here?" I ask.

"In the back," Dante murmurs.

Jost thinks to ask a more useful question. "Is this normal?"

"That, maybe," he says, pointing to the Rems leaping out from the garbage bins, but then he swipes the image to the next feed. "This isn't."

The stream shows a crumpled steel door lying on its hinges in the alley. One of the Rems is caught underneath it. It's a woman from the look of her long hair, but I can't see her face and she isn't moving. The feed shifts to show Remnants inside a concrete holding area, much like the sally port we entered through.

"The Guild must have given them some fancy explosives to

get through our doors," Dante says. "They're not here to blow us up, they're trying to reap us."

"Can they get in?"

"Doubtful. The holding areas are triple reinforced—two layers of concrete and steel supports in between. Anything they used to get through that would kill them, and we have our own booby trap that will be triggered if they try to take out the other door."

The camera feeding us the stream of the holding area circles to the next corner of the room, and I feel my heart thumping hard in my chest. I've barely glimpsed the footage before the stream changes again, but the last image is all I can process.

They have Erik.

SIX

THE ALARM DOESN'T FADE AND ITS WAIL pierces the air, pounding in my ears. Thoughts and ideas tumble through my head as quickly as they evaporate. How did this happen? How did they know to bring Erik here? Has the Guild found us?

Are we being watched?

Dante wastes no time pulling rifles from a storage unit in the safe house. He starts to hand me one but hesitates, and I understand what he's thinking. He doesn't want me to go. Maybe Sunrunners don't think much of girls, but I have my own tricks. I refuse the rifle, reaching for a short knife with a serrated blade.

"Jost and I can handle this," Dante says.

"He's right. Those things are after something," Jost says. It's a warning. Jost thinks they've come for me, but there's no reason to believe that. Except that they chose this safe house to attack. And that they took Erik as a prisoner. So actually there are several reasons to think that.

"Maybe," I grant him, "but they aren't going to get it."

The security stream doesn't show anyone near the main entrance, so we head there.

"Don't you have more men?" I ask Dante as we slip into the darkness outside.

"They're around. Some aren't in yet, others are probably already sleeping before they take the early patrol shift," Dante says.

"Should we—I don't know—wake them up?" I suggest.

Dante grabs my arm to stop me, and his eyes look black in the night as he peers down at me. "It's for your own good that I'm not getting anyone involved yet. Once Kincaid knows about you, he'll expect an audience with you—and probably a whole lot more than that. And I won't bring anyone else in until you explain things to me."

"I already did," I whisper.

"No, I want the *whole* story. It's not a coincidence that they're here, and I want to know what happened with that aeroship."

Before Dante can say anything else, Jost pushes him away from me. "Don't touch her."

Dante whirls on him, but then calms himself. Instead of forcing it, he heads toward the building's edge. If Erik weren't in danger, I'd run now because I'm suddenly afraid of Dante's intentions. He knows I took down that ship last week. I said something over dinner that spooked him, but nothing that truly gave away me or my unusual abilities. He didn't respond this way when he saw the techprint. He was curious then, but now he seems to be repressing fury and I know it has nothing to do with the Remnant attack. He's angry with me.

I'm so preoccupied with this that we're near the alley before I can process what we're about to do. Emergency lights flood the area, bathing the alley in more light than we've seen on Earth, even during market hours. The unlit parts of the street creep along the corners of my vision, casting shadows into the small alley. Bodies seem to fade in and out of sight.

They're here, and they see us coming.

"Get out your weapons," Dante hisses.

The small knife in my hand feels light and useless. I wouldn't even know how to use it. I may as well try to punch our attackers. I should have asked Dante more about the Remnants. In fact, there are a lot of things I wish I'd asked Dante now that we're staring down a group of maniacs.

It's their eyes that scare me. Pupils dilated and stretched past the irises, extending into an infinite nothing. They move with unnatural grace, leaping without fear of falling and bounding in long strides. The Remnants play with the shadows, popping in and out of sight, seeming to shift and change shape before my eyes. The darkness licks along their limbs, branching like poisoned veins across their arms and faces, but as one glides closer, the black streaks deepen in his skin. They're *scars*, not tricks of the filtered light.

"Can you weave us out of here?" Jost asks in a whisper, balancing the butt of his rifle against his shoulder and peering along its long, thin barrel.

"I can likely freeze the moment, but there's nowhere to go." I see no point in hiding my weaving abilities from Dante if we need to use them. My eyes automatically draw out the strands around us. They're tangled in a mutilated web. There's no discernible pattern in the chaos. I can see Earth's strands. I can touch them, but this world is too unpredictable for me to know for sure what would happen if I created a large warp in the strands.

"I imagine your friend would feel pretty raw if you left him behind," Dante adds. It's in the weight of his words, how carefully they're chosen, how they flow slowly from his tongue—he knows what I am. I don't know how, but Dante knows I'm a Spinster.

"One thing at a time," I snap. "I thought we'd deal with the maniacs first."

"Let's see what you got," Dante says.

"Find Erik," I command Jost.

He nods, but I can tell I'm more inclined to help Erik than he is, so I remind him in a low voice, "He's your brother."

"He's over there," Dante interrupts us.

Erik is wrestling with one of the Remnants, trying to hold his attacker's body back with one hand while the Remnant grips his other.

"Erik," I cry out to him, and then instantly regret it because his head turns toward my voice. For a second, he loses his focus on the Remnant he's fighting. But before the strange woman can attack him, Dante sends a shot tearing through her body. The Remnant woman trips back and goes limp. It buys Erik enough time to get to us.

"Glad you showed up." He's panting.

"Me too," I say, hoping he doesn't notice I'm shaking. "How did you know where we were?"

"*I* didn't," Erik says meaningfully. "*They* did."

"What's he doing?" Jost asks, and I turn to discover Dante has moved away from the group and farther down the alley. At first it looks like he has things under control, but then a Remnant backs him against a tall chain-link fence.

Without thinking, I lurch forward, sprinting toward the pair with my knife in hand. The Remnant pins Dante to the ground, hands gripping his neck. Something whistles past me, but I don't stop until I've reached them. My hand lashes out with the knife and slices across the Remnant's back. The blade vibrates as it tears along flesh, and it makes my hand tremble.

It's not the kind of wound that will slow him down, but it does make him angry. Dropping his hands from Dante's neck, the Remnant lunges forward onto his palms and hisses under his breath. Dante is free, but now the Rem is after me.

Knife still in hand, I thrust it forward to scare him off. But he laughs. It's a completely normal, human laugh, and it makes me lose my grip on the handle. I recover, but I've lost my defensive posture. Now instead of inching him back, I'm vulnerable. Slowly he moves toward me with a low growl, moving erratically and pushing me farther and farther toward the fence.

I open my mouth to call out to Jost when a brick cracks against the Remnant's skull. He crumples to the ground, and Dante waves for me to follow him.

"Dante! Adelice!" I look over and see the boys beckoning to us. We sprint toward them and when we reach them Erik grabs my arm. The others keep moving but he holds me back.

"Do you trust this guy?" he asks in a soft voice, even though we're nowhere near anyone.

"Do I have a choice?" I pull forward against his hand.

"This could be a trap."

"If you want to take your chances with them," I say,

wrenching my arm free, "be my guest. Those things are from the Guild, which probably means they're after us."

I turn my head enough to gauge his reaction. His eyes narrow a bit, but he starts running. "Who says they're Guild?"

"Dante. He's our one chance at getting out of here."

"That's your problem, Ad," he shoots back. "You only hear what other people tell you."

Before I can ask him what that means, we've caught up with the others, so I let it go. Remnant bodies litter the entrance to the safe house, and I turn away as Dante starts picking off the few survivors trying to crawl away.

"Is that necessary?" I ask as he circles around, checking each one to be certain they're all dead.

"You saw what they did, and you want to let them go?"

"They're people—"

He interrupts me, "They're what's left of people."

The Remnant trapped under the door stirs, and Dante's rifle swings toward her, but not before I see her face in the floodlight.

She's nothing like the woman I remember. Her previously smooth skin is sallow and waxy. A few of her teeth are broken into stumps, and her eyes, once luminous emerald, are still beautiful but something deadly sparkles in them now. Hideous scars run jagged across her flesh, but they don't shimmer or flicker—these are not superficial scars, they're deep and permanent. She struggles against the door that pins her to the ground, and without thinking I reach for the wild strands of the world around me until I latch onto a golden thread of time. It whips through the air as I draw it into a warp. The strand is longer than I expected, and it cracks against the natural elements around it, distorting the air into a blur of color and light.

"Stop!" I cry, but he already has, bewildered by my actions. And then it strikes me that Dante's not looking at the warp in front of him, but at *her.*

"Who is she?" Jost asks.

Jost moves closer to my side, placing a hand on the small of my back to let me know he's there. But he has no idea what we're facing—*who* we're facing.

Had she come for me? Had they sent her after me? Realization dawns in agonizing ripples. They'd removed her. I hadn't given much thought to Cormac's words before—*she was found and removed*—even when Erik warned me she might still be alive. But whether it was from my inability to comprehend what the Remnants were or my unwillingness to, I hadn't seen this coming. It seems I've grossly underestimated the Guild's cruelty. Again.

"It's my mother," I say, trying to pin the statement to the reality of seeing her here in front of me.

Jost's hand slips and grabs the fabric of my blouse. I can hear his sharp intake of breath, but Dante stays calm, unmoved by my announcement. *Almost* as if he expected it.

"It *was* your mother," he tells me, but his words are forced and he doesn't move to get around my warp. "You've been keeping secrets."

"Can you blame me?" I ask.

"Then they came for you," Dante says, and I know it must be true. It seemed arrogant to jump to that conclusion before. Now it's merely a fact. He addresses his next question to Erik. "How did they catch you?"

Erik steps into the light to face him. "The man I was trading with sold me out to the Guild."

Erik had known the man was curious about his Guild paraphernalia. He must have figured out that Erik was a valuable refugee. And we'd let him walk into the trap alone.

"Why send *her* though?" I ask. The shell in front of me seems unaware I'm her daughter. I can't see any benefit in using her against me.

"To scare you," Dante says in a cold voice. "Whatever you've done to earn their wrath, they want you to know they're coming for you and they'll use any means to destroy you."

It sounds like he's speaking from experience.

"Are you going to kill her?" I choke the question out. It might not be my mother anymore, but the thought of standing back and letting him murder her claws across my body, squeezing my heart until I'm sure it will shatter. It will be like losing her all over again.

But Dante hesitates at my question, and the pained look on his face mirrors what I feel. He's closer to this situation than he's letting on. The Guild must have taken something from him, too. "Not unless you ask me to."

Whatever the Guild has done to her, forcing her into a half-life, I can't bring myself to end it. I think of the boxes in the storage facility. It's possible the rest of her waits inside one, and if so, wouldn't it be possible to save her—to mend the damage done to her in the sterile clinics of Arras? The technology exists to make a Remnant, perhaps it exists to fix one.

"I can't let her go without angering Kincaid," Dante says. "The security feed will catch it, which means I'll have to take her in."

"Do you have holding areas here?" Jost asks.

"Not here. Kincaid has holding facilities on his estate, but I can't protect you from him if I take you there. A refugee is one thing, but a renegade Spinster is another," Dante tells me.

"I'm guessing after this"—I gesture to the warp—"you couldn't protect me from him regardless."

Dante's attention turns to Erik. "You got a good bit of credit for that Guild paraphernalia, right?"

Erik nods.

"Then let me put this in terms you'll understand. Adelice is the most valuable Guild paraphernalia on Earth," Dante says. "Kincaid will want her."

And like that I'm an object. Something to be collected and used and sold, like a machine.

"What if we don't want to come along?" Jost asks.

Dante faces him, his shoulders drawing up so that his slight difference in height feels more formidable. "He'll come after you. We may not have looms here on Earth, but you can't get far if Kincaid wants you. Your best option for staying alive—and keeping her safe—is to come as an invited guest. Otherwise, he'll see you as a threat."

"We've been threats before," I say, taking my place beside Jost.

"You don't need more enemies than you already have," Dante warns us. "The Guild overstepped their bounds here tonight. Kincaid won't overlook this. He'll want retribution from whomever he can get to after this. At this point, you need him as an ally."

"I won't be of any use to him," I warn Dante. "The strands here are different. I can hardly control my abilities." The warp

I'd made to protect my mother was nothing like the large domes I'd built around Jost and myself in the Coventry. It would have stopped a direct bullet but he only had to change position. I'd barely been able to grab the correct strands.

"You aren't dealing with the precise patterns of Arras here. This is raw space-time—you can't control it like you're at a loom," Dante says. "Not that I imagine most Spinsters could do what you did."

Jost steps closer to him and nods at my mother. "What will we do with her?"

I'm grateful he's changed the subject. I don't want to explain more about my skills, especially since I'm only now grasping that here I can touch the raw matter of the universe.

Dante's face is grim, but he's gentle as he lifts the remains of the steel door from my mother. Jost keeps a gun leveled at her, but Dante reaches to take her into his arms. She claws at him, howling, but her injuries prevent her from causing too much harm. Keying in the passcode, he holds her cautiously and eventually she goes limp in his arms as we wait for the door to swing open.

"We have facilities where I can restrain her," Dante says. "She will be fine there until we can move her in the morning. You should rest."

He tilts his head toward a hallway lined with doors.

"Sleeping quarters," he tells us, and then he disappears down the gray corridor without another word.

For a moment, I question if I've done the right thing by keeping her alive, and if I'm making a mistake by sending her with Dante now, but soon worry gives way to a panic building inside me. It rushes through my limbs and stops me in my tracks. The boys freeze alongside me and I feel their concern. But I can't put words to my dreadful realization yet.

This is what the Guild does to traitors, and I committed treason of an extraordinary caliber when I ripped us from Arras to Earth. We might be safe here temporarily, but there's no way to protect those we left behind, and now I know what the Guild does to those they perceive as threats—the monsters they create from them.

And if I don't find the resources to get back to Arras soon, there's no way to prevent them from doing this to Amie.

SEVEN

IN MY SLEEP, I FACE THE GHOSTS that come for me. A wave of Remnants with Amie in the middle, reaching for me. I can only watch as Amie is swept into the crowd of soulless monsters. A new figure emerges where she vanished: a woman with wrists dripping red. The Remnants are gone now. I open my mouth to scream but no sound comes. Blood pools at her feet as she dissolves slowly into a puddle and then another woman rises from it. She's naked, a long scar marring her belly, and her hair on fire. My mother. She points to me accusingly. Her eyes hollow. Dead. Because of me. I will the dream to change, coaxing my mind to wake up, reminding myself this isn't real. But when I open my eyes, I'm at a bar, a whiskey perched in front of me. Next to it rests a tiny card. I lift it to read the inscription.

Drink me.

I look around, wondering where this dream has taken me. The place is familiar, although it lacks the color of the real location I encountered in my travels in Arras. Here the bar isn't rich mahogany but a slab of ebony in a gray world. My eyes fall on the swinging doors. He'll arrive any minute.

Cormac. The worst nightmare of all. But it's not him. He's stockier than Cormac with the same easy swagger, but his face is shielded by a fedora cocked too low.

Even as I fight the dream, I drift in and out of consciousness until light breaks into the room. Suddenly Jost's arms are around me, waking me.

"I was dreaming," I murmur.

"Nightmares?"

"Yes."

His arms tighten around me, coming to rest in a cross on my chest. I feel the steady thump of his heart against my back. "You can rest now."

I relax into the security of his embrace, but I don't sleep. We've been on the surface barely over a week, and I've discovered so much. *Too much.* Seeing Valery, which I am increasingly sure was not my imagination. Being attacked by my mother. The strange experience in the Old Curiosity Shop. Cormac must have a hand in it all, but to what end? Does he hope to scare me back to Arras?

The events of the day crowd my mind, each bringing a question that I can't answer. Sleep becomes impossible while knowing my mother is locked somewhere in the safe house. I replay the attack and rewind farther and farther into my memories of her and my father.

My parents were never risk takers. They'd hinted at rebellion in whispered conversations, but the only openly anti-Guild action they ever took was to try to keep me from being retrieved. If there was more to their treachery, it was as hidden as the mysterious tunnels under our house. I wish I could talk to my mother or that my father was alive to direct me. I resented when they got involved with academy issues or offered unwanted advice about classmates. Now I ache for their guidance.

I close my eyes, trying to wash the memory of them from my mind, but they persist in the space between sleep and wakefulness. My parents were affectionate. Kind to each other. But what I remember most is how my father adored my mother. How he tried to fill the void of the third child the Guild would not grant or remedy the scars of her thankless job. Now she's a monster created by the Guild. I squeeze my eyelids tighter, willing myself to sleep, but images from home haunt me. Love notes. Morning routines. My mother pinning up her hair. I catch a glimpse of an hourglass scar behind her ear and startle awake, but close my eyes again quickly lest Jost wants to talk.

Did I imagine it? Have I added the scar to my memory as I try to understand who my mother was, or have I simply over-looked it for years?

My fingers touch my own scar. It feels the same as ever—slightly raised, but hardly perceptible. And yet it throbs, an-nouncing me for who I am. My father's words linger in my mind—*remember who you are*—but I'm no closer now to under-standing who I am than I was that night.

As each second ticks by, I see the lies surrounding me. The secrets everyone kept from me. When did my parents dig those tunnels and why didn't they tell me? How did Enora upload the program that led me to the truth on the digifile? Who gave her access? On Earth, the darkness is everywhere, and I'm trapped in it. How can I discover who I am when my world is built of secrets and shadows?

I only know one thing: I'm no safer here than I was in Arras. That's one message Cormac's made clear. He knows where I am, and he's still pulling the strings. So if Kincaid is the most powerful man on Earth, I'm going straight to his compound. Enora told me once to make allies. She couldn't have been more right.

We travel into the mountains the next day in a death trap Dante calls a crawler, which looks like a cage with wheels. Kincaid's estate rests on several acres located comfortably outside the Icebox but still under the Interface. Far enough away to supervise his business there while still having room to wrap an intimidating perimeter fence around his land. And though I've yet to meet him, our first glimpse of his home colors my impression of what kind of man he is. The estate is extravagant in the worst sense of the word. Kincaid must be a man who tries hard to impress if this is where he lives. We can't drive close enough to the estate to park the crawler there, so Dante stops outside one of the long, winding pathways to let us out. My mother is sedated and bound in the back—for our safety, according to Dante.

The opulence of Kincaid's estate takes me by surprise. I shouldn't have expected it to be any different, based on the Sunrunner's safe house in the grey market, but it pulls at me— the luxury off-putting in a world where there's not enough food to feed the population. It's nearly an entire metro unto itself, and I can't help thinking it puts even the compound of the Coventry to shame. In the center, the main house governs the landscape with its red-tiled roof and twin spires watching over the grounds. There are balconies that overlook the magnificent spectacle below. Palm trees and shrubbery line the walkways, and everywhere I turn faces frozen in marble stare back at me, locked in a permanent display of horror and beauty for those deemed worthy to enter the estate.

Pillars loom overhead, creating an artificial lighting system that mimics the sun. It's bright and warm, and the light sparkles off the water in the pools and fountains, nearly blinding me. But tucked behind the stately buildings and manicured gardens, a series of smokestacks billows against the Interface.

"Jax will show you in," Dante says, gesturing to a lanky boy waiting at the top of the stairs. "I'm going to see to our prisoner."

"I want to see her. I need to talk to her," I say as Dante turns away. I have so many questions for her. No matter what the Guild has done to her, she might still have answers. And I miss her.

"I promise you can later, but right now she needs to be secured for—"

"Our safety," I finish for him.

"Exactly," Dante says through tight lips.

The friendliness Dante exhibited toward Jost and me on our first meeting has cooled. He brought us here, starting out at first light, and he barely spoke to us as we took the twisting roads through the mountains to reach Kincaid. Maybe my talent unnerves him, but I suspect it's something more.

"Welcome," Jax calls as he bounces down the steps.

"Kincaid is expecting us," Dante says.

"I'll take care of them," Jax says, "and I have a message for you once you're done, uh . . ." He stares at my mother in Dante's arms, undoubtedly wondering why we've brought a Remnant onto the estate.

"I'll find you later," Dante says, carrying my mother away.

Jax is so skinny he looks years younger than Jost or Erik. But his eyes are surrounded by wrinkles, and they light up when he grins widely as he sticks his hand out to shake each of ours, repeating our names as we introduce ourselves—the greeting so easy and natural that I can't help but relax a little for the first time since yesterday's crazy events.

"I had them put some drinks in the assembly room for you," Jax tells us. "Kincaid is in a business meeting, but he'll join you at lunch."

"What's that?" I ask, pointing to the smokestacks.

"Power plant. It hosts the grids for the estate and the Icebox," Jax says.

"That's where you store the solar energy you collect?"

"It's a bit more complicated than that. We utilize a hybrid photovoltaic system with a coal-based generator that—"

"So basically it's where the power comes from?" Erik stops him.

"Yeah," Jax says with a laugh. We follow him into the main building, trailing behind as he chatters about the locations of toilets and how to call a servant. But I'm mesmerized by the statues that lurk in every corner and the detailed portraits that hang from the carved wooden panels. Tapestry after tapestry with precise, intricate embroidery chills my blood. There are faces everywhere, frozen in time, watching me as I enter the house. Between the patterns and colors and ornamentation, my head begins to hurt. The assembly room contains a variety

70

of seating choices, arranged in clusters. Against the far wall, a tall hearth, at least twice my height, lords over the room. My feet sink into the plush, woven rug as I melt into a sofa. The sofa is very elegant and very small, and I perch on it uncomfortably. Jax excuses himself, leaving the three of us alone in the grand room.

"Drink?" Erik asks, lifting a crystal decanter toward us.

"No, thank you," Jost says, and his formality irks me. Will we ever move past this awkwardness between the two of them?

"Not at the moment," I tell Erik.

"If it's poisoned, at least you'll be rid of me." Erik shrugs, nonplussed by our refusal, pouring a bit of the amber liquid into a tumbler. He shifts back, draping his arm around the sofa and throwing a leg across the seat. He looks at ease in this setting, not at all put off by the oppressive grandeur of our surroundings.

"So should we take a look around?" Erik asks a few minutes later, depositing his empty glass on the table.

I scoot a coaster under it, afraid to mar the pristine wood. Something tells me this Kincaid fellow would notice.

"This place has to be crawling with security," Jost points out. "Maybe we should wait a day or two before we label ourselves troublemakers."

With their cards on the table, the brothers glare at each other and then inevitably turn to me—tie-breaker extraordinaire.

"Jost is right," I agree, although I hate to take sides. "And they're probably listening to us now. I bet we wouldn't get far."

"Well that only leaves the elephant in the room then," Erik says. "Your mom."

Suddenly I want to jump up and go exploring. Anything to avoid this conversation, but I can't ignore it forever. "So my mom's a Remnant."

It's liberating to say it out loud, as though I've taken the first step in accepting the fact.

"Yes, but what is a Remnant exactly?" Jost asks. "How did the Guild do this?"

"I interacted with them. They're as smart as we are, maybe even more cunning, like they've been tuned into some primal frequency," Erik says.

"But how?" Jost's question feels more desperate this time, and I think of his wife.

"We know the Guild can remap and alter. They did it to Enora," I remind him, taking his hand.

"They seem to have perfected their technique," Jost mutters.

I frown. He's right. Enora's alteration backfired horribly, resulting in her suicide, but the Remnants seem fully functional. "Listen, there's something I haven't told you," I whisper. I relay the story of the clear cubes tucked away in storage at the Coventry.

"What do you think they are?" Jost asks.

"Souls," I say without hesitation. "Dante told us they remove the Remnants' souls, and the strands I found were too thin to be full people. I knew that then, but Loricel told me that people who die before they're ripped lose part of their strand. I think it's the key to understanding this. Spinsters rip people so the Guild can reuse them."

"So they separate the soul from the body?" Jost muses. "But why? It seems like a lot of work for no good reason."

"Take Enora. They didn't remove her soul, so it didn't work."

"But why wouldn't they remove Enora's soul if it was going to cause a problem?"

"I can't say exactly, but if I had to guess I think it comes back to something Loricel told me. Cormac was scared to do it to me. That's why they tested it on Enora, and when it backfired, they couldn't be sure I wouldn't have a similar reaction," I tell them.

"But they were planning to map you," Erik says.

"No," I say slowly as the pieces start to fit together. "They'd already mapped me. Cormac was positive they could splice my skill set into another Spinster, someone ready and willing to do what they asked. Someone who wouldn't reject the manipulation."

"Who?" Jost asks.

"My guess?" Erik says. He pours another drink and doesn't meet our eyes. "Pryana. She's as power hungry as Maela, but easier to control. That must have been why she was there that night."

I'd forgotten Pryana was there on the night of our escape. Her presence had seemed so trivial. Pryana blamed me for her sister's death after Maela, the manipulative Spinster in charge of our training, made an example of my refusal to rip a thread from Arras. Maela took out an entire academy instead, Pryana's sister included, and ever since, Pryana had been eager to rise to a position of power over me. Of course she's the Spinster Cormac would choose for the experiment. He enjoys making me squirm.

"But if the technology hadn't worked, they'd have jeopardized you and her," Jost says.

"They weren't going to use me," I remind him. "They were going to take Loricel's skills. If they did that, they wouldn't have to manipulate me much, only enough to make me Cormac's perfect bride."

"You know, I have to feel a little sorry for Cormac," Jost says. "You are quite the catch."

Erik raises his glass and says, "I'll drink to that."

For a second they grin at each other, but Jost's smile slips first.

"How would they have done this? Who has the ability to alter a person's personality and memories? Their skills?"

"Someone at one of the other Coventries," I guess. "Loricel told me she once assisted with the memory wipe of the entire population of Arras for the Guild, which means others helped."

"It's hard enough to keep the entire Western Coventry in line. I can't imagine how they managed it elsewhere," Erik says.

"Maybe it's not Spinsters," I say. The memory of the mapping session niggles at my mind. It was overseen by a doctor. Loricel wasn't present at all.

"Kincaid better have answers," Erik mutters.

"And I promise you I do," an airy voice proclaims. The man appears out of nowhere, but behind him I spy an elevator door sliding closed. As soon as it shuts, the panel blends in with the carved wooden wall. "But your guesses aren't bad. You're close, children."

I ignore the "children" comment. As one of the Coventry's

newest recruits, I've dealt with my fair share of simpering adults. Instead I stand in greeting. "Kincaid, I presume."

"Dear girl, you presume correctly!" His voice peaks, and Kincaid claps his hands in delight. He's wearing a smoking jacket, tied at the waist, and what appear to be velvet house slippers. We're not the only ones dressed down for the occasion.

"Care to tell us which part we were close on?" Erik asks, not bothering to straighten up.

Kincaid's taut features slacken when he takes in Erik's overly comfortable appearance, and I frown in disapproval. Erik gets the message and sits up.

"All in good time," Kincaid assures us. He extends his arm to me. "But first, strangers must become friends."

EIGHT

MY STOMACH FLIPS WITH ANXIETY AS WE take our places at the long dining room table. The table could seat a good portion of the Western Coventry's Spinsters. It's set formally with an array of cutlery and folded linen napkins. Crystal goblets are already filled with cold fresh water and thin red wine. A feast is placed before us by a valet. Some of the dishes are familiar staples, like a basket of bread, but others are new to me. I'm particularly drawn to a dish of fresh broccoli and roast fowl—chicken, perhaps—spread over a delicate brown sauce that wafts the aroma of garlic. I'm pleased to see that the greenhouse I spotted on the edge of the estate is being put to use. It doesn't feel like the kind of meal one serves to prisoners, so I presume Kincaid views us as guests—as Dante hoped he would.

Kincaid presides at the head of the table. Dante sits at the other end.

"Your house is lovely," I force out as naturally as possible.

"The *estate* is to my taste. Before the war it was called the

Enchanted Hill. It belonged to a fellow named Hearst, but he's dead now," Kincaid says.

What an odd thing to say. Of course he's dead.

"So you're refugees," Kincaid says, ignoring the plate of food in front of him.

I nod, scooping broccoli into my mouth.

"I've seen the footage from the incident at the safe house—unpleasant business," Kincaid continues, flicking the air like the attack was a mere annoyance. "A renegade Spinster is quite the treasure. I'm sure the Guild would love to have you back."

I set my fork down and meet his gaze. "I'm not going back."

Beside me Jost and Erik stop eating, waiting to see how this will play out, but Kincaid wheezes a low chuckle.

"I'm not going to give you over to them if that's what concerns you," he says. "The Guild and I are neither strangers nor *friends*."

His words reassure me, but I can't continue eating despite how warm and savory my first bite was.

"Eat, child," he prompts me.

"I'm afraid I find talk of the Guild rather unappetizing," I admit. My thoughts straddle two realities: this one, where Kincaid is telling me about his relationship to the Guild, and the one I know exists elsewhere in this prodigious estate. I feel safe for the moment, but knowing my mother is here, locked away somewhere on this property, makes me feel again like the girl who was dragged from her home by a retrieval squad. I hadn't been able to eat more than a bite or two of the dinner Mom cooked for me the night of my testing, so it's only fitting that the awareness of my mother—alive and imprisoned—is enough to revert me to the girl I used to be.

"We're of the same mind." He gestures to his untouched plate. "The victims of the Guild usually are."

My curiosity is piqued. "Victims?"

"I have a rather sordid past," Kincaid admits.

"Don't we all," Erik quips, but the mood at the table remains heavy.

"I was once an official myself."

The confession catches me off guard and I grip the table-cloth in front of me. Why didn't Dante mention this before?

"I'm in exile," Kincaid says, tearing apart a roll and slapping several pats of butter on it. He's surprisingly thin if this is how he eats.

"Exiled to Earth?" I ask.

"Cormac and I had a disagreement about the way Arras should be run. Unfortunately when it came time to take sides, I discovered most of my friends shared Cormac's antiquated notions. The Guild wouldn't accept change if they could stop it, and with the looms they could. They didn't see the merits of progress."

"And you do?" Erik challenges him.

"When I came back here, I had nothing," Kincaid says, his knuckles white around his butter knife. "Earth was dying. I built this city, creating a refuge of stability that could stand up to the Guild, and helped stabilize the solar energy trade."

"He monopolized the solar trade," Dante corrects, and then grins, but the smile stops before it reaches his eyes. Kincaid doesn't notice.

"'Take mercy on the poor souls for whom this hungry war

opens his vasty jaws,'" Kincaid tells him. He turns to us and simply says, "*Henry V.* Shakespeare."

How romantic of him.

"Well, I'd call my work progress. There would be no power under the Interface without my efforts, so it's best for everyone that I oversee the operation. My ideas weren't welcome in Arras—especially among the likes of Cormac Patton. Who could have imagined that being exiled would prove so liberating? Turning against the Guild was the best decision I ever made."

"Then we have even more in common," I say, willing my voice to stay steady regarding this news. "We're both renegades."

"Ahh, yes. I like that, having things in common with you."

His words are honey sweet, meant to be endearing, but they grate against my ears. I know better than anyone that having been part of the Guild doesn't automatically qualify one as a villain, but I'm reluctant to take his admission at face value.

Before the conversation can continue, a woman sweeps into the room. The train of her low-backed gown trails behind her. Despite its high neckline, only sheer mesh covers her skin, and across it a snarling dragon breathes fire. The embroidery is elegant and lends an exotic air to her entrance. Her hair nests on top of her head and tendrils curl down against her neck. When she turns, I stifle a gasp. Her cosmetics are less tasteful than the ones she wore in Arras. Her skin is painted milky white, her cheekbones rouged deep pink, and her lips drawn into a tiny red heart, but her toffee eyes are the same, even with the petite peacock feathers that dance at the ends of her lashes.

Valery.

"Darling, you're late for lunch." Kincaid's tone is simpering, and I get the impression he's putting on a show.

I meet Jost's eyes and then Erik's, and I know we're debating the same question. Do we say something or pretend not to recognize her?

In the end, Valery chooses for us. "You can't rush perfection," she simpers back, and the whole act is quite sickening. "That's something Adelice knows."

"Then you've met our delightful new friends," Kincaid cries in his giddy, childlike way. "Tell me how!"

"I was Adelice's aesthetician at the Coventry before I sought sanctuary with you," she says.

I can't keep the words from tumbling out. "I thought you were dead."

"Thought or hoped?" The venom she displayed to me in our last conversation before she disappeared from the Coventry drips from her words, but she smiles brightly to cover it. We had been friends once, but Valery disappeared before either of us had come to grips with the suicide of Enora, my mentor and Valery's lover. "Loricel aided my escape, and Kincaid granted me safe passage."

"Any enemy of the Guild is a friend of mine, and how fortunate I am to make such a lovely friend." He draws Valery's hand up to his mouth, and I see a flash of her red fingernails. Instantly I'm reminded of a moment I witnessed in the hall of the High Tower. Her red fingernails on Enora's back.

"But you're—" I choke the last word back. If Loricel had managed to help her escape, why did she lead me to believe Valery was dead? It isn't my place to bring up the past, not before I've had a private moment to talk to Valery about her change of . . . heart.

Valery arches a perfectly shaped eyebrow at me, a challenge. "Forgive me, Adelice. We parted under trying circumstances."

"There's nothing to forgive," I murmur. "If I had known you were alive, I would have tried to help you."

"Others helped me," Valery tells us. "Earth is far from the ideal hiding place, as I'm sure you're discovering, but Loricel made a compelling argument."

"Which was?" Erik asks.

"Run or be ripped. Not much of a choice. I might have done it years ago if I'd known about Kincaid. He immediately opened his home to me."

"I had not thought I could love again until Valery entered my life," Kincaid says, raising her hand to his lips again.

My head is starting to spin and I stare down at my plate, wondering if food might help me digest this news, but I discover it's gone, stripped away by the valet while I was distracted. My fingers reach for a lock of loose hair and I twist it nervously. Valery and Kincaid can't have known each other more than a few days. It doesn't make sense.

"My dear, your arm," Kincaid says.

Without the jacket I left in the drawing room, the burns I suffered from the falling aeroship debris are evident. They've healed into rough scabs that are more unsightly than painful. I shrug it off, flashing a smile at Dante, whose eyes narrow.

"An accident," I assure Kincaid.

"They look like chemical burns," Dante says. It's an innocuous comment, but he's already accused me of bringing down the aeroship our first day on Earth and I know he's tallying this as further evidence.

"I insist that one of my men take a look at it. Don't let your time in the Icebox fool you," Kincaid says. "We're not all barbarians here. We have our own renewal-patching methods available."

I thank him although I have no intention of taking him up on it.

"Ahh, dessert," Kincaid calls as a server appears with another platter. "Sweets for my sweet." Valery giggles and nuzzles his hand.

"If I ever act like that, promise to kill me," I whisper to Jost.

"Deal," he says without hesitation.

This is why our relationship works.

Across from us, Erik is chewing on his cheek in what I'm guessing is an attempt to bite back laughter at the absurdity of the scene in front of us.

Despite the whirl of emotions I'm feeling, I take a spoonful of the custard in front of me. It melts across my tongue and floods my mouth with the slightest sweet creaminess. One more bite reveals spicy chocolate swirled through it.

"Lovely, no?" Kincaid asks with greedy eyes.

"It's delicious," I admit, but I set down my spoon. I've been a gracious guest, but I have something I need to do.

"Kincaid has excellent taste in everything he procures," Valery tells me. There's a warning in her voice and I search her face for a signal, but it stays placid under her mask of cosmetics.

"Dante said you could help us," Jost says, clearly having grown impatient with the doublespeak.

Kincaid leans forward in an ominous way, dabbing the corners of his mouth with a linen napkin. "We're going to help each other."

NINE

THERE'S NO LOGICAL REASON TO GO TO her, but I excuse myself from lunch early, ready to hold Dante to the promise he made when we left the safe house. Given the events of the past week, I'm reeling as though my world is turning so fast, spinning so uncontrollably, that I can't count on my feet to hold me upright. When I left the Coventry, I was an orphan, but now my mother is alive. It's too much to process. I knew who I was a week ago, but I'm not so sure anymore, and my mother is the one person who might have the answer.

The guards give me a little grief when I ask to see my mother, but Dante himself called in the request, so they acquiesce.

Of course, I'm not sure that I want to see my mom.

They're keeping her in the highest-security facility they have on the estate. A guard leads me there past dusty paintings, rolled-up rugs, and discarded busts, which they must have no additional room for in the main house. As we walk, he explains what will protect me from her trying to attack. I never thought I'd have to be protected from my mom. It seems like uncertainty is the only sure thing these days.

"It's a huge power drain," the guard tells me as he leads me down a barely lit corridor, past dozens of empty cells. "We usually don't keep Remnants more than a few hours before . . ."

He hesitates, but I already know the answer.

"Before you execute them," I finish.

"It sounds horrible," he says. "But we've tried to help them. We've done everything we can. There is no redeeming these creatures."

"Creatures?" There's disgust in my voice, but I know I'm being a hypocrite. Don't I think of them the same way?

"You've seen them. What they can do. You can waste your time feeling sorry for them if you want, but not all of us have that luxury." He keeps his face turned from me as he speaks.

I wonder who he lost to this dirty war between worlds. It's in his voice—the pain of it.

"So why are these such a drain?" I ask, shifting the topic back to the cells, which look ordinary enough to me.

"These ones aren't. We primarily use them for holding Rems before termination. But our newest visitor is going to be staying awhile. She's been patched up and healed, so Dante wants to be sure she doesn't try to escape."

"You catch a lot of Remnants?" I ask, wondering at the need for so many enclosures.

"A fair few," he hedges before abruptly adding, "We're here."

He stops at a small gray door and enters a code. The door zips open and I follow him into the high-security cell. The room is lit by halogen but only enough for me to make out her shape lying in the corner. There are two sets of bars between us, which seems a bit excessive.

"You want me to stay with you?" he asks, but I can hear how much he's hoping I'll say no, so I shake my head.

"I'll be fine," I say confidently. After all, it is my mother.

"Okay," he says, but he doesn't sound convinced. "Whatever you do, don't stick your hands through the bars."

I glare at him. "Or she'll bite me, right?"

"No," he says, pretty patiently considering how surly I'm being. He pulls something from his pocket and tosses it through the bars, but it doesn't make it into the cell. Instead it cracks and sizzles as it makes contact with an invisible wall between the bars. A moment later a thin layer of ash drops to the ground.

Well, that explains the power drain.

"Don't you think that's a bit much?" I ask, staring at the ash.

"You've seen them in action. What do you think?"

He has a point, but I don't tell him so. "I'll keep my hands to myself," I assure him.

He gives me a bemused look and leaves me alone. My mother stays in the corner, not acknowledging my entrance.

"Mom," I call softly. Then I feel silly. Whoever this woman is, she's not my mother anymore and she's not likely to remember she once was. But to my surprise, she turns her head to stare at me.

"Mom." I try again.

She rolls over, keeping her eyes on me. They've cleaned her up, given her fresh clothes, and brushed her hair. It strikes me as odd that they'd bother with such things for someone they don't consider human.

I smile, hoping to make her feel safe, to coax her into speaking to me.

She bares her teeth.

"Mom," I say again, this time more sternly. Ironically, I'm channeling how she used to sound when I was being reprimanded.

She closes her lips back over her teeth and then she starts to crawl toward the bars. This was a horrible idea. Why did I want to see my mother like this? What does it matter if they terminate her? This woman is nothing like the parent I lost.

When she reaches the bars, she uses them to pull herself up. And then she brushes off her pants and turns her eyes to mine. I notice a scar, thicker than the rest, glinting silver-white on her forehead.

"Adelice," she murmurs, but it sounds more like a hiss.

It's not my mother's voice. Still, she remembers me.

"I'm not sure why I came," I admit. My words bounce around the mostly empty room, leaving a faint echo.

"You came to see your mother," she says, "but we both know I'm not really your mother, Adelice."

I've seen Remnants attack, and the amount of destruction they can inflict, and yet, listening to her speak so coherently shocks me. She'd howled when we took her into the safe house.

"You thought I'd be some kind of zombie," she says.

I nod.

"You assume that because we attack you, we're animals, but we're not," she says angrily.

"Then what do you do with the people you take?" I ask. "Why attack at all?"

She looses a hollow laugh. "Survival, child. We can't all make it here."

"We'd stand a better chance if we worked together," I say.

"An idealistic dream," she scoffs.

It's in the way she says it. The way her eyes seem to lock on mine but still look right past me. There's something missing, something vital. Never has *Remnant* seemed like such a fitting term.

"How do you know who I am?" I ask.

She stares at me and her lips curl up at the corners. "You're hoping I'll admit to some latent memories, I assume. That deep down I remember being your mother."

I back up a few steps. Each of her words stings a bit more than the last.

"Rest assured, I do remember my life before," she says, keeping her eyes on me. "I remember getting coffee and making dinner and wasting every night trying to rescue you. What I don't remember is *why*. Why I did any of it. But that's not the only reason I know your name, Adelice.

"We were prepped to look for you," she admits with a wicked smile. "We were shown pictures, told about who you were and that we must retrieve you at any cost."

"Retrieve?" Nothing about what she's telling me is a surprise except this.

"Or kill," she coos.

That's more like it.

"I remembered you, of course. I could foresee every stupid move you would make. Coming to rescue your friend. It was my idea to snatch him. I would be embarrassed by how predictable you are—how much you let those boys influence your actions—if I cared. If I was still trapped in Meria's pathetic mind-set. But I'm not. That's why he put me in charge of the troops. Because I'm perfectly in control of myself. And because I know you." She turns her eyes from mine and the scar comes into harsh relief, cutting across her cheekbone. Her clothes prevent me from seeing how far it goes.

"He?" I ask, even though I don't need to know who she's talking about.

"Your jilted fiancé," she mocks. "Cormac misses you desperately. Tell me, Adelice, would you have invited me to your wedding?"

"Probably not," I say coolly, although invisible screws twist my insides. "Maybe you can come to my funeral."

She finds this very funny.

"I was told you were dead," I tell her.

"Your mother is dead," she says. "She died after she was stuck in cold storage for months."

"Is that where you were?" I ask, thinking of the threads I removed as a Spinster.

"There were a lot of us that needed the procedure. I had to wait my turn."

So they froze her until they could pull her soul strand. That means somewhere in Arras there's a lab devoted to preparing Remnants to come to the surface.

"Will you tell him this?" she asks.

"Who?"

"The Sunrunner," she breathes. "Dante."

I stare at her. How does she know his name? "No," I murmur. "Not yet. Why do you care if Dante knows?"

"I could lie and tell you we were prepped on him," she says, "and we were, to a point. But I know Dante very well. It's another reason Cormac chose me to lead the new contingent. You should ask Dante why I'm here. Why he didn't execute me."

"You're here because Dante wants me to help him and he figured killing my mom wasn't going to ensure my loyalty," I say defiantly.

"Ask him when you're ready to learn the truth then," she says.

I'd suspected Dante was hiding something, but why does my mother know what it is? I've had enough of this conversation so I rap a couple times on the steel door and wait for the guard to open it.

She may not be my mother anymore, but she knows me as well as my mother once did, and that's what scares me.

Dante is waiting outside the cell block as though he's anticipating my next move. Lounging against the door, he looks agitated, even more so than he's been since the Remnant attack. He's dressed down from his flashy attire into a pair of jeans, and he's fiddling with something in his hands. A digifile.

"Is this the best place to have this conversation?" I ask him in my most confrontational tone. Seeing him here, I'm sure that he knew my mother would direct me to talk to him.

"No, let's go to the fountains. And, Adelice"—he pauses— "keep the questions to yourself until we get there."

I do as he requests but only because I'm not sure what to ask first, and because the time it takes us to walk outside and down into the gardens allows me to calm the anxiety that has built up inside me since my mother pushed me to speak with him.

"The surveillance can't hear much with the water," Dante says as we sit on the edge of the fountain. It's cold and water sprays my back slightly, but I don't care.

"I know. Jost and I used this trick to block the audio transmitters in the Coventry," I tell him.

Dante fidgets with the digifile, flipping it from hand to hand. "He's smart. Seems nice. Do you love him?"

It's a totally inappropriate question and it catches me by surprise. "I'm not sure that's your business."

"Fair enough," Dante admits. "I was merely interested."

Interested in what? Me? He didn't ask flirtatiously—more like an old friend trying to catch up on the latest news. But we're not friends. Not yet.

"I brought this so I could scan your techprint," he says.

"I have questions first," I say, holding my arm to my waist. "Lots of them."

"I know that, Adelice," Dante says in a quiet voice. "I do, too. I think some of the answers we're looking for are encoded in that hourglass though."

It never occurred to me to try to scan the techprint my father left on me. I'd accepted my father's simple explanation that it was to remind me who I was, but now that I've learned it is the sign of Kairos, I realize it might hold more answers.

"I have one, too," Dante says, revealing his wrist to me.

I swallow hard. Why has he waited so long to show me this?

"What does yours say?"

"Nothing spectacular. I had reasons for seeking refuge here," he says. "It was my ticket in, and it helped me get in with Kincaid."

"He's more than a Sunrunner," I surmise.

"Much more," Dante says. "I can show you new ways of looking at the world, Adelice, but first, I need to see what that techprint says."

Ready for answers, I thrust my wrist out to him. He takes it gently, and his hand is warm on my skin, sending the oddest sensation of comfort traveling up my arm. The digifile takes a long while to scan.

"Sorry, we only get the castoffs that refugees bring from Arras," he apologizes, and then the information displays. I can't read what it says, but the words reflect in his wide eyes.

"Did you find what you were looking for?" I ask.

Dante waits a long moment before he responds, and when he does, his hand grips my wrist tightly.

"It says I'm your father."

TEN

THE MOMENT LOCKS IN PLACE, MY MIND frozen like a blank screen as shivers ripple from my fingertips to my throat. Suddenly I'm falling, but I never jumped. It's the sensation of the world slipping away.

This is what my mother was trying to tell me, why she pushed me to seek answers from Dante. How is this possible? Dante is barely a year or two older than me.

A voice calls me back, and I find I'm still on the edge of the fountain.

"Come on, you're getting wet," Dante says.

And in that moment, he sounds downright *fatherly*.

"You're lying," I say, pulling my arm from him.

"It's right here," he says, holding out the digifile. "Your parents encoded it in your techprint."

"My father is dead," I spit at him. "Benn Lewys died on the night of my retrieval. Whoever you are, whatever happened between you and my mom, nothing changes that."

I don't stop running until I'm back inside. He doesn't stop calling after me.

Jost's bedroom is across from mine. I stare at his door, knowing it's late, knowing I don't want to talk, knowing he's asleep.

But also knowing that the door will open if I twist the knob.

I do it. His room is too dark to see much. A single beam of light from the security system outside evades the blackout curtains, cutting across the floor and falling on Jost's still form. I tiptoe to his bedside and watch him sleep. A pillow is twisted in his arms and his hair covers his face. He breathes slowly and rhythmically, and I count each inhale and exhale, willing the steadiness of it to calm me.

When it doesn't, I climb into bed next to him. He rolls over and wraps an arm around my waist, but his eyes don't open.

"You're still dressed."

I press into him. I don't want to explain why I'm awake. I don't want to share what I've seen or learned today. Not yet. Not while I still don't understand any of it.

"Can't sleep?" he asks.

"I haven't even tried yet," I admit.

"Do you want—"

I know he's going to say *talk*, but I don't give him a chance to ask. I don't want to talk. I don't even want to think, so I stop the question with a kiss.

He doesn't object.

In fact, his whole body says yes. His fingers find my jaw and he holds my mouth to his. His grip loosens and his hands slip into my hair, holding me to him. The room falls away. There is only him, and the wonder of how soft his lips are. This is the only real thing I have left. The taut muscles of his back, coiled like wire, as he hovers over me. The way my body aches to float up, to close the space he's left open between us, but his hands hold me in place.

I stretch against him. His touch erases the agony I feel in my chest, leaving traces of fire where our skin connects.

"I need you," I murmur into his ear, and he responds by drawing me up, his hands cocooning my back. He cradles me gently as our limbs lengthen and intertwine like vines growing into one another until I can no longer remember where I end and he begins.

But the barriers between us remain intact, and his lips leave mine as he drops them to my ear. "What are you running from, Ad?"

He knows me too well. I rejoice in this knowledge even as I deny it. "I'm not running."

Jost drops to his back, his hand wrapping into my own. "I won't make you talk, Adelice, but I wish you would."

I'm not ready to face this—not even with him, so I turn to him and run a tremulous finger down his cheek. "I'm not running from anything," I whisper. "I'm running *to* something. I'm running to you."

He doesn't ask to talk again.

ELEVEN

THE LIBRARY SPANS A SPACE AS LARGE as the dining hall in the Coventry, books tucked behind lattice doors. Someone has lit a fire in the hearth, and its heat radiates through the room. I'd never imagined so many books could exist. My experience is limited to the fifteen or twenty hidden in my parents' room. Here stories from men about the nature of the universe mingle with tales of all-powerful creators. I come from a world created by men, but on Earth, they don't know how we came to be, whether we are the product of spectacular chance or divine intervention. I find poetry and prose, history and science mixed together into a world of words and thoughts.

Most of the history books are dated. None of them were written after the building of Arras or the Exodus from Earth. I doubt anyone writes books anymore. I flip through them, looking for clues that will link this reality with the one I knew once, but the volumes are full of history I've never heard of, places with names that are lost, and people who died long ago.

"I collect them." Kincaid's proclamation is nonchalant, but I can tell by the tilt of his head that he hopes I'm impressed.

"My parents did, too," I say.

Kincaid slides onto the sweeping arm of a sofa, leaning forward. "So you were raised to be a rebel."

"No—I was raised to blend in," I correct him.

"And yet here you are. A girl who reads books and runs from the Guild while your mother sits in my prison," he says with a smile that stops on his cheeks. His eyes stay snakelike, darting ever so slightly at the smallest of my movements.

"Is that a problem?" I ask.

"Not for me. Not yet," Kincaid says. "My informants within Arras tell me the Guild is none too happy about your unexpected departure from service. It seems you were more than another Spinster to them."

I keep my gaze leveled on his beady eyes, forcing myself not to blink.

"Don't fret, child. I'm thrilled you came to me. Any enemy of Cormac Patton is a friend of mine. 'The signs of war advance,'" Kincaid quotes. "But I wonder why you are here. What are your plans?"

I'm not sure I can trust Kincaid. I know I don't like him, but he's opened his home to us. He's also as eager to destroy Cormac as I am. I turn my attention back to the shelves. "I want answers about this world and Arras. I was hoping to find a book about Kairos."

"That will be a problem," Kincaid says, a note of apology in his voice. "Not many books have been published since the Exodus."

"That's unfortunate."

"It is, isn't it? I never took to the Guild's desire to limit the arts. They felt the arts were too dangerous to the controlled history, but I think it's barbaric. It's one of the reasons I settled here. The Guild occupied this estate for a long time. Apparently they weren't interested in cultivating the arts in Arras, but they were keen on preserving those they took control of on Earth. I have been a much more attentive owner. My staff takes care to attend to the sculptures and libraries, so I'm certain you will find many treasures in my home."

I'm not exactly interested in Kincaid's artistic ambitions, but I nod to show I appreciate his effort. "What is Kairos?" I prompt.

"The correct question is, *who* is Kairos?" Kincaid says.

"Kairos is the name of a scientist, or at least, he's come to be known as that. I'm told you bear his mark," he says, returning to my original query.

I hesitate but then I stretch my arm out to confirm it. I see no point in hiding this information. He already knows I'm a traitor to the Guild.

"Who was he then? Kairos?" I ask.

"That's complicated," Kincaid stalls.

"Come on. I showed you mine," I press.

Kincaid's mouth twists into a bemused grin. "He was the scientist who started the Cypress Project. Rumor is that he didn't hold with the Guild's ultimate plan. Bit of a legend here actually."

"What happened to him?" I ask.

"He vanished." He sweeps a hand through the air, opening

it with a flourish. "Poof! Some of the people left behind after the Exodus dubbed themselves the Kairos Agenda, determined to continue his work."

"They rose up in his memory?"

"More or less," Kincaid confirms. "Unfortunately, their ambitions died out as the resistance to Arras grew more futile."

"But the Agenda had a plan to fight back against the Guild?" I ask.

"The Agenda believed Kairos left behind a machine."

"A machine?" I ask in a breathless voice. "What did it do?"

"No one knows. It's only known as the Whorl. Its myth is almost as legendary as Kairos himself. Some believe the Whorl could give Earth control over Arras."

"Instead of the Guild controlling us," I say.

"I believe it could do more than that. Kairos wanted to end Arras's dependence on Earth. His machine would have to do more than simply control Arras. I vowed years ago to find it and finish Kairos's work. If Arras became independent from Earth, this planet could prosper again. I 'have no delight to pass away the time; unless to spy my shadow in the sun.'"

"Shakespeare?" I guess.

"An indulgence of mine," he says.

I make a mental note to procure a volume of Shakespeare's collected works to add to my book of sonnets. Studying them might give me better insight into Kincaid.

"If you're right, with the Whorl, both worlds could exist?" I ask. It's too much to hope for.

"I'm almost certain of it, but I've had my own men searching for intelligence on the Whorl for years." Kincaid sinks back against the sofa, and my pulse quickens. He might have the information about the Guild.

"No luck?"

"False leads and dead ends. It probably doesn't exist." Kincaid pauses before adding, "But one can hope." He stands and offers his arm to me, and my heart sinks. I loop my arm through his and he leads me away from the library.

"So that's all there is?" I ask. "Rumors? Lies?"

"Oh no," Kincaid says, patting the hand that rests on his forearm. "I have more to show you."

He leaves me with promises of answers tonight, but little else.

"It's an old film about the Cypress Project. Kincaid hopes it will enlighten you," Dante says. His tone is formal as he leads us into a room with a large white screen at one end. I've been avoiding him since the day in the garden, but even though a few days have passed, none of the tension hanging like a cloud between us has dissipated. I wonder if Jost and Erik can sense it.

The walls of the theater are papered in crimson brocade, and the exaggerated figures of women bear torches overhead, glowing gold in the dim room. The carpets here are so plush they look like velvet and the row of armchair-like seats is equally divine. It's nothing like the spare white room where we watched vids at the Coventry.

The Cypress Project. Greta spoke of it in the Old Curiosity Shop, and Kincaid mentioned it earlier today. He was following through on the answers he promised me. "The Cypress Project is Arras? Is that why our capital is named Cypress?" I say.

"I suppose," he murmurs. "It would certainly be a reminder of their cleverness."

"But they didn't want anyone to know about Earth," I say.

"Not subsequent generations, but the original population of Arras was quite proud of their achievement."

"A film is like a vid?" I ask, pointing to the screen.

"Yes." Dante excuses himself, obviously eager to get away from me. I'm not sorry to see him go. The awkwardness between us is getting harder to hide, and I still haven't told the others about Dante's claim.

We take seats and wait for the film to start. Kincaid enters but he doesn't sit with us; instead he chooses a small sofa placed to the side of the room. Only Valery sits with him. He nods to me, and I turn away, embarrassed to be caught staring at him.

Blurring light streams past me and life bursts onto the screen. The images are in black-and-white and they crackle although there's no sound. Dante returns and sits next to me. I focus on the screen, feeling Jost's arm drape around my shoulders.

Tanks roll through cities. Soldiers march in proud lines. Women wave from windows. A man with a smudge of a mustache screams from a podium. Planes drop bombs overhead. Then a man with a shock of white hair appears, speaking directly to the camera. I can't hear what he's saying, but he looks congenial and important.

"Who is that?" I ask Dante.

"The scientist who discovered the strands," he whispers.

I suddenly realize that the great scientist Loricel first told me about—the one whose name was long since forgotten by Arras—is the same man Kincaid told me bore the name of the mark on my wrist: Kairos. He moves across the screen, and the camera follows to zoom in on a small machine comprised of whirring gears.

"A loom," I breathe.

The scientist demonstrates the loom for a group of men. I glance in the direction of Kincaid, who was once an official in Arras, then jerk my eyes back to the screen. Kincaid is watching us as we watch the film, and now I feel his eyes on me.

The film shifts to footage of girls waiting in line to be weighed, to have their eyes checked, and their hands measured. Many smile and wave to the camera. One curls her arm up and stares out fiercely before dissolving into laughter.

"Are those . . ." Jost's voice is full of surprise.

"The original Eligibles," Dante finishes. I forget the tension between us, too wrapped up in the film. "We have to assume from the film that they are. I truly wish we had the sound so we could hear what they're telling us. Most of the other records have been destroyed. The Guild has worked very hard at ensuring confidentiality regarding the Cypress Project."

But it's obvious to me what's going on, especially as the screen flashes lists of items approved for transport followed by written guidelines for safe addition and eligible participants.

"Wait," I say as something slowly dawns on me. "Those eligibility requirements weren't for Spinsters."

"No, families and individuals had to prove their health and value to earn a spot in Arras's weave."

"And those that didn't?" I ask.

"You've seen the evidence," Dante responds. "Not everyone on Earth migrated to Arras, but they didn't die out either as the Guild had hoped. Those who were left behind adapted to the changing surface conditions. The war ended quickly. Hitler, the man who started it, had no one to fight, and there were bigger problems to grapple with here."

"They picked who got to come along." The unfairness of it grates against my sense of justice.

"They assumed the war would destroy the rest. The few records that have stood the test of time indicate that the war lasted for several more years, stretching out almost an entire decade. The Icebox was less affected as most of the fighting continued in what was known as Europe," he says.

"Was known as Europe?"

"We have enough information to conclude that most of it is gone now. A large portion of Arras's population came from Europe, as many of the Allied troops hailed from there. The rest imploded after they left. And of course, many died during squelched riots. The survivors were driven into the Icebox." Dante keeps his eyes on the screen while he tells me this. He relates it like a newsman on the Stream.

We watch the few remaining images flit across the screen. The program ends with a happy family—two parents, a daughter, and a son—beaming out at the audience. I wonder who they were. And whether they thought this would consign them to immortality, and how they would feel to see the theater sitting in a ruined world. An empty, forgotten Earth.

As the last image vanishes, the lights in the theater come up. I blink against the brightness. Kincaid stands and politely claps.

"I hope you found that informative." There's something weary in his voice, a heaviness that doesn't suit, and I realize the film has moved Kincaid to tears. He's touched by something that happened hundreds of years ago.

"I think it raises more questions than it answers," I say. I bow my head a bit in an attempt to hide the surprise I can't quite wipe from my face.

"It's the story of how our worlds came to be." Kincaid spreads his hands. "You cannot expect one film to explain everything."

TWELVE

DANTE FOLLOWS ME OUT OF THE THEATER, but Jost keeps a protective arm around my shoulder. I know I can't avoid Dante forever, and now that I've seen the film, I shrug off Jost's arm and kiss him swiftly on the cheek. He doesn't like it, but he gives Dante a terse nod and leaves us, heading back into the main house while Dante and I tarry on the stone path. The lights have dimmed to near twilight, but I can see the outlines of the wild plants and hear the trickle of the nearest fountain.

"Have you told anyone about us?" Dante asks me.

I shake my head. "I wouldn't know what to say."

"I can barely believe it myself," Dante says.

"But you suspected it. Why?"

"You said your last name was Lewys and, well, because of your mother," he says.

"You know her?" I ask.

"Of course, she's your mother."

I'm having a difficult time composing sentences, and

thoughts, for that matter. It doesn't make sense. It's not possible. "So you *knew* her."

"Yes," Dante confirms.

"But Benn Lewys was my father," I say, trying hard to sort this in my mind.

"Benn was my brother," Dante says.

"He didn't have a brother," I say.

"No, his brother left." Dante blinks several times as if resetting himself. "I left, because the Guild was coming after me."

It doesn't explain anything, especially not his claims about his past—our past—or how he wound up on Earth. Still, my mother hinted at this, so I concentrate.

"But," I say, struggling, "you aren't old enough to be my father."

"About that," he says, scratching his temple.

"Yes?" I prompt.

"Things are different here."

"Do you have time machines?" I ask sarcastically.

"We don't need them. Time doesn't flow rapidly on Earth like it does where we came from. Arras is a construct, so its time is not bound to the same physical laws that time on Earth is. For every month that passes on Earth, a year passes in Arras. So if you're sixteen years old—"

"It's only been sixteen months since you left," I say. If he's right, then half a year has passed on Arras since we left. It will be spring again, and Amie will graduate primary academy soon.

"I feel like I've barely been away, but here you are. I didn't know," Dante says. "I wouldn't have left Meria if I had known she was pregnant."

He wants me to understand. He wants forgiveness.

"It doesn't matter," I say. My words are glass, smooth and cold, and I know he can see right through them. "You still left her."

You left me, I add silently.

"You don't understand. *Meria* refused to come with me," Dante explains. "She didn't want to run. I showed her the mark of Kairos so she could come if she changed her mind."

"Why does this matter?" I ask, gesturing to the techprint—a symbol that's lost its original meaning to me. Now it's another secret—another lie.

"Credentials," he says. "It's not just the mark, but also the information the techprint contains. Most refugees and dissenters hide theirs along their hairline."

That's why the girl checked our necks, but because my father had burned mine into my wrist she almost didn't see it. "Why is mine here?"

"Priority access," Dante says in a grim voice. "If you'd made it out that night, our channels would have rushed your clearance. Kincaid's men in Arras verify information, but the placement of your techprint would have granted you priority passage through a loophole."

"A loophole?" I ask.

"It's an exit from Arras. It's how most refugees make it to Earth.

"I told Meria all of this. If she had left . . ." He pauses and searches my face as though he wants to tell me something, but he changes the topic instead. "You can't imagine what it was like. A girl with fiery hair walks into my life with that mark, and you're so like her, but—"

"My father marked me, not my mother," I interrupt.

Betrayal flits across Dante's face. His voice is raw when he speaks. "She must have told him about it."

He's hurt that she revealed his secret to her husband. His brother. "Yes," I say, "because she loved him. Because he was a good man."

"I never said differently." But his body is saying it now. Every expression, every gesture, every pause is wounded. But then his posture changes, shrinking down before me. In my short time at the estate, Dante has never seemed vulnerable.

"I knew you the second I saw you," he says. "I couldn't explain it, even to myself."

"That's why you invited us back to the safe house," I say.

"At first I thought you were Meria, altered a little, toying with me."

"Mom wouldn't do that," I say defensively.

"The spitfire I knew would have, but I figured out pretty quickly you weren't her," Dante says.

"When you saw me kissing Jost."

"I wouldn't have put that past Meria, but no, I knew it wasn't her. It was obvious you didn't know me, but when you showed me that techprint and started telling your story—"

"You realized—"

"No, I don't think I understood anything until I scanned the techprint," he admits, "and even then, I wanted to deny it. But from the moment I saw you, you were as familiar to me as air in my lungs. I didn't know why."

"That sounds about right," I say. I'd spent my entire first meeting with Dante trying to determine why he seemed so familiar, but how can you know someone you've never met? I can see my father—I can see Benn—in him now. Both are fair with dark features. Dante a younger version of the man I knew. "You had no idea about me?"

"No," he says.

"But then how do you know you're my father? If my mom married your brother—"

"It says so here," he says, touching the print on my wrist.

"They never told me," I say. The deception twists hard in my chest. Did it make Benn any less my father if he wasn't biologically related to me? Does it matter that he never told me?

"They were protecting you," he says. "The only way to protect my family was to run. If the Guild knew I had fathered you, they never would have let you be born."

"Because you weren't married to my mother," I guess.

To my surprise this makes him laugh. "No matter what their politics are, no one in the Guild is that morally rigid. No, it would have been because they thought you would be too dangerous. I think you proved them right."

"But why?"

"A child with your genetics can't be controlled."

"My genetics? How would they even know my genetics?"

Dante hesitates and his eyes grow distant, reflecting only the rippling water of the fountain. "They know everyone's genetics. They knew your mother's and they knew mine. That's why they wouldn't let me marry her. You've been in the Coventry. You know women need permission to give birth in Arras, but anyone can get pregnant," he reminds me.

"But what do they do if they don't get permission?" I ask.

"Earth isn't the only world with a grey market. There are secrets in Arras, Adelice, but they're bought at a cost."

108

"Then why didn't you stay? If there was somewhere to hide—if you loved my mother?" I ask.

"It was too late. If I'd left earlier, I could have set up in the grey market, but we didn't know anything was wrong until my marriage request was denied. We knew then that whatever was in my file meant I couldn't stay in Arras."

He had wanted to marry her. The Guild hadn't merely denied my mother's request to have more children or placed my parents in menial jobs, the Guild had dictated the course of their lives with one simple denial. One that colored how my parents perceived each demand of their government thereafter.

"But why would the Guild want you?" I ask.

"Like I said, I have my secrets." He runs a hand through his hair, evading my question. "Did your family have the radio? The books?"

I nod a yes.

"And the stories of Earth?"

I shake my head slowly. "Loricel, the Creweler at the Coventry, was the first person who told me about Earth. They must have forgotten."

"Impossible. They chose not to tell you," Dante says.

"So they knew, but why would they train me to fail at testing?" I demand. "They could have brought me here."

"Meria had no desire to come to Earth," he says in a cold voice, and I realize then that sixteen years in Arras may have given my mother time to move on and build a life, but Dante hasn't had the same advantage. His scars are fresh. The damaged parts of him are still tender.

"This isn't possible. Nothing you've told me makes sense.

You can't be my father, and Arras doesn't run on an accelerated timeline." Each of my words is louder than the last, as though volume can erase the information Dante has given me.

Dante pauses to consider this, and then he stands and walks to a fern lilting near the fountain. "Spinsters use a loom to see the fabric of the universe," Dante says. "They work within the constructed weave of Arras."

"Except Loricel, the Creweler," I point out. "She could capture the threads without a loom. They even used her to help gather the raw source materials here."

"That's an entirely different level of skill," Dante says, his forehead wrinkled in concentration. He's trying to explain things and I'm interrupting him. "Very few *women* have that ability."

The way he emphasizes *women* sends ice through my veins. Loricel alluded to this once, in her studio at the Coventry: *There are rumors of departments where men work with the weave, but the Guild always denies it.*

"It's different for men," he continues. "We don't need looms, but we can only alter things that already exist."

I can't hold back the questions now. "*We?* You can weave?"

"I can alter," he clarifies. "Same materials, different results. Spinsters can create, while Tailors can only alter what's already present. I'm a Tailor."

"That's why you ran." Loricel was right about the secret departments employing men, and they had wanted Dante to be part of it.

"You met some of us there, I'm sure. A medic who healed you or maybe an assistant of some sort," he says. "They were Tailors."

110

My encounter with the medic who healed my leg during my retrieval is hazy from the Valpron I was administered that night, but I can recall how easily Cormac had him ripped. Cormac did it as a reflex, like the man was the least important person in the world. If these men exist within Arras, the Guild has a very different way of handling them. "Why aren't we told about this?"

"Alterations are a specific skill. If the public knew what Tailors could do to them—how we can manipulate a person's body *and mind*—there'd be little point to our skills. A renewal patch is alteration on a very limited scale. It's the closest the public comes to knowing what we do. We're more useful if we operate in secret. *I* ran before the Guild could force me to become a Tailor for them."

"They wanted you to be a Tailor?" I ask.

"Oh yes."

"So you ran away from your family?"

"You ran, too," Dante points out.

"That's different. My parents forced me to run."

"Why do you think they did that?" he asks.

"They lock Spinsters away." I think of the doctor and nurses and the clinic where they were going to map and alter me. "The medics went home for the night. They had lives. Only the Spinsters were kept in a cage."

"Did they invite you over for dinner?" Dante asks. "You don't know anything about them. What they do to Tailors— it's a fate much worse than being placed on the loom."

Worse than false windows and constant surveillance? "I doubt it."

"Tell me, Adelice, how many Tailors did you know before you came here?" Dante asks.

"That doesn't prove anything," I start.

"Had you ever even heard of Tailors before?"

"No," I say in a quiet voice.

"Spinsters are locked up," Dante says. "Tailors *disappear*. We are forced to exist on the periphery or to go along with the Guild's schemes and adopt fake lives and occupations, chosen by the Guild for whatever diabolical plot they've concocted."

"And since you wouldn't go along with that?"

"They would have killed my family," Dante continues. "When a Spinster is retrieved, everyone celebrates. When a Tailor is retrieved, he vanishes. And often his family does, too. No one can know Tailors officially exist because of what we do. Tailors can't create like Spinsters or Crewelers, but we can alter their creations."

"How?"

"Sometimes it requires special tools to adjust a person or a thing."

I'm reminded of the clinic at the Coventry, where I lay on a cold, steel slab as a dome of gears and wheels mapped my mind.

"Tailors can remove memories, adjust emotions, even undo things entirely."

"Undo?" I repeat in a whisper.

"Watch," he commands me, and as I do, his finger slips into the leaves of a fern near the door. At first it looks like he's massaging them, but then I see what he's doing. He's teasing apart the very strands that make them up. Most objects, even people, look like one thick thread on a loom, but I've seen them close enough to know that they are comprised of multiple thin threads twisted delicately together. Dante is pulling the fern apart. At first nothing happens, and then he tugs against a strand and it separates from the others. It's golden in his fingers and as he pulls it slips out from the other strands. The effect is instantaneous.

The fern's leaves wilt, withering into brown, drooping, then shriveling until they become so brittle that the plant crumbles into dust before my eyes. A moment ago it was alive and now it's nothing. It scatters like ash to the floor.

My eyes are wide as Dante releases the golden strands and they vanish, evaporating like smoke when met with too much air.

"You ripped the time right out of it," I say breathlessly. "I never even realized threads had time strands."

"They aren't easy to see." Dante brushes his hands together as though they're dirty. "I unwound it."

"But why would time exist within a strand?" I ask.

"All things have a season, Adelice. You and I, we both have natural lives to live. We've been granted so much time and when that's up . . ."

"We die," I finish for him.

"If something doesn't kill us first." It's an attempt at humor, but it falls flat. Probably since we both know that people like us aren't likely to die of old age.

"If you can pull the time from a plant, then you can pull it from a person." I shudder at the thought of seeing that.

"Yes." Dante pauses and his jaw tenses under his smooth skin. "Or you can warp it. You can divorce it from the natural order of things to suit your purpose, which is exactly what the Guild has done."

"Warp," I repeat, and then it hits me. The *Bulletin* story we found with the photograph of Cormac. The propaganda film. I knew hundreds of years had passed in Arras, but no one could tell me exactly how many. Loricel was cagey about how long she had acted as Creweler. Cormac never seemed to age. At the academy we studied civic responsibility, not history, because Arras's history never changed. It moved along pleasantly. It was orderly. Nothing in Arras progressed except technology.

Not even its leaders.

"How many years?" I ask, because I need to hear him say it, even though all the pieces are falling into place now, beginning to reveal a secret I could never have imagined. "How many years have passed on Earth since the Exodus to Arras?"

"Sixteen years, give or take. On Earth, it's probably close to the year 1960, but we can only guess. It's hard without days and seasons."

I've never been good at math, but even I can figure that out. If sixteen years have passed on Earth, nearly two hundred years have passed on Arras. Generations in Arras have lived and died before those left on Earth have even forgotten the war.

It doesn't make sense. It isn't possible. "Are you telling me that Cormac Patton is over two hundred years old?"

Dante's eyes shift to mine, and I see fire in them. "That's exactly what I'm telling you."

THIRTEEN

STEEL SNAKES AROUND MY WRISTS AND PINS me to the table. I struggle to see in the blinding light, and the smells of whiskey and renewal patches cause me to thrash against the cold metal. His Stream voice—the one that's both patronizing and charming—melts in my ear. It oozes into my consciousness as his form comes into view.

"Darling, why struggle? You can't stop this."

I slam my chest against his, but it doesn't help, and his breath stays hot on my ear. I feel Cormac's lips press down against my skin and my body bursts into flames, my bones cracking and shattering, my blood rushing into my hands and feet. I've lost the ability to fight him, and all I can do is scream.

I wake with a start. I can't escape Cormac any more than I can escape my dreams.

Cormac, who can't die, who never ages, who uses Arras-knows-what technology to maintain his youth eternally. With each minute that passes here, many more pass in Arras, giving Cormac time to build a plan of attack. He won't ever let me go because he has an endless amount of time to devote to finding me and destroying me.

In the Coventry, when I warped moments of privacy for Jost and me, I imagined lingering there, living an entire life safely away from my responsibility to the Guild. I never knew the Guild had done the same, creating a timeline that allowed them to move forward with unspeakable plots against those who rose up against them on Earth and in Arras. They'd corrupted the very strands of the universe.

Jost, Erik, and I breakfast in the sitting room of my suite the next morning. Through one door is my bedroom, and on the other side is the room they've given Jost. I thought the accommodations of the Coventry were luxurious, but these rooms border on lavish: heavy blue curtains line the walls and the intricately carved hearth looks to be hundreds of years old. I'm not sure I could even use it if I wanted to. Overhead, winged angels watch us from the painted ceiling. A valet brings coffee and pastries on a silver cart, but my choice of topic causes us to leave the food untouched. I've kept this from Jost and Erik for far too long, waiting until I could grasp it myself, but they need to know what we're up against.

"So you're saying Cormac is over two hundred years old?" Erik says. "I thought he looked good for his age."

"Yeah, it seems like renewal patches are even better than we thought," I say.

"But how?" Jost asks. "How would no one notice that?"

"I think that's a question for Kincaid," I say. "He must know about this if he was a Guild official once. He was probably here at the beginning." The fact that Kincaid could also be two hundred years old sends bile rising in my throat.

"Are there more Tailors like Dante here?"

"I don't know, but there are Tailors in Arras. Dante claims the Guild retrieves them like they do Spinsters, but that all traces of the boys and their families disappear," I say.

"Makes sense," Erik says.

"How does that make sense?" Jost asks incredulously.

"Well, if I was trying to hide the fact that I was two hundred years old from everyone, I'd cover up how I did it, too. If they use the Tailors to cover up their conspiracy, they have to ensure no one knows the Tailors exist," Erik says, "and the Tailors have nowhere to go. They're dependent on the Guild, even more so than Spinsters."

"Unless they run," I say quietly.

"And then they're stuck here," Erik adds.

Earth isn't exactly a paradise, and the Guild has made sure it's even less possible every year to inhabit it, by stealing more and more of the planet's resources. What the Tailors do is monstrous, but deep down I feel sorry for them. I know what it's like to be caged, to feel like you have no options. The Guild systematically destroyed every option the Tailors had. How could they fight that?

"Dante said Tailors are everywhere in Arras. Medics. Guards. Doctors," I tell them. "Did either of you know about this?"

"I would have mentioned it," Jost says, and Erik gives an awkward laugh. At least they're trying with each other.

"But why would they cooperate?" I wonder.

"Why do Spinsters?" Erik asks. "Given the right incentive, anyone can be bought."

"Not anyone," Jost says.

There goes the friendliness.

"I haven't told you the weirdest part yet," I interrupt. Taking a deep breath, I reveal my true relationship to Dante.

Erik blinks and Jost frowns. They either didn't hear me or they're in shock.

"So your dad is nineteen?" Erik says.

I nod.

"And you never knew he was your real father?"

"Oh, do you mean I never knew my real father was my father's brother, who left my mother pregnant and escaped to an alternate reality before I was born?" I ask in a scathing tone, hoping the cracks in my voice aren't too noticeable.

"So you didn't know," Erik says.

"I went from being an orphan to having two living parents—"

"Sort of," Erik interjects.

"Not helping, Erik."

"He's your father," Jost says. The frown has slipped from his face, and he's far away again.

"Yes," I confirm.

"He missed everything," Jost says in a voice so low I barely hear him.

"Sorry?"

"He's been away your whole life," Jost says.

"It's okay. I didn't know what I was missing," I say. The second the words launch from my lips I want to take them back.

In my own confusion, I hadn't even thought of how Jost would take this news. Jost is thinking about Sebrina. Each day we spend on Earth is weeks in Arras. Each second that passes,

Jost's daughter slips further from his fingers. She doesn't know what she is missing either.

But he does.

"I'm going to digest breakfast," Erik says, although he hasn't eaten a bite. Nothing about his tone is casual. He must have picked up on what was going on long before I did. Proof, once again, that the brothers are more attuned to each other than either would like to admit. He slips into the hall with a faint farewell, but I see his eyes turn back to his brother. He wants to comfort him, but he doesn't know how.

"I'm sorry, Jost," I say as the door shuts behind Erik.

"For what?" Jost asks, but there's an edge to his voice.

"It didn't occur to me," I admit. "I didn't think about Sebrina."

"It's not your responsibility to think about her," he says, but it's these words that reveal that the edge in his voice isn't anger, it's pain. I've hurt him. Not by reminding him of Sebrina or of how quickly he's losing her, but because I hadn't cared enough to think about it in the first place.

"I was so caught up in what Dante told me," I say, but the excuse sounds lame. "I didn't even think about Amie until now."

"Amie's a lot older," he reminds me.

"And very impressionable," I say, thinking back to how eager she was to be tested. How fascinated she was with the *Bulletins*, fawning over the Spinsters and their beautiful dresses. "She's in danger, too. Cormac knows about her and she's getting closer and closer to the age of Eligibility. We can't waste time here. We need a plan."

"Do you think Kincaid can help us?" Jost asks, and I can tell he doesn't think Kincaid can—or will.

"I think it's worth finding out," I say. "We need help. Resources."

Jost's head snaps back and he stares at me, his eyes on fire. What did I say?

"Sorry I couldn't provide for you," he says in a low rumble.

I'm caught off guard by his reaction. I stumble to find words that aren't angry or annoyed. "I didn't ask you to."

He doesn't respond.

"Is this some sort of male-ego thing?" I ask. "I'm not a damsel in distress. I don't need you to save me."

"Maybe I want to save you." He's practically growling now. He's not angry. It's something else. Something primal. Something I've never seen in Jost before, and I understand. He couldn't save Sebrina, but he wouldn't lose me.

"That's noble—"

"There's nothing noble about it," he says. His lips are on mine then and they crush so hard that I feel his teeth cut against the soft flesh of my mouth. I'm torn between pushing him away and pulling him closer.

The latter wins out.

But I don't let him control the kiss. I push back harder as his arms circle my waist, pulling me roughly to him.

"Romantic," I murmur through our fighting lips.

"Wow. This is your idea of romantic?" he asks. His grip on me loosens and his hands drop from my back. "I need to work on this with you."

"That's exactly what I had in mind," I say, drawing him to me. I trace his shoulders, my fingers trailing along his chest until I bunch his shirt in my fists and force him to me. He doesn't resist. He wants the world to fade away, too. Even if it's only for a few minutes.

His mouth forces mine open, and my body reacts in interesting ways. First, there's the tingle in my fingers I always feel when we kiss, but it spreads out, gathering finally into throbbing energy. We break apart, panting, and then I push him back against the fireplace and kiss him again. His body presses into mine, and he flips me around so that now I'm gripping the stone mantel. The stone is cold, sending shivers rippling through me, but I don't care. His hands twist and grab my wrists, pinning them up over my head as his lips trace the hollow under my jaw.

"*This* is romantic," he says.

"I couldn't agree more," I murmur between his kisses.

We continue for a while, laughing and teasing and always kissing, but then he pulls back and his face grows distant. He's stopping us again.

He doesn't want you, the voice in my head mocks me. *You're not her. You aren't his perfect wife.*

No. I refuse to believe that. There are more important things than my insecurity right now.

"Jost." I call him back to me. He doesn't respond until I take his hand.

Tears pool in his eyes, and I feel the hot prickle of tears in my own.

"What are we going to do?" he asks.

"We're going to talk to Kincaid," I say firmly. "We can't make a move until we know how to get back to Arras. Kincaid will know how."

"How can we trust him?" Jost asks.

I understand his hesitation, even more so because we both have so much to lose if Kincaid betrays us. Kincaid was Guild once, but so were we. And if the Guild has done anything nearly as terrible to him as they have to us, I can't blame him for abandoning them. I can't blame him for wanting to destroy them.

"We don't have a choice."

FOURTEEN

I LINGER IN THE GARDENS THAT AFTERNOON when the artificial lights are turned high enough to feel like the sun, replaying Jost's kiss in my mind. Even as a memory it pulls me apart, shattering me into a thousand glorious pieces that only he can put back together.

I feel eyes on me first, drawing me back to the present, and when I finally spot the man tucked behind a large statue, he saunters out. His smile is too wide, and as he approaches me, he bows. He's about my height, but his features mimic Valery's—a thick sweep of black hair and sloping, brown eyes. The lighting system fades as he gets closer to me, and I start to feel apprehension ripple through me.

"Scheduled maintenance," the stranger explains. "You must be our new guest."

"I'm sorry," I say, my eyes flickering to the doors that lead back into the main house. "I don't know everyone here yet."

"No, don't apologize," he says. "I'm Deniel."

"You're a Sunrunner?" I guess.

"Yes," he says. His finger traces the air. "But I'm also a refugee from the Eastern Sector. You're a refugee, too."

I swallow hard but nod, wanting to keep things friendly. I have no reason to feel so nervous. Kincaid's estate is impenetrable, but I've had little contact with any of the other Sunrunners. I curse the empty-headed romantic reverie that allowed me to let my guard down.

"I saw the Eastern Sector," I say, recalling my goodwill tour with Cormac.

"There is so much beauty there. No doubt the remains of the culture we brought from Earth." Deniel's voice is so low he practically purrs. He offers his arm, and I take it tentatively. Relief floods through me as he leads me back toward the house, and I relax. "I left there long ago."

"To come here?" I ask, trying to keep my voice even and pleasant.

"I worked the grey market in Arras until I was forced to come to Earth." He speaks into the distance, not bothering to look at me.

"You must have left a lot behind," I offer.

"Yes, but I keep my past close. My *ojiisan* gave me a piece of ivory. It is very old," he says quietly. "Your skin is smooth and pure like it. Would you like to see it?"

I agree, but keep my eyes on the doors we're nearing, counting the seconds until I can excuse myself.

Deniel draws out a smooth, sculpted piece of ivory. He holds it so close to me that I can barely see it. It is flawless, I think, and then he presses it to my chin. As his thumb twitches, I realize the ivory is actually a handle—a thin silver blade extends from it.

"Beautiful and deadly, like a woman," he murmurs.

In an instant the blade is at my throat and Deniel forces me into the hall of the main house. My skin stings where the blade has slashed a shallow cut near the hollow of my neck. He presses his full weight against me and breathes hot and fast against my ear. I expect him to push me down to the floor, but instead the panel I'm crushed against trembles and rotates back. He drops the knife from my throat as he shoves me through the hidden door.

The room is out of place at the estate, lacking the opulence of the other chambers. It's spare with cinder-block walls and a long, slick table. I fight the panic spreading through my limbs. It threatens to lock me down and make me an easy target. I turn to see the dark concentration in Deniel's eyes. The room reminds me of a clinic, like the one where I was mapped in Arras. A realization that does nothing to stem my panic.

"I don't like dangerous women," he breathes, lingering in the doorway.

"Am I dangerous?" I ask, locking my gaze on his.

"You won't be for long," he says, edging toward me. His eyes bore into me, studying my face and then my body. It makes me want to hug myself protectively, but I stay still, waiting for the right moment.

Deniel inches closer, clutching his knife between us, moving me backward into the room.

"You wouldn't be stupid enough to fight," Deniel spits, saliva peppering my ear. There's a note of amusement in his voice. "Do you think the Guild will let you go?"

The frozen part of me melts at his words. Clearly he doesn't know me very well.

The blade presses into my throat again and his hand moves to my shoulder. He's left the panel ajar. I only have to get there and then I'll be back in the corridor. I feel the tug as his fingers dig into me. But he's not merely scratching me, he's ripping me open, tearing into my strands. His touch burns across my shoulder, blazing onto my neck.

The strands of the room come into focus—brilliant and tempting—and as my eyes fly to Deniel's face, I realize I can see him and the shimmering threads that comprise him as he must see me now. His strands aren't bright and golden, they're tarnished brass and pulse with a near-crimson light. Without thinking, I claw at his shoulder, rending the tightly knit threads there, and the skin ruptures in the spot, blood spewing from the laceration. Deniel pulls back with a shriek of agony, clutching his wound. For a moment he looks like he may pounce again, but I raise my hands defensively, feeling his blood dripping down my long fingers. His shock and outrage mirror the raw anger I feel. His eyes slide to my fingers and the calculating look returns. Obviously he's estimating how much damage I can do to him before he can stop me. But rather than attack, he laughs, shaking his head, his knife still raised.

I scream as loudly as I can.

It startles him, but he jumps at me, lunging to cover my mouth and losing his knife in the process. I know he can do plenty of damage to me without it, so I kick him hard. It only makes him angrier. I'm reaching to tear at him again when a guard bursts into the room and tackles Deniel.

Erik rushes in behind him and pulls me up from the floor, ushering me away from the mayhem as more of Kincaid's men appear. The tears come then. They spill heavy and hot down my cheeks, washing the fear from my body and leaving me to tremble over what's happened.

I watch as Kincaid's men lead Deniel away to a fate worse than what he'd planned for me. I'm sure of that much.

"Are you okay?" Erik asks, taking my shoulder. When I don't respond, he pulls me into a hug and I let him. I count his heartbeats, trying to breathe in rhythm with him, but his heart is racing too fast to calm me.

He takes me to my room and pulls a dress from the wardrobe. I look down and realize mine is torn. It flaps at the shoulder, ripped in the attack. I reach for my zipper and start to pull off the damaged gown. As I do, Erik throws his hands over his eyes.

"Sorry," he says, his voice muffled by his hand.

"Are you covering your eyes?" I ask in disbelief. The gesture surprises me.

"I'm being a gentleman," he says, still looking away.

"That would be a real first," I tell him as I slip the dress over my head.

"I guess I'm a changed man," he teases.

"You can turn around now," I say after I'm sure that I'm completely covered.

When he does, I can't help but notice that his cheeks are a little pink.

"Zip me up?" I ask. My hands are still shaking too hard to manage the last bit of zipper on the back of the dress. I pull my hair up and Erik tugs at the slider in a slow, gentle motion, one hand on the small of my back.

"What's going on?" Jost asks, coming into the room. I pull away from Erik and fall into Jost's arms while his brother explains what's happened. Jost's eyes travel between our faces, growing darker until they flame with anger. He jerks away from me and heads down the hall, forcing Erik and me to follow after him.

"Where are you going?" I call, but he doesn't respond so I sprint to keep up with him.

"I'm going to have a little chat with Kincaid about his men," Jost says through gritted teeth.

"I don't think that's a very good idea," I murmur. "We're his guests—"

Jost cuts me off. "And one of his guests was attacked. He needs a lesson in hospitality." He whirls to face us, but I can't think of anything to say that will stop him now that he's reached this point.

"You don't think he's going to do something about this on his own?" Erik points out. "I doubt Kincaid will be happy to hear this has happened."

"I think Kincaid is the one who sent him," Jost says.

"Why? What purpose would that serve?"

"Everything serves a purpose," Jost responds. "We can't trust him. Do I have to remind you that he was Guild? The only thing we can trust is that he knows how to lie."

"Maybe we should get Dante," I suggest quietly, trying to draw down the volume of Jost's voice so we aren't overheard.

Before we can talk Jost out of it, he's bounded down the stairs to the main floor of the house. It doesn't take long for us to hear the shrieking castigations coming from the assembly room.

"Yes, sir," a guard says.

"This is poor form. What will my guests think?" Kincaid squeaks.

"He's prepared to make amends for his . . . mistake," the guard says.

"Oh, amends will be made," Kincaid says.

For a moment we hang back, but something pushes me forward.

"Adelice," Kincaid croons when I get close enough for him to see me. "I have been informed of what happened. In fact, I was about to send for you."

"I'm sorry for interrupting. It was rude of me," I say, "but I was hoping you had learned why he attacked me."

"The boy is new, came in with a refugee group only a few weeks ago," Kincaid says. "He had an introduction letter and everything. Standard protocol for someone who has come in through our contacts in Arras."

"You should reconsider your contacts in Arras," Jost says.

I put my hand on his arm as much to calm him as to warn him to be careful what he says to Kincaid.

"Deniel," Kincaid says, "is going to be seriously punished."

"That's not necessary," I say. "I'd like to know why he did it, but I don't want him to be hurt."

"I want him to be hurt," Jost says.

"You should listen to your friend," Kincaid says. "It's not sensible to allow a man like this to prowl around."

"And"—comes a voice to my left—"it's important everyone gets the same message."

I turn to Dante and stare at him. "Which is?"

"You aren't to be touched."

I follow Dante's gaze to see it burning into Kincaid. His

words are fiercely protective, and it feels strange. It's not something I welcome exactly. Jost might treat me like I'm breakable, but his actions are rooted in his loss of Rozenn, something I'm only beginning to understand. Dante barely knows me though. He can't turn on fatherly emotions like that. I don't want him to.

"I couldn't agree more," Kincaid says from behind me. His voice is low and even, not his usual airy, bouncing tone. "None of my guests are to be touched . . ."

"We can put him in the cells until—" the guard begins.

But Kincaid waves off the suggestion and gestures for him to be silent by raising his hand merely inches from his face. "I want Adelice to sleep tonight. How can she if definitive action isn't taken now?"

"I'm fine," I say, but I know I'll ask Jost to stay the night. Then I'll be able to sleep.

"Bring him into the gardens," Kincaid says, ignoring my input. The guard nods and walks a few steps away to use his complant more quietly.

"And how do you plan to make her feel safe after this?" Dante asks Kincaid, coming into the hall's light. He's dressed in a thin tank-style shirt and soft flannel pajama bottoms. His shirt reveals a techprint on his biceps—three braided bands circling his arm.

"Don't worry. You'll be pleased," Kincaid says.

"Your defenses were penetrated. This may not be the only threat. I'd like permission to investigate further." Dante isn't asking him.

Kincaid's jaw twitches, but his mask of authority stays in place. "That won't be necessary. I assure you that your daughter is my priority. Remember that."

My eyes fly to Dante. How could he have told Kincaid? Dante claimed it would be a secret until I decided I wanted to share the information, if that day ever came. But Dante looks confused. He has no more idea how Kincaid found out than I do. I consider how quickly security responded to my screams when Deniel attacked me. They couldn't have heard me unless they were watching me.

Which means it isn't Dante's fault that our secret is out. It's mine.

FIFTEEN

SOMEONE LAYS A THICK FUR COAT OVER my shoulders after Kincaid announces that the punishment will transpire in the garden. I turn, expecting to see Jost behind me, but it's Jax. I haven't seen him since our first day here. He doesn't speak now, but he gives me a resolved nod as he slips to the back of the security team that's amassing for Kincaid's verdict. With the lighting system dimmed, the chill outdoors is reminiscent of the Icebox, without the lurking, shifting shadows. There's no need for me to watch the corners and hidden spaces around the plants and fountain; the monster is in plain sight now, no longer able to hide.

Deniel is dragged across the uneven masonry of the brick path, his knees scraping against the rough surface, but he doesn't speak or cry out. He keeps his head low, his ink-black hair falling over his eyes. When the guards bring him to Kincaid's feet, they drop him there and one nudges Deniel's head up with his knee. I gasp at the sight of the man's bloodied mouth and crooked nose. It looks like the guards have already put him through some significant punishment before they brought him to Kincaid.

"Who do you work for?" Kincaid asks in a singsongy voice. The amusement in it isn't lost on me.

Kincaid is enjoying this.

Deniel doesn't respond to the question. Instead he lolls forward again, his head drooping to his chest. Kincaid snaps his fingers and one of the guards bends forward, taking Deniel's chin forcefully into his hand and jerking it up.

"I'm waiting."

"No one." Deniel's answer oozes slowly from him, and I notice how swollen his cheekbone is. It balloons out, swallowing the space around his eye and forcing it shut.

"Let's try that again," Kincaid says.

I barely make out the guard's fingers tightening, but Deniel strains against the force, clawing at the hand that holds him.

"You could have had a fine life here, son," Kincaid tells him. "The Guild forced you to run because of your ability, but while the Guild abuses Tailors, I value them. I would have valued you."

Apparently the time for secrecy has passed. Dante isn't the only Tailor on the estate. It seems Kincaid collects them.

Deniel tries to splutter something against the guard's hand, but Kincaid continues. "The time for excuses has passed. You have betrayed my trust."

"What's going on?" Valery says, her voice elevated a decibel sharper than normal. She flies into the courtyard, her silk dressing robe rippling behind her. It's loosely bound by a sash at her waist, and it does little to hide her flawless lithe figure, which does a lot to distract Kincaid.

"Darling, go back to bed. I'll join you soon," Kincaid assures her.

"I can't sleep," she says, crossing her arms against her chest. "What are you doing to Deniel?"

"Deniel attacked Adelice."

I can't help wondering why Valery even cares, but she swoops down to Deniel and stares him in the eye. How does she know him? If he's new here, as Kincaid said earlier, I can't imagine their paths crossing. I've rarely seen Valery out of her chambers except for dinners. Now she lingers before Deniel as if she's trying to tell him something, but then her words come freely, in front of us.

"This is how you repay my kindness." Accusation drips like poison from her words.

Deniel hesitates, still staring Valery in the eye. "We have our parts to play."

Valery doesn't respond. She rises up and turns to Kincaid. "I assure you I had no idea he was a traitor when I brought him here."

"You know him?" The question sputters from my lips before I can stop it.

Valery winces, but taking a deep breath, she turns to me. "He was a refugee. We met fleeing Arras, and I helped secure his place here. I made a mistake."

Mistake hardly seems to cover it. If Deniel fled Arras at the same time as Valery, he was sent here for some purpose and I have the scratches on my shoulder to prove it. She led him straight to his prize without hesitation. Without thought. But my ire softens when I meet her eyes. Valery helped him because that's who she is—even if her graciousness no longer extends to me.

"You were trying to help him, darling," Kincaid says, placing an arm around her waist and pulling her close. "It was a lapse in judgment. Now go to bed."

He kisses her full on the lips, and I see it: whereas Valery melts and simpers into Kincaid's arms during dining times, she's stiff during this act. Unyielding. She doesn't want his attention. Not now.

And still she goes to his bed, with the slightest glance at Deniel as she passes.

"Hold on," Kincaid says. He gestures for Dante to come over, which he does reluctantly. "Will you do the honors?"

Dante's eyes flicker to mine, and I know that whatever punishment Kincaid has in mind, I don't want to see it. Is it too late to excuse myself? Beside me Jost takes my arm and pulls me close to him. Dante's attention turns back to his boss and he shakes his head.

"I'm not playing your games, Kincaid."

"Games?" Kincaid echoes with a guffaw. "My interest in your daughter should please you."

Dante's shoulders stay set, his lips a firm line of refusal.

"No?" Kincaid asks, but he sounds indifferent. He wags a finger at a burly guard, who steps forward. "Show Adelice that we will protect her. Show her what I do to those who would betray her."

The guard nods, and Deniel is lifted to his feet. The guard's eyes stay on Deniel's chest, but Deniel remains passive and remote. Then he gives a loud groan as the guard's fingers reach toward him.

My pulse leaps, pounding against my veins, and as the guard reaches forward, Deniel's strands glimmer to life again.

I can see them so clearly now, more so than I did when he attacked me. His strands are thin, well worn, patched with newer strands. Some grafted in seamlessly and others barely attached. Whoever Deniel is, he's endured a fair amount of alteration. Who did this to him?

Through the center of his jumbled weave runs a slender golden strand. The last pure thread remaining within the man. Another set of strands moves within Deniel, pushing apart the threads and patches, making straight for the man's core. With a great wrench, the guard rends apart Deniel's threads, below the tear that I gave him. For a moment my concentration is broken and I can only see the crimson that drips thin across the guard's hands, but then the golden strand pulls slowly from Deniel and he starts to melt away. I am fastened to the sight, unable to turn my head.

First, Deniel's skin shrivels. The blood stops flowing from his chest until only a seeping puddle remains on his shirt. His eyes sink into his skull and his head lolls back, and I know he's dead, but it isn't over. The golden strand pulls cleanly from him, and the shriveled skin cracks and falls away. Deniel's bones follow, until the only thing that remains is a pile of dust at the feet of the guards.

Kincaid steps forward, surveying the guard's work. His face is grim, but there's a gleam in his eyes he can't quite hide. And then, without a smile, he says quietly, "Dust to dust."

SIXTEEN

THE NEXT MORNING, A KNOCK ON THE door to my quarters startles me. I've been sitting at the desk, absently brushing my hair. When I open the door, a younger valet is waiting with a silver tray perched on his fingers. A small ivory card with my name penned in elegant writing rests on it. I take the card and nod a thank-you to the valet.

"My instructions are to wait for your response, miss," he says in a clipped tone.

"Okay, give me a moment." I turn into my room, and after some hesitation, shut the door. I can't stand the thought of him waiting there, watching me. I'm not fond of the idea of shutting the door in his face either, but, well, choices.

I unfold the card:

Adelice,

Please accept my sincere apologies for yesterday's unfortunate interlude. I want you to feel secure here, but I don't wish you

to think ill of me. To relieve the tension from last evening,
I've arranged a small play for you and your friends' amusement
in the theater. I hope it will show you the positives of having
Tailors available for our use. Please let me know if you are
available for the presentation at three o'clock.

Most sincerely yours,
Kincaid

My eyes flick to the ticking clock on my nightstand. It's already noon. I scrawl my acceptance across the bottom, trying to sound enthusiastic and failing miserably.

I don't want to go, but this isn't so much an invitation as a summons. I traipse back to the door, nearly tripping over my dressing gown, and give the card to the valet, who does a good job of not looking too annoyed at having had the door shut in his face.

"Thank you," I say, but he merely tilts his head in acknowledgment, pivots to the right, and moves down the hall.

I've barely shut the door when another knock forces me to open it again. On the other side I find Jost standing there with two large turquoise boxes. Another valet is walking hurriedly down the hall, carrying more of the same boxes. I raise an eyebrow at Jost.

"A gift from our amiable host," Jost says, nodding to be let in.

"I see you've been invited to the show then," I say.

"And what a show it will be," Jost mutters. He crosses to the bed and sets down the boxes. I walk over and lift the lid of the one with the tag addressed to me. Inside I find a cloud of pink tissue paper. I push it open and pull a silk gown from the box. It's a lovely pale pink and the fabric swims down my body when I hold it up. The décolletage is a sunburst of crystal. I turn it over and study the draping back, finding another sunburst to decorate my derriere.

"Pretty," Jost says. It's as much enthusiasm as he can muster up for something as shallow as clothes.

"Let's see what you got," I say.

"Oh, I hope mine is purple and shows more skin," he says with a wink.

"If you are going to be a smart-ass, I hope it does too."

He lifts a pressed black suit jacket from the box. "No such luck."

"You'll look dapper," I say.

"I'll be uncomfortable."

"I never knew you were so anti-tux," I say.

"Tuxes are for men like Cormac."

"And what's for a man like you?" I ask, pulling the jacket from his hands and tossing it down on the bed.

"Careful, you'll wrinkle that," he starts, but as I latch my arms around his chest, he stops.

"How very conscientious of you," I murmur as I move closer to him.

"What can I say? You know what a conscientious guy I am," he says, but the words mute as my lips meet his.

"I think the dress is pretty. It will be beautiful when you're in it," he says, pulling away from me.

"Should I try it on?" I ask.

Jost hesitates for moment, his eyes growing serious.

"We're alone here and we have hours to get dressed."

He sinks onto the bed and watches me with serious, widening eyes. For a moment, I feel shy, my bravado failing me, but my fingers grip the sash of my robe, and I hope he doesn't see how they tremble as I begin to pull it open. His hand reaches up to grip mine, stopping the shaking, but also stopping me from opening the robe. For a second I expect he's going to pull it open himself and I wonder what his hands will feel like there. Somewhere my mother's voice calls to me, but it can't compete with the roar of blood that floods through my body, igniting every inch of my skin.

"You don't have to do this, Ad," he whispers instead. His hand pulls mine away from the belt and we stare at each other for a long moment, and then I listen to my body and sink against him, my legs straddling his lap, my arms wrapping around his neck. His breath is hot against my collarbone and as he slides his fingers through my loose hair a shiver runs down my spine. He's bringing his lips to mine when another knock interrupts us.

"What is it, annual knock-on-Adelice's-door day?" I grumble.

Jost's hands fall from me and he grins shyly and then casually pulls me up to my feet.

"Come on, Kincaid is probably inviting us to another wild party."

"Can we be so lucky?" I ask.

But it's not a valet waiting outside the door. It's Valery. Her cosmetics are perfectly applied, less drastic than the first night we saw her here, but she still looks exotic with her wide, dark eyes and midnight hair. She's wrapped in the same robe she wore last night, but it's clear that she's done up for this afternoon's event.

"I thought I could get you ready," she offers. Her eyes flash to Jost, who's standing awkwardly by my bed.

Like old times, I think. I want to send her away. She might feel the need to hide under a painted mask when she's with Kincaid, but I've got more important things to do than getting primped for a charade of civility.

"That sounds nice," Jost answers for me, grabbing his tuxedo box. "I should get dressed. Check in on Erik."

Check in on Erik? Erik is the last person he'd want to see. He's trying to avoid where we were going a few moments ago. "Sure," I say. "Help him tie his bow tie. Curl each other's hair."

I don't try to hide the annoyance in my voice.

Jost smiles and shakes his head slightly as if to remind me to watch myself. "I'll see you later." He kisses my forehead at the door, then looks to Valery and back to me. "You two have fun."

Fun is probably the last thing we'll be having, but I give him a small smile.

Valery wastes no time once he's gone.

She rushes to my bed and lifts the silk dress from the heap I've left it in. Smoothing it out, she crosses to my closet and hangs it carefully on the closet door.

"Lovely," she says, surveying the gown. "You should wear your hair down. We'll put some waves in it."

I open my mouth to ask her why she's doing this, but then I shut it again. It's the friendliest Valery has been since we discovered her here. Perhaps she feels badly about what happened with Deniel. I can't exactly blame her for being cold to me after Enora's suicide.

But I can wonder what she's up to.

"It's good I came now. They don't have the kind of tools I had at the Coventry. This will take some time," she says.

I follow her into the bathroom and she urges me toward the sink. There's no fancy chair for me to sit in while she dampens my hair, so I bend awkwardly and she presses my head down under the flowing water. It's freezing and my body tenses.

"Sorry," she says absently, and I feel the water grow warmer. A moment later, her long fingers run through my hair, massaging shampoo into my scalp. It feels good for a moment but then her fingers grow more frenzied in their actions until she's practically scraping me with her fingernails. I wince, and she repeats her apology. She lets the water rinse out the soap and it slides into my eyes. I squeeze them shut but feel the sting of the shampoo. She lifts my head and wraps a thick towel around me, offering me a washcloth to wipe my eyes.

When we return to my room, I sit at the vanity and she pulls the towel from my head. Water drips down my back, and my robe sticks to my skin from the moisture.

I feel a comb running through my hair and water gushes to my shoulders as she pulls it into a straight line.

"You should cut this," she says. "Less work."

"I like it long," I say. My mother's hair was long. My mother's hair *is* long, I correct myself, but I push the thought back out of my head, fighting against the helplessness I feel when I think of her. I don't want to imagine her roaming around her cage, deep in the cells under the estate.

"As you wish."

"You don't have to do this," I say. "I mean, I can get ready on my own."

"I'm sure you can, but Kincaid expects a certain level of aestheticism when it comes to his guests."

"I can put on cosmetics," I snap.

"Fine." She drops her hands and steps back from me. "I thought we could talk."

I soften a little at her words, feeling ungrateful and confused at the same time. "I'm sorry. I didn't want you to feel like you had to do this. You aren't my aesthetician anymore."

"I know that. I liked doing your cosmetics, Adelice," she says. "I'm not offering out of obligation."

"In that case, thank you," I say.

She retrieves long, thin pieces of fabric from her pocket. Her eyes meet mine and she pulls one taut between her hands, and for a moment I'm scared of the stranger I see reflected there. Who is this?

But then she takes a section of my hair and wraps it with precision around the fabric, tying it off at the end.

"Like I said, we don't have the same tools at our disposal here."

I swallow hard and nod. "Is that why you wear your cosmetics differently?"

"Kincaid likes the geisha aesthetic. It's an old Earth style," she responds in a quiet voice. "I often do my cosmetics to please him."

But that's not the only thing she does to please him. Still, today her face, while lined and painted, reflects the aesthetic of an Arras woman. I wonder if she's trying to send him a message after last night's spectacle, reminding Kincaid where she comes from.

She repeats the action until most of the hair framing my

face is wrapped up into the rags. She faces me and leans in, taking my chin in her hands and studying me. Her breath smells of cinnamon.

Even here, after everything that's happened, Valery is the essence of poise. Her skin silky, everything about her soft. Her fingers, though, are cold on my face and they pinch my skin as she turns my head to inspect me.

"How am I holding up?" I mutter through my nearly closed mouth.

"Well enough. A little cosmetics and no one will see the damage."

I frown. Damage?

"None of that," she says in regard to my dubious expression. "It makes it worse."

In fairness, I've been through a lot. I'm not exactly looking forward to another round of cosmetics, but if it gets Valery talking, it will be worth it.

She reaches for the bag she brought and pulls out a cream, which she smooths over my face. Her brushes dance over my cheekbones, glide against my eyelids, and line my lips. For a moment, I close my eyes and imagine I'm in my quarters at the Coventry. Enora will meet me to take me to training or a meeting or a carefully prepared feast. This will have been a dream—or will it have been a nightmare?

I'm not sure.

"Open your eyes," Valery commands. I do so, and she brushes a mascara wand roughly through my lashes. I catch a glimpse of her in the mirror. She's concentrating, which makes her look like she used to—engaged in her work. She did truly enjoy it. She hadn't been lying about that. Her robe has fallen off her shoulder and there I spy it—a thick purple mark running across her olive skin. It creeps toward her neck, but doesn't quite reach it. A lavender scar. Her eyes catch mine staring in the mirror, and she tugs the robe back up.

"Let's get that dress on," she suggests.

I stand and let my dressing gown fall to the floor in a puddle.

"You should be more careful." Valery clucks under her breath.

My eyes follow hers and I see a patch of blue blooming on my calf.

"Probably from Deniel's attack," I say, shrugging it off.

"There are plenty of things to hurt yourself on here," Valery says, but her words are colored with warning. She draws my gown into her hands and waits.

I've worn enough of these dresses to know only one thing works under them. Nothing. She drops the dress over my head and I let the straps fall over my hands. The dress slides gracefully into place.

"Lovely," she says.

"We didn't talk much," I say.

Valery pauses and pain flashes across her face. "I know."

"You didn't want to," I accuse lightly.

"No, I didn't."

I start to ask her why, but she steps to the side and pulls the rags from my hair, which bounces down into soft curls that fall across my shoulders. I watch her in the mirror. She came because she wanted to do this. She wanted her old life, if only for a moment. She tugs one side of my hair up with a sparkling comb and stops to look at our reflection. I can't bring myself to smile, but Valery positively glows. We look glamorous and polished. We look like ghosts from Arras.

"Beautiful," she says with pride in her voice. She places her hand on my shoulder and I'm transported back to another time. Another world. My imagination sketches in Enora where she would have stood in the Coventry.

"Do you miss her?" I whisper.

Her hand falls and her expression changes. She steps away from me, still meeting my eyes in the mirror.

"I don't want to talk about her with you."

"So what? You've replaced her? With Kincaid?" I challenge.

"I never want to hear you mention Enora again," Valery snaps. "She's dead, and you have no right to even think of her."

"Someone has to," I accuse. "She tried to help me. She knew what was going to happen to her, that's why she gave me that digifile."

"And what did that cost her?" Valery asks. "Helping you, getting you that digifile. Enora trusted too many people, and it destroyed her."

Enora had revealed her concern, showing her hand by giving me that digifile. Had the person who helped her get it betrayed her to the Guild? It doesn't matter, because I understand why she did it. "She led me to the truth even after her death, and you don't care."

"Caring won't bring her back. It will only bring us pain," Valery warns.

"I dream of her—of how I found her. I'll never stop thinking of Enora," I say in a determined voice. Valery might dismiss Enora's memory, but I won't.

"Don't worry," Valery says in a sharp tone. "After a while you'll stop dreaming."

But dreams are the least of my concerns. After she leaves, only one thing consumes me: the lilac scar licking up her shoulder. She's hiding it, and I have a suspicion I know why.

Valery has been altered.

SEVENTEEN

THE CURTAINS RISE AT THE BELLOW OF a trumpet. Three men appear, pointing and crying out as a specter rises in the distance. The ghost's voice booms out over the theater. I melt into my plush seat, consumed by the action. My heart pounds as the ghost cries for revenge against his murderer.

"Here," Valery says, pushing a booklet into my lap.

I don't want to look away from the action, but I flip through the pages to please her. More than ever, I want to make amends with Valery. It's a program, featuring images of the actors in the play. "Before" and "after" shots. Each actor has been made up as someone else, with a note on which famous film star he or she is portraying. The actors aren't only playing roles in Shakespeare's play, they've been made to look like actors from the past. The surreality of it isn't lost on me.

I peer at one of the actress's images as the scene changes. It's dark but I'm struck by the subtle changes that have been made, enabling her to look more like a classic film star named Veronica Lake, according to the program. Her hair is longer, waving over her face. Her nose more pert. Lips more full. The differences are pronounced—perhaps too much so to be achieved by a powder brush and eyeliner.

As the next scene begins, Kincaid appears onstage. He sports a trim beard and a black mourning ensemble but the hint of a smile betrays the somber moment. As the ghost's request for retribution is repeated along with the truth about his murder, my throat swells.

One of the actors clutches his side, where a thin crimson ribbon pours from his ribs. His performance is haunting. Even from where I'm sitting, I see the pain reflected in his eyes. Ophelia goes mad, casting flowers, and I weep for her, the girl locked away and used by Hamlet and Horatio and the king. I weep over Hamlet's confrontation with his mother.

Kincaid's age is the only thing that distracts me. He's too commanding. Too self-assured to play Hamlet. He doesn't understand his character's dilemma.

I could do better.

Only Valery seems as moved as I am by the performance, which surprises me. Jost and Erik sit up straighter during the final climactic scene, and we watch, waiting to see who lives. No one breathes until the final line has been spoken.

"That was beautiful," I murmur.

"Were we watching the same performance?" Valery asks hollowly, but before I can ask what she means, she excuses herself.

"It's late," Jost says beside me. "Are you hungry? It's well past supper time."

I start to nod, but then shake my head. "I'll join you after I freshen up."

I'm surprised when he turns to Erik and they begin discussing the play. As I exit, their conversation grows louder.

Valery lingers near the stage door, peering through. Her shoulders are hunched close to her craning neck, and I'm struck by the overwhelming need to know what she's doing. I creep up next to her, but the oak floor groans beneath my feet, giving me away.

She spins, her fingers splayed against the slope of her collarbone.

"What are you doing?" she demands.

"I could ask you the same thing," I say, but she shushes me.

"I was looking for a friend," Valery says, her eyes darting to the ground as she speaks.

She's lying, but why?

"You could try going in," I say, reaching to push open the door.

Valery shifts to block me. "I'm not playing a game with you, Adelice."

"Then stop pretending that you aren't up to something. Stop pretending we're friends, and tell me who you are and what you're doing."

"I'm surviving," Valery says, spitting the words at me. "No thanks to you, Adelice. Judge me all you want, but you might want to look in a mirror."

She dashes away before I can recover from her stinging rebuke. She might be right about me, but that doesn't mean she wasn't lying. I slip through the door instead of going to the powder room. Something drew Valery back here, and I'm going to find out what.

There are plenty of corners to hide in, shadows cast by

pulleys and bits of the set. Here is where the spell of the play gives way to props and costumes. The story fades to flat, choreographed illusion. But it's not the wooden trees or the series of curtains separating the world of the stage from the audience that chills my blood. A woman rubs black-and-blue marks developing on her neck, and an actor dressed in a soldier's uniform moans on a table. Jax is there, attending to the actors. He spots me hiding among the shadows and gives me a quick smile. I try to smile back, but the scene before me is more horrifying than anything that occurred in the play.

The violence was realistic because it was *real*.

"What about my face?" the woman who played Ophelia asks. "Can you change it back?"

"I suppose," Jax says, examining the marks from where Kincaid nearly strangled her during the show. "If you want to go through the alterations again."

She winces at the suggestion. "I think . . . I think I do. I don't like looking like someone else."

"I'll let them know." Jax pats her arm and hands her a pack of ice for her bruises. He turns to me, but he closes his mouth as quickly as he opened it, turning hastily back to his work. Jax is the only other Sunrunner who's been friendly to us since our arrival. The rest keep their distance, but he seems interested in us.

I roll up the program filled with old film stars. These people are Kincaid's homage to the past—*his* past. Whatever he offers his actors must be substantial for them to endure so much pain. It can't be a simple process to have your entire face altered to look like someone else.

This is the benefit of Tailoring that Kincaid wanted to show me.

"Shame, shame," Kincaid's high voice says, startling me. "Spying on us, eh?"

I start to defend myself, but he continues before I can think of a good excuse for being back here.

"She was quite good," he says. He smears a rag across his forehead, wiping off some of his elaborate stage cosmetics. "Got a bit carried away. I hate to leave marks on them, but it's part of the play."

"She wants her face back," I say.

"Pity, but the boys can fix her."

"How would they do that?" I ask. I try to keep my voice steady, hoping he doesn't hear the tremble in it that betrays my true feelings. If there is a way to reverse alterations, I could save my mother and help Amie remember. But maybe it's easier to change a face than to undo the kind of damage the Guild inflicts.

But Kincaid is still glowing from his great theatrical accomplishment and doesn't seem to notice. "'All the world's a stage,' Adelice," he says. "'And all the men and women merely players. They have their exits and their entrances; and one man in his time plays many parts.'"

"I'm not interested in being pseudo-intellectual," I say. "Can they fix her?"

Kincaid glowers, but his tone stays even as he answers. "They'll have her original measurements on file. It's a shame, considering how lovely she is as Veronica, but I did promise them they could be altered back. If she wants to continue in my employment, she'll get used to a bit of alteration for the good of the performance."

I force a small smile, but bile rises in my throat. I can't imagine being so far indebted to Kincaid.

As we watch, the stage crew emerges from the shadows, leading the injured actors away. I bite my lip to keep the accusations from tumbling out. When I turn back to Kincaid, anger blurs my vision, bringing his strands into harsh relief, as Deniel's had been when he attacked me. Kincaid's central time strand glimmers. It's not like the golden strand I witnessed being pulled from the young Tailor. It's tarnished with age, although there's a thin, bright fiber braided through the central portion. I blink, trying to dismiss the sight, unsure of what I'm seeing.

"Sir," Jax says, appearing beside us, "we've assessed the injuries and cleared most of the cast for release."

"Very well," Kincaid says. "There's an issue with the voltage drop near the pavilion. No one can get it to dim properly."

"Probably the variable resistor. I'll take a look at it and check the estate's grid for any faulty circuits," Jax says. He seems giddy at the possibility.

"Please do it quickly. We mustn't keep the party guests waiting," Kincaid says in a low voice.

"Are all the Sunrunners also Tailors?" I ask after Jax leaves.

"A very small portion of them are Tailors. Sunrunning takes up plenty of my workforce," he answers, "but Jax is one of the few that's gifted at both. He and your father."

I can't think of anything to say to that. I know so little about Dante.

"Do you have more questions?" Kincaid asks. "About the performance? I do hope you enjoyed it. We needed some revelry to erase that . . . unpleasant experience."

He thinks I'm back here to see him, I realize. It doesn't even occur to him that what he's done has only increased my anxiety about the Tailors and men working on his estate. I have lots of questions, but Kincaid won't answer them.

"No," I say, weighing my response. It takes every ounce of energy I have to say what I say next. "I wanted to compliment you on your performance."

Kincaid beams and claps me on the shoulder. "We'll have more shows now that there is such a large audience."

"What about intel? Looking for the Whorl?" I ask. It's a question that's been on my mind since yesterday. Deniel came too close to getting to me, which means the Guild knows I'm here. "Shouldn't we be coming up with a plan to stop Cormac?"

It's a stupid move bringing this up now, but I can't push it out of my mind any longer.

"My men are looking," he assures me. "When we have news on the Whorl, you will be informed and then we can move forward. No reason not to enjoy ourselves in the meantime though."

"And once we find it?" I ask.

"It's the key we'll need to rid this world of Cormac."

"And to rid Arras of him, too?" I prompt.

Kincaid waves me off. "Of course, sometimes I forget."

Forget about what? I wonder. That Arras exists or that he vowed to separate the worlds? I can't bear to ask him.

Kincaid shepherds me toward the dressing room, prattling on about the various plays he'll put on for my delight, but as he does, I glimpse a soldier lolling forward lifelessly. I hope he's only unconscious.

*　*　*

Dinner is more like a festival. We dine at small tables in the main garden. Large solar lanterns strung overhead shine like small blue moons against the sparkling Interface.

I haven't seen the Interface since we came here from the Icebox. The lighting system always masks it, creating the illusion of a real sky most of the time. But Jax has managed to dim the lights to near twilight, and now I can appreciate the Interface's strange and terrible beauty as its rugged strands writhe above us.

There are toasts with champagne, and tiny bits of cheese passed on silver trays, but I'm heavy with thought.

"Are you okay?" Jost whispers at my side.

I turn on my best false smile—the one I perfected during my time at the Coventry. He doesn't seem to notice, so while my face beams, my heart slips down.

Kincaid is surrounded by men and a few of the actors. None of the players bear wounds or bandages from the performance. The woman still wears Veronica's face, but she smiles and laughs and hangs on the arms of a fellow actor. If they aren't sad, why should I be? Kincaid took care of them. None of them seem to be in pain.

"We'll do another," Kincaid promises. "Perhaps *Titus*?"

A few of the men whoop in approval. Only the actress's smile falters. The slip reveals her terror, but her mask is back on before anyone else notices. I hope she'll leave, run away from the stage and Kincaid, but based on how well she plays her part now, I doubt she will. She's acting again. It's in her blood.

Valery is absent. I see Kincaid glance to his side a few times, but she's not there. The play upset her enough that she risks Kincaid's displeasure, or perhaps she knew he would be so wrapped up in his own ego that her absence would go unnoticed.

"You aren't eating," Jost says, pulling me toward a table laden with platters and plates.

"I'm not hungry," I say. I loop my arm through his and press my face to his shoulder.

"You should eat," he says.

The din of the party grows louder as a man demonstrates a dance. His hands flail out and he reaches for the actress. She spins gracefully into his arms.

I look at Kincaid. I imagine he'll be bouncing in giddy beat with them, but instead he's engaged in deep conversation with a guard. His fingers stroke his small false beard. He issues an order I can't hear, and when he turns back to the spectacle, our eyes meet. He smiles, but his eyes stay hard, absent their usual sparkle. Unreadable.

Kincaid can act after all.

EIGHTEEN

I SLEEP SO HEAVILY THAT THE NEXT morning I have no memory of the prior night. When I look back at the time since Deniel's attack, it seems like a dream, even though I feel far from safe. Sleep is the dark and lovely escape of my childhood, and nightmares are now an inevitability of my waking existence. They'll come for me again and again, but in sleep, I'm finally free.

When I was little, I would lie awake and listen to my father checking the locks on our doors. The only thing I needed so I could drift away was the sound of locks clicking in place and if I heard them, I rarely had nightmares.

Once, soon after my parents starting training me to hide my gift, I dreamed I was tangled in a web, held captive by sticky strands that wound slowly around my short legs. They wrapped up my entire body until even my eyes were glued shut from the clinging fibers, and I waited to be devoured.

My father woke me that night, and I was still screaming even after he switched on the lamp that hung over my bed.

Only cocooned in his strong arms did I calm down enough to relate the dream in choking, gasping sobs.

"You're safe," he whispered into my hair.

"But you weren't there," I sobbed.

He could have lied to me—told me he would never leave me—but instead he pulled away and took my trembling chin in his warm, rough hands. "When I'm not there, remember you have the strength to free yourself."

"But I didn't," I protested.

"You will," my father said, brushing back the wisps of copper hair caught in my tears.

I fell asleep in his arms and woke the next morning to find him sleeping in a crooked heap next to me. He'd stayed with me through the night. Looking back, it was almost as though he knew our time together was drawing to a close, as though he couldn't bear to deplete my strength before I would need it most.

Now sleep asks no more of me than it once did. It is a refuge for me like it was when I was a child—perhaps the last refuge I have left.

My father is the first person I think of when I wake—my real father. The man who brought me up and locked the doors at night to keep me safe. I only knew him as a parent—someone who cared for me, providing food, shelter, and security—but now I know there was more to Benn Lewys. In the Coventry, I blocked the memory of my retrieval night, letting it fade into a fuzzy, Valpron-tainted recollection. If I didn't think of it, it had never happened. The fact that I would never see my father again could burn out of my mind along with the other moments too painful to recall.

But now, knowing that Dante is my biological father and that Benn kept his own painful secrets tucked away, I want to remember. And for the first time since my retrieval, I have a conduit to my past.

I find Dante piling large glass panels and coiled wire into the back of a crawler.

"Going somewhere?" I ask, suddenly glad that I'd pulled on thick blue jeans rather than a dress.

"Yeah," Dante says, pushing another panel into the cargo bed. There's the hesitation of a question in his voice. He knows I'm up to something.

"I want to come with you," I say, twisting a loose strand of hair tightly around my finger. "Maybe I could learn the family business."

Dante slams the cargo door closed and wipes his hands across his jeans. "Sunrunning is hardly the family business."

"Still, I'd like to see it." I'm not exactly lying. I would like to understand how Sunrunning works, but I'm more eager for some time off the estate with Dante.

"I don't know. I was planning to go alone—"

"I don't feel safe here anymore," I say in a low whisper, confessing my weakness to my father as I would have as a child.

"Fine," Dante agrees. Apparently he's as vulnerable to my entreaties as my father once was. "I'm leaving in ten minutes. Meet me out here."

I dash back in to grab a few supplies—a bottle for water and a jacket in case it's cool in the open-air crawler.

Unfortunately, my quick supply run puts me in the path of Jost and Erik. I'm not eager to make a party of it, but I can't say no when they ask to come along. It means Jost and Erik can help Dante collect the solar panels after they're charged. Dante doesn't seem too happy about it, but he doesn't renege on his agreement to let me come.

"And you're sure this is safe?" I ask Dante, my attention locked on the crawler. It has the same terrifying, cage-like appearance of the one we traveled in to the estate with the added bonus of no roof.

"Perfectly," Dante says, balancing a thick glass panel on his shoulder. "Get in and stop worrying. I thought you were a rebel."

"I haven't quite hit the suicidal stage of rebellion though," I mutter.

"What every father wants to hear," Dante says. He looks away as soon as it slips from his mouth, but awkwardness crackles in the air around us. I can appreciate his attempt to lighten things between us, but I can't laugh about this yet.

"How far are we going?" I ask as the engine thunders to life.

"Until we see the sun," Dante says.

"We'll be outside Kincaid's territory?" I ask.

"Yes," Dante answers, not taking his eyes off the road that leads from the estate.

The ride is as rough as I predicted based on the appearance of the crawler, but when we get closer to the border, where Dante will gather the solar energy to sell in the Icebox, light creeps across the edge of the Interface. We've been past the border before—the night we came to Earth—but we hadn't stayed long enough to study the relationship of the worlds. Day never came once we'd passed under the Interface into the metro of the Icebox, only an artificial morning created by the solar charges in the street lamps. I had looked at the sky that day and it hasn't changed since. At the time I was sad to think I had left the moon and stars behind without so much as a goodbye. In a moment I will see blue laced with cottony clouds. I will see the sun.

And when I do, we'll be deep in Guild territory.

"But what is it the border of?" Erik asks as we cross into the bright light of morning. We're out from under the Interface now. Arras's cover doesn't reach this far along the rocky, mountainous shoreline.

"The Interface between Earth and Arras," Dante says over the rumble of the crawler's engine. That's hardly more than we knew before though. The relationship of Earth and Arras remains hazy, although we see the parasitic effects of Arras every day. "There's a Guild mining operation nearby."

"Only one?" I ask.

"One active mine. Once they expend a spot, they move to another. We estimate there are about one hundred active mining locations at any time, but there are thousands of abandoned ones," Dante says. "Arras always needs more. It's growing every year." His eyes flicker to the sky directly over us.

If Arras is up there, it's hidden from view, even at the boundary of the Interface. Dante parks the crawler in a patch of grass, and I leap from it, kicking off my thin flats and stretching my toes in the cool blades. It tickles my skin and I'm reminded of home, of the grass woven into the yard I played in as a girl, and I have to fight the ache of longing that tumbles

161

through me. Turning around, I look at the world the sun touches. There's some vegetation, although it's sparse and unruly. I stare up, unblinking, into the bright sky, looking for an aeroship like the one we saw the first time we were here. But no ship comes and soon purple spots blossom in my vision. Dropping my gaze, I stare out to the other side and catch my breath—across the top of a far series of mountain peaks runs a long fence. Metal. Sharp. Modern. On the way here, Dante warned me that one of the Guild's mining operations was located nearby, and here's the proof. I don't want to know what lies beyond that fence.

Jost and Dante are busy checking equipment, ready to get started with the operation as Erik and I watch. They move with purpose, unloading thin panels from the small cargo space in the crawler.

"How does it work?" I ask.

"Basically, these collect the solar energy," Dante says as he mounts a panel on a rack behind the vehicle.

"And that?" I point to a cord snaking its way from the rack to the back of the crawler.

Dante opens the cargo door wider and I spot a long, squat control board. "It monitors the intake of solar energy as well as the panel's temperature level with bypass diodes. Collection occurs in cycles so the panels don't overheat and crack. We need to hook them up to a solar tracker to ensure the rack tilts them toward the sun. It takes hours to fully charge a panel."

"So we'll be here awhile," Erik says, pivoting around to take in the entire view—how the raw weave blocks the sun, the Guild's fence, the sparse vegetation. "Arras lies over it . . ."

I have to assume so, based on our escape from Arras, when

I ripped an exit through to the mantle that we now see over-head.

Erik takes a few steps back, surveying the world around him. Then he leans down and touches the ground. A moment later his eyes rise to the border between the sun and the weave.

"Then this is where it begins," he says softly.

At first I don't follow, and then it hits me: everything Lori-cel told me and everything I've learned. Arras has to begin and end. And it does, I realize. At four distinct points. Dante called them resources, but I know them as something different— coventries. Four distinct coventries.

"It's hard to fathom," I whisper. "But it must be."

We both start turning, looking for what we know is nearby. If only I knew what it looked like.

"There!" Erik points to a spot in the distance.

"Come on," I call, picking up my pace until I'm jogging to-ward it. If we have hours to kill before the panels are charged to capacity, we might as well look around.

"Whoa!" Dante calls, but we don't listen.

In the distance, barely close enough to see, something rises up in a wind tunnel. Sparks fly off the twisting strands, and all around the building are large gears and tubes. My eyes follow the tubes back as they snake off. I know where they lead—to a Guild mining site. One of the ones Loricel had to visit each year. The ones I would have been responsible to maintain as Creweler. I pull back. Nothing good can come of going there. Even from a distance I can feel the frozen deadness of the area, the corrupted world around the drill site.

But I walk backward, staring at the strange cloud that rises farther and farther up into the sky until it covers the sun, and the dark, glittering strands that stretch out past it, covering the Earth. It's separate from Earth and separate from Arras, and around it strands radiate, knitting together into the Interface, as though it's creating the Interface's weave.

We've found a coventry.

"Is that . . ." Erik's voice trails into a question.

"A coventry," I guess. It rises like a tower, tubes and gears taking it above the surface of Earth. Due to the Interface, we can't see the actual compound where we once lived. The tower fades past the mantle like a castle nestled in the clouds. But I know it's there.

"How?" he asks.

I drop down to my knees and drag my finger along the ground, drawing a square. "Think of it this way. Arras has four coventries, right?" I don't wait for him to answer me. "They each rest on the border of the Endless Sea—or that's what we're told."

"But why is it here?" he asks, his eyes on the wind tunnel circling the tower.

"It's not really," I say. "It's up there, but that tunnel actually plumbs the elements of Earth and sends them up to Arras. Spinsters use them on the loom. We weave them into Arras, but we have to mine them from somewhere."

"So you take that"—he points to the twisting strands— "and make it into Arras."

"Yes," I say. "That's why we have to be in the coventries. To keep Arras bound together correctly."

"But if you're right about this," Erik says, "then the coventries aren't part of Arras. They're located in between Earth and Arras."

I follow his eyes up to stare at the snaking tunnel. We can't see the compound, but I know he must be right. Hadn't I always suspected everything about the Coventry was false? From the programmed windows carefully created to display a perfect setting to the strange walls in Loricel's studios that she'd overridden to use exactly as she wanted. The garden filled with creatures and plants that should never have been able to coexist. The constant need for security. The coventries were between Earth and Arras, and that's why we didn't fall to our deaths when I ripped us through Arras to Earth. We'd been close enough to the surface in the Coventry.

"That's why we have to rebound in," I tell him, recalling the small station situated right outside the compound walls. "It's why they guard us so closely. They don't want us to know where we are."

Dante and Jost stride up in the middle of my explanation, looking angry and out of breath.

"Are you trying to get killed? Do you know how close we are to the mines?" Dante asks.

"I know," I say.

Jost looks at my drawing in the dirt, and I repeat Erik's and my conversation as his eyes search the sky. "But the Guild officials must know how this works."

"Maybe," Erik says. "The Guild is funny about what it does and doesn't share, and there are enough ministers occupied with keeping their heads up their—"

"They aren't worried about it," I finish for him.

Erik grins. "Sure, sweetie."

"Did Maela know?" I ask him, gesturing to the strange site. "Did she ever mention anything about the mines?"

"Perfect example," he says. "I don't know, but I doubt it. You see, Maela doesn't care about anything unless it directly affects her. She doesn't care what you are weaving or why. She does as she's told and she takes any opportunity she can to advance."

"So she's indifferent?"

"It's the preferred disease of Arras," Erik says, and his smile becomes anything but amused.

"We shouldn't stay here," Jost says in a low voice. "They must keep guards near here."

"He's right. Not that there are usually refugees from Arras running around the base of the slubs to worry about," Dante says.

"Slubs?" Erik asks.

"You'll feel it," he says. "The areas near the drill are dead. The Guild has mined all the resources and left an irregularity in space-time."

Loricel told me Earth was frozen around the mines, and I could feel the coldness creeping over my skin as we moved closer to them.

"I want to see the mines now," Erik says, and before we can respond to him, he's heading in the direction of the tubes.

"Me too," I vote.

Dante groans but turns to follow him. "I knew why you wanted to come today, but I hoped you'd chicken out."

"We're too young and reckless to chicken out," Erik calls back.

"He's going to get us killed," Jost growls, even as we follow him.

"Not if I get us killed first," I say, trying to lighten the mood. He doesn't laugh, so I take his hand and drag him after his brother.

We catch up with Erik, but no one speaks. There's a sense of shared purpose in the silence, and we walk for so long that the sun shifts in the sky. First it moves high and glares over us and then it begins to dwindle down. We're hours from the crawler and the solar equipment, but I won't turn back until we see the mines. The area we're exploring is outside the mountain range, and by the time we finally reach the steel fence, the sun hangs low. Not far from the fence, I spot a small creek a short way off. The rushing stream seems so vital after being under the Interface, where everything is inert, lifeless, or artificial.

"I'm going to fill up a few bottles," Dante says. "Water near the source mines is pure, and we'll need it for the hike back. Stay here until I return."

"I'll come with you," Jost says. "No one should be alone."

I open my mouth to protest, but he holds up his hand.

"Please, Ad. You'll draw more attention if there are guards," he whispers.

I'm itching to get to the mining site and I don't want to waste time refilling water bottles but I bob my head in agreement.

"Stay with her until we get back?" Jost asks Erik.

Erik looks genuinely surprised by the request but a little pleased as well.

"You look as out of place as she does," Jost continues, as if he can't bear to actually be asking a favor of his brother.

"Sure," Erik says, but now he doesn't look happy.

Dante and Jost stride off toward the water, and I fidget as their outlines grow small on the horizon.

"Promise me that you won't let me clock him," Erik says through gritted teeth.

I can't exactly blame him for being mad. I'm not very happy myself. "Promise."

As soon as they're far enough away, I start toward the fence.

Erik grabs my arm to stop me, but I drag him along. "They'll be back in a few minutes," he says.

"Dante is going to rush us out of here. I want to take a look around without him hovering over us," I say. "Are you coming with me or waiting around?"

Erik follows me. Now that we're so close, I feel pulled to the fence. It's not what I would expect. It's thick steel, and sturdy, but I don't see any cameras or guards. It looks more like a boundary than a safety measure, which makes it easy to climb. As soon as I'm over it, I spot the mines. Erik holds a finger to his lips. Like I need him to tell me to be quiet. And then I see it.

A light moves not far from a nearby truck. It's held by a worker. It looks like he's escorting a group. I'm too curious to keep from taking a few steps forward to look more closely. The truck is parked near a grove of trees and it's unlikely to be seen, but I understand the need for caution.

"Ad," Erik says in a low voice. I hold up a hand, indicating I know what I'm doing.

The group continues, moving closer to the actual drills. For a moment my attention wanders to the mining spot. I've seen pictures of the drills, but I hadn't come close to understanding their enormity. They are massive, even larger than the aeroship we saw when we first arrived. Since mine operations are shut down for the night, the gears don't grind into the ground. Instead they sit ominous and dangerous in a cavernous hole in the world. Part of me wants to creep closer to see how far the abyss extends, but then movement catches my eye. The group stops at the perimeter of the site, and I see him.

Leave it to Cormac Patton to wear a suit into a labor camp.

"Is that . . . ?" Erik whispers as he comes up beside me.

I nod. "Someone should explain occupational-appropriate attire to him."

Erik chuckles lightly and tugs at my shoulder. It's clear he wants me to step back farther away from the tree line. But I don't need him to protect me. I pull away and move a few steps forward. I expect him to go back to the fence, but he follows me.

"If he sees you," Erik warns.

"He won't."

And I know I'm right—unless he's looking for me. Cormac is paranoid enough to always be on alert, but he can't expect us to be here in the belly of the Guild's operations. It would be stupid of us to come so close to their operations after our escape.

The mining group is too far away for me to hear them, so I gesture toward a cluster of boulders that's closer to them. Erik shakes his head, but I ignore him and tiptoe forward. We're still near enough to the grove that if anyone from the Guild group looked up, they would see only darkness and branches.

Cormac and the other men's attention stays on the mining

site, and I tread quietly to the rocks. Straining, I can barely make out their conversation.

"How long until the site is expended?" Cormac's voice, even from a distance, sends a tingle of apprehension running through me. I wasn't sure I would ever be so close to him again. For one moment I consider running forward and pushing him into the drill site. It's not a bad plan except that Cormac is only one cog in the machine of the Guild. Their operations might stall for a bit but his death wouldn't be enough to destroy the entire system—even if it would be satisfying.

"You realize Jost is going to kill you." Erik's eyes dart around us, dutifully watching for trouble. "If Dante doesn't first."

I shush him and turn my attention back to the group. The space behind the rock is tight and Erik leans in against me to stay hidden. I'm not sure he's ever acted this nervous around me.

Cormac is nodding. "We'll need to expand farther in then. Unless you think we can risk the stability here longer."

The man next to him, who I can't help noticing is dressed in jeans and a plain shirt, responds, "I don't think so. We risk a temporal collapse if we continue, but expanding won't be easy. The natives are already restless in these parts, and Kincaid's men are getting greedy."

"They get that from Kincaid," Cormac says. "No doubt he's filled their heads with talk of his glorious revolution against the Guild. If they only knew him like I do."

"Several Sunrunners have picked fights with miners in the last few weeks."

Cormac waves off the warning, unconcerned. "We'll send more Remnants in."

"Will you be bringing her here soon?" someone asks him.

"Perhaps. If we open a new site, Pryana will have to come for a visit." But his tone stays noncommittal.

So Pryana is slated to be the new Creweler. This is bad news. Pryana is a talented Spinster, but she's never shown the wisdom necessary for the powerful position of Creweler, the woman who oversees the entire pattern of Arras. Everything about her is wrong for the job.

Cormac dismisses most of the group, but one man lingers by his side.

"Sir, what if—"

"Believe me, Hannox, I'm considering it. I think Pryana can handle it. We haven't had to really test her yet," Cormac says to his companion.

Hannox: the man on the other end of the conversations overheard in Arras.

"And if she can't?" Hannox asks.

"We'll deal with that when we know it's a problem," Cormac says, ignoring Hannox's concern.

"Until then we should keep up the search for Adelice, I assume," Hannox says.

"We know she's with Kincaid," Cormac says. "But I've had no word from the spy for weeks."

"Sir, it's not been very long on the surface," Hannox reminds him. "Give it time. Word will come. Until we've recovered her, we'll ration source material?"

"Yes, our supply is stocked for several months. I want skeleton operations at drill sites, and every surface resource focused on finding Adelice," Cormac commands.

"Sir, if she's dead—"

"She isn't," Cormac says. "And stop calling me sir. Dammit, Hannox, we've known each other one hundred and seventy-five years."

"Yes, *sir.*" Hannox adds a bow and a salute to emphasize the point.

Cormac waves him off with a smirk. "See to the operations. I'll take care of our missing Creweler."

"I'll liaise with the handlers and check for new intel," Hannox promises.

"We'll have images and details sent down so that they can recognize her, but under no circumstances are they to know why we're looking for Adelice," Cormac warns.

"What if she's on Arras?" Hannox asks.

"She's not smart enough to get into Arras undetected," Cormac says. "But I'm increasing security and surveillance around her sister. If Adelice is up there, she's going after Amie."

"Someone's spying on me. On us," I whisper. The thump of my heart is so loud it nearly drowns the words. They're coming after me, and even worse, they're watching Amie.

"No surprise there," Erik responds, tugging at my arm. We stay crouched behind the rock until Cormac and Hannox begin moving back to the camp.

"Who do you think it is? The spy?" I ask Erik after the men are out of earshot.

"It could be anybody," he says. He nods back to the grove of trees and I follow him. My footfall is soft, but I feel heavy. Pryana might be capable of performing the tasks I'd hoped to keep from the Guild, but Cormac doubts her skill. My head turns over everything we've learned, sorting and tagging it into appropriate slots in my memory. Cormac even confirmed the disparity in time acceleration in Arras. He sent a spy weeks ago—was he talking about Deniel? That had happened only two days ago.

As soon as we're back over the fence, Jost slams his hands into Erik, catching hold of his shirt. "That was stupid," he says quietly, but his tone is fierce and angry.

"It's my fault," I say. "Erik tried to stop me."

Jost doesn't apologize to Erik, but he drops his hold on his brother.

"Come on, Ad," Jost says, turning away from Erik.

"I don't care what Kincaid will think," Dante says, his hands clenched in tight balls at his sides. "If any of you go running off again, I'll shoot you."

"Noted. I'm sorry," I say to him. But I'm not.

"We should head back." Jost's words are simple, but I can see the tension in his jaw. I know it won't allay their anger, but I tell them about what we overheard at the mines and about Cormac's presence. Jost keeps relatively calm, considering that was exactly the kind of danger he wants me to avoid.

"It's bad enough that they know you've settled in with Kincaid, but if they get intelligence that you've left the estate—"

"They won't miss the opportunity to get to me," I finish for Dante.

"There's an old ammo factory up the way. Our intel says they use it to weaponize and release new Remnants. It's likely there's some transport there," Dante tells us, shifting from foot to foot. I can't help but notice his eyes swiveling around us. It's not like him to be so worried. "If their spies informed the Guild that you're Sunrunning, then we need to get out of here before they come looking for you, and the crawler is hours away."

"Won't there be Remnants?" I ask.

"We'll stick together and check things out first," Dante says. "We don't have much of a choice, I'm afraid."

"I'm not sure that I like this plan," Jost says.

"Cormac Patton is on Earth, and he's looking for you—" Dante begins.

"Looking for Adelice," Erik corrects him. "She's his blushing bride."

"Oh shut up, Erik," I say, making a gag-me face. "Maela's missing you too, I'm sure."

"So I'm home free," Jost says in a voice that can only be described as joking.

Everyone turns to stare at him.

"What?" he asks, confused.

"Did you crack a joke?" Erik asks him slowly.

"Oh shut up, Erik," he says, mimicking my face.

"Now you can both shut up," I say, turning on my heel and moving alongside Dante. I need to think about what I've heard, about where to go from here.

NINETEEN

THE AMMUNITION FACTORY IS WELL KEPT ON the outside, but
when we enter we're met with cobwebs and rust. Each step
sends dust swimming into the air. The roof is glass, made
opaque by years of neglect, and only a hint of light breaks
through the muck. An abandoned conveyor belt hosts a line of
rusted stools and little else, and images in faded paint still
decorate the walls. I slow down to study them.

A man in a uniform, rifle in hand. A woman gazing at him
in admiration. THE GIRL HE LEFT BEHIND IS STILL BEHIND HIM.

Another poster urges viewers to KEEP THE DANGER OVERSEAS.
A woman smiles, her hands full of bullets. A shadow passes
across the overlarge portrait. I turn, but no one's behind me.

"We lucked out. This place is empty. Let's find the store-
room," Dante calls, and I jog to catch up.

As we cross the factory, I reach for the arm of the person
beside me, but come up empty. The other three are ahead of
me and yet I would have sworn I felt Jost right beside me a moment ago.

"The Guild leaves these here?" Jost asks as we come up on a row of motocycles.

"It's where the Remnants are outfitted when new batches are brought in. They wake up here and are herded out into the Icebox with transport and weapons," Dante explains. He gestures to a stockpile of firearms along the wall, tossing a rifle each to Erik and Jost in turn.

"How did you know it would be empty?" I ask, refusing a weapon of my own.

"I didn't."

Something dashes along the periphery of my vision. It's probably a wild animal, but it's enough to raise goose bumps along my arms. There's no reason to discuss the Guild's methods since we've found what we came for, so I grab the handles of a motocycle. "Let's get these out of here."

As we wheel the cycles out of the building, my dread dissipates a little until Jost asks, "Where's Dante?"

He isn't with us. We wait by the door, but he doesn't come, and then an acrid odor drifts out to where we're standing. I don't waste any more time. The air stings my eyes when I reenter the factory. Sulfur prickles along my nostrils. It smells like a fire, but who would be stupid enough to light one here? A body materializes, fading in from a shaded corner, but it's not Dante.

Question answered.

The factory isn't empty. The shadows weren't tricks of my imagination. I spot Dante as he sends an old stool cracking across the head of a Remnant. He yells something that I can't make out, but I think it's a warning.

A Remnant leaps in front of us and Erik doesn't lose a

moment—he knocks off a shot. He doesn't hit our would-be attacker, but the Remnant skitters away from us, disappearing back into the dark recesses of the factory.

"Should we be shooting in here?" I scream, but no one answers me. The acrid odor is replaced by smoke, and I see the beginning licks of a fire. It grows larger, consuming the machines, which pop and crack in the heat. We need to get out of here *fast*.

The inferno is building inside the ammunition factory and I can't think of a worse place to be trapped. We're only steps from the exit, but I whip around, grabbing for strands, and move and tuck and weave to build a trail of protection behind us. The rush of fear makes it easier to see the wild strands, but their unruliness slows me down. I have to look closely to differentiate the time strands from the matter. As we reach open air, the Remnant that Dante hit over the head jumps toward me, landing so close that I panic and miscalculate my work, yanking the wrong strand. It wrenches out from the strands surrounding it, brushing against the flames. It slides across the plant, shooting sparks that amplify the raging fire and then the factory shatters into smoke and debris.

Black plumes billow up from the burning plant, and as soon as we're a safe distance away, I drop to my knees, hacking against the fumes I've inhaled. It could have been worse. No one seems to be hurt and we have what we came for.

I'm stumbling back to my feet when Dante grabs hold of my shirt and pushes me back down. "Want to leave any more proof that you're here?"

"It was an accident," I mumble, but it sounds weak even to my ears.

"Like that ship you unwound from the sky? You claim to want answers, to want to help us fight the Guild, but what I see is a stupid girl bent on blowing things up." His words sting.

"Maybe next time I'll let them kill you," I scream. He's hit his target though; I'm wounded by his accusation.

"Get control of it or don't use it," he seethes, towering over me. "You jeopardize everything because you don't know what you're doing."

A hundred jibes tumble into my brain, but before I can settle on the one that will be the most hurtful, a Remnant limps from the plant's remains. Erik's on his feet, heading toward him, when Jost jumps in front of him.

"Let him go," he commands.

"He's going to run back and tell the others where we are," Erik says.

"And by then we'll be long gone," Jost says. "We aren't ready to take on another pack and these cycles will get us back to the crawler. The Guild will come to investigate what's happened, so we need to get out of here."

"So you're going to let him go rat us out? These cycles better have lots of gas, because the second we stop they'll catch up," Erik scoffs.

"Cormac already knows we're on Earth," I say, trying to defuse the situation.

"He doesn't know you're *here*," Erik reminds me.

"Let's go," Dante says. His anger at me still flames in his words, but he sounds distant now. Determined.

I'd lost track of how far we'd traveled to find the mines, but I know the crawler is hours away. With the motocycles we can get back to it fast, but I know it might already be too late. It won't take the Guild long to realize something has happened. I can only hope they assume the explosion was caused by the Remnants. I can't imagine that they haven't had problems controlling them before, especially if the Guild keeps them locked in a factory.

The only roads between here and where we left the equipment are cracked with age. It's probably not a top priority to maintain roads out here, but it makes riding the cycle trickier. I've nearly skidded off course twice but manage to keep my motocycle upright. It's a good thing too, because we've lost Dante and Erik, who are now so far ahead of us they would never hear a crash. It's cold out here as night really settles in, and save for dark piles of bones that I hope are those of animals, there's not much to see.

I'm finally getting the hang of riding the cycle when it begins to make a spluttering noise. Jost responds by speeding up to cut off the others, and by the time they turn back, I'm waiting next to the immobile motocycle.

"Out of gas," Dante proclaims, and we redistribute so that I am now riding with Jost.

"How much farther do we have to go?" Erik asks.

"Not much longer, especially now that we can keep pace with one another," Dante says, and I feel heat flood my cheeks.

We race through the crumbling roads, zipping around large cracks and holes. My suspicion that I was holding Jost back was right. The ride is terrifying. It's harder to trust the safety of the cycle when I'm not the one controlling it. Whirling through the crisp air, my hair beats across my face, and I clutch Jost's waist. The speed results in a sort of paralysis of mind and body, and I keep my eyes shut. The only parts of me that seem to be working are the arms that squeeze around him tighter with each jerk of the motocycle, and then the hum of the motocycle fades down, and I realize that we're coming to a stop. Carefully opening one eye, I peer over Jost's shoulder, not sure what to expect.

The crawler sits before me, and I can't believe how happy I am to see it, considering I hate riding in it. Dante wastes no time gathering the charges and panels. Shame over our screaming match seeps into my chest. Dante came out here to do work, and I messed everything up.

"Did you get any solar energy?" I ask him, trying to make conversation.

"Enough," he says with a grunt. He hoists a panel onto his shoulder and turns away from me.

"Enough?"

"Enough that Kincaid might not ask questions about where the hell we've been all day," Dante says.

He ignores me as the boys help him load up the back of the crawler. Erik throws me concerned glances, but no one says anything more about what happened at the ammunition factory.

"Sit up front?" Dante asks when we go to leave. I'm surprised that it's a request and not a demand.

I look to Jost, and he leans down to my ear and whispers, "You should talk."

I take the front seat and wait for the lecture to begin, but when Dante finally speaks, it's not what I'm expecting to hear.

"You should know why I agreed to let you come along—"

"Because you knew I wanted to see the mines," I guess, but Dante shakes his head.

"I didn't take you to see the mines or to learn about Sunrunning. I brought you because I didn't want to leave you at the estate with Kincaid after his little play," Dante says.

"Kincaid doesn't realize he's scaring me," I say, fully believing it. Kincaid thought unwinding Deniel and staging that play would help me feel safer. In his own way, he's as twisted as Cormac Patton.

"He knows what he's doing, Adelice. Kincaid is many things, and you would do well to remember that," Dante warns. "But I'm sorry, Adelice. I shouldn't have attacked you like that."

"No." I stop him. "It was stupid of me. I clearly don't know what I'm doing here."

Dante pauses, shifting the crawler into a higher gear. His eyes flick over to me. "I think we should work on that. You have a magnificent talent, but it won't do you any good if you can't control it."

He's being reasonable, but I still feel smaller as he speaks. The words are a carefully disguised reprimand—once again, he sounds like my father. I dreaded Benn Lewys's gentle rebukes more than any punishment he could dole out, usually because I knew he was right. Apparently Dante shares that quality with his brother.

"You're probably right," I mumble.

Dante opens his mouth, but then he shuts it again. We're both trying. Only we have no idea how to do this. The rest of the ride, I concentrate on thinking about how to approach this problem, how to accept what we are to each other, but when we pull through the estate's gate, I'm no closer to a solution than I was before.

TWENTY

THE ESTATE IS QUIET, HEAVY WITH SLEEP, when we arrive. We part ways with murmured good nights, eager for baths and beds, but Jost takes my hand as we climb the steep stairs into the mansion. He holds my hand when we get inside, but he doesn't ask what Dante and I were talking about on the ride home.

An angry voice echoes through the silence, and I freeze. Jost tugs me along but not before I overhear the argument.

"You are not to remove her from this estate again," Kincaid commands. "I expect better judgment from you."

"It was a simple gathering trip. We set up the panels and enjoyed some sun. It was fine," Dante says. His lie is smooth and believable.

"This is a warning. Consider what would happen to your precious girl if they caught her. She's here under my protection." The song is out of Kincaid's voice, his words fierce and demanding.

"I appreciate that," Dante says.

"Do you, Dante?" Kincaid asks. "You have a strange way of showing it."

Their voices fade, but I'm sure Jost heard it, too: Dante lied for me. I can't digest what it means, any more than I can understand Jost's silent treatment.

"Come on," Jost says. "I'm tired."

But before we can continue toward our rooms, Dante speaks. He's quieter than he was with Kincaid, so I dart closer to his voice, coming from the large assembly room. I hide in the shadows of a neglected piano.

"It was a long day, Jax," Dante says. I imagine him running his hands through his hair as he speaks.

"Trouble?" Jax asks.

"Remnants. Mines. You name it."

Dante is telling Jax what really happened, which means he trusts him, unlike Kincaid.

"Do I want to know how you got yourself into that mess?" Jax asks.

"My *daughter*." The word is overemphasized, as though Dante is tasting it to see if he likes it.

"She must take after you," Jax says, clearly amused.

"Don't start," Dante warns. "She could have gotten us all killed, and she might as well have sent Cormac an invitation to our outing. It was so obvious that we were there."

"What are you going to do about her?"

"Knock some sense into her?" Dante says. "I don't know. She's stubborn. Oh, don't give me that look. I know: *she gets it from me*."

"She's been through a lot," Jax says. "Her life in Arras. Her mother. Even what that scum Deniel tried to do to her. Give her the benefit of the doubt."

"I'm trying, but I don't want to see her get killed." There's a pause in the conversation, and I realize I've stopped breathing. "I barely know her."

"Do you want to?" Jax asks him.

"Yes, I do." There's certainty in his words, and I find I'm relieved.

"Did you manage to get any solar energy above the quota?" Jax asks, changing subjects.

"No. I'm sorry. I know how important it is to your work . . ."

Jost guides me away, urging me to the elevator. We're both too tired to take the stairs tonight. I have no more interest in Dante's conversation, but plenty to contemplate. Dante wants to know me. I'm not sure how to feel about that.

When we reach our suite, Jost fills a basin of hot water in his bathroom and brings it to me. We're both filthy, covered in dirt from the road and ash from the explosion at the ammunition factory. I dip my hands in the basin, rubbing them clean. I'll take a bath later.

"Dante was upset," Jost says finally, and it's evident from his clipped tone that he is as well.

"According to Dante, I have no control over my talents," I say.

"You sure about that?" he asks.

"I'm always right," I joke, trying to lighten the mood.

"Don't I know it," he says, unamused. Sullen Jost has returned. Until today's disastrous events it felt like our relationship had turned a corner, as though we were finally moving

184

forward. I thought he could be happy again. But shades of angry Jost are showing themselves, and suddenly I don't want to discuss anything with him. Not that he'll want to talk anyway. He never does when he's locked inside his own head.

So instead of telling him anything more, I watch him stand and move to the washbasin. I keep watching as he strips off his dirty shirt.

Why don't I want to go to him? Not so long ago, seeing him like this, being alone with him, would have been enough. But now I feel like I'm the only one wanting, and it's making me numb.

I force the hurt down and go to him. Before he can turn to me, I wrap my arms around him and bury my face in his back. He smells like sweat from our adventures earlier, and when I press my lips to his skin, all I taste is salt.

As I kiss his shoulder, I feel him exhale and then, to my surprise, instead of pulling out of my embrace, he wraps his hands around my wrists and pulls me closer to him.

A shiver runs through me, and I kiss him again. My arms thaw, followed by my chest, until my entire body responds to the contact. I push up on tiptoes to kiss his neck. Then his ear. He spins me to face him but he doesn't push me away. His arms twist around my waist. But he doesn't kiss me, he tucks his face against my neck, trailing his lips along until they're in my hair.

He breathes in deeply and murmurs, "You smell like smoke and fire."

I smile a little and somehow I know he is smiling, too.

But I don't let him continue; instead I bring my lips to his. He meets my eagerness, and this kiss is different. His body reacts to mine, crushing closer to me, each of us trying to fuse with the other. I can feel the desperation in our embrace, but there's want there, too. A need for closeness. A need for something we've been denying too long. Something we could lose any moment.

And then he presses me onto my heels and I realize as I stumble back, still kissing him, that he's leading me to his bed.

I don't need to think about it. I just have to keep going.

He lays me down gently, and the bed is too small, and I don't care, because Jost is on top of me and he's kissing me and I want him. And he wants me.

It's right.

It's right.

It's right.

I bury my face against his chest as he moves back to my neck and I reach for his pants.

His hand grabs my wrist.

And like that the need—the desire—is gone. It sucks from the room, leaving only dry air in its wake.

"Ad," he manages between breaths, "I can't."

"Won't," I accuse. It's the same way he reacted in my room before the play. He pulled away from me then. He's been pulling away since we got to Earth.

"Don't start this again," he says, standing up and grabbing a shirt from the dresser nearby. "I don't want to argue."

"Considering you force us to drop it every time we're in this situation, I wouldn't call it having an argument," I snap, smoothing my shirt back into place.

He turns from me and leans against the dresser, and I can't decide if I should slip out. Is this my cue to exit, because he's done talking? Or does he expect me to stay? It's hard to know since he isn't telling me anything these days. After a few minutes I stand to leave, an embarrassed blush creeping onto my neck.

"Don't go," he says softly.

I stop and wait.

"This isn't easy for me," he continues.

"And it is for me? Do you think I'm happy here?" I wonder if I'm even capable of happiness anymore, but I don't say this to Jost. Too much moving forward. Too much planning the next move. There's no time for happiness, and it's becoming clear that there's no possibility of it with what we've discovered here. If we can't get lost with each other, what's the point?

"I could be happy with you anywhere if . . ."

And there it is: *if.* I'm not sure what I expect him to say. *If you were happier. If you hadn't brought Erik. If we weren't caught in the middle of a war. If. If. If.*

"Don't you understand that we can't sleep together?" he finally asks. It's the last direction I expected this conversation to go in.

"Is that what this is about? Sex?" My voice peaks on the word.

"Ad, if we have sex, we can't go back."

I stare at him for a long moment, hoping he'll elucidate what he means, because it makes no sense to me.

"Wait," I say slowly, starting to grasp the heart of the problem. "Is this because of purity standards?"

"Of course," he says. "If we have sex, we could go back to Arras to rescue the girls, but your skill is our most powerful weapon. We'll never get to Sebrina or Amie without it."

It's hard to tell which emotion wins out at this proclamation: anger, annoyance, relief? They mingle and leave a sour taste in my mouth.

"You know purity standards aren't real, right?" I hate how condescending I sound, but I thought Jost was smarter than this.

"How do you know that, Adelice?"

"Seriously? Because Cormac told me but also because half of the Spinsters were sleeping with officials and valets." I bite my tongue to keep from using Erik as a definite example of this phenomenon.

"Are you willing to risk the girls on a hunch?"

That does it.

"Why don't you ask your brother?" I say, without hiding the seething frustration in my voice.

"So he screwed Maela. That hardly proves your point. She didn't have any talent anyway."

"Well, what about Enora?" I ask. "I'm sure she and Valery, you know . . ."

"Do you know?" he counters. "Did either of them tell you? Have you asked Valery?"

So that's it. We're going to have an argument without any way to prove that I'm right without risking I'm wrong. *Perfect.*

"Cormac wouldn't have been planning to marry me if sex was going to destroy my skills," I argue, because I'm sure that was where most of his attraction to me lay.

"But he knew how to map you. He could have fixed your skills after or given them to someone else and kept you home . . ."

Barefoot and pregnant. The thought is enough to make me sick.

"You are going to have to trust me on this, Jost. It's a lie.

Ask Erik," I say, crossing my arms over my chest. "On second thought, don't. That would be weird."

"Come here," he says, the hostility of his tone dropping off. I bury my face in his chest and marvel at how soft his shirt is and how, even now a world away, it still smells the same as it did in Arras. His scent makes something ache in my chest, but I'm not sure if it's longing or sadness now.

"Ad, it won't be much longer, and then . . ." He trails off, and I can almost hear the hesitation in the air.

"Then?" Surely he won't reject me then.

"Then we can be a family," he says, and now I understand.

If sex is the topic Jost is skirting around, then family is the one I'm trying to avoid. I want Amie and Sebrina back, but I'm not sure I'm ready to be a family. Going back for the girls isn't where things end, it only puts me in more danger than ever. Danger I want to avoid placing the girls in.

"What if we can't be?" I whisper.

Jost's eyes narrow and I can see the condemnation in them. "Because you don't want her."

I want to deny this. I want to explain the danger and my need to protect Amie and Sebrina, but I can't. So I don't say anything at all, which is probably worse.

"I didn't ask you to be her mother, Ad," he says quietly, but his tone is anything but soft. It tears with accusation. "Why did you even tell me she was alive?"

"How can you ask that?"

"It's what I'm honestly wondering," he says. "Why are you even here now?"

"I-I-I care about you," I stammer, shocked at the way his words cut. "We belong together."

"Maybe we did in Arras, but what about when we get them back?" he asks. "I can't abandon my daughter. I thought you understood that. What about your sister?"

"It's different," I admit.

"Because she won't come between us," he says wisely.

"No, it's not that. I can't be a mother. Amie won't need me that way." *And they'll both be safer without me,* I add silently.

"I didn't ask you to be," he repeats.

"No, you might not have, but, Jost, you're going to be a father—"

"Ad, I've always been a father," he says in a tired voice. "That never went away."

But you didn't seem like one, I want to say. He's right. I've always chosen to ignore how awkward his past made me feel, especially when it came to his daughter. And I've denied how things will change once she's back. I won't be able to protect her or care for her. Even my being with Jost would be a risk to her.

"I can't waste time waiting for you to be ready. I won't be like you and Dante. I don't want to be a stranger to Sebrina. Maybe we need to focus on a plan for now," he suggests.

My eyes meet his and I understand exactly what he's saying, and something twists and snaps in my chest, leaving a hollow ache in its wake. But I want him to say it. I want him to own it.

"Instead of?" I ask quietly.

"Instead of worrying about us."

I have to push against the raw ache in my throat to keep my voice steady, but I manage to ask, "Like, we'll figure it out later, or like, we'll remove the 'us problem' altogether?"

"Altogether," he says in a firm voice.

Why had I wanted to hear him say it? So I wouldn't have to dissect exactly what he meant by "instead of worrying about us"? Because this wasn't the answer I was hoping for, even if it's the one I knew was coming.

I want to crumple onto the floor. Part of me wants to sob and beg, making me feel like a traitor to the person I thought I was. As the rawness builds in my throat, I nod, without a single tear, and turn on my heel. The door feels like it's a million miles away and with each step I nearly lose my resolve, but Jost doesn't say anything to stop me and that helps.

The tears sting my cheeks as the lock clicks behind me.

TWENTY-ONE

THE SCENT OF JASMINE FLOATS THROUGH THE room as the faucet pours water into my claw-foot tub. As I step into the water, its chill surprises me. It's warm, but not the hot bath I was expecting. I sink in and feel goose bumps rise all over. I take a deep breath and push myself completely under the surface. My hair swirls around me and after a few seconds of weightlessness, I open my eyes. The world swims before them and the water burns, but I don't shut them again. I stay this way until my lungs feel like they'll collapse from the effort of staying underwater.

When I rise from the bath, I feel reborn, and yet my face is still too pale and the scarlet of my dyed hair has finally faded into a recognizable copper. I slip into the same dressing gown despite discovering a tear in the sleeve. The mirror lies to me, offering an unchanged reflection when everything about me is different.

* * *

I don't leave my room the next morning. I stay in my dressing gown, torn sleeve and all. It's clean and otherwise comfortable. Someone brings me food, but it grows cold on the serving tray it arrived on. A cart of sweets and delicacies and none of it looks good. There's wine, too. But I don't want to drink it. I tried to lose my grief in a bottle when Enora died, but I want to feel this. I want it to tear at me so that my heart is scar tissue when it heals—harder to break and less sensitive to pain.

The truth is, I don't feel anything. I don't feel sadness or anger. The numbness is crippling. The only thing that seems true in this moment is that this was inevitable.

How do girls my age in Arras get married? Do they fight with their husbands? I can't remember my parents fighting. But marriage is different from being in love, I remind myself. It's permanent—legal and binding. I couldn't walk out of a marriage like I walked out on Jost last night. He has no claim to me, and I have no claim to him.

I'm still in my dressing gown when there's a hard rap on my door. I open it expecting to see Jost.

Dante takes in my disheveled appearance and my fallen face, but he doesn't comment. He's too tense. Excited, maybe. He looks like Benn right down to the crease forming between his thick eyebrows.

No. *Anxious.*

"Come on," he says, pulling me into the hallway.

I clutch my robe together. "I'm not dressed."

"There's not time," he says, dragging me along.

I wrench my arm free. "Okay."

I retie my robe as modestly as possible while trying to keep pace with him. I'm more than a little surprised when we run through the grand marble entrance and right out the front door. We pound down the side staircase so quickly that I grip its long carved railing to keep from falling down the brick steps. Dante leads me past the drive to the outer road, where a group of crawlers wait. These ones are armored. Their roofs are made of thick metal, but looking closer I see there are holes in the tops. A Sunrunner pops up through one and I realize what they're for: scouting. Dozens of men are loading up crates and weaponry.

"What's going on?" I ask, suddenly fearful. We were in Guild territory yesterday; did they track us back here? Is Cormac coming after me?

Kincaid appears over Dante's shoulder. He's wearing a thick black vest, not unlike the ones the guards at the Coventry wear. I know they are worn for protection there, but Kincaid doesn't seem like the type to put himself in harm's way. Not unless something important drives him to it.

Kincaid slithers up to me and watches the men. His eyes glint in the false daylight of the artificial lighting system.

"We're going on a mission," he tells me. The omnipresent glee is in his voice. All around us men test rifles and pull on vests, but you'd think Kincaid was going camping.

"What?" I put my question to Dante this time, unsure I'll get real information from Kincaid. A Sunrunner dashes past us, knocking against me slightly and pushing me into Kincaid.

His gloved hands catch me, but he releases me as soon as I'm steady. His eyes flick to the offending man, and I wonder what punishment is in store for him.

"We have info on the Whorl," Dante says. "One of our scouts found some information in the Heart."

"The heart?"

"Heartland, middle of former America. It's in the dead center of the Interface's cover."

"I thought it was mostly abandoned," I say.

"It is. There are a few outposts though," Dante says. "Kincaid's intel indicates the Whorl may be hidden in one of them. They're heading to check it out."

"I want to go, too," I say.

"Impossible," Kincaid says, his focus remaining on the flurry of activity surrounding us. "I want you to stay safely on the estate."

"Not a good idea," Dante says to me. "It's several days of travel and rough company. I'm staying behind with you—"

"I'm not a child," I say, feeling a bit petulant despite my claim. But as soon as the words escape my lips, I spot Jost loading a bag into one of the crawlers. "He's going?"

I don't know how the question comes out because I feel the familiar paralysis of last night in my chest.

"Yes, he was the first to volunteer. He's very single-minded," Dante says. "They're leaving quickly, and I didn't want you to miss saying goodbye. I know you want to go with him, but—"

I hold up my hand to stop him. "You win. I'll stay here. Bye."

"I knew you would see reason. Which is why I'm sure you won't mind staying on the estate during our absence. Under no circumstances are you to leave. I've informed security," Kincaid says.

"What?" I ask, my voice breaking. I clamp my mouth shut

to stay the tears rising in my throat. I won't let them see me cry. The Guild knows we're here, and the answers I've been searching for aren't here on the estate. Kincaid is putting me in a purported net of safety, but I feel trapped, like bait dangling from a snare.

"It's for your own security," Kincaid assures me. "I would hate to see you fall into the wrong hands. Dante is staying as well. It will give you a chance to get to know each other."

The prospect of growing closer to a man who doesn't hide his disapproval of me is small comfort.

"Valery will be traveling with me, but I'm leaving Jax behind. He should be able to maintain grid operations in an emergency," Kincaid says to Dante.

While they are distracted, I dash off. Dante calls out after me but he's swept back into the conversation before he can stop me. I don't stay to watch the preparations. I gather up the hem of my robe so I don't trip over it and flee back to my room.

Sensation is creeping through the blessed numbness—a horrible clawing that rips at my chest. But before I can shut the door behind me and figure how to feel about this, a hand pushes it open and Jost ducks in. His eyes are flat and cold, but the trance melts as we stare at each other. I'm glad we're not immune to each other's presence.

"I'm leaving," he says. His tone is clipped. Formal.

"I heard . . . saw . . ." My words stumble out of me, and I want to sink into a puddle on the floor from embarrassment. Where is the girl who sat in her room, not crying, not feeling now? Why has she abandoned me at this precise moment?

"They have info on the Whorl. If they find it, I need to know," he says.

"Why? You can't do anything with it," I point out.

"We could control Arras and if we do, I won't rely on anyone else to help me get to Sebrina. Every second we waste here, I lose minutes with her! I don't trust any of them to care about that," he says. "I don't expect you to understand."

"I do understand." The words explode from my mouth.

"I thought you did, but I can't expect you to care about Sebrina the way you care about Amie or your agenda. If you want to get caught up in their war, so be it. I'm going after my daughter."

He's drawn a line down the room, the edge from our argument last night creeping into his voice. It's a line I'm not welcome to cross.

"Leaving doesn't change anything," I say.

"I know," Jost says coolly. "I don't want it to."

Okay, *that* hurt.

"To be clear, I want you to rescue Sebrina, too," I say.

"I know that, Ad," Jost says, "but you aren't willing to fight to help me."

That hurt, too.

"I've never stopped fighting," I claim.

"It doesn't matter," he says. "You aren't responsible for her."

"Sooner or later, you'll have to let someone else in, Jost Bell," I say.

"Why?" he asks.

I hesitate.

"I never wanted it to be like this—" he begins.

"You should go," I say, cutting him off. "I guess this is goodbye."

Jost reaches out and tucks a loose strand of hair behind my ear, and I shatter, falling piece by piece back to the dome of safety in Arras. Back to stolen kisses. The memories mix together, muddling into something black and viscous, and the words I should say die on my lips.

"No, I'm not saying goodbye." He walks out, sending my world spinning.

TWENTY-TWO

I STARE BLANKLY AT THE DOOR. THE only light streams in from the opened curtains, and everything around me is washed out and colorless. It feels false, even though this is reality. This is the real world. My real world, and I don't want any part of it.

I'm still sitting there when Erik pushes the door open and peeks into my room. "Hey, you."

I can't manage a reply.

"I heard," Erik says, the blue of his eyes deep and concerned, "about Jost."

"I'm so tired of this," I say through gritted teeth. "I'm so tired of fighting with him."

"But he's gone now."

I swallow, trying to digest the bitter truth of his words. "Yes. He is."

"Which means you don't have to fight anymore." Erik moves beside me, hovering next to my vanity and waiting for me to speak.

I glance up at him. His expression is hard, but there's something beneath it. Conflict.

"Erik—" I start to say.

"Don't," he says, putting a finger on my lips. I close my eyes and a tear falls, cold against my heated skin.

"You're crying," he says, and his hands drop from my face.

"It's . . . it's not you," I say, because it isn't.

It isn't him. I know how he feels. And part of me wants to crash into him and forget. Forget Jost. Forget everything that's happened since we left Arras. But Erik deserves more than I can give him. He deserves more than I can give anyone.

"For once let yourself feel something, Ad!" Erik yells, losing his composed attitude. "You can't push everything down and make it disappear."

"I feel alone," I mumble.

"You aren't." Erik stands over me shaking his head. "You have me."

"You deserve better," I say to him, standing so that he can't peer down at me like he's looking into my soul.

"You're the closest thing to a friend I've had for a long time." He fingers the tear in my sleeve, and I pull my arm back. "So you can't push me away, because I'm not giving up on you."

"I feel like a lost cause. I'm tired of running and fighting, Erik. I don't know what I'm doing anymore. They didn't even take me on the mission because I'm so useless. I guess I'm ready for this to be over," I admit.

"This isn't you," he says. "Adelice Lewys rips the world apart. She attacks Remnants. She's a little stupid but not helpless."

"Do you really know me, Erik?" I ask, and the words taste

sour. They build in my throat, unleashing themselves with an anger that pushes me forward to stare at my reflection screaming in the vanity mirror. "About him—about anything. I don't even know why I'm doing this. I don't know who I am anymore!"

I lash out at the image in front of me, flinging brushes and cosmetics across the room. They clatter to the floor, bottles shattering. The destruction calms me enough for me to break the hold of the mirror.

Erik's shoulders drop, but his hands curl into fists. "I do."

I stare at Erik as he bends to gather the scattered glass from the floor, wondering how he can be so certain. Of me. Of what we're doing here. Isn't he the boy who was angry for being ripped to Earth? How has he grown so much?

"Look, Ad," he says, dropping to kneel next to me. "You are extraordinary."

"I don't want to be extraordinary," I say softly, not meeting his eyes.

"I don't mean your skills. You're not extraordinary because you can weave, you are extraordinary because you have a good soul. Much better than mine. Or Jost's. Or pretty much everyone I've ever known," he says.

"A good soul who let her father die, who lets her mom sit in a prison cell. You know why Jost left, because he doesn't think I can handle Sebrina."

"Handle Sebrina?"

"Like be her mom or whatever."

"That's a lot to ask anyone," Erik says.

"But if I loved him wouldn't I have said I could, wouldn't I have fought for it?" I ask.

201

I want him to answer me, because this is the question pressing at my chest, bearing down on my lungs. An answer would be my oxygen.

"You mean you can't fathom how you would respond to someone you've never met in a situation you've never been in?"

I know the point Erik is trying to make, but it falls flat.

"Ad, he's scared. Not just of not getting to Sebrina," he says, "but of losing you."

"Of losing me?" I repeat.

"You're in more danger now than Rozenn ever was. People are chasing you. People who want to kill you or use you. He knows that."

"So he's protecting me?" I don't buy it. The pain in Jost's eyes wasn't from loss, it was from betrayal. I know that. I betrayed him, and the worst part is that I'm not even sure how.

"He's protecting himself."

"I'm not even sure we ever loved each other. I mean, not like my parents," I say.

"It's not that simple," Erik points out. "Your parents loved each other, but your mother also loved Dante."

"I know. That makes it even harder to understand. I know she loved Benn, my father, but why didn't she ever mention Dante?"

"She was protecting you, but she was also protecting herself, like Jost. Some things are too painful to bear. Jost can't stand even thinking about losing you, and he almost has several times. He thinks if he shuts you out he won't lose you." Erik pauses and puts his hand on my knee. "But some people have too large an impact on our lives for us to imagine we can forget them. I know if I'd known you a week and lost you, I'd miss you the rest of my life."

"I'd miss you, too."

I see something hidden behind his friendly demeanor and the burning force of it frightens me. But he's slipping back into our safe relationship now. The one where he doesn't betray his brother. The one where I don't have to choose.

"You going to be all right?"

"Yes," I say. And somehow, despite the empty echo in my chest, I know I will be. "I'm going to wake up tomorrow and it will be a new day. Promise me something?"

"Anything," he says.

"That you'll drag me out of bed if I don't get up tomorrow," I say, stumbling a bit over the sadness creeping into my words.

Erik sighs, but agrees. "I promise. And what are your plans after you manage that?"

"I'm going to have Dante teach me how to alter."

"You know how to have a good time," Erik says.

"I'm quite the party girl," I agree.

"Can I come?" Erik asks.

"Sure," I say.

"I wasn't invited on their little hunting trip," he says. "And I'm getting a bit bored around here."

"You could swim," I suggest. "There are about ten pools."

"No trunks," Erik says, wiggling his eyebrows suggestively. "I'd have to skinny-dip."

I know my face is on fire right now, but I grin despite myself and push him out of my room. I have plenty to do today. Like cry away this ache so I can start tomorrow in a new world.

TWENTY-THREE

THERE ARE THOUSANDS OF STRANDS WEAVING IN brilliant discord through the greenhouse once I focus in on them. It's taken me nearly a week to get to the point where I can see the strands on Earth without adrenaline pumping through me, and it's now over two weeks since the mission left, making me feel like an empty well drained of every resource. Without the organized weave of Arras, it's been harder to command my skill—both in manipulating the natural strands of the universe and in seeing them.

Now as I stare at them, I try to home in on one. I could grab any number of the overlarge room's strands; the space around me is full to bursting. A low hum fills the air from the backup generator Dante has turned on to give us more light. The old halogen bulbs illuminate the room but their constant flickering seems to warn of their impending demise. Between that and the buzzing of the generator, it's harder to feel the strands' vibrance. The problem isn't that I can't see the strands, it's that

Dante wants me to find one specific thread—the time strand located within a petite orchid.

I'm trying to slip my fingers into the weave of the flower. I hold the strand at an angle, keeping a finger on the particular one Dante has asked me to find. I'm sure it's easier for him to point one out than for me to find and grip the precise strand he's referring to, which is exactly what he's trying to show me. I gingerly grasp the golden thread and tug to pull it into a warp. My touch is gentle but the thread cracks through the air, splitting a petal in two. The pieces fall bruised to the ground. My eyes meet Erik's; he's watching from a nearby stool. He came for moral support, but I know we're thinking the same thing: we're going to be here forever.

"No," Dante says. His tone is patient, which has the strange effect of making me feel *very impatient.*

"It's occurred to you that this is hopeless, right?" I ask, dropping the strand in defeat and settling back against a table full of pots and plants. It creaks under my weight. I know how it feels.

"Only if you tell yourself it is," Dante says simply, but he cracks his left knuckles as he speaks.

Never mind. The Zen master is getting a bit tired.

"If you are in a fight, your skill has to be controlled. What would happen if you grabbed the wrong strand?" It's not a question. We've both seen what happens, but I'm getting tired of him constantly bringing up the ammunition factory as an example.

"We'd get out alive. That's what matters."

"Is it?" he demands. "And how can you be certain you would, with such a cavalier attitude?"

"I haven't killed any of us yet." I stop fingering the strands around me and plant my hands on my hips.

"You nearly did at the factory. You weren't in control," he says. "I'd call that dangerous."

"I'd call that *lucky*. It bought us time."

Dante shrugs, rubbing the frond of a tall potted fern. "We view things with a different perspective, Adelice. Your escape from Arras was brave but too risky. When you wield your power like that, you put everyone in your path at risk."

"No one was hurt," I argue, but this time my argument sounds small and weak, because I know he has a point.

"Perhaps not, if that makes you feel better, but how would you feel if someone was caught in the tear? If Jost, for instance—"

"I don't need a lecture. I need you to teach me."

"You're missing the point," he says. "You already know what to do. You have to learn to control your skill."

So I've been told. Repeatedly.

"I'm trying!" I explode.

Dante sighs but his face softens. The crease in his forehead vanishes. "Close your eyes."

"But—"

"Do it," he snaps. "You need to find the time strand moving past you. You must isolate it if you want to protect the objects and people around you."

"No sh—"

"Feel for the pulse," he says firmly.

"Time doesn't have the pulse, the matter does—*the life*," I argue, but I keep my eyes closed. I can feel the matter around me. If I concentrate I can hear its crackling vitality under the room's ambient sounds.

"Time's pulse is different. It's more like the wind— ephemeral, always changing a little. Matter is vibrant, throbbing with energy. Time is like a whisper. You can only catch it if you listen closely," he murmurs. "Accept that you're a part of it and that it's a part of you like the beat of your heart."

I clear my mind and reach out with my fingers. I don't grab anything, I caress the strands around me. They pulsate, pounding with vital life. Strands of matter. I'm shocked at the sensation in my fingertips. Maybe I didn't concentrate so intensely in Arras, but every strand I touch throbs through me. I drop them and focus on the space around me, tuning out everything but the thrum of the world. And then it's there—a tinny whistle that fades in and out of my hearing. Almost metallic, it oscillates between a faint rhythm and a heavy, inelegant hammering. I let my fingers reach out, trying to match the sound with the tactile sensation. They close over a thin strand and I feel the intensity of its pulse shift, growing louder and more demanding in my hand.

"Better," Dante says, breaking my concentration.

As I open my eyes, he fingers a glowing strand of time.

"I'm glad you approve," I say. "But I can't stop and concentrate in a fight."

"Of course not," he agrees. "That's not what I'm trying to make you understand. You must let go to unleash your ability. You are strongest when you aren't trying."

I try to hold back a groan, but I can't. "Then isn't training the exact opposite of what I should be doing?"

207

"Don't think of it as training, think of it as honing."

"A differentiation worthy of a politician," I mutter. "Maybe I'm not cut out for this."

"You were made for this," Dante says, placing a hand on my shoulder. "We both were. Weaving and altering skills aren't accidental. They're your genetic legacy. But you have to accept your gift. Once you do that—once you make it a fundamental aspect of who you are—it will be as simple as breathing."

Something I'm looking forward to, especially if it means I can stop training and get some sleep. It's going to be tricky, considering my parents trained me to ignore my weaving ability, not to accept it. I practiced that for years, and now Dante thinks he can undo that preparation.

"What happened to your hands?" he asks.

I hold out my hands and he inspects them.

"A Spinster punished me," I say.

"By trying to destroy your fingers?"

"I wove razor wire and steel." I pull my hands back, suddenly self-conscious about the scars that are still visible from Maela's revenge.

"You're lucky to have fingers at all," he says. "But, Adelice, your skill lies as much in your mind as your hands. Stop being so tentative, it's making you clumsy."

"That's what's holding me back?" I ask.

"I've seen you let go when you need to. In that alley to save your mother and in the ammunition factory."

"I thought you didn't approve of my use of my skills," I say.

"I didn't. You reacted brashly," he says. "But you relaxed and channeled your ability in those instances. Your hands didn't stop you. Don't let that stop you now."

I nod, embarrassment growing a lump in my throat.

"I think we're done for the day," he tells me. "There's a problem with the photovoltaic array at the power plant that I need to look into."

"Is Jax helping you?" I ask. "I haven't seen him in a while." Jax and I aren't exactly friends, but after Erik he is still the friendliest person on the estate.

A shadow passes over Dante's face. "He's on the mission."

"He is?" I ask. "Sorry, I thought he had stayed."

I consider accompanying Dante to the power plant, but even the sight of the smokestacks makes me cringe. I'm still embarrassed by my mistake at the ammunition factory. If Jax isn't going to be there, I'm not sure I want to go with Dante. Thinking of the plant, I recall what he said earlier. "What happens if I catch someone in a warp?"

"In the best-case scenario, you merely trap them in the caught time."

I know that from experience. I count on it actually.

"What if it's more serious?" I ask quietly.

"You could damage their thread. Maim them. Kill them. That's why it's imperative you learn to focus on time. Grabbing matter uncontrolled is too risky. You know how delicate we are. One wrong move and you could rip someone in half."

"What I really want to know is how to alter," I admit.

Dante stops and gives me a heavy look. "I assumed so. It's not as glamorous as it looks."

"I saw what they did to Deniel," I say. "I'm aware of how *glamorous* it is."

"You saw the worst thing that Tailors do," he says.

The worst? Yes, what happened to Deniel was horrible, but

what about removing people's souls or altering their memories? What about the other ways Tailors and the Guild take away people's lives? Take away the very essence of who they are?

"Tailors can help people, too, Adelice. A trained Tailor can patch a thread and heal someone," Dante says.

"I've only seen them do that to people *they* hurt in the first place," I say, planting my hands on my hips. It's true. My only experience with renewal patches is seeing them misused by men like Cormac and Kincaid.

"I need to know what I'm doing," I say. "You've been teaching me this so that I don't hurt anyone, but what I did to Deniel when he attacked me—that could have been worse. I need to understand how alteration works."

"Fine. I'll give you an hour, but then I have to check on that array." But the look on Dante's face says it's anything but. He doesn't want me to see this or understand this or do this. But why? "Maybe your friend will volunteer."

I'm not imagining the way Erik swallows before he nods. "Sure."

"Maybe we could start with something smaller and less prone to bleeding?" I suggest.

Dante's jaw tenses but he bobs his head in agreement, gesturing to the fern he'd been fiddling with. It's only a plant, but I don't like the idea.

"I can unwind this," he says, "or I can change the shape it grows in, make the leaves longer. I can steal strands from another plant and wind them through it, and create a hybrid."

"Could you make it look like another plant?"

"Sure," he says with a shrug, and as we watch he tugs apart the fern and then carefully adds its strands into a small bush.

The plants blur and shift, growing, changing in front of our eyes until the stubby little bush is a baby fern.

"You are possibly the best gardener ever," Erik says, clearly impressed. "Don't tell my brother I said that."

Dante grins despite his earlier foul mood.

"Make it grow," I say.

He runs his hands over a leaf and it blurs, stretching into a long green leaf.

He turns to me. "You try."

My hands tremble a little as I reach for the leaf. I try to focus and see the composition of it, where to slip my fingers, what pieces to manipulate, but I can't.

"Relax," Dante says. He moves behind me and places his hands on my shoulders. It's a strange gesture, but having him there makes me calm.

The plant's composition comes into focus and I concentrate harder until I'm reading it like a code. Each strand woven neatly through, certain threads knit tightly while others are loose. But when I pull on the strands, the plant crumbles into dust.

"Does that make me the worst gardener?" I ask Erik.

"Let's say you don't have a green thumb," he says.

"Try again," Dante urges. "You got the time with it."

"I killed it," I say in a bleak voice.

"Don't look at it that way."

"Is there another way to look at it?"

After a few more tries, I manage to get a leaf to stretch. It's only a quarter of an inch, but it boosts my confidence. "I want to see how you alter a human."

"You already saw that," Dante reminds me softly.

"I saw a human unwound," I say. "What good is my alteration ability if I don't know how to use it?"

"I think being able to rip someone's flesh apart is a pretty good way to use it," Erik offers.

I shoot him a look. "The more I see outside of a stressful moment, the more I'll be able to control my alterations when there's a crisis."

"So you want to practice on me?" Erik asks.

"Spoken like a true volunteer," I say, giving him a sweet smile.

"Don't try to charm me, Adelice Lewys," he warns, but I already know I've won.

"Why don't you watch for now?" Dante suggests. He reaches for Erik's arm, but Erik doesn't extend it.

"Wait, that seems like you're going to touch me," he says.

"You aren't being terribly open-minded," I tell him.

"Forgive me," Erik says sarcastically. "I'm attached to my skin. Literally."

"Never mind, we'll do it on Ad," Dante says. "You'll be able to see as well."

I don't hesitate in thrusting my arm out to him. I sink back into my head, trying to clear my mind of distractions, waiting for my own composition to come to life but Erik pushes my hand down.

"Do me," he commands.

"I guess chivalry isn't dead," Dante mutters.

"What was that?" Erik asks.

"Nothing."

But I can tell from the pinched expression on his face that Erik heard. He doesn't want to admit why he's so eager to volunteer, and I don't want to think about it. About what it means. That Erik is protecting me, because I not only don't need Erik to protect me, but I also don't want him to.

I don't want anyone to.

Erik holds very still as Dante pulls a thin blade from his pocket. But he doesn't cut him. Instead he traces along the bare flesh of Erik's wrist. I feel my stomach flip over, but as it does, I see what Dante is doing. He's tracing the lines of Erik's weave. A moment later, his fingers slip down and a trickle of blood appears at the spot.

I look to Erik's face, momentarily abandoning my interest in the procedure. This can't feel good. His teeth are clenched together but he gives me the barest of determined nods. He's putting on a show for me, no doubt.

I shouldn't have let him volunteer for me.

When Dante's done, there's the lightest hint of a scar traveling up Erik's wrist, but it's thin and hard to see. I wouldn't notice it if I wasn't looking.

"What did you do to me?" Erik asks, examining his hand. There's some smeared blood on his wrist, but other than that and the small scar, you'd never guess that he'd been altered. It was so fast, so expert.

The thought makes me sick.

Anyone can be changed in an instant.

"I added some of that plant to your DNA," Dante tells him.

"What?" both Erik and I say in surprise.

"What effect will that have?" I ask.

"He'll probably turn green and start producing tomatoes." Dante's face splits into a full grin.

"Not funny."

"You two are very gullible," Dante says. "All I did was stretch your strand and then fuse it back together. That's why there's a scar."

"Oh," I say in a small voice, but I can tell Erik appreciated the joke.

"Any side effects?" Erik asks.

Dante hesitates but when he answers there's no two ways about his answer. "No. There won't be."

It's the calm, even voice my father used with me when I was a kid. If I asked if there were monsters in the closet, there weren't. If I asked if I would be taken away at testing, I wouldn't. If I asked him if I would make friends at academy, I would. The same even tone used to tell me what I needed to hear. Sometimes he was right about the monsters, but he'd been gambling on some of the others.

Of course there were monsters everywhere in Arras.

But why lie to Erik? What side effects can come from alteration?

"I'm starving," Erik says. "Being a lab rat takes it out of you. Anyone else interested in food?"

"I'll join you in a minute," I hedge, knowing it's me he's waiting for. "I want to change first."

Erik accepts this explanation and heads out of the greenhouse, flexing his wrist a little, like it's sore.

"What did you do?" I ask as soon as he's out of earshot.

Dante opens his palm to reveal a bloody chip of metal and circuits.

"What is that?"

"Tracking chip," he says.

"How did you know it was there?" I ask. I take the chip even though it's covered in blood.

"A guess."

"But they can track our sequences in the mantle," I say, confused. I turn the chip over in my palm, looking for a clue as to why it was there. Why bother when they could call up a personal identifying sequence and remove the individual strands so easily?

"They can track through most of the mantle, but the looms don't see everywhere. There are slubs, irregularities in Arras's weave, much like the ones near the Guild's mines here."

"Are the slubs caused by accidents?"

"There are no accidents in Arras," Dante says in a quiet voice.

No, there aren't, which means any irregularities, any slubs in the weave are man-made. It wouldn't make sense for the Guild to put them there. They wanted total control. So why are they there? "I was tracked," I tell him. "They put a transmitter in my food when I went out on a goodwill tour with Cormac."

"I doubt it's still there," Dante says. "Transmitters like that break down too easily within the body, or pass through altogether. I'm surprised they bothered."

"Why?" I ask.

"Probably to track you more conveniently. Perhaps Cormac didn't want to use the looms, or maybe he wanted to be able to follow your movements throughout the day."

That does sound like Cormac, but why bother with Erik?

"I wonder if they've been tracking him this whole time," I say, feeling more sick every minute.

There's a pause before he answers. "Probably not."

That's not reassuring.

"Do I have one here?" I ask.

Dante reaches for my arm. "I don't see a scar," he says.

"Erik had a scar?" How had I not noticed this?

"It was a pinprick. I wouldn't expect the average person to pick up on it. But altered skin is different. I doubt even Erik knew he had it."

"But why would he have it?"

"I don't know, Adelice," Dante says. "I guess the question I'd be asking if I were you is, how well do you know your friend?"

I don't know him at all. I only know what he's told me, what Jost has told me—but still I'm certain of my answer. "He didn't know. I trust him."

"Even if he's lying to you?" Dante asks, wrapping the chip up in a handkerchief and putting it in his pocket.

"He's not lying," I say. "He didn't know it was there."

"That's not what I'm talking about," Dante says in a soft voice. "Your friend sees the strands."

I knew that. I'd known that since my first training session at the Coventry, when Erik reacted to my proclamation about the fake windows. I'd even seen him grip the strands when we came through the Interface to get to Earth. It wasn't news to me, and yet I'd never stopped to consider what it meant. "I'm sure lots of men can."

"The strands of the Interface or the knit of Arras's weave perhaps, but Erik is hiding something," Dante muses out loud.

"If you were going to implant a tracking chip in someone, why would you do it?" I ask instead.

Dante hesitates and then looks me directly in the eyes. "There are two reasons I would implant someone with a chip. Because I didn't want to lose them, or because they were dangerous."

I don't like either option. Mostly because even though I trust Erik, I know it's both.

TWENTY-FOUR

DANTE LOCKS THE GREENHOUSE BEHIND US. I'M not sure why a bunch of plants and potting tools need to be secured, but I know Dante wouldn't tell me even if I asked him. In evening's dim light settings, the glass is black. I trail a finger along a pane, considering something Dante said earlier.

"I wonder how our family got a pass to go," I muse.

Dante chuckles, moving toward the main house. "I should think that's obvious given your ability."

"You said we were made," I remind him. "They didn't choose the original Spinsters for their skills—they had none!"

"But they chose our families based on a list of physical and mental requirements. Decisions were based on potential," Dante says, as I trail beside him.

"And then they made them into Spinsters," I finish. "But wait, my mother wasn't a Spinster. Or my sister."

"Most genetic abilities skip around in a family," he explains. "Not everyone gets the same eye color or body build, for instance. Remember the footage of the injections and surgeries in the film? It was genetic manipulation."

"So the scientists gave us the gene?" I ask.

"I'd be lying if I said I understood half of it. Weaving is a cultivated recessive gene. Once it was added to a person's genetic composition, it might reveal itself but that wasn't certain. The first crop of Spinsters was very small and very weak. Early on, while the scientists created serums that increased ability, they depended completely on the looms."

Dante claims ignorance, but he's full of information.

"And those that didn't have ability?" I ask.

"They were put into the population to breed more Spinsters."

"And Tailors," I add. "So now the Guild is trying to isolate those genes so that they can replicate them?" I guess.

"It will be much easier for the Guild to have total control over Spinsters. You're right, Adelice," he says. "I think they plan to make a dominant gene that can be spliced into hand-picked specimens. Then they can decide which girls to grant the ability."

Girls who are easier to manipulate, I think. Girls who are obedient.

"My grandmother told me families fought the retrieval squads," I say out loud. "All those women in the film looked eager to join."

Dante's mouth thins into a tight line and he tilts his head thoughtfully. "You shouldn't believe everything you see in a film, Adelice, but I suppose you're right. The circumstances here were terrible during the war, but I think things changed in Arras."

"Changed how?" I ask.

"Nations merged, and laws were adjusted to meet everyone's expectations. Conflicting national identities merged to create a cohesive whole. Those changes, coupled with resentment over having daughters whisked off in the night with little to no expectation of seeing them again. There was an adjustment period," he tells me.

"How do you know about this?"

"Our family," he says after a pause. "They took care to chronicle things despite the laws against it."

"Were they members of the Kairos Agenda?" I ask. My parents had never told me these stories, even though they knew what I was—they kept this information from me.

"Not really." Pause. I can tell he's holding something back. "They were pacifists. My parents wanted to live comfortably and easily."

"Until you showed your abilities?" I ask.

"It wasn't my parents who asked me to run. They should have," he says. Pause. "With the increasing amount of propaganda thrown at them, like the film, for instance, most Arras citizens stopped seeing the danger of the Guild's absolute control. Bombs weren't being dropped, so people went along with it, even as the laws got stranger and more restrictive. The Guild required everyone to marry and have children, who could then be tested for the gene. It's how Arras wound up with marriage laws and skills testing."

"So this trait could reveal itself in a male child?"

"I'm living proof," he says with a flourish.

"Then why not use men at the looms?" I ask. The Guild seemed eager to keep women in small boxes, carefully placed on specific shelves. If men could weave, why not give them the opportunity and keep women even more pressed under their thumbs?

"How powerful would a man with weaving abilities be?" This time he pauses for emphasis. "More powerful than an official without?"

I nod. "That makes sense."

"And at first glance, there's no problem. But the war the Guild escaped from was fought by men hungry for power. What if a government was put into place to act on behalf of citizens and a young man demanded power from them because of his ability? It would have been disastrous to the peace the Guild had cultivated."

"They were no better than those other men," I say.

"Intentions are fickle things," Dante says. "I believe the Guild intended all their rules to safeguard against power struggles and war. If they carefully monitored and controlled the female population with a male government, things could be regulated. Boys with weaving ability remained untrained and away from looms."

"Now the Guild tells us only women can weave."

"Denying an ability doesn't make it go away. More boys were born with the gift. Some went away and came back different. Changed," Dante tells me.

"Is that why so many Tailors fled to Earth?" I ask.

"It's safer for them here," Dante says.

"Too bad it's so much more dangerous for the rest of us with them here," I say.

"Not every Tailor is evil, Adelice."

"You aren't," I say.

Dante hesitates before he responds to this, running a hand over his cropped brown hair. There's a pattern to his nervous habits. "I'm not really a Tailor. Not in my heart. I never wanted my skills."

"Just like I'm not really a Spinster," I admit.

"Exactly," he says.

"You can warp, then?" I ask.

"No, that's a Creweler's skill," he says. "I'm powerful, but not as talented as you are."

"Why?" I ask.

"Good genetics?" He shrugs, giving me an awkward smile.

"So both Spinsters and Tailors need tools like looms to manipulate the weave," I say.

"No, Tailors can't work looms," he reminds me. "Their power is more insidious than that. You know that the true nature of their ability lies in alteration."

"Tailors alter objects and people physically. Spinsters use looms to weave and embroider."

"Correct," Dante says.

"Is that why the Guild is so afraid of Tailors?" I can't imagine how dangerous that talent could be unchecked. Spinsters can be kept under control by preventing loom access.

"It's certainly why they control them so stringently. But never forget that there are Tailors who go along with the Guild. We aren't all bad or evil, but you can't blindly trust us either," Dante says. "If you suspect a man—or a boy—of being a Tailor, keep him at arm's length."

The warning isn't as generic as he's trying to make it sound. He's telling me to keep one particular boy away, but while

Dante may not have a reason to trust Erik, I do. I steer the conversation away from Erik, knowing things could get volatile. "How do they find Tailors? There's no required testing of boys like there is for girls."

"Once they understood the true nature of male weaving ability, they started cataloging boys born to parents who had been part of the initial experiments. Many didn't come back. Cities were segregated so the Guild could attempt to control marriage, ensuring ideal female offspring."

"They've been successful enough at keeping women under their control," I say, not bothering to hide my distaste.

"Spinsters can be powerful, but they allow themselves to be controlled by the Guild. They resign themselves to patterns in return for privilege."

Dante clearly doesn't understand what it feels like to be dragged from your family. I acted out of fear for my safety. I let them cage me in the Coventry for too long because I thought they were in control. I didn't act because I thought I didn't have a choice.

"It's not always easy to accept that you have power," I say instead. "Especially when the world is dedicated to telling you that you don't."

"You're an exception, Adelice," Dante says. "And that's thanks to your parents."

His words are complimentary. He means them. But his mask slips for a moment, revealing his scars again.

"They understood," I say, the realization hitting like a sudden gust of wind on a static day. "They knew what I would face, because of you. Because you ran."

"I felt like half of myself in Arras—always hiding my gift instead of embracing it. Here, I thought I might be able to do something with my skill," Dante admits.

"How did you find the courage to leave?" I ask.

"Stories," he answers in a conspiratorial whisper. "Stories are dangerous and useful things."

TWENTY-FIVE

THE POOL STRETCHES OUT BEFORE ME. A dozen squat white lampposts line the space, their soft glow mirrored in the water below. It's the indoor pool's only light source now that no sun shines through the windows overhead. The water is as smooth as glass, gold-flecked tiles peeking through the cerulean surface. Although it's quiet, I spot a shape moving forward under the water. Erik strokes evenly across the pool, the barest ripple following him. His hair is a golden halo flowing behind him. I wait by the side, surprised by how long he can stay under the water.

His head breaks through, shattering the water's surface. He rubs at his eyes and smiles at me. "Ad, you scared me. What are you doing here?"

"I see you found swimming trunks," I say. I'm not ready to address the real reason that I've come.

"Sort of. I'm using the fishing-village version," he says. His arms perch on the side of the pool, and his eyes are as bright as the brilliant tiles.

I slip my shoes off and roll down my stockings. "And what does this version consist of?"

"Sorry," Erik says, pretending to fan himself. "You're distracting me. What did you say?"

I frown at him, sitting down and dipping my feet into the water. It's warmer than I would have expected.

"When I was a kid, working the fishing boats in Saxun, we took off as much of our clothes as possible, without revealing our, uh, *treasure*, and jumped in," he says, his lower lip inching up into a crooked grin.

"You have a treasure?" I say, widening my eyes in feigned innocence.

"You gonna pillage it?" he asks.

"I walked into that one," I admit with a groan.

"Yes," Erik says, "you did."

His finger traces a spot on my calf, leaving a trickle of water on my bare skin, and I swat his hand away.

"That's one huge scar," he says. I frown and look to see what he means. A thin, pale line slants across my leg. "Where did you get it?"

"I don't know," I say, drawing my knees up and clutching them to my chest. "It's probably from my retrieval night. They used a claw to pull me out of the escape tunnel. The renewal patch must have left a scar."

"It shouldn't have," Erik says, squinting to get a better look at it. I don't care about the scar. It's only a remnant of a past life.

"Erik." But I stop on his name, searching for the right way to ask him about what Dante told me about the tracking device. It doesn't take me long to realize there is no right way.

"You're going to chew off your lip," Erik warns me, and I relax my mouth into a tight line. "Just ask me."

"I want you to tell me how you wound up at the Coventry, how you got out of Saxun," I say. The words jumble into one long exhalation.

"Why?" he prompts, seeming to disappear from the conversation. I know he's upset. Erik distances himself, asking questions, when he feels cornered.

"I need you to tell me the truth," I say in a quiet voice. He'll vanish entirely if I push too hard.

"I can't," Erik says.

"Why? I promise it won't change anything."

Erik turns from me and stares up at the glittering ceiling. His arms spread wide against the the lip of the pool, revealing the sharp sinews of his upper body, built by years of handling fishing boats. "You can't promise that. It will change things between us, Adelice. There are things in my past that I'm not proud of—"

"You think I don't have regrets, too?" I ask. "My father was murdered. My mom is a monster. My sister is in Cormac's clutches as we speak. And that all happened before I got to the Coventry and started messing things up."

"This is different. Those things happened *to* you, Ad." Erik hesitates, pausing to look at me for a fleeting moment before he turns away again. "The things in my past—they're choices *I made*. I can't blame anyone else for them."

"You aren't going to tell me?" I ask. I swish my feet through the water, watching the bubbles swirl around my toes. I know what he's hiding, and he has to know that, too. He sees right through my feigned interest. He knows I want to catch him. If

Dante's theory is correct, Erik's secret breaches our trust completely. If he could be honest now, we can rebuild it.

But he doesn't want to.

Neither of us speaks, the silence extending so long that my toes shrivel and pucker in the water. "I know."

"Know what?" Erik asks casually.

"I know that you can see the strands. I know that you can touch them."

"That doesn't necessarily mean anything," Erik says.

"No, I *know* it does, and I'm hoping you respect me enough to tell me what it means." I wait for him to rise to my challenge, but he stays silent.

"I can't take it back once I tell you, Ad," he whispers finally.

"I know that, but I need to hear the truth from you." My voice is a plea, cracking from the pressure of my warring emotions. "Right now I'm betting my imagination is making things worse than they are."

"I doubt it." Erik scratches the top of his head and pushes out of the pool so he's sitting next to me. Our feet dangle under the surface of the water, dangerously close to each other.

"I left Saxun to pursue a career with the Guild," Erik begins, and I nod to show him I'm listening, that I care about whatever part of his story he's willing to share—as long as there are answers at the end of it.

"I wasn't cut out for fishing."

"The pretty ones never are," I joke, trying to lighten the mood. Erik gives me a small smile but his face stays serious. "What I've never understood is how. How did you get the Guild's attention?"

"I gambled," he said. "They brought a friend of mine into

service, which is pretty rare, and when they came to Saxun, I approached a Guild official and told him I had something they wanted."

"Risky," I comment. "What was it?"

Erik takes a deep breath and speaks slowly. This is what he wants to avoid talking about.

"I showed them I could alter," he admits.

Somewhere deep down I had known Dante was right, even if he hadn't tied it up in a neat bow for me. He'd told me to keep Tailors at arm's length, and I knew he was talking about Erik, but I didn't want to believe it.

"You're a Tailor?" I murmur in a voice so low that I'm not sure Erik can even hear me.

"I am," Erik says.

My hand flies up and slaps him hard across the cheek before I even consider what I'm doing. "How could you keep that from me?"

"How was I supposed to tell you?" Erik says, rubbing the splotch of red left by my hand.

"It's pretty easy actually," I say, dropping my voice to mimic his deeper one. "Adelice, I can manipulate strands like you."

I know it's not that easy, but I wish it were.

"I wanted to tell you, but you don't know everything about Tailors. Do you know what they do to us?" he asks.

Dante told me what they do to Tailors. They take them away like Spinsters, but Tailors are controlled even more tightly. The Guild wipes out their families systematically. They imprison them and ask them to do things to people—take away their memories, alter their feelings and personalities—I can't even imagine what else.

"I wanted out of Saxun," he says. "Doing alterations was my ticket. I didn't know what I was getting into."

"Does Jost know?" I ask.

"No," Erik says quickly. "Ad, aside from other officials and my best friend, Alix, from Saxun, you're the only person who knows."

"Not even Maela?"

"You're the first person I've ever told."

"How did you even discover you could do it?" I ask.

"We don't have to trade stories about our first time," he says. "Like so many first experiences, it was an accident. I have no reason to believe the Guild would ever have known about me if I hadn't approached them. I thought Alix might tell them, but I couldn't spend my life in Saxun, especially once Alix was gone."

"So you left and did whatever they told you to do?" I ask. I'm making it sound more dramatic than it was, but the betrayal is still raw, each new revelation stinging the tender, damaged skin of our relationship. Even worse, I know I'm judging him.

"I left without saying goodbye," Erik says. "I was young and careless, and it never occurred to me that I might not see my family again. Saxun didn't have a lot of Spinsters, let alone Tailors. There was no one there to guide me, to explain my skill to me. I thought I was special."

"You thought you would be worth something to them?" I guess.

Erik nods, a far-off look settling over his face. "I thought I would be somebody. Now I know the best thing I ever did for my family was to leave them like I did."

"They didn't go after your family because you volunteered?" I ask.

"Alix helped me get access to a grey market Tailor. New privilege card, new last name—no questions," he says. "They didn't go after my family because they didn't know about them."

"That's your face though, right?"

"Changed the name, kept the sexy," he says.

"Why bother?" I say.

"I didn't want my family to know where I went," he says. "I was scared that the Guild would reject me if they knew I was the son of a fisherman." A dark look passes over his face. "I was being a complete jerk, but it may be the only reason Jost is alive today."

"I doubt he'd see it that way," I say. Erik left his family without concern over how they would feel, and his recklessness saved them. The night of my retrieval I only thought of my family and me. I was too selfish to warn them, and I destroyed them. Funny how selfishness comes in shades of destruction and salvation.

"He doesn't," Erik admits. "Why do you think he hates me?"

"He doesn't hate you."

"He doesn't like me," Erik says.

I can't argue with that.

"You need to tell him," I say, grabbing Erik's hand. "He'll understand."

"No," Erik barks. He clutches my hand so tightly my nerves gasp in pain. "Promise me you won't tell him—that you won't tell anyone."

"I promise," I say, and he releases my hand. "But I still think you should tell him."

"You don't know Jost like I do," Erik says, but the second the words leave his lips, he sighs.

"Did you do the things the Guild asked you to?" I ask, steering our conversation away from Jost.

"Yes," Erik says. "I always did what they asked. I never saw any reason not to."

He didn't see anything wrong with manipulating people's minds? With unwinding their bodies? "Why did you change your mind?" I ask. I need him to redeem himself. "You told me you were trapped at the Coventry. You helped me escape."

Erik's face hints at a smile, but it's a sad one and he shakes his head. "I get to keep a few secrets."

"Yes, you do." I incline my head and meet his eyes. "I'm sorry I slapped you."

"You're stronger than you think, Ad," Erik says, his hand reaching for his cheek.

"I'll keep that in mind."

"I definitely didn't deserve to be slapped though," Erik says, his voice dropping to a whisper. "There are repercussions for slapping your friends."

"There are, huh?" I ask, waiting to see what Erik's idea of a fair punishment for a slap is. His hands stay on the tiled edge of the pool, but he leans in toward me, shrinking the space between us.

And then his arms reach up and pull me down into the pool with him. We plunge into the water, and I struggle frantically, kicking my legs and pushing against Erik's arms. When we surface, I gasp for air, spluttering a stream of foul-mouthed names at him.

"You're only a little wet," Erik says, dropping his hands from my waist.

I throw my arms around his shoulders, clutching at him. "No, idiot, I can't swim!"

Erik's head pops back a fraction of an inch to appraise me.

"Not everyone was raised in a fishing village," I remind him.

"You like water. You love the ocean," he says.

"I do, but that doesn't mean I know how to swim. My family didn't live near the ocean. I doubt even my mom knew— *knows*"—I correct myself—"how to swim. The closest I've come to swimming is my bathtub."

"Your bathtub at the Coventry was huge," Erik says, a guilty look settling over his face. His arms wrap tightly around my waist and I relax against him, feeling safe enough to enjoy the gentle airy pressure of the water.

"I could touch the bottom of my bathtub," I say.

"Here," Erik says, pushing me away from him. I shriek and splash, trying to stop him. "Put your feet down."

My legs are still stroking against the water in frantic, helpless circles. "Don't let me go," I tell him.

He nods, and I relax my legs, surprised when my toes find the smooth grid of the tiled floor. The tension in my chest deflates a little, but I don't let go of Erik's arm. I make a mental note to ask my mom if she knows how to swim. She has no reason not to tell me. Another innocent question to fall back on.

"I'm going to teach you how to swim," Erik says, drawing me back to the moment. "I'll never forgive myself if you drown."

"I'm not in the habit of jumping into large bodies of water," I say, "but I'd like to learn how to swim."

Erik's hand squeezes my hip and I rest against him for a moment until I disentangle myself and take a tentative step without his help. Now that I can touch the bottom, my initial panic is subsiding. Still, I don't go more than a few feet from Erik. He nods encouragingly and stops me when I get too close to the deep end.

After a few minutes, I remember I'm still fully dressed and I tiptoe to the end of the pool, careful to keep my head above water. Erik glides toward me, his hands lifting me out of the pool.

"Thank you," I say, allowing myself to linger a moment on the edge, his hands still low on my hips.

"Don't worry, Ad," Erik says, pushing out into the water. "I'll never let you go."

TWENTY-SIX

"Dante told me Tailors aren't all bad," I say to Erik as we exit the pool complex into the cool night. The air creeps along my damp skin, whistling a chill down into my bones and I clutch my towel tightly.

"We aren't," Erik says. "I personally have a disproportionate amount of badness."

"You talk big, but what can you do?" I challenge him.

"Are you asking me to alter something?" Erik says, stopping in his tracks.

I pause, realizing I've upset him. "Only if you want to."

"What do you want me to alter?" he asks.

"Make something beautiful," I tell him, thinking to add, "without hurting it."

If Dante is telling the truth and alteration can be used for positive ends, I need proof of it. It feels like I've only seen it used for destruction on Earth. I used it myself, by accident, to bring down the aeroship and to destroy the factory. It makes me uncomfortable that even my alteration training is focused on one thing: honing my unwinding skills to protect myself in a fight. I want to see something that proves being a Tailor doesn't make me a monster—any more than I already am.

Erik stops me and pulls me toward a manicured bush near the walkway. "Do you know what these are?" he asks.

I shake my head. Despite being pruned, there are no leaves or needles—nothing to indicate what kind of plant it is.

"Rosebushes." Erik reaches into the branches that tangle over one another like a series of veins.

"There are no roses," I say, wishing there were. My desire is fervent and sudden like in the moment before being kissed.

"They've died. These bushes were in bloom when we came to the estate. What happened?"

I shake my head. I have no clue.

"He uses Tailors to bring them in and out of season," Erik says. His fingers move over the branches so swiftly I can't quite see what he's doing. But even though I've always suspected there was something special about Erik, seeing him now I'm in awe. The branch in his hands trembles slightly as new leaves burst forth in a shower of green, and as I watch a bud develops from a tight knot into a cocoon bursting with life. The leaves unfold gently, revealing the treasure underneath.

Erik pulls it from the bush and holds it out to me. I manage a small smile. My father used to bring my mother flowers, but no man has ever given me one. I take the rose and press my nose into its soft bloom, inhaling the sweet scent. The rose is snow white, and its petals velvet against my fingers. My eyes peek up at Erik, who is smiling, with his hand still outstretched. There's a spot of blood on the top of his hand. I drop the rose and grab it.

"You've hurt yourself," I say.

"Every rose has its thorns, Adelice," he says, pulling it back from me and stooping to retrieve the rose. "It was worth it."

"Can you show me more?" I ask, gingerly holding the rose to avoid being pricked. "What else can you do?"

"Yes." Dante's voice breaks the moment. "What else can you do, Erik?"

Erik's eyes dart to mine, but I shake my head. I haven't told Dante anything of my suspicions.

"I'm sorry," I murmur.

Dante steps forward and regards me with barely concealed fury. "Why apologize to him? He lied to you, Adelice."

"He wouldn't be the first person to have lied to me," I remind Dante.

"You didn't forgive me quite so quickly if I recall," Dante says.

"I didn't know you."

"And you know him?" Dante asks. "What else haven't you told her, Erik? What have you done for the Guild? Why were they tracking you?"

"Tracking me?" Erik says. He looks from Dante to me. I give him a tiny nod to confirm it's true.

"Dante found a tracking chip in your arm."

"That's what you were playing at," Erik says. His voice pitches up an octave. "Whatever you found, I didn't know it was there. The Guild can't track me here. I knew you had an endgame for *practicing* on me."

"And I got the information I needed," Dante confirms. "I suspected you could see the strands. I knew you weren't some simple Guild assistant."

237

"Congratulations," Erik says. "But I've already told Adelice everything. I have nothing to hide from her."

"You've told her everything you've done?" Dante asks. "And she's still standing beside you?"

"You told me that not all Tailors are bad," I remind him. "We've all done things we'd rather forget. Who Erik is today is what matters."

"Believe what you want," Dante says in a low voice, "but ask him if he would have told you if you hadn't figured it out."

Erik stiffens next to me as though he's bracing for this question, but I already know the answer. Erik only told me because I confronted him. He would have kept his secret his whole life. But what Dante can't understand is that I don't fault Erik for that. There are ghosts I would rather bury than face. I can't blame Erik for feeling the same way.

"You're a hypocrite," I say to Dante. "Tell me the secrets you're hiding."

Dante's jaw twitches but he doesn't open his mouth to answer my question.

"That's what I thought," I say to him. "In the future, don't give me advice that you don't plan on following."

I pull Erik's arms, leading him out of the garden and back into the house. My clothes are still wet, but now I feel the heat of anger.

"I'm sorry about that," I blurt out.

"Don't be," Erik says, raising a hand to stop my further apology. "He's looking out for you. I'd be the exact same way if our positions were reversed. He's probably trying to keep you safe."

"By keeping me away from a friend?" I ask. "By trying to turn me against you?"

"Friend, huh?" Erik says, not quite able to keep his lips from turning up into a crooked grin.

"Don't get cocky," I say. "The pickings are slim here."

"I'll take the position however I can get it," Erik says. "And, Ad, don't be too upset with him. If you knew the things I know about Tailors—the things I'm sure Dante knows—maybe you wouldn't trust me ei—"

"Stop," I say, placing a hand on his chest to bring his attention away from his diatribe and back to me. "I trust you, and I don't care what's in your past."

"That's philanthropic of you," he says, "but—"

"No!" I say. "Stop trying to convince me otherwise, because you won't be able to. I know you, Erik Bell. You've got a good heart—whether you like it or not."

Erik thinks on this a moment and then draws me into a hug. "Like it."

"See?" I say, lingering in the warmth of his arms. "Your choices are getting better every day."

TWENTY-SEVEN

I TELL MYSELF I HAVE QUESTIONS ONLY she can answer, but in truth, I visit her to stem the waves of guilt that roll through me without warning, brought on by the most innocuous things. The scent of roses drifting through the garden, the sting of hot bathwater, a bite of dry pot roast—they bring her back to me. I don't want to attach the prisoner locked securely in the bowels of the estate with my mother. But no matter how well I understand the situation, my brain is no match for my heart.

My mother's curled up in a ball in the corner of her cell. She doesn't move when I enter. For a moment, I think the worst: that she's dead. And confused feelings swirl up inside me. Anger. Bitterness. Sadness. Relief. I wish I could lean forward and reach out to her. With her eyes closed, she looks peaceful. She's not wearing cosmetics and her hair is clumped around her head, but it's still her. She lifts her head, and the shift reveals a large purple scar running up her neck.

What did the Guild do to her? Can I undo it?

She stares at me without speaking and I see the wheels

turning in her head. She's going to play with me, but I won't let her.

"Meria," I say. I can't bring myself to call her Mom after our last meeting.

"Adelice," she murmurs. "Come to check in on your prisoner?"

"You aren't my prisoner," I remind her.

"Sure, your whining didn't land me in here." She sits up. She's thinner than the last time I saw her. Under her threadbare shirt I can see the jut of bones, and how her clothes hang on her. She's all points and angles.

"Are they feeding you?" I ask.

Her lips squash a smirk. "Yes, scraps."

Scraps like she is an animal. No wonder she's so thin.

"I'll make sure you get real meals," I promise her.

"That's so sweet of you." Her voice is flat, as colorless as the walls around us.

"I have some questions for you."

"And I have all the time in the world to answer them." She blinks slowly.

"Can you swim?" It seems silly and frivolous to ask a starving woman this.

"Are you planning to drown me?"

I plant my hands on my hips and stare down at her. "Do you see any water in here?"

"No, I can't." She speaks each word with halting, dramatic emphasis.

"Never mind," I say. "This was a stupid idea."

"Your question was stupid."

"Fine." My fists ball up as they did when I was a sullen

child. If she wants a real question, I have those, too. "How did you get to Earth?"

"Planning to return home?"

"Do you remember?" I ask, bypassing her question.

"Of course I do," she says. "We took a loophole."

"Were you running to a loophole on the night I was retrieved?" I ask, abandoning any hope of a casual conversation.

"Your parents really failed you that night," she says, not answering my question.

"Do you remember?" I ask, unsure I want the answer.

"I know what happened," she snaps. "The retrieval squad came and you were too stupid to warn your parents. They tried to run. There was a slub in Romen. You would have been safe there, but you didn't warn them, so they couldn't escape. You killed your parents."

Her words sting.

"My parents aren't dead," I say. "Benn is. But you're alive, and so is my biological father."

"So Dante told you?" she asks. "I wondered if he would. I didn't think he had the courage."

"Why didn't you tell me?"

"Why would I tell you?"

It's frustrating to sit here and talk with a woman who shares my history and holds the secrets to the past I can't remember, but who doesn't see herself as part of it. She looks at her memories from the outside.

"I don't suppose I'll be calling him Daddy anytime soon," I say.

"That child couldn't be a father," she says. "He can't see past himself. He didn't even realize she was pregnant."

"You were pregnant?" I prompt.

"Meria was pregnant." The words are oozed venom on her tongue.

"You are Meria."

"I am no one," she says.

And I see the truth of it in the flat deadness of her eyes. I hear the resignation seeping through her voice. I feel it as the words hang between us. It's true because she believes it.

"Where can I find a loophole?" I can't keep talking circles around this subject. I can't listen to my mother denounce me, my family, herself.

"Around," she says with a shrug.

"That's so helpful."

"Don't you think someone as powerful as your host would know the answer to that question?"

"My host is gone at the moment," I say. Then it occurs to me that I might be giving her too much information in telling her that Kincaid is away. Maybe it's a good thing she's so securely kept.

"And he left you behind?" The question digs at me.

"I'm tired of your games," I tell her. "I just . . . just wanted to see you."

"In the future," she begins, and my breath hitches, caught on the unexpected hope rising in my chest, "don't bother."

It stings, even though I know this is a game. I turn without a goodbye and leave her there. On my way out, I decide:

I'm never going back to her.

Erik is at dinner, alone. I'm not hungry, but I knew he would be in the dining room. When Kincaid left to find the Whorl, I expected meals to become less formal. But even though Valery doesn't join us and Dante rarely does, the kitchen still serves a full five-course meal.

"Do you know anything about loopholes?" I ask Erik, sipping the last of the coffee that was brought with the dessert tray.

"Like bunny ears for tying your shoes?" he asks.

"Yes, of course that's what I mean," I say in a flat tone.

"I guess I don't know then," Erik says. He hasn't touched his coffee, so I steal it.

"I can't believe you drink that stuff," he says.

"I can't believe you don't." I slurp a long draft of it for emphasis.

"Why?" he asks.

"It hits me right here," I say, poking my forehead. "Like tiny explosions."

"Right," he says as he fiddles with my old digifile, barely interested.

"Why didn't you pawn that?" I ask.

"It's useless down here," Erik says, but he doesn't stop playing with it. "Why did you ask about loopholes?"

"Something my mom said."

That gets his attention.

"At the risk of sounding like my brother, you know it's a bad idea to visit her, right?" Erik asks. He abandons the digifile and looks at me.

"I know," I admit. "But it feels like she's the only connection I have left."

"You have me," Erik says.

"Not what I meant. My last connection to a time when life

244

wasn't confusing." My words are all wrong, betraying me. I can't explain it to him. I barely understand it myself.

"And she told you about loops?" Erik guesses.

I nod, trying to sort my thoughts into coherent strings of words. "Dante called them loopholes. There must be one in the Icebox with that many refugees winding up there. Someone in the grey market must know."

"Do you even know what a loophole is?"

"No," I say. "But I have an idea."

"Well, that's something," Erik says.

It's more than I usually have. "But what now?"

"That's the easy part. We go to the Icebox."

Most of the house has retired for the evening. There's no way to procure a security detail to leave the premises at this hour and Kincaid has left strict instructions that I can't leave anyway. But thirty minutes later we're sitting in a crawler. I've traded my skirt and blouse for one of the few practical outfits Kincaid has supplied me with: a mink coat layered over a flowing silk tunic and close-fitting black trousers with supple black leather boots that reach my knees. There are a few credits crammed in my pocket—the leftovers from the items we pawned upon our arrival here. The Icebox is down through the mountains, and it sprawls around the estate like a metro built on a tributary.

"So you stole a crawler?" I ask.

"I borrowed it," Erik says.

"Without permission," I add.

"Flexible morals," we both say at the same time.

"Jinx," Erik says.

"Uh-oh, bad luck for me," I say.

"Nah," he says. "In Saxun, it means you owe me something."

"That sounds like trouble," I say, unsure I want to be further in Erik's debt. "What do I owe you?"

Erik shoots me a wink from the driver's seat. "I'll think of something. So what now?"

"We figure out . . ." I pause. I have no idea what we need to figure out next.

"Good plan," he says.

"I'm known for my high-quality planning skills."

The grey market is as delightful as I remember. But Erik says nothing when I toss a few credits to a refugee begging on the sidewalk.

"I don't care how he uses it," I say, suddenly self-conscious of my move. "He needs it more than I do."

"I'm not judging you," he says. "He probably does need it more than you do."

He smiles so genuinely then that my insecurity melts, replaced by something much warmer that tugs at me.

Something that forces me to turn away.

"Wait," I say, twisting back toward the opposite direction, returning to the refugee.

"Ma'am." The refugee tips an imaginary hat at me.

"You're a refugee." I point to the scrawl of information on his makeshift sign. "How did you get here from Arras?"

The beggar's eyes dart from me to Erik and back again. "Don't remember."

"I promise," I start, squatting down to him, "we're only looking for one to use ourselves. We need to go back."

His eyebrows tilt in surprise and he mumbles a few unintelligible words that sound like oaths.

"Please," I press, reaching out to touch his hand.

"There's a depot in the grey market. Find the speakeasy on First," he says, but he grabs my hand with sudden passion. "You can't go back. It's suicide."

I pull my hand away, managing a smile.

"Come on," Erik says, offering me his hand. I accept it, thanking the refugee for his information. The man's face stays gray in the halogen of the fading lighting system. We have enough time to find the bar he's talking about, on First Avenue, before the streets go dark at curfew.

"Want to grab a drink?" Erik asks, threading my arm around his.

"Erik, you read my mind."

TWENTY-EIGHT

THE SPEAKEASY IS DARK, LIT BY SMALL solar sconces along the walls. High booths afford their occupants privacy, and a few eyes twitch up to meet my curious gaze as we pass each booth. We both immediately look away, uncomfortable. This isn't the kind of place you come to make friends. Erik's hand presses into my upper arm, shepherding me forward until we find an empty booth near the back. I sit down. Erik slides in, hesitating for a second before he scoots right next to me.

"It's better if we look like we're together," he says.

"Better for who?" I ask, cocking an eyebrow, challenging him to come up with a reasonable response.

"For both of us," he says. "People don't bother couples on dates."

"Ahh," I say with a sigh. "Sure."

"Plus, you make me look good."

I frown, but he hangs an arm casually around my shoulder. He's pretending, but I can't help but realize I like how his arm feels there. Safe, warm.

"What's this?" Erik says. He traces the crook of my elbow.

His fingertips sear my skin, and I gasp, shaking my head, trying to focus. Dark flecks pepper my pale arm around a thin red scratch, but I barely notice them since I'm consumed with the fire scorching under my skin.

"Freckles," I say, pulling my arm away, unsure where the scratch came from.

"Those aren't freckles," Erik says. "Are you being careful during training?"

"I don't remember hurting myself, but it's nothing. It doesn't even hurt," I assure him.

"What'll ya have?" a waitress asks in possibly the most bored tone ever. She could pass for a stewardess in Arras except her skirt stops too short, revealing more of her lengthy legs than I'm used to. Her head cocks to the side, examining the small platform stage behind her.

"What do you have?" Erik asks.

"Same as everywhere, hon," she says with a shrug, her eyes still occupied elsewhere. "Gin. Whiskey. Moonshine."

"Moonshine?" he asks.

"I didn't make up the name," she says.

She couldn't have, I think. She's probably never seen the moon. I can't imagine she's gone exploring past the Interface's border.

"Gin. Do you have tonic?"

"Sure, sure." She doesn't write anything down, but I hear her call out the order to the stubby bartender.

"So what now?" Erik asks, turning his attention back to me. His voice is low.

I take a deep breath. "I'm not sure."

249

"You know, your mother was probably toying with you," Erik says gently.

"I know." But the words are thick on my tongue. I don't like thinking of the monster wearing my mother's face.

The waitress plops down two smudged glasses and asks what else we need.

"There was a place around here," Erik says. "A loophole. Do you know what happened to it?"

"The refugee shelter? Sure," she says with a smack of her lips. "It's gone now."

"Yes, we assumed that," Erik says in a measured tone. "Do you know where it was?"

"Yeah, next door, down the stairs. But it got closed up a long time ago."

"Who closed it?" Erik asks.

"Owner, so far as I know. She still lives there. She rents this place, too. She comes in for a drink now and then, but she keeps to herself."

"Do you know her name?" I ask.

"Nah, not really my job," she says, her eyes elsewhere again. "You need anything else?"

"No, thank you," Erik says.

"If it was next door," I start, but my thoughts are too jumbled for me to continue speaking. It could still be there, and if the owner is there, we could ask her. I know Erik is thinking the same things.

"It's risky," he says.

He's right. It's dangerous to go asking around after the loophole, especially knowing nothing about the owner.

"To almost-solutions," Erik says, raising his glass. We clink, but I don't take a long draft like he does. It's too strong for me. I take a small sip and let it burn my throat before setting the glass back down.

"Strong," I say with a grimace.

"You didn't have any dinner," he reminds me. "You should probably take it easy on that—not everyone can handle liquor like Cormac."

"I have no desire to drink like Cormac," I say, but the conversation jogs my memory. I hadn't eaten dinner because Erik was already done with his and playing with the digifile I'd brought from Arras. I stare at him and he responds by raising an eyebrow.

"The digifile," I say in a quiet voice. "I've always wondered where Enora got that program. The tracking program."

Erik's arm drops from my shoulders and he leans away from me for a moment.

"It was you," I say when he doesn't speak.

"I'm sorry, Adelice. I should have convinced Enora to drop it when she came to me. If I had done more, she might be alive now."

"You didn't have anything to do with her death," I say, but then it strikes me that might not be true. Erik is a Tailor. A fact I keep forgetting.

"I didn't," he assures me, as though he can read my mind. "At that point, things were out of control. I think Cormac suspected me after the State of the Guild."

"You finally made an impression on him," I say. Cormac had written Erik off early on during my time at the Coventry.

"Adelice," Erik says, taking a deep breath, "I worked for Cormac."

"We all worked for Cormac."

"No," he says with emphasis, "I worked for Cormac. He had Tailors all over the coventries, spying on the operations and keeping tabs on Spinsters."

"And you were keeping tabs on me?" He told me that during our last hour in the Coventry, but I haven't brought it up since then. Now I wish I had.

"Would you let me off the hook if I said it was really complicated?" he asks.

I look at Erik then, measuring him up. I can appreciate secrets and regrets. I have plenty of my own, and I've decided not to let them dictate who I am. Erik deserves the same chance.

"Actually, I would," I say.

A chaotic mix of instruments starts playing. No, not playing. Warming up. Each musician individually tuning his instrument, filling the air with a clash of rhythm. The solar lights around us dim even lower, and then the band starts to play. It's nothing like what I expect to hear. The song is vibrant, alive. The notes dip and bounce and a few couples make their way to the small space in front of the stage. Once they're there, they become as alive as the music. One waves her hands in front of her, kicking her feet out behind her. Her partner watches for a moment and then joins in. Another woman spins away from her lover, her skirt fanning around her. In Arras, we only had slow songs. Elegant, carefully timed waltzes or quiet songs to sway to. Nothing like this.

"Want to try it?" Erik asks.

"I'm not sure I'm that rhythmically gifted," I admit.

We watch for a few more minutes, and then Erik slides out of the booth and offers his hand to me. I bite my lip, pondering the likelihood that I'll wind up splayed on the dance floor on my butt. But Erik leans forward and says, "I won't let you fall."

I put my hand in his and he pulls me from the booth. He keeps his eyes on me. He doesn't close his hand over mine, but I feel something weighty in his gaze. It never leaves me. When we get to the floor, his fingers close around my hand and he throws me out with great force. I'm not wearing anything that can fan out or impress anyone, but I'm sort of thankful. At least in pants and boots I can stay on my feet. Erik grins at me, and I narrow my eyes, but then I giggle. I can't help it. I feel his hand tug on mine and before I know it I roll back into him. My other hand meets his waiting palm without a thought and when we touch everything is electric. Full of life. I pull out of his embrace and spin under his arms. Then I attempt to mimic the woman who's kicking up her heels.

I fail.

We both spend more time laughing than dancing, but I feel light, like I'm full of air. Like I don't have a care in the world. For a moment, I'm truly happy.

Then the vibrance of the music fades down into a soft rhythm. A woman steps forward and begins to sing. Her voice is low and hoarse, but it's beautiful. She sings of love, of belonging, of loss. My heart gives a thump in my chest. I can relate to this song.

Erik pulls me back to him, and I let my head drop to his shoulder. His arms curve around my back and we sway softly.

Neither of us speaks. I think of the night back in Arras when we waltzed in the garden. How his hand felt on the bare skin of my back. The moonlight painting his hair silver.

"Are you feeling okay?" Erik asks softly.

I blush. "Yes. It's warm in here."

"It is and we were really, uh, dancing a minute ago. Do you want to sit?"

I shake my head. It's okay to dance. It's okay to linger in this moment because of the music and the mood. I won't have any excuses once we sit back down.

Erik's hand rests on my shoulder and I curl my arms a bit more tightly around his neck. I know we're both feeling the same thing. I can sense it from him, like the low humming energy of a solar panel. It comes off him in waves—the things we can't say to each other.

Something's changed between us, but it's not until I look up at his face that I understand. I see the curve of his jaw with its trace of stubble. The way his nose bends slightly to the left—not enough to be called crooked but not perfect. For a moment I wish we were in the moonlight so his hair would be silver and his eyes would be gray, and when he looks at me, I see what I feel reflected back. We don't say anything, and I pull away from him, escaping with excuses of needing the powder room.

But I can't escape this for long.

TWENTY-NINE

I STUMBLE INTO THE POWDER ROOM AND splash water on my neck. The mirror reflects a girl with flushed cheeks and tumbling chignon. I pin up my loose hair, but the redness stays on my cheeks.

"Remember who you are," I whisper to the girl in the mirror. My fingers trace the techprint on my wrist.

No matter what has changed, I can't do this to Jost. I won't do it to him. It's not who I am.

I smooth down my glossy tunic and tug my boots up a bit. The club is warmer when I leave the powder room. More people have found their way inside despite it being well past curfew. A group of men watch me as I cross the dance floor to our booth. They don't bother hiding their stares, and I realize with a sinking feeling that they're clad in pressed slacks and vests with rolled-up sleeves and gold pocket watches. The only other person here dressed as smartly as they are is Erik. On Earth only one group of people has access to such stylish clothing and expensive accessories: Sunrunners. Even if they're here for their own pleasure, they've noticed me. I'm not supposed to be off the estate grounds let alone running around in bars.

I slip into the high-backed booth, grateful for the anonymity of the pocked red vinyl sides. "We've been spotted."

"Oh yeah?" Erik pops his head over the booth and lets out a low whistle.

"How long until this gets back to Dante?" I wonder out loud.

A tumbler of clear liquor slams down on our table and I look up to find the answer to my question.

"That was even faster than I imagined," Erik mutters.

"So I say to myself, 'I'm going to check on Adelice. Talk it out, because I'm mature and responsible and so is she,' and do you know what I found?" Dante asks as he plops onto the bench across from us.

"I bet you're going to tell us," I say, folding my arms over my chest. I'm not the least bit sorry for leaving the estate.

"Do you actively look for trouble?" Dante asks. "Or are you stupid?"

Erik's arm pulls away from my shoulder, landing on the table as he leans toward Dante. "We're not Kincaid's property, and you would do well to remember that. We had business in the Icebox. That's all you need to know."

"Business in the Icebox, huh? Looks to me like you're drinking gin in a speakeasy," Dante says.

"Let's go, Erik." I scoot across the squeaking vinyl bench, but Dante holds his hand up.

"I'm sorry for what I said in the garden. You have to understand how hard it is for me to trust a Guild-trained Tailor," Dante says.

"Half of Kincaid's men were Guild, and you trust them," I point out.

"That's not entirely true." But Dante doesn't offer to elucidate for us.

"Why wouldn't I trust Erik?" I ask, my voice growing with the clamor of the music. "He trusts me enough to tell me—"

"Ad," Erik stops me. "It's okay. Your father is right."

"He's not my father," I say.

The table falls quiet, the music invading the silence between us. No one knows what to say—least of all me.

"I don't want to tell you what to do, but if you leave without me, they'll follow you," Dante warns. "What did you come here looking for?"

I take a deep breath, willing my words not to shake with rage. "We're looking for the loophole."

"The loophole?" Dante repeats slowly.

"My mother told me about it," I admit. Dante sinks back against the booth and takes a long swig of his drink.

"She's trying to cause trouble," Dante says.

"I know that," I say. "It doesn't mean I can't learn anything from her."

Dante's eyes swivel to the door and back toward the dance floor. "We need to get out of here."

"Why should we go anywhere with you?" Erik asks. His hand closes possessively over mine, but I draw it back.

"Because I have something to show you."

Erik lifts my mink coat for me, and I shrug it over my shoulders. We both know we have to go with Dante. As we exit the speakeasy, my eyes stay on the ground. I expect my father to drag us straight back to the estate, but instead of leading us out into the quiet, black streets of the grey market, Dante gestures for us to follow him down a narrow alley wedged between buildings.

"I'm not sure I like where this is going," Erik whispers.

"Where's your sense of adventure?" I ask, but for once I keep my hand threaded through his.

"Oh, I have not had enough gin for this kind of adventure," Erik says.

We stop near a full-to-brimming Dumpster, and Dante glances around us. I doubt he can see anyone in the ink-black night, but thankfully that means they can't see us either. Dante pushes on a stone and it sinks back into the wall as a slab slides over, revealing a hidden door.

"Someone is making a killing building hidden passages," I mutter.

Inside the entrance it's dark, but Dante flips on a handlight and starts into the darkness. The handlight provides enough illumination for us to see a few feet in front of us but not much more than that. Once we've walked for a few minutes—faithfully following Dante, despite the fact that we have no idea where we're headed—he stops and shines the light on the wall. He flips open a panel, flicking some switches. A series of solar lights flares to life, dimly lighting the rest of the tunnel. With the lights on, some of my unease dissolves.

"Where are we?" Erik asks. If we're far enough from the entrance to safely turn on the lights then it must be safe to ask questions.

"You wanted to know what a loophole is," Dante says. "I'm taking you to one. There's a crawler up ahead, we'll take it to the ship."

Ahead of us the tunnel seems to stretch on for miles. I'm simultaneously glad that I don't have to walk the whole way and nervous to be back in a crawler. Dante hoists himself into the crawler and turns it on. Erik boosts me into the front seat and then jumps into the back. He leans over me and pulls a harness strap up over my shoulder.

"Buckle up," he whispers.

I nod, not bothering to tell him the harness is the only thing convincing me to ride in the crawler.

"You don't like these things, do you?" Dante asks.

"I do not," I admit.

He grins at me, but I notice his own harness is buckled. "You aren't a fan of many vehicles," he says. "You didn't like the motocycles either, and something tells me you're going to like this even less than last time."

"I am?" I whimper, tightening the straps that hold me in. Erik's hand comes to rest on my shoulder but it does little to abate my fear. Dante is right. I don't like being in the open air or the wild momentum of vehicles like this. A motocarriage is a smooth ride and, perhaps more important, it has a roof. But motocycles and crawlers feel out of control. There is nothing to grip, so I focus on Erik's hand when the crawler lurches forward.

The name *crawler* made sense from the moment I saw the vehicles. They look like metal spiders, after all, and I saw the way they rumbled over the rocky terrain when we went Sunrunning, but now I really understand where they got their name.

The tunnel is rounded, but there's no road, only broken tracks, and as we progress down the shaft we zip up the side of the concave walls instead of navigating the old tracks. Dante drives the crawler farther and farther up the wall, accelerating until my hair is whipping against my face. It's almost painful, but given that we're now riding parallel to the tracks below us, I can't convince my arm to reach up and pull it back. My hands are frozen to the harness, clutching it, but Erik's hand stays on my shoulder. I focus on it, using its warmth as an anchor.

We rumble back down to the floor, riding over the broken tracks, zooming through the tunnel. We're moving too fast and my voice won't carry over the rushing wind, but when Dante finally starts to slow, approaching a cluster of lights, I ask, "What was that?"

"They used this tunnel to shanghai men into slavery on boats during the last century. Now we run refugees through it. One second you're drinking a whiskey, the next second you have an exciting new life at sea."

My legs shake as I pull myself out of my bucket seat. I cling to the frame of the crawler and take Dante's hands when he offers to help me down. I tentatively step over the side, but I can't bring myself to let go of the bar. Dante reaches up and grips my waist, bringing me to the ground. I wobble a bit, but Erik steadies me when Dante lets go.

"You didn't like that ride," Dante says.

"No, I don't exactly have a fondness for death traps," I admit.

"That's funny given how often you throw yourself into dangerous situations," Erik says. We follow Dante to stairs that take us to a bustling dock. A large glass dome rises over us and through it I can see the Interface. When I look out into the distance, the ocean stretches before me, infinite and black.

Workers run back and forth, shouting over steam that's blowing in from a round hatch in the side of the dome. Through the hatch, the dock extends. I spy something tethered to the end of it. I make out a door and a couple of windows set into a blue metal wall. Men pass us in a hurry, but even in their haste they stop and raise a fist to their left shoulder, bowing their heads to Dante. He raises his fist in response but doesn't nod.

A man in a gray jumpsuit rushes past us and skids to a stop. It's Jax.

"Dante," Jax says, his face splitting into a grin. He doesn't welcome him with the same formal greeting as the others; instead the two men grip each other's arms.

"Is she around?" Dante asks him. "I should probably get this over with." His eyes flick to us. Nothing like making someone feel welcome.

"Yeah, Falon hates surprises," Jax says. He pushes his goggles up onto his forehead a bit higher, grime smearing across his skin as he does it. "Last time I saw her she was checking some passenger manifests."

"Why is she interested in passenger manifests?" Dante asks, frowning at this bit of information.

"Ask her yourself," a voice snaps behind us. I turn and find myself face-to-face with a girl. I take a step back as her eyes narrow to focus on my face.

"You," I say, recognizing her almost immediately. It's the girl from the night of the crashed aeroship—the one who encouraged Jost and me to make a run for the Icebox.

"I looked for you in the Icebox like I said I would," she says. "I thought you had disappeared." There's an edge of recrimination in her voice.

"Dante found us first, but you've found me now," I say.

"Dante found you, huh?" She looks to him, cocking her head to the side and raising an eyebrow. "You might have mentioned that."

"Don't start, Falon," Dante says, his voice low. "You know our channels are being watched."

"And what's his excuse?" she says, pointing to Jax.

"I didn't need any more info getting out about Adelice. Jax was following orders," Dante explains.

Falon's nostrils flair but she turns her attention to me. "Adelice, huh? So you're the one that's got half of the Guild in an uproar."

"Only half? I must be slipping," I say, giving her a small smile.

She doesn't return it. "What's she doing here?"

"I think we should talk in private," Dante says, taking her by the elbow.

"Don't start patronizing me, Dante," she says.

"Don't force me to."

"You're so Arras sometimes. It disgusts me." She practically spits the insult at him.

I step toward Erik until I feel his hand on my back. Things are getting ugly pretty fast.

"Falon, a word." Dante reiterates his request. After a pause he adds a hesitant, "Please."

They walk a few paces off. It's noisy enough here with the steam and activity that we can't hear them.

"What was that about?" I ask Jax, who shifts from foot to foot nervously.

"Dante didn't message us that he was bringing you. He hasn't been to the dock in weeks," Jax explains.

"Because of me," I say with a sigh.

"How did you know Falon?" Erik asks beside me.

"Jost and I ran into her the night we arrived on Earth. She came to see about the ship I took down." I relate Falon's warning from that night to Erik.

"You didn't think to mention this to me?"

"I guess I sort of forgot with everything happening, and you and Jost were fighting." Even as I make the excuses I know that's what they are, despite the truth streaking through them.

"Security is tight between things with Kincaid and the Guild. It's not your fault . . ." Jax trails off, wiping his palms on his pants.

"I thought you went with the mission," I say to Jax, recalling what Dante said about Jax not being around.

"Nope, but I've been here most of the time," he says. Dante lied to me about Jax to cover up where he was really going. It's a good enough reason to be dishonest, but it doesn't sit well with me.

Falon and Dante are walking toward us, and neither looks happy. Dante tries to slip a hand into Falon's but she avoids him. He settles for a quick squeeze of her shoulder, but the grim expression stays on his face.

"That explains that," Erik mutters to me.

"Lover scorned," I say.

"And then he shows up with a pretty girl after weeks of no contact," Erik says.

"I'm his daughter," I remind Erik.

"Do you think she knows that?"

Good point.

The whispers die on our lips as they come closer to us.

"I apologize for my rudeness," Falon says. She offers her hand to Erik and they exchange formal introductions. "Dante has caught me up on everything."

"Everything?" I ask, looking at Dante. Has he told her he is my father?

"Everything," Dante says, pressing his lips together.

"Okay, then," Erik says, breaking the tension. "Can you show us the loophole?"

"We're making a run in ten minutes. You have good timing, Dante," Falon says. Her eyes look black in the dim light.

"Not really," he says. "I caught wind of some intel coming from within Kincaid's web."

"Good to know you're still paying attention," Falon says. She strides off. With her leather pants and simple black braid she's intimidating, but we follow her as she exits through the dome's hole onto the dock.

"Give her a few minutes," Dante says. "She'll warm up. She doesn't like to admit when she's worried."

"And she's been worried about you?" I guess.

"I've been preoccupied and with Kincaid hovering over you it's been even harder to slip out."

"So Kincaid doesn't know about this operation?" Erik asks.

Dante takes a deep breath and then slowly shakes his head. "A lot of these people run refugees for him. It provides a cover and a living, but Kincaid doesn't know about this place or everything our operation does."

I look around at the workers. It's a strange mix of

people—many our own age, but plenty of older adults. They have belts with tools and goggles over their eyes or hanging at their necks for easy access. As we pass through the burst of steam that hangs over the dock, I see what's at the end of it. The doors and windows I spotted are part of a metal box that hangs suspended from a balloon drifting in the air. Great steel ribs circle the envelope, locking in its shape. The aeroship is tethered to the dock by thick ropes. It's the same type as the one I crashed on our first night here—the one I assumed was Guild.

I whirl on Dante. "Where are we? Who are these people?

Dante spreads his hands wide, gesturing to the bustle of activity around us. "Welcome to the resistance. Adelice, you're in the heart of the Kairos Agenda."

THIRTY

DANTE LEADS US ON A SHORT TOUR of the facilities, past instrument panels and groups poring over blueprints.

"What are they working on?" I ask.

"The grid," Jax says, pointing to the panels. "We're getting close to self-sufficiency."

"You're building a power grid?"

"The only way the Icebox—or any future city on Earth—can exist is with a power source," Dante says.

"But Kincaid—"

"Is shortsighted," Dante interrupts me. "He can only think of destroying Arras. He's never considered what it will take to rebuild Earth after that. If we're going to repopulate civilization, we'll need access to power, and the last thing I want is to rely on Kincaid when that day comes."

"We're experimenting with an exclusively solar-based system," Jax tells us. "We don't have access to coal at this point. That's still under Kincaid's control, but I've built a photovoltaic array that is entirely dependent on solar energy. It will be easier when we have a power station with permanent arrays, but we'll have to wait until the Interface comes before we can fully utilize my system."

Jax and Dante answer more questions about their plans, but I stay silent. Not only is the Agenda alive, it's growing. Dante and the other revolutionaries aren't planning for war, they're preparing for what comes after. As annoyed as I am that Dante hid this from me, I admire his foresight. It's not something I'm naturally gifted with.

They take us to the aeroship and we step inside it to find a spacious viewing area that overlooks the ocean below us. Outside, a corridor exits onto an open-air deck, with ladders onto the rigid body of the ship. I can't bring myself to ask the question waiting on my lips as I look around.

"They're pulling the tethers," Falon says, coming up to us. "I checked with the pilot and we have a confirmed rivet set up along the gathering route."

"How many are coming through?" Dante asks.

"Only one with credentials, but he's ensured passage for a few others," Falon says.

"And what are we going to do with them?" Dante asks. "Kincaid is watching the Icebox too closely right now. It will be hard to get them safely established inside."

"You'll figure something out," Falon says, her words more threatening than supportive. She won't look at Dante, clearly still angry with him over the last few weeks.

"I don't have the sway," Dante says, grabbing her arm.

"Since when?" Falon demands.

"Since Kincaid got ahold of her," Dante tells Falon. Their eyes swivel to me.

I love being in the middle of fights.

"Well, we can't leave them now. They're safely in the slub and they've been promised passage."

"They'll have to stay with the Agenda then, until we can distract Kincaid," Dante says.

"Kincaid is already distracted," Falon reminds him.

"But he won't be for long, and your trick won't elude him. He'll be on the lookout for activity."

"Anyone care to fill us in on what you're talking about?" Erik asks. I'm glad I'm not the only one who's having trouble following the conversation.

"Kincaid is on a fool's errand," Dante says in a grim voice.

"A fool's errand?" I repeat, my heart dropping into my stomach.

"The intel on the Whorl was a distraction to get him away from the Icebox," Falon says. "We needed to be sure that he was busy."

"Why?" I demand, feeling sick: not only had I pinned my hope on them coming back with the Whorl, but, more important, Jost had as well.

"We have good reason to believe the Whorl is under Guild protection, and we couldn't look for it with Kincaid nosing around," Dante tells us.

"Does that mean you know where it is?" I settle into a chair, waiting for answers.

"Not yet, but we're closing in on it—" Dante says.

"The most important thing"—Falon interrupts him—"is that we get to it first. We can't risk the Whorl falling into Kincaid's hands."

"Why not? Kincaid wants to use it to sever the worlds," I

say. Getting to the Whorl was my best option for escaping the Guild once and for all. Even if Kincaid couldn't be trusted, he could be used as a resource.

Falon's head swings to the left and right as she looks to see who's around, and then she shakes her head. "Kincaid isn't Agenda."

I suck in a breath. "Then who is he?"

"That should be obvious," Falon says.

"Humor me."

"He's the bad guy."

"Then we can't go back to the estate," Erik says.

"That's exactly what you have to do," Dante says in a rush. "What do you think will happen if you disappear from the estate?"

"You expect us to wait around and pretend we're on Kincaid's side?" I ask.

"If you place any value on the Agenda—" Falon begins.

"I don't even know what the Agenda is planning!" I explode. "Where are we going now? Why should I trust any of you? You never came for us, and Dante's been keeping secrets from us the whole time." The questions and accusations flood from me, unleashed in a tidal wave of recrimination.

"I couldn't tell you about this," Dante says in a low voice, trying to draw me down from my rage. "It wasn't safe."

I wiggle in my seat, folding my arms over my chest. "And now was the right time?"

"No," Dante admits, "but you were going to get yourself in trouble. You've both made that clear."

"Maybe a little trouble is needed around here," Erik says. I nod in agreement.

"We have enough trouble without a bunch of kids adding to it," Falon says.

"Don't get self-righteous with me," I say, leaning forward and jabbing a finger in her direction. "I don't care if Dante is my father, you and I are the same age."

"You been in a lot of gunfights? Have you watched your best friend die in your arms?" Falon asks.

"I've watched more than one friend die," I seethe. "I've seen people I love made into monsters and I've escaped Cormac Patton. Let me know when you manage to rip yourself out of the Coventry."

"So the rumors are true. You aren't only a Spinster," Falon says. For the first time since we met, approval glints in her eyes.

"No, I'm the goddamned Creweler," I say with as much venom as I can muster.

"Well, she certainly has your attitude problem," Falon says, leaning back in her chair and looking at Dante.

"Don't get me involved with this," he says, putting a hand up.

"You got yourself involved when you left me in Arras," I say, jumping from my seat and crossing to the first door I see. Erik is at my heels, but he doesn't stop me when I exit into the next corridor.

"Who is he to treat me like that?" I mutter.

"He's your dad," Erik says.

I turn and hit his shoulder. "He will never be my father."

"I know that," Dante says, closing the door behind him. "I'm not trying to boss you around. I wanted to protect you from this."

"You had no right to keep this from me," I say.

"I'm sorry," Dante says. "I kept it from you at first because it was protocol. I wasn't about to drop this into your lap, but somewhere along the line, I didn't want to tell you."

"Because you don't trust me," I accuse.

"No, it's more than that. I may not have been there when you were born. Arras, I might have a hard time wrapping my head around this—you aren't the only one struggling with what this means," Dante says. "And despite all of it—despite the fact that I knew you deserved to know—I couldn't tell you."

"Why not?" I demand over my swollen throat. Erik wraps an arm around my shoulder and steadies me, which makes it harder to hold my tears hostage.

"Because—like it or not—you're my daughter, Adelice." Dante pauses and dares to bring his eyes up to meet mine. "And I love you."

He doesn't offer me any more placation; he quietly exits back to where we left Falon. Erik pulls me into his shoulder and I free my tears, sobbing.

"I don't know who to trust," I whisper.

"Me," he says, rubbing my arm. "And Jost. No matter what, you will always have us."

I know that, but even as I cry in his arms, the distance between us feels like too much to overcome. It's a distance we've created out of necessity, and if we breach it, I can't guarantee I won't lose Erik, but I know one thing.

I will lose Jost.

"Erik, I can't lose you," I say. "I can't lose either of you."

His arms tighten around me, and for one second I want him

to storm the wall we've built between us. I want him to help me forget this. But instead he only whispers, "You won't. I won't let that happen. I promise I'll never let you go."

And even now, wrapped in an embrace, we're a million miles from each other.

We stay on the observation deck, watching the aeroship pass along the Interface. A series of hooks and pulleys built along the ship's external skeleton grip and gather the strands of the Interface. We're not flying, we're crawling across the web of strands. Dante approaches us as the skeleton's gears and hooks latch and lock, tethering us to the Interface semi-permanently.

"This is a loophole," Dante says.

As he speaks, strands of the Interface rotate violently, curling in on one another in rapid and graceful precision until a long funnel of chaotically woven strands extends in a gentle diagonal toward the ship, opening a few feet from the deck. I take the risk and look up into the mouth of the loophole. It's hollow as I expected, a perfectly round shaft of strands that stretch and swim in a kaleidoscope of color. My eyes squeeze shut and I listen for the music of the strands. It comes in a surge of violins, the notes sharp and lingering. This is all I need. I could climb through there and go back. But back to what?

"How did you do this?" I ask.

"Arras doesn't control every talented person," Dante says with a shrug.

That's the understatement of the century.

"You have people on the inside," I surmise.

"Of course," Dante says, "a resistance wouldn't be much good without spies."

"What do your spies say about me?" I ask, recalling that Falon recognized my name immediately from her intel.

Falon appears at my side. "It's my job to keep tabs on what's going on up there. And girl, you're all over my stream."

"They put me on the Stream?" The color drains from my face. There's no way I'll ever make it back into Arras safely if everyone there is looking for me.

"A stream of information," Falon assures me. "I have a web of spies, people who pass info to me from inside the coventries and ministry offices."

"The same people that pass Kincaid info?" I guess. "You sell it to him."

"Information is good business," she says. "I can control what Kincaid hears and use the money he pays me to buy some people off him."

"Buy people?"

"Refugees don't come here for free. If they don't have the credits, they owe their sponsor," Falon says. I detect a note of disgust in her voice.

"That's how Valery wound up at the estate," Dante says.

"Speaking of, how is Deniel?" Falon asks him.

At the mention of his name my stomach constricts as though a wire is coiling tight around it.

Dante hesitates and shakes his head. "Gone."

"Gone? Where?"

"Not where," Dante says. "He was unwound."

"What?" Falon asks, unmistakable anger in her voice.

"He attacked Adelice, tried to alter her. He was a spy," Dante says.

"A spy?" Falon echoes. "Who authorized his credentials in Arras?"

"I'm not sure," Dante says.

"Too bad," Falon says, sighing. "He was talented. I should have known when he asked to go to Kincaid. We could have used a Tailor like him."

"A crooked Tailor does bad work," Erik reminds her.

"True. I guess we got lucky," Falon says.

"How does this work?" I ask, still mesmerized by the tunnel of swirling light and color.

"It's a convolution of space-time. They've twisted the strands of the Interface with those naturally occurring on Earth," she explains.

"The slub is at the other end," Dante says.

"Who puts in the slubs?" I ask.

"We make some, but others are pre-existing," Dante says. "There were slubs in Arras when it was created."

"We've been utilizing this slub for months, but if Deniel was a spy it may have been compromised."

"What happens if the Guild discovers the slub?"

"Sometimes nothing," Falon says. "They use it to send spies through. Sometimes they send a battalion of Remnants instead, *if* they want us to know they know. Worst-case scenario is Protocol One. They adjust the whole metro."

My mind flips back to a hazy memory. The night of my retrieval. "They change the citizens' memories."

"Yes," Falon says. "It's a combined effort. Spinsters reweave the whole piece, removing the slubs, and meanwhile the

Tailors adjust the collective memories of the population. All without ever knowing what the other group is doing. And then the passage is closed. There's no way for the refugees to get through."

I turn and stare into the loophole, watching the colors swirl and the light shifting around the twisted strands. It calls to me. But that's only a space between. Arras isn't my home anymore, no more than Earth is. If I could, I'd lose myself in the raw beauty, build a life in the very fabric of the universe, among the possibility. But I have plenty holding me here and plenty calling me home. There's no time for staying in the space in between actions.

"They're coming," Falon announces.

I look but see nothing. I shut my eyes and listen. The strands hum and if I strain I can hear the twang of time running tinny through the soft melody of the matter around it. Combined, the sounds are quite lovely, but if I wasn't paying close attention it would sound like static. I retrain my focus and hear voices. Shadows cast themselves down the convolution of the loophole and a small band of people slide through. There are only five or six of them.

"Evening, Walter, what ya got?" Falon asks, exchanging a salute with the man heading the group.

"Only a few. Five adults. One kid."

I look closely at the group. I hadn't seen a child, but then he's there, clinging to his mother's leg. He meets my stare, eyes saucer-wide. He's dressed in a typical academy uniform, but he can't be too old. He must have started academy this year. I smile at him, but he darts behind his mother's skirt.

His mother is stoic, looking at us warily. Her dress is worn and I notice that she pulls her thin sweater sleeve up to hide a tear in it. She holds her head high, but I spy a few dark spots by her ear that stretch to her neck. Bruises.

"This is the one with credentials," Walter says, leading a tall man over to Dante and Falon. The man turns his head so they can observe the hourglass techprint hidden along his hairline.

"What can you do?" Dante asks.

"Me?" the man says. "Nothing. I have intel for Dante."

Dante doesn't betray that the man has found him; instead he turns and looks to the woman and child. "And this intel secured your passage for six?"

"I wasn't leaving her," the man says. "Not after what's been done to her. I know what happens to people who come here on credit, but believe me, my intel is worth our passages."

"Fair enough," Dante says, "but that still doesn't explain what you know that's important enough to grant you passage."

"That's for Dante to know," the man says. He lifts his chin as if to press the point.

"You're talking to Dante, ole windbag," Walter calls over.

"Sir." The man's stance changes and he bows low, raising his fist to his shoulder. "I apologize. I thought you'd be . . ."

"Older?" Dante guesses. "I get that a lot." His eyes flick to mine.

"I need to speak with you privately."

"You can tell me here," Dante says.

"No, sir, I can't," the man says. "I'm under orders from Alix to tell you alone."

Dante stiffens at this information, but he inclines his head in agreement and the two return to the empty corridor inside.

"What can that be about?" I wonder out loud, but Erik

doesn't respond. When I turn to repeat the question, there's a dazed look on his face.

"Erik?" I prompt, touching his arm lightly. "Are you okay?"

"Yeah, I'm fine," he says, but I notice how he swallows against the words.

Out of the corner of my eye, I spy the female refugee watching us, her son still huddled against her. She shivers in the breeze created by the slow movement of the aeroship.

"Hold on," I say to Erik.

Approaching the woman slowly, I bend and run a hand over the boy's finely cropped hair. He smiles at me. I shrug off my coat and move to wrap it around the woman's shoulders. She steps back and shakes her head.

"I don't need it," I insist.

"I couldn't," she says simply. "I can't pay you for it."

Whatever happened to her in Arras, she's unwilling to owe other people for favors, but there are going to be a lot of things she can't pay for on Earth with that attitude. Thanks to Jost, I know the one way to get her to agree.

"I'm not doing it for you," I tell her. This time she lets me wrap it over her shoulders. Jost taught me a parent's love trumps everything else, even pride.

The woman swallows hard and mouths, "Thank you."

I give her a small smile and turn away, tears pricking my eyes.

Warm, scratchy wool falls over my shoulders. "Adelice Lewys, you have a good soul." There's a trace of huskiness in the thick words.

I tug the corners of Erik's jacket closed. "So do you, Erik."

He shrugs and looks away, but I grab his hand.

"You do," I say.

Erik opens his mouth to respond, but suddenly a group of men appear on the deck, shouting instructions and dragging the ropes that tether us to the slub in the Interface. They throw the tethers up and stop our progress. I catch Falon's arm as she rushes past us.

"What's happening?" I yell over the din of activity around us.

"The estate is under attack," she calls. "Dante's ordered us back."

She doesn't linger to answer any of the million questions I have. The estate is under attack? Has the Guild come after me? Do Kincaid's men know I am gone? And then one question stops me cold:

What will happen to my mother?

THIRTY-ONE

THE AEROSHIP MOVES TOO SLOWLY FOR MY taste so I pace the length of its deck until Dante appears, with Falon at his side, carrying a stack of vests in his arms. I haven't seen him since Falon informed us what was going on, but as he approaches he lifts a finger to my lips.

I shake my head. "No, I have to know what's going on. Who's attacking the estate?"

"It's a group of Remnants," Dante says. "They're probably after your mother."

"My mother?" I repeat in disbelief.

"A rescue mission?" Falon asks, holding out a vest for me to slip into. "Remnants aren't loyal like that, Dante."

I dare a glance at Dante and his eyes stay cool and distant. He's lying to Falon—and to me—but why?

"Kincaid can't know you're gone," Dante says. "He'll have been alerted to the attack, so we can't waste time. We need to beat him back there."

"We need to get to my mother," I add. No matter what's

happened, I can't stomach the idea of her falling back into a Remnant pack.

"Of course," Dante says absently.

"And what exactly is your plan?" Erik asks, examining the pockets of his black vest.

"How are you with ropes?" Dante asks as he glances over the side of the deck.

Nothing about that question is comforting.

"But won't we be walking into an attack?" I ask, taking the offered vest.

"No, we'll be *dropping* into an attack, but it can't be helped. We don't have time." Dante hands a thick black bodysuit to me and then one to Erik. "You'll want to be wearing these."

I can't bring myself to ask why.

"And we're going to take the aeroship in over the Icebox?" Erik asks. "That's risky."

"We don't have any other choice," Dante says, his tone growing weary. From the look on Falon's face, he's already tried this argument with her.

"We'll fly Kincaid's standard as we approach," Falon explains. "We can only hope that in the chaos, no one looks too closely."

"It will be fine," Dante says. "Kincaid isn't back yet. Jax and I can deal with any problems that arise."

"I sure hope so," Falon responds, but she looks skeptical.

Erik and I change, backs turned to each other. Neither of us speaks, but I'm sure he can hear my heart beating. It's as loud as a drum, pounding against my chest.

"Zip me up?" I ask, once I've shimmied into the tight suit.

Erik pulls my zipper up and then plants a soft kiss on the

back of my neck. The world around me stops, strands glimmering, swimming in a vital tangle of life and energy. I live a lifetime in the softness of those lips and the heat of his breath on my skin. I don't say anything. Instead I shrug on my vest and stride from the room, unable to look at him.

Dante examines my vest and shows me a thin metal carabiner attached to a harness that will hold me to the rope as we rappel. I step into the harness and pull it over my legs. Dante grabs the carabiner. "Fall back."

I eye him nervously, but allow my weight to shift back. I sway, but my head never hits the floor—Dante grips the carabiner and the harness holds. He grabs my arm and pulls me onto my feet with an approving smile.

"All you have to do is pull this under your leg. One hand here and the other here." Falon demonstrates gripping the rope above the carabiner and then bringing the rope between her legs. Her other hand grips the rope against her tailbone. "Then push off and fall by slowly letting the rope slide in your hand. Don't let go though."

"You make that sound easy," I say, taking a deep breath and mimicking her demonstration with the rope.

"Don't overthink it," she says. "Take these." She holds out a pair of gloves. "We don't want to damage your hands."

"Thank you." I don't tell her they're already damaged—that every bit of me is cracked and broken in some way.

She leans into me, whispering in my ear, "If anything happens, get to the tunnel and find me."

I nod, but Dante steps between us to appraise my harness one last time.

"We're here," he says. No one appears on the deck to throw

the tethers, and I look to him, confusion written across my face.

"We can't stop," he says. "We don't know the nature of this situation and we can't risk the aeroship. It's the only one the Agenda has."

Because I destroyed the other one, I realize. I nod my head, trying to look brave, but I'm failing miserably.

Dante leads me to the only side of the deck without a railing. Four ropes are waiting in coiled piles. He yells but his words are caught in the wind. Then he grabs a rope and slings it over the side of the ship. It unfurls in the air, staying anchored to the deck. He pulls the rope between his legs. Positioning his hands, he leans back into the open air and jerks his head as if to say *Join me*. Erik and I look at each other. He winks.

"Any advice?" I ask Jax as we near the ropes.

"Slide fast," he says, patting me on the shoulder.

I wrap the rope around my thigh and then clip the carabiner around it. My hands grip the rope tightly.

"Go!" Dante shouts over the rush of air around us.

He disappears over the side along with Jax.

"I can't do this," I call to Erik.

"You have to," he says, and then as if to dare me, he lets go, sliding furiously from my side.

I relax back into the wind and close my eyes, feeling the rope in my hands. It's just a strand, I tell myself as my blood pounds through my veins and into my frenzied heart. The breeze kisses my cheeks and roars in my ears. Retightening my grip, I push off the deck and into the air.

THIRTY-TWO

I'M SUSPENDED IN THE AIR, THE ROPE anchoring me. As I fall back, my body twists until I'm hanging upside down.

So much better.

I'm hovering above Earth, swaying with the forward movement of the aeroship. Using every bit of strength I can muster, I heave my body up until I'm clinging, right side up, to the rope. Taking a deep breath, I relax my fingers for an instant. I plummet several feet before my fingers tighten over the rope and stop my progress.

"Okay," I say to myself—because I'm hanging from a rope, alone in the middle of the air, "you know how it works, now let go."

I have to repeat it several more times before I let myself slide. The effect is instantaneous. I zip down the rope, and despite my gloves and suit the friction burns across my skin, leaving a trail of fire running through my body. Gravity pulls at my hair, loosening it to fly around my face. I dare to look down at the ground hurtling up to meet me. The rope tears at my gloves, but I control my descent until I'm dangling several feet from the ground. The aeroship continues to glide overhead and it pulls me slowly through the air as I try to convince myself to let go and drop the last few feet.

"Took you long enough," Erik calls out.

"I stopped for tea—what took *you* so long?" I respond with a shrug of the shoulders. I can't help feeling a little full of myself at the moment.

"Let go," Erik calls. "I'll catch you."

I stare down at Erik, who's jogging along to keep up with me.

"Ready?" I call, and despite my better judgment, I release my grip on the rope.

It is not an elegant landing. Erik catches me, but he buckles against my weight and we both crash to the ground.

"Way to stick the landing," Dante says, looming over us.

"Shut up and help me," I say.

Once we're on our feet, we survey the situation, discovering we're not far from the estate.

"I sent Jax in," Dante explains. "We shouldn't show up at the same time."

"Let's not sit around talking then," I say. "We've got an estate to save."

At first nothing seems wrong, but the closer we get to Kincaid's, the more uneasy I feel. The first sign that something terrible has happened is a hole blasted in the large perimeter fence.

"Explosives." Dante kicks at a pile of debris around the shattered portion of the fence.

"Guild," I murmur.

"It's probably Remnants, but the Guild might not be far behind. Cormac knows that you've been holed up here," Dante says.

I'm not prepared for the scene we stumble upon once we reach the main grounds of the estate. Several of Kincaid's precious statues lie in ruins on the ground, marble heads and arms sown along the brick walkway. As we get closer to the great house, we discover something far more disturbing though—bodies.

Kincaid left a skeleton crew behind when the mission went after the Whorl, and it had often felt like we were the only three people left on the estate, but now I see how wrong I was. I trip over the legs of a corpse, falling onto a body covered with thick alteration scars.

"Remnants," Dante says, helping me to my feet.

Most of the other bodies scattered across the grounds are Kincaid's men and a few servants I recognize from mealtimes. My heart leaps into my throat when I spot the corpse of a blond woman, still wearing the face from the play Kincaid put on a few weeks ago. Apparently the Tailors never got around to altering it back.

"It looks like we missed all the action," Erik says, but as if to prove him wrong, a blast booms from the main house, sending showers of brick and tile ricocheting in our direction. Erik throws me to the ground as Dante sprints toward the building.

"He's not armed," I cry. "He's going to get killed." I rush forward, but Erik grabs my arm to stop me.

"He'll be fine. He's got powerful skills at his disposal," Erik says. "Let's stick together, Ad. We don't know what's going on in there."

Inside a battle is being waged on Kincaid's ornate carpets and marbled floors. There's too much smoke to see who is who and we're only in the house for a few minutes when Erik pushes me into an alcove previously occupied by a statue. Before I can process what he's doing, he's grabbed a Remnant. A crack shatters the air and Erik momentarily loses his grip, but then his fingers sink into the Remnant's flesh with a wet *split*. The man looses a shrill wail as his shredded skin opens in a torrent of crimson. But Erik doesn't unwind him. The Remnant turns on his heel to escape, and we rush through the hallway.

"Where's Dante?" I call to Erik.

"Doesn't matter. We need to get you out of here," Erik orders me.

"I'm not leaving him!"

"Ad, the Guild might be after you, but these Rems don't have the self-control to capture someone," Erik argues, shoving me behind him until we're near the stairway that leads to the upstairs guest rooms. But instead of directing me up, Erik reaches out to press a carved face in the woodwork. A panel swings open like the one Deniel pushed me through when he attacked me. I stare at Erik in wonder.

"How—" I start.

"I figured it might come in handy to explore," Erik shouts over the clamor of gunfire in an adjacent room. "I'm a bad houseguest. I snooped. There're hidden passages all over this place."

"Where do they go?" I ask, unwilling to enter the dark passage.

"It doesn't matter." Erik pulls me into it, and before I can respond, the panel swings closed behind us. The insulation muffles the sounds of battle and I grope along the walls, wondering what terrors lie hidden in the dark. Erik's hand closes over mine and he guides me.

Then Erik drops my hand, and suddenly the wall shifts, swinging to reveal another passage. I catch myself against the frame, which is a good thing because behind me a well-lit set of stairs curves down, spiraling toward an unknown destination.

"Sorry," Erik says, reaching out to steady me. "I'll go first."

"I'm not helpless, you know."

"Never said you were. I just know where the stairs go," he says.

The stairs empty into the basement of the estate, and I recognize the passage leading to the cell block. My mother is there, and regardless of everything that's transpired between us since I found her on Earth, my feet fly toward her cell. Erik follows. The familiar buzz of the electrified bars is absent.

"The security system is off," I whisper. I turn to gauge his thoughts and notice he's holding his left arm.

"What's wrong?"

"Nothing," he says, shifting away from me.

I turn to face him and stare at the blood seeping through his sleeve. "You're bleeding!"

"That happens when you get shot," he says. He tries to smile and fails magnificently, the grin faltering into a grimace of pain.

"We need to get you medical help."

"There are people worse off right now," he says. "Let's find your mom and Dante."

I start to protest, but he pushes past me toward the cell block.

There's no guard stationed outside. The hair prickles along my scalp like a biological alarm, but the sound of Dante's voice turns my panic into curiosity even as ice fills my veins. I press against the wall and listen, hoping to understand why he's here instead of fighting with the rest of Kincaid's men.

"Meria, I can't change what they did to you," he says.

"Don't pretend to care, Dante. They didn't take my memories. I know you left me. Left us."

"I am sorry," he says.

"Meria might have been once, too. But I don't care now," she responds. "Surely you have more important things to worry about than the next prisoner Kincaid is going to execute."

"I won't let that happen."

"Why? I'd kill you if it weren't for these bars," she says.

"Would you?"

My mother lets loose a hollow laugh that's nothing like the bell-like laugh I remember from my childhood. "I'm not Meria. No matter how much you want me to be. No matter how much she wants me to be. I am not your friend or your lover."

"That doesn't change anything for me," he says.

His shoes click against the floor and I suck in a breath, sure I'm about to be caught. Instead a lock snaps open.

"What are you doing?" Meria asks in a suspicious tone.

"I'm letting you go," he says.

I have to clap my hand over my mouth to keep from screaming.

"You want me to prove I'll kill you?" she says, and I hear the smile in her voice.

"I'm drugging you first," he says.

"This doesn't change anything," she warns him.

"That's not why I'm doing it. Some things don't change no matter what's happened," he says. "Even things that fade with time and distance aren't ever really lost."

Her shrieks grate on my ears and I know what he's done before I hear her body hit the floor. This is my only chance to stop him. I take a deep breath and round the corner. Erik stands silently behind me.

"Ad," Dante says in surprise. He's hovering over her body. She looks like she's sleeping—or worse. Dante looks from me to Erik, his hand running through his hair as he takes in our sudden appearance. "Erik—are you okay?"

"Fine," Erik mutters.

"What are you doing?" I demand, unable to dismiss what he's done to her.

"It's not what it looks like."

"It looks like you drugged her and are planning to drag her into the desert and leave her," I say.

"Okay, then it's exactly what it looks like," he says, a note of confusion in his voice.

"I heard it all," I say. Only some of her words stung, but I still feel their vibration on my skin. She isn't my mother, I remind myself. "You can't let her go. For Arras's sake, it's a war zone out there."

"Which makes it my only chance to get her out without suspicion. I never should have brought her here. Once Kincaid returns he'll blame her for this attack."

"She wants to kill you," I remind him, slowing down my words. "She wants to kill me."

"I know."

"And you're okay with that?" I ask him.

"I would prefer she didn't want to kill us," he says. "Adelice, you don't understand."

"I'm trying to," I say.

"Kincaid has humored me by keeping her here, but after a raid like this there's no way he'll keep harboring her."

"Why does Kincaid care?" I ask. "He can't supply the precious energy to keep the cell electrocuted anymore? He needs it to put on his sordid plays and watch his films? Even if you drop her off hours from here, sooner or later someone will kill her.

"Why won't you save her?" I demand. "Alter her back—fix her."

"You can't patch in someone else's soul," Dante says, his fingers circling his temples. He leans against the disarmed bars that once held my mother captive.

"The Guild has the remains of her strand. They have the remains of all the Remnants' strands. If we could get to them—"

"There isn't time for that," Dante interrupts me. "Whatever happens to her out there can't be worse than what Kincaid will do to her."

I touch one of the bars. It's not dangerous now that the

electricity is off. I need something tangible to hold on to. "What if she kills someone else? What then?"

"I can live with that," he says.

"I can't."

"It's not up to you. You think what the Guild did was bad, but . . ."

"But?" I press. "What will Kincaid do, make her into a doll to play with?"

"I wish it was something as nice as that," he says.

"You brought us here. You told us Kincaid was our best option—"

"I told you Kincaid was your *only* option," he corrects me. "You made a choice, and it brought you here."

"You brought me here." I step forward, wagging a finger at him.

"I had no other choice."

"Really? Or was it simply to satisfy your curiosity?" I ask.

"Partially," he admits. "But, Ad, things are happening. Kincaid is coming back. They have information."

"Good."

"I don't think it is." Dante hesitates. He stops and lifts my mother onto his shoulder. She hangs limp over him, like a rag doll on a child's shoulder.

"And why are you telling me this now?" I demand.

"Because Cormac is after you, Adelice, and we don't have time. We can't stay here much longer."

"But what about Jost?" I protest.

"We'll wait for him, if he comes back with the others."

"If?" I repeat in a hollow voice.

291

"When," Dante says, moving past me toward the corridor. "I can't explain now. You two need to see to that wound."

"But I don't—"

"You can do it." Dante stops me. "Erik can help you. Tell no one, not even Jost, what you saw tonight."

He doesn't bother to wait for our promises.

THIRTY-THREE

WHEN WE PEEK OUT FROM THE BASEMENT, we find the halls quiet. Tattered tapestries hang precariously from the ceiling and the paneled walls are marred with tiny holes, but no one is in sight. In Erik's quarters, I run the faucet until the water is warm, but when I reenter the bedroom, the harsh scent of whiskey prickles my nostrils.

He gestures to the bottle of liquor on the table.

"No, thanks," I say with a shake of my head. "Should you be drinking?"

"Disinfecting," he says as he pours some over his bloodied biceps, wincing as it hits his skin. He immediately covers it with the wet washcloth I've dropped on the bed.

"Should I lock this?" I cross to close the door, wanting to be helpful as much as I want to avoid looking at his wound.

"If the attack is over, security will do a sweep. Might as well leave it open or Kincaid's goons will break it down."

"I wish that made me feel better." I force myself to go to

him and tentatively lift the cloth to examine his wound. A blob of red blood oozes not far from his muscle.

"Flesh wound," Erik says in a casual voice, but I catch him wince again as the air hits it.

"Is there a bullet in there?" My words are strangled with some unrecognizable emotion. I want to cry and kiss him at the same time.

"It went straight through," he says. "It'll be fine once the bleeding stops."

"I can fix it," I remind him.

"I wasn't going to ask. I could do it myself, but two hands are better than one when patching," Erik says. "If it makes you uncomfortable—"

I stop him. "Walk me through it." Taking a steadying breath, I pour a little whiskey on my fingers. I'm less convinced of its disinfectant powers, but there's no harm in trying. Further inspection reveals an exit wound on the other side of his arm.

"Concentrate," Erik says. "See the strands."

It sounds so serious and profound coming from Erik that I giggle, but he balks at my nervous titter and draws his arm away.

"I'm sorry," I say. "I can do this."

"Once you stop laughing and see the strands," Erik begins, a bit sourly. "Draw together the damaged ones and connect them. It's like the loom, Ad. Fix the hole."

I close my eyes and focus on the fear pounding its war song in my chest. When I reopen them I can see the strands that weave together to make Erik's arm and a stream of pulsing red fibers on his biceps calls out to me. I don't exactly know what I'm doing, but I work at the shrill, off-key notes of the damaged strands until they grow harmonious, knitting together and healing.

"Not bad," Erik says when I step back to survey my work, the room resolving into a world of physical objects.

Suddenly exhausted from the effort, I drop down on his bed. I roll onto my stomach, clutching the pillow to my chest. He wipes the excess blood from the newly patched wound and takes the ruined washcloths to the bathroom. As he goes, I consider what to say to him about Dante and my mother. I don't have to talk about it, but I want to. I'm just not sure why. To make myself feel better? To talk through it? Those reasons make sense, but one thing holds me back. An unspoken tension that hangs between Erik and me. Talking about my mother and Dante means I'll have to talk about the issues that he and I are constantly skirting around.

I mention it anyway.

"It's not too late to stop him," Erik says.

"Should I?" I ask, confusion infusing my voice. I know I should stop him, but deep down, I don't want to. I'm not sure why though.

"No," Erik says in a firm voice.

"Why?" I ask, wondering how he can be so certain.

"Because he loves her," he says.

"I know that. But loving someone doesn't mean you make the best decisions about them," I point out.

"No. Love can be blinding," Erik agrees. "But if he believes she's in danger, he's already thought through his options. He's chosen the best one."

"Maybe someone who can be more objective should be making the decision," I say.

"Perhaps, but someone who is more objective won't fight as hard as the person who loves her," Erik says in a low voice. "One man will step aside when confronted while another will die. If you try to fight him, consider that."

We aren't only talking about Dante and my mother anymore.

"He'll lose her either way," I murmur.

"Doesn't mean that he shouldn't try," Erik says.

"She loved someone else though. My father, my *uncle* . . ." I struggle with putting words to my thoughts, trying to sort out my tangled family tree. "It's so confusing. Dante isn't my father, not in my heart."

"I understand," Erik says.

"My father died for me and my mother," I say.

"He was a good man," Erik says. "A better man than I am."

"You've leapt more than once for me—and for your brother." It's the first time I let it slip that I know we're talking about the three of us as much as we're talking about the convoluted love triangle in my family.

"I'd leap for you again," Erik says.

I drop my head onto the pillow to avoid his eyes, and at the foot of the bed I spot a book. My book. I reach for it, running my fingers over the green canvas cover.

"Sorry," Erik says. "You left it here weeks ago. I meant to return it, but . . ."

He doesn't finish the thought and I lift my head to look at him, raising an eyebrow.

"I was reading it," he admits.

"What did you think?" I ask, pulling the book of sonnets closer. I trace the gold-foil *Shakespeare* on the cover.

"I comprehend about half of it," he says honestly. "But it's beautiful."

"I'll never understand why people in Arras don't write anymore," I murmur.

"You don't?" Erik asks. "It's easy enough to understand."

"Do tell," I challenge him.

"Why aren't there films anymore? Beyond Stream-approved programming. Why only the *Bulletin* and fashion catalogues?"

I pause and consider this. The insipid forms of art we are permitted in Arras are empty. They lack depth. There is a certain artistry to the design of clothes, the application of makeup, the structure and decor of a building, but it lacks meaning.

"Words," Erik says.

Of course he's right. The books in my parents' cubby. I'd boasted of reading them, but I never considered why they were contraband. Words can tell a story. But they can also convey an idea.

"Words are dangerous," I say.

Erik nods.

"But they're also beautiful," I say, holding the book out to him. "You said so yourself. How can the Guild turn their backs on poetry?"

"They've turned their backs on more than that," Erik says.

I know he's right, but the realization makes me hate the Guild a little bit more.

Erik drops down beside me and grabs the book. He leafs through it and stops on a particular page. "This is my favorite."

"Which one?"

"116."

I shake my head. I hardly have them memorized. "Read it to me."

A strange look passes over Erik's face, but he clears his throat. I don't understand why until he begins to read.

"'Let me not to the marriage of true minds admit impediments. Love is not love which alters when it alteration finds, or bends with the remover to remove.'" He pauses and dares a look at me.

"Do you like it because it mentions alteration?" I tease, but secretly I hope my cheeks aren't burning.

"It seems very applicable to our current situation," he says.

"Continue," I urge him.

He reads the rest of the sonnet, stumbling a bit as he goes, and yet it slides smoothly off his tongue. The words curl around me, and lull me. When he finishes, the final line hangs in the air between us.

"Why is it your favorite?" I ask.

"Because it's true," he murmurs. "That's why Dante took your mother. It's why your father died for you."

"Careful, Erik," I warn him. "You're in danger of becoming downright sensitive."

He smiles but the expression doesn't reach his eyes. "Wouldn't want that."

And once again I've disarmed the moment, cracked a joke to avoid real conversation. We slip into our familiar banter, abandoning the book and talking late into the night about plans and futures and strategies, but never about us.

Never us.

THIRTY-FOUR

AT DAWN, ARTIFICIAL LIGHT STREAKS THROUGH THE room; it highlights Erik's face, showing off the curves of his nose, the angle of his cheekbones. He's stunning in his sleep, but soon his eyes flutter, and I turn away, not wanting to be caught staring.

"You look lovely," he murmurs dreamily.

I'm caught off guard. My heart is beating so fast that it aches in my chest as I lie next to him, close enough to touch him, but not daring to. I like that he said it and it's this realization that pushes me up on my side to face him. I stretch my fingers out, searching for the courage to reach across the space between us. Erik catches them and brings my fingertips to his lips. He kisses each softly, and tingles fall down my neck.

"I'm sorry for what she did," he says, keeping my fingers clasped loosely.

"You couldn't have stopped her," I whisper, allowing myself to trace his jawline.

"I should have tried. Your hands are beautiful."

"Not anymore," I say.

"They're more beautiful now. Flaws make them perfect."

He lets my hand fall away as I swallow against the words sitting in my throat. The things I want to say to him—and then the door swings open. The one I left unlocked last night because I hadn't planned to stay here.

"Erik, have you seen Ad?"

I'm still sleepy enough that it takes a second for everything to fall into place. Jost is back, looking tired and road weary, and he has found me on Erik's bed. I don't have to think hard to know what this looks like.

"Never mind," Jost says, stumbling back outside.

I'm off the bed before Erik can respond and I dash into the hall and down the stairs. A breeze brushes past me and I notice that one of the doors to the garden is propped open. I take my chances and walk into the still morning, taking in the destruction wrought the previous day. Jost stands surveying the scene, with his back to me, and overhead the Interface flashes as though Arras is peering judgmentally down.

"Jost, wait!" I call, but he strides away.

"Hey," I snap, when I do catch up. I grab him by his arm. As soon as his eyes meet mine, my angry rebukes and excuses seem like too little, too late. He's already decided I've betrayed him, and part of me wonders if I have.

"What, Ad?" he challenges me. "I can't wait to hear what you have to say about this."

I stare at him, weighing each possible response. They're all lacking.

"Don't tell me you're speechless," he says. "I know that can't be true."

"Erik and I are friends," I remind him.

It's definitely the wrong thing to say.

"Really?" he asks, his voice raw. "Looked like a little more than friends to me."

"We broke up," I say. "You left me."

"To find answers. Answers we both need," Jost says. "Did you run to Erik right away?"

"I didn't run to Erik." But in the back of my mind poetry plays. The flash of Erik's eyes meeting mine. I didn't run to Erik, but I found him anyway.

"I was gone a few weeks," he says. "I've come back with nothing and then this. Did you do it to prove me wrong?"

"Prove you wrong?" I repeat. It's impossible that's what he said. It's impossible he thinks that's what has happened in his absence.

"Yes, I told you we couldn't risk *that*, so you wanted to prove me wrong. Is that it? Tell me something, Ad, did you choose Erik to see if you could drive us even farther apart or was he the first guy you ran into?"

The accusation cuts through the fragile thread holding me to him.

"So can you still do it? Can you still catch the threads?" he asks. At that moment, I realize that my skill is more important to him than anything else. More important, even, than the fact that he believes I spent the night with Erik. More important than whether we can ever get past this.

The back and forth of the last few months. Feeling so close only to sense a wall between us. My growing friendship with Erik and subsequent guilt. The assumptions and distrust. It all overwhelms the happiness I once felt with Jost. Memories of us, the want I felt for Jost, it's all washed away as my shame shifts to indignation.

"My talent—that's all I am to you, isn't it?"

He stares at me, trying to understand what I'm saying.

"Was I ever more than a Spinster to you?" I ask. "Or did you always see me as a means of revenge?"

His jaw drops open, but he shakes his head. "If you believe that—"

"What am I supposed to believe, Jost?"

"If I made you feel that way, I am sorry," he says, his expression softening a little. "I wanted to get back to the girls. I wanted to make sure we were safe, so we—"

"Could be a family," I cut him off. "But you never once asked me if that's what I wanted. I'm not capable of it. Can't you see that? I'm a danger to them."

"I guess I assumed," he says quietly. "But apparently I assumed too much."

"Don't you dare," I seethe. "Don't you dare make me feel bad because I needed someone to listen to me. Don't you dare, Josten Bell."

"I wouldn't," he says.

"And as for my *skill*"—I spit the word out like it's rancid—"I wish it were gone. Maybe then I wouldn't have to put up with any of you anymore."

"So you'd give up your sister to not have responsibility?" he accuses.

"No, I'm still going to find her. But maybe if I can't warp or weave, then you guys will be forced to do something useful for once."

"I am doing something useful. I've been out there searching for the Whorl so we can get the girls back before it's too late. Before time takes them away from us!" Jost grabs my arm, his fingers squeezing the soft flesh.

"And what good has it done us?" I ask. "We're no closer to saving the girls than we were weeks ago. We've lost nearly two years in Arras, Jost. Two years."

"You think I don't know that?" he growls. "You think that every second that passes doesn't remind me that Sebrina is slipping away?"

"I've been training," I say. "I can alter, unwind. Don't tell me that I've done nothing."

"You have done something," Jost says. "You've become a weapon. Did you fight yesterday? Fulfill your purpose?"

I hate that word—*weapon*. But I hold my ground and don't miss a beat. Jost won't win this argument. I won't let him. "I'm no one's weapon. No one is using me. I'm not being dragged around looking for a mythic answer to our problems."

Jost gives me a rueful smile. "Enjoy your pedestal, Ad."

"You're the one who put me up there."

Jost turns to go, but it's at exactly that moment that Erik appears, dressed only in his jeans. He must have heard me chasing after Jost, which means he's been listening to us fight.

"The problem isn't the pedestal, Jost," Erik says. "It's that when we fall off, you won't help us back up. We can't all live according to your rigid moral standards."

"So you slept with Adelice," Jost counters, "to prove me right? To show you're as good as the dirt you landed in?"

Erik's eyes meet mine and I see pain in them. "You have it

wrong. Nothing happened, but from now on what does happen is between Adelice and me," Erik says, edging closer to his brother, "because I'm in love with her."

Well, that's out in the open.

"You're in love with yourself. You've never cared more about someone else's happiness than your own. You wanted her so you took her. Like you wanted to leave Saxun, so you did. You never consider anyone else," Jost accuses.

I know what Erik has gone through. I know he's struggled with what might have been if he'd stayed in Saxun. *I* know it. But Jost doesn't. Because Erik and Jost barely talk to each other unless they're arguing, and I'm sick of it.

"Don't stop now," Erik says. "Tell me how I should have stopped what happened in Saxun. Tell me how I could have stuck around and wasted my life fishing. Tell me that I should have stood in the shadows while you ignored the only good thing you had going instead of falling in love with Adelice."

"You don't know the first thing about love."

"Maybe I don't," Erik admits, "but I know a thing or two about fighting. When are you going to step up and fight for something, little brother? I never held it against you that you didn't share my ambitions. When you came to the Coventry, I didn't judge you for watching and thinking. And when you went after Adelice, I didn't blame you. But there comes a time when you have to figure out what to fight for and *actually* do it."

I might as well not even be here, because their gazes are locked on each other.

"And what do *you* fight for?" Jost asks.

"Adelice," Erik says without hesitation. "You had your

chance. I'm not waiting around any longer. I've held back because I felt bad. But this time you lost, and it had nothing to do with me."

"Anyone care what I think?" I ask in a quiet voice.

"No!" they respond in unison without turning to me.

"Fine." I walk away, leaving both boys in the dim glow of halogen, but before I can flee to my quarters, two Sunrunners step into my path.

"We're going to need you to return to your room, miss." A row of stitches runs up the side of one's face. He must have seen some action last night.

"I'm on my way," I tell him, maneuvering around the pair toward the door.

"You too," the man calls to Jost and Erik, interrupting the brothers' heated argument.

"In a minute," Jost responds, not bothering to look at the Sunrunner.

"This estate is on lockdown. Our orders are to shoot anyone who resists us," the Sunrunner warns. "If you have a room, I suggest you go to it."

I wait long enough to see both Erik and Jost slinking back toward their rooms before I disappear into the safety of mine.

THIRTY-FIVE

THE NEXT MORNING MY DOOR IS LOCKED from the outside. I try the windows, but none of them open. I can't even exit to the adjacent sitting room. When my breakfast arrives under heavy guard, I know that I'm Kincaid's prisoner.

"When will we be allowed out?" I ask the guard, who has brought me a plate of cold boiled eggs and dry toast.

"They're sweeping the area. There's been a breach of our perimeter," he says, already moving to leave.

"Tell me something I don't know," I mutter.

The man's eyebrow cocks, but he doesn't say anything else. I manage to stomach the cold egg and toast, if only because I've had little to no food for the past two days. It's definitely not up to Kincaid's standard cuisine, but then again, there's probably no one to cook after the attack.

I try my door after he's left, but it's still locked. I could attempt to alter it, but without having any clue what is waiting on the other side, I decide against it. My alteration skills are dicey at best, and I'm as likely to destroy half of the wall as I am to get the door to open. I'll give it a day before I start to rip the place apart.

Jax arrives with my afternoon meal, and I sigh with relief when I see his friendly face. He brings my plate into the room, closing the door until only a sliver of light is left, so it doesn't lock behind him.

"Jax, thank Arras," I say. "What's going on?"

"Kincaid is furious. He thinks the breach came from the inside," Jax tells me, setting my plate down on my vanity.

"And he's keeping us in lockdown until he figures out who it was," I guess.

"No," Jax says, his face sagging. "He's already decided who it was."

I bite my hand so I won't scream. If Jax is walking around with the other Sunrunners, and I'm locked in my room, that must mean I'm the prime suspect. Or Jost and Erik are.

"Dante's gone," Jax continues. "And so is your mother."

"I know," I murmur.

"Kincaid thinks you had something to do with it."

"I didn't." I tried to stop him, but I don't tell Jax this. The less he knows, the less likely he is to get in trouble himself.

"I can't stick around," Jax tells me, "but I'm working on something."

"And I'm supposed to wait?" I demand, balling my fingers up so tightly that my fingernails pinch into the soft skin of my palms.

"You don't have a choice. I'll get you out of this, but I need you to listen to me. Don't eat your dinner."

"I couldn't eat if I wanted—"

"Don't even touch it." Jax stops me. "Throw it out. Hide it. When we come for you, pretend you are asleep."

They're coming for me. I can't quell the rising panic at this thought. Tonight they're coming for me. "Who is coming? Why?"

"I can't stay, but you can trust me," Jax says, pulling open the cracked door and disappearing. It clicks behind him.

I don't have any other choice.

I stay in bed, the contents of my dinner stashed in a drawer in the vanity. I'm too afraid to move for fear that they'll come without warning and catch me awake, ruining Jax's plan. When the lock to my door finally clicks open and feet shuffle across my floor, I squeeze my eyes shut and try to stay still.

"She's out." I hear Jax's voice, which puts me at ease.

"Be sure, I hear she's dangerous," another man says.

"I said she's out. Don't worry, I've got her." Hands slide under me and lift me up. I'm cradled against Jax's chest.

"Keep quiet," he whispers.

The sensation of being carried off is surreal. I can't open my eyes to see what path he's taken or where I'm going, but my mind involuntarily guesses each step of the way. The light filtering through my eyelids grows brighter and the air cooler.

"Put her down there."

"Okay." Jax squeezes my hand when he lays me back on a metal slab, and I struggle to keep my breathing slow and rhythmic. Where am I? What's going on?

"You can go," the other man commands.

"One thing first," Jax says. A moment later something crashes into the exam table and falls to the floor. My eyes fly open—I'm unable to keep them shut. Jax rushes over and helps me off the table. I have to step over a body when I do it.

"Is he dead?" I ask, staring down at the man.

"I knocked him out," Jax says. He squats to riffle through the lab coat the man is wearing, pulling a thin plastic card from the man's pocket.

"What is that?"

"Security clearance," Jax says. "We don't have much time."

I follow him out of the exam room and into one of the corridors of the estate's lower level. It looks like the hallway that leads to the cells, but I've never been here before. Nondescript steel doors line the corridor.

"These are the alteration labs," Jax explains. We turn left and immediately meet with a set of security doors. Jax holds the security card to the scanner and the doors glide open to allow us entrance.

"Where are we going?" I ask, checking over my shoulder.

Jax doesn't answer. Instead he pushes open a white door. Privacy screens partially obstruct several hospital beds, and on the near wall, lit boxes display black-and-white images. I step closer to examine them.

"So this is where he makes his toys," I say, remembering Kincaid's strange play and the actors adjusted to perfection for our entertainment.

"Not only his toys," Jax says. He flips a switch on the wall and a light buzzes on behind a bank of mirrors. Only then do I see the images hanging across them. The light casts shadows across the film and a variety of shapes appear before me.

I wander closer and peer at the sheets. "Is this . . . ?" I let my voice trail into a question.

"A brain," he confirms.

"And the others?"

"Chest. Hands." He rattles through a list, pointing to each picture. Some of them are obvious, such as the spindly bones of a hand and foot, but others require concentration to see clearly.

"He uses these to perform the alterations?"

"Tailors use them," he corrects me.

Tailors, like Dante or myself or Erik.

"X-rays give us a basic pattern to work from. They guide the measurement process," Jax explains.

"What do you need measurements for?" I ask, my alarm building to a frantic pulse.

"Remember the actress who wanted her face back after the play?" he asks.

I nod.

"A Tailor uses measurements to change someone's features. It's not always necessary, but it speeds the work along," Jax says.

"Why are you showing me this now?" I demand. Being in this room gives me the creeps, and it further reinforces the idea that the Guild is using Tailors in their efforts to map and alter. I had been close to going under the Tailor's instruments in Arras. I don't like being so close to them here.

"You didn't look closely enough," Jax prompts.

I stare closer but it's still a mass of murky white and spindly bones. Jax's long finger trails to the bottom of the X-ray I'm studying and I follow it. There's a mass of meaningless numbers and codes. Measurements of some sort, I assume, but it's what's underneath the gibberish that stands out:

SUBJECT: LEWYS, ADELICE

"This is me?" I ask aloud. I'm not really speaking to him, only trying to wrap my head around what I'm seeing.

"You aren't the only one," he murmurs. "You deserve to know what Kincaid had in store for you."

I scan the next image. Valery. Erik. And the next. Jost.

"How did they get these?" I ask loudly. Jax shushes me.

"They don't have surveillance in here, do they?"

"Would you keep records of your misdeeds on tape?" he asks. "But it's still not a good idea to yell."

Good point.

"I don't understand where they came from," I repeat, trying to fit the pieces together. "I never agreed to be mapped."

"Do you think Kincaid's the kind to ask? This isn't the first time Kincaid ordered us to drug you."

"And you did it? Before now?" My fingers jab at him.

"Dante wanted to see what Kincaid was up to." Jax spreads his hands apologetically and backs a few steps away from me.

Of course Dante would risk me to learn more about Kincaid. It doesn't even hurt anymore to realize that, not after his attitude about abandoning my mother. But how had I missed it? The dreamless nights, the world fading from awareness to black to light again. I thought I'd stopped dreaming because I felt safe, but now I realize more sinister machinations were at work. Did someone carry me down here at night without me knowing it? But when I stop to think, I remember the strange dots and scratches on my arm that Erik noticed in the speakeasy, and the silvery scar we discovered at the swimming pool.

My torn dressing gown the morning after Jost and I broke up. The strange bruise on my leg that Valery pointed out when she dressed me for the play. The clues have been there. Kincaid's men weren't even careful enough to prevent them, and still I hadn't seen them until now. That didn't answer the most important question though.

"Why?"

"What?" Jax asks.

"Why would he do this? What's his endgame?"

"Kincaid is twisted," he says but there's discomfort in his voice. He has no more idea than I do. Jax is another cog in Kincaid's machine, but he feels the creepy, sinister implications in the X-rays, in this room. Whatever Kincaid is up to isn't benign.

"What else do you do here?" I ask.

"We do the alterations," Jax says, hesitating a moment. "And this is where Kincaid gets his renewal patch."

"That's how he's still alive, isn't it?" I ask. "What are these patches?"

"He uses donor threads to keep from aging," Jax says. "We take the time strands from other people and insert them into Kincaid's own thread."

"*Donor* implies willingness," I mutter.

"There's nobody more willing than the dead," Jax says.

I recall the bright time strand I spotted within Kincaid. Was it the one pulled from Deniel after he attacked me? It doesn't matter. It is despicable and unjustifiable however Kincaid came by it. Is this how Cormac and the other Guild officials stay alive too?

"We need to tell Jost and Erik," I say, heading to the door.

"First, we have to take care of something more important," Jax says. He gestures to the privacy screen, and my heart sinks into my stomach. He pushes it to the side, revealing Dante, unconscious, lying on a table. An IV runs from his arm, and a mask regulates his breathing.

"What happened to him?" I breathe.

"He's sedated," Jax tells me.

"Wake him up," I cry.

"It's not that easy—"

"Wake him up!"

Jax fumbles through the cabinets and emerges with a vial of liquid. He sucks the medicine into a long syringe and takes a deep breath.

"Hold his arms," Jax orders me. I do as I'm told. Before I can ask him what he's planning to do, Jax slams the syringe into the center of Dante's chest. The effect is instantaneous. Dante's eyes fly open and he gasps against the mask covering his face. I pull it off him and he stares at me in confusion.

"It's okay," I say.

"Ad?" It's the only word I can make out. Dante's words are confused, a jumble of consonants and vowels.

"We need to go," Jax says. He offers Dante a hand, while I gently pull the IV needle from his arm. "We'll explain everything in a minute."

"We need to get to Erik and Jost," I say, wrapping Dante's other arm over my shoulder to help steady him.

Dante pushes us away. "I can walk."

Jax and I exchange a concerned look, but we let Dante walk.

I stay close to him in case he stumbles, but he doesn't head for the door. He trips his way to the next privacy screen.

"There's someone else in here," Dante says. "I got glimpses between doses."

"Who?" I ask, moving to push away the screen, my heart pounding in my chest.

"It's Valery," Dante says, beginning to tremble.

"The drugs are messing with his system," Jax says, grabbing a scratchy white blanket to place over Dante's shoulders.

Valery lies sedated behind the other screen. A bag drips nutrition into her arm, but from the look of her skeletal form, she's been here awhile.

"How long has she been here?" I wonder out loud. I can tell from the sallowness of her complexion that this is more than a couple days of sedation. I barely recall Kincaid mentioning Valery was going on the mission.

"She never left the estate," Jax says in disgust. "Kincaid lied to us. It took me a few days to piece together what was going on down here, and then I had to convince someone to let me in on the job. Kincaid doesn't trust me, he knows I'm too close to Dante."

"I'll get her. She won't be able to walk on her own," Jax adds.

"And then what?" I ask, beginning to feel the familiar panic crawling through my skin.

"You need to get your friends and run," Jax says.

"They've got the whole place on lockdown," I argue. "There's no way we're getting out of here."

"Don't worry about that," Jax says. Despite the seriousness of the situation, he winks at me.

"Jax is an expert at causing a commotion," Dante says weakly.

"You're going to distract them?" I guess. "How do you plan on distracting Kincaid's whole security force?"

"With a very big boom."

"And then what?" I ask. "Where will we go? We have no—"

Dante holds up a shaking hand to stop me. "We do have a plan. I know where the Whorl is."

"What?" I ask.

"The Whorl is on Alcatraz Island," Dante says in a small voice. "That was the intel the man who came through the loophole had. Kincaid doesn't know, but we'll have to move quickly. We'll need supplies—a raft and dry suits. This place won't be easy to get to."

"I'll take care of it," Jax says. "You guys worry about getting everyone ready to go and I'll make sure there's a crawler waiting with what you'll need."

"Get ahold of Falon. Tell her what's happened and where we're heading." Even in his weakened condition, Dante is coherent giving orders and making plans.

"What about Valery?" I ask. "We can't leave her here."

"Jax will take care of her. Get her clothes and get her to the crawler." Dante looks to Jax for confirmation, and Jax nods.

"I'll message Falon from Valery's quarters," Jax says.

I look at Dante and his face is determined as he gives one final order: "Let's get the hell out of here."

I rap so quietly on Erik's door that he doesn't respond so I knock again. When he answers his door, his shirt is untucked and his hair tousled but I can tell he hasn't been sleeping.

"Can I come in?" I ask. It's my job to convince both Erik

and Jost to come, something I plan to approach with separate tactics, while Jax works on a distraction and gets Val and Dante out and into a crawler. The plan is straight and to the point, so I'm positive it will go all wrong.

Erik looks flustered to see me, which is unusual, but we haven't talked about what he said to Jost. If he meant it. Or how I feel about it. Because I'm not sure yet. I duck in under his arm and push the door closed.

"I have something I need to tell you," I start, but before I can continue Erik leans into me, resting his arm on the door behind me, and suddenly I can't seem to breathe. He's so close to me that I can see the golden flecks around his irises, like stars swimming in the ocean.

"We've needed to talk for a while," he murmurs.

This close I can see that his lower lip is slightly fuller than the top one. I want him to lean closer. In this moment, I forget about Kincaid and Valery and Jost. I want him to kiss me.

Instead I push him away. Erik sighs and drops onto his bed, leaning his head into his hand. I'm immensely jealous of his hand in this moment. How he runs it through the mess of his hair.

"Not about us," I stop him. "There's trouble. More trouble than I can explain right now."

"Well?" he says expectantly.

"We have to get out of here. I'll explain later."

"Explain now." He grabs my wrist to stop my frantic pacing.

I gawk at him and pull away. Before I can respond to Erik's demand, the door bursts open and a man stumbles in. At first I think we've been discovered, but then Jost appears in the doorway behind him.

So this is how it ends. The betrayal numbs my body into paralysis.

But Jost surprises me, releasing his fist. It makes hard contact with the Sunrunner's jaw. He bounces back but doesn't fall and soon he's tussling with Jost. They wrestle each other to the floor and I jump up, looking for a way to help without accidentally ripping apart the room or anyone in it.

The Sunrunner pins Jost to the floor, his arm coiled around his neck.

"Little help here," Jost gasps against the pressure.

I whip around, looking for something to attack the Sunrunner with, and as I do, the room spins to life, full of purple and gold and crimson. I could use my alteration abilities.

"Do it," Jost croaks.

Before I can, Erik jumps in, surprising the Sunrunner enough that he loses his grip on Jost, who reverses the hold, pinning the other man to the ground as Erik unceremoniously cracks the medicinal bottle of whiskey over our attacker's head, knocking him out.

"What's going on?" Jost demands, his breath coming in heavy, fast pants.

I look to Erik, but neither of us speaks. I hadn't planned on convincing both of them to come at the same time. That would require a miracle.

"Do you know what he was going to do to you? I got to know Burris on the mission," Jost continues, pointing to the man on the floor. "Kincaid doesn't send Burris to bring you tea. Trust me. He sends Burris to kill you—or worse."

"Why would anyone want to kill us?" Erik asks in a cool voice.

"That's what I'm asking you," Jost says.

"Why don't you ask Burris?" Erik says, crossing his arms defensively, abandoning the brief brotherly camaraderie.

"Because he's not currently very talkative," Jost says, "and because he already told me."

"Told you what?" I ask.

"That he caught a spy and was going after her," he says. "I assume he means you."

My heart thumps when he looks at me. "We have to get out of here."

"And go where?" Jost asks. "Kincaid will be after you."

"We know where the Whorl is," I say, trying to keep my head clear and my words rational despite the trying circumstances I've found myself in this evening, but when I finish relating the night's events, neither of them acts surprised. Erik places an arm around my shoulder, but I shrug it off, aware of Jost's tensed jaw.

"Why are we still here?" Jost asks, his gaze glued to the floor. "If Dante knows where the Whorl is, we need to go."

"We have to wait for Jax. We can't get past security without a distraction," I tell him. Our eyes meet for a moment before I look away, confusion blooming in my chest.

"This ought to be good," Erik mutters, "and by good, I mean very, very bad."

THIRTY-SIX

Jax's distraction comes in the form of blowing up a garage that sits far enough from the main house that we aren't in imminent danger but close enough that the security force acts swiftly, giving us the opportunity to slip out of an entrance at the back of the house. As smoke pours from the wreckage, we flee the estate in the stolen crawler, Dante and Valery tucked safely inside with a bag of food and water. Jax has kept his word—everyone is too busy to see us go and the gates are unattended. I don't look back at Kincaid's playground. There's nothing left for me there. Jost drives north, following a rough map Dante has drafted.

"Hopefully, the men notice I'm gone first," Jost says, his hands white knuckled on the steering wheel. "They'll probably assume I'm out somewhere killing Erik. It's actually a fantastic alibi."

"Yeah," Dante says, from the backseat. "Because it's very believable."

"To be clear," Erik says, "you probably won't kill me though?"

"The night is young."

"Let's get to the island before we kill each other," Dante suggests in a mild tone that grows weaker as the adrenaline wears off.

We collapse into silence after this, the somewhat good-natured threat still hanging in the air. Although it's clear now that everyone knows about the drama between Jost, Erik, and me.

Now that we're off the estate, the road grows wild the farther we get from the inhabited Icebox. I turn around, hoping to stem the rolling nausea from our ride. "Dante," I call, leaning my chin against my seat, "do you think Jax will be okay?"

We'd left him at the estate to deal with the fallout of the explosion. Dante grins. "He'll be fine. He's headed straight to the Agenda to let them know what's happened so we can rendezvous with Falon later."

"That night when I caught you in the cells," I say, hoping this question doesn't destroy Dante's mood, "did you get my mother out?" I've been wondering since I found him strapped to the exam table, not knowing when or how he'd been taken.

Dante swallows hard and nods, but he doesn't give me any details.

Her freedom means she'll come after me again, but I have new enemies to worry about. The woman I knew as my mother is already dead. Even if I alter her I don't think I can erase what's happened. Would she remember what she's done? The people she's killed? I've spent enough nights contemplating how my own actions have led to deaths: Enora, my father, the nameless threads I ripped in cold blood. I was passive in those actions but I feel their blood on my hands like the sticky, black substance that coated my feet on the night of my retrieval. I can't dismiss the past, it lives in my head and infects me. Even with her soul back, her morality intact, would my mother be able to calm the bitter truth of what she's done?

And I know one thing for certain, my mother would want me to push forward, to find the Whorl, to get to Amie. I haven't given up on that yet. I won't let Arras and Earth be severed without reaching Amie first and removing her from Cormac's control.

But Loricel's words *the good of the many* whisper in my mind. I can't sacrifice a world for a sister as much as I can't sacrifice an opportunity for my mother. If I did, the groans of the dead would haunt me, calling to me, slowly driving me insane. Loricel asked me to think about my choices. At a loom to help others she made decisions. I have no loom now—merely passion swelling up inside me like a flooding dam ready to burst into action. Sometimes the only way to serve the greater good is to fight.

We pass along the coast in silence, weaving through abandoned metros, past service stations crawling with vines, tiny saltbox homes, and an endless series of unlit relics. No signs of life appear. I wonder what lies at the heart of the Interface. Someday, when this is over, I will explore and rebuild Earth. If I find nothing, I'll build my own world.

I look behind me. Erik rides silently. Even if Jost knows nothing happened between Erik and me, it's meaningless. I didn't kiss Erik, but I wanted to. I ripped a deeper void between them than can ever be patched.

Erik didn't kiss me that night either, because he loves his brother despite everything that's passed between them.

Now that we've driven beyond the Interface's boundary, overhead a sprinkling of stars peek out and the moon perches in the gray night sky. In Arras, a Spinster moves the time along, determining how the light will fade, whether the sunset will be orange or rose or purple. She places a false moon in the sky. Earth is a world born from nothing but potential. I think of the books in Kincaid's library. The ones that contain theories on Earth's origin, positing everything from a cataclysmic spasm in the universe to a creator placing it here, placing us here. I've seen in Arras what comes of the idea of a creator; I like the idea of randomness better. That we are born of infinite possibility and fade back into the fabric of the universe to feed new life. That the moon perches overhead simply because, and nothing more. I don't want to live my life at the hands of another, I want to live my life now, deciding my own fate.

Whatever lies ahead of us on Alcatraz could change everything, but I choose the path of self-determination. Whether we find the Whorl—if we accomplish the separation of the worlds—I will listen to myself. My fingers find the techprint on my wrist.

I'm not meant to remember who I am. I have to *discover* who I am.

Alcatraz Island is full of men and women with scarred skin that shimmers and shifts. It's not the decrepit old facility we expected. It's full of white light that bounces off metal tables and blank walls. There are no bars on the cells, only thick glass. The prisoners beat against it, lick it, scratch at it, leaving bloody streaks from deeply torn nails behind, but we can't hear them. We hear only a low hum from the energy powering this place. It must take so much of it, I think. The hum grows louder until it's pulsing thick in my ears and I can feel it there in my head, under my skin, behind my eyes. I try to shake it out but it won't fade. I tug on Dante's hand. He's closest to me, but he keeps walking forward, down a hall toward the black doors at the other end. He can't hear me in here either. I cry out, but I can't hear myself over the pounding in my ears. Around us more Remnants gather at the transparent walls of their cells, and they start thumping against the glass. Their faces constrict into masks of ferocious concentration. Their hands are balled in fists. I don't have to hear them, because I can feel it. The ground beneath me shakes and concrete pillars spit dust over us as though the prison will collapse at any moment.

I run to Jost and pull on his arm, warning him to hurry, that they're going to break loose. But when he turns around his hair grows lighter, and he morphs into Erik. I scream.

"Ad!" Dante's call startles me from the dream and I arch in my seat, running a hand over my bleary eyes.

"You were asleep," Erik says. He's grabbed on to my seat, clutching it for balance.

"It was a nightmare," I murmur, my mouth full of cotton.

"No one here to drug you," Erik says with a wry smile, but it's too soon to laugh about Kincaid's betrayal.

"You want to stop for a second?" Dante asks, pulling Erik back in his seat. "Walk around?"

I shake my head. I want to put distance between Kincaid and the horrors of the estate. I want to move forward. More than anything I want to get to the Whorl—my future—and get on with it. I'm not eager to have total control of Arras, but I can't let someone else have it either. Certainly not Kincaid. The Whorl will give me a chance to right so many of my mistakes.

The world outside the crawler is dark with night, and above us the sky is black and full of stars and milky bands of light. The ocean laps against the road, and I can see where parts of the pavement have crumbled and fallen into the sea.

"You think that bridge is safe?" Erik asks, his focus ahead on the faded burgundy bridge in the distance.

"Probably not," Jost answers. "But we don't have to cross it anyway."

He takes one hand off the wheel and points outside to something planted firmly in the ocean—a towered compound rising up from the water. The familiarity of the stone towers unnerves me.

"What is that?" I breathe.

"Alcatraz Island," Dante says. "It was a prison before the Exodus. The Guild keeps the Whorl there now. That man who came through the loophole—he found out about it."

"After all these years," I say, staring across the ocean, "you've found it."

Jost slows the crawler when we reach a patch of shoreline that's intact. It's full of rocks and long, winding grass.

"High tide," Erik informs me, helping me out of the back of the crawler.

"How do you know?" I ask.

"Fisherman's son," he reminds me. "The water has risen as close to the shore as possible. When the tide goes back out, the shore will stretch farther out."

"What's underneath it?"

"The water? Rocks and seaweed and seashells."

"Seashells?"

"You've never seen a seashell?"

"No, I have. On the Stream, at least. But I've never seen the ocean until now." The fake one programmed into my window screens at the Coventry don't count.

"I never taught you to swim." Erik's words are an apology as he sweeps a finger along my jaw.

I bite the inside of my cheek, daring to say the thing I shouldn't. "You will."

I wander down to the fringe of the water with Erik, wishing it was daylight and warm enough to slip my toes in and feel the sea. The water goes on forever, at moments peaceful and then bursting with a wave that washes down with mighty force, nearly reaching our feet.

"It's beautiful," I murmur.

"I ran from my village," Erik whispers, "but I never stopped missing it."

"Was it like this? The Endless Sea?"

"Yes and no. It was calmer. Why control the ocean if you can't *control* it?" he points out.

"Why control it at all?" I wonder aloud as I stare at the magnificent, powerful waves. I can imagine how lovely the ocean's strands would feel on a loom, strong and slick and ancient, but they can't compare to standing here, looking out and never seeing where it ends.

"Mind giving us a hand?" Jost calls, and I turn to see he's spread a thick plastic sheet on the ground.

"What's that?"

"Our raft. I mean, if we're still going," he replies, pain edging into his words. Is that what it will always be like? Hurting him to exchange a few words with Erik? Would it be better to hurt Erik by ignoring him to spare Jost? Behind me the ocean laps on, beating against the shore in rhythmic bursts, reminding me that I'm small and insignificant.

Erik and Jost set to work, inflating the raft until it's a large boat that, to be honest, looks a little flimsy considering we have to get out past these waves.

"How will we get out there?" I ask, staring at the frail raft.

Jost and Erik exchange a look, a first since we fled the estate. The fact is that the ocean is their territory and there's no sense denying that now.

"We'll push you out," Erik says.

"How?" Valery asks, alarmed. She's been quiet most of the trip, but I don't blame her for speaking up now.

"You'll sit in the raft and we'll swim it out," he replies.

"Is that a good idea?"

"I'll help," Dante volunteers.

"You spend much time in the ocean?" Jost asks.

Dante shakes his head. He's their equal in size and strength, but even I know that doesn't mean he has the skill to navigate this water.

"We can do this," Erik assures us. "Fisherman's sons, remember?"

I swallow and force a nod. I like this idea less and less, but I have to trust that they have the skill to do it. Meanwhile Dante passes foam suits to us.

"Put this on," he orders. "That water is cold enough to kill you if you go in."

If we go in, I think, I'm not worried about the cold. But I struggle to get my suit on. In the end, Valery and I help each other with the difficult zippers on the thick, fitted suits. Jost and Erik have theirs on before we've sealed the sleeves, making them waterproof. When the suit is on, it flexes enough for me to move, but it's tight.

"And once we're out there?" I ask, forcing myself to think ahead. I don't like the idea of sitting in a raft while two of the people I care most for in the world drown.

"Paddle," Jost says, swinging a long stick up for me to see.

I eye it apprehensively. "You want me to do what with that?"

Jost swings it in a small circle, dipping the flat end of it and then raising it back up for a split second before dipping it through the air once more. "I'll call beats from behind. Right and left. If we're going to get across this current, we'll need to time things well."

Behind him the water smashes hard against the rocks, each wave unpredictable. How are we supposed to get across that?

"We have four paddles," Jost says. "Ad and Dante will each take a side in the front, and we'll take the rear once we've got you over the surf."

"And me?" Valery asks, her voice lacking the miffed tone she usually takes when she's left out.

"You sit in the middle and look pretty," Erik says.

She gives him a scathing look, but lets him help her into the center of the raft.

"What if we go over?" I ask. The wind has picked up and it bites against my face.

"If you go over, we can't help you," Jost says. "Once we're out there, you're gone. This current is fast."

I find myself looking for a bridge or a boat or something that isn't going to result in my drowning, but I know we don't have time. Since the tide is still high, Dante and I wade in a few feet behind the raft. A wave crashes down across my ankles and I'm surprised at its force. I can't imagine how we'll ever get past the surf.

Erik's arm slides around my waist, taking me by surprise. He steadies me as I climb into the raft and hands me a paddle.

I must look nervous because he leans down to my ear. "Dip it in when he says *right*. As soon as we get past the big waves, I'll be there behind you."

I nod, which makes my ear brush against his lips.

Jost and Erik push the raft hard against the tide and we catch a large wave. For a moment Jost's head disappears below the surface, and a scream rises in my throat but he reappears, pushing us harder. I don't like this, especially when the raft catches a wave and we ride up, threatening to tip over. My nerves twist with each surge of water, but the brothers get us past them. Once the rolling tidal waves are behind us, they both hoist themselves over the side and onto the raft. They have to be freezing, even in their suits, but they set to paddling immediately.

The current tries to push us west, to the middle of the ocean and away from the island, but we beat on against it. I dip my paddle in unison with Jost's orders, although the wind catches his voice and carries off many of the commands. At a distance the waves seem small, but as they crest closer, my heart pounds. I concentrate on timing my paddle strokes to control the helpless panic threatening to break over me with each new swell.

The prison is in sight, towering on the horizon. It stretches across the island, demanding my total focus. All of the answers lie there.

A wave seizes us, and I miss the beat. The force of the ocean knocks the paddle from my hands, and without thinking I reach out for it. I barely have time to register the panic and take a final breath before I go under.

The water is black and cold, and it pushes me with ancient force. My arms stroke against the pressure, but it pushes me farther down until my muscles are on fire. Slowly the burning dissipates and I relax, letting the water take me down, down, down. I open my mouth and let it flow into me until I am the ocean itself. But when the last of the air seeps from my body, I gulp against the pressure until my lungs stop trying and everything goes black.

THIRTY-SEVEN

GLASS SPLINTERS THROUGH MY BODY, the ice-cold water bursting like shards into my skin. And the darkness—a void that presses me into nothing. I'm dead or very close to dead.

Cormac is going to win.

And then life rushes in at me and ebbs quickly out. *Bam!* My eyelids flutter. I see blue, then black. *Bam!* And the water gurgles from my throat. *Bam!* I suck at the air. I hack against the water, and my chest blazes.

"Adelice!"

I want to respond. I want to respond.

"Ad, I won't let you go. Stay with me." Erik's cry is more urgent and his lips are on mine, like a kiss that pumps into my chest, breathing into me.

Lifesaving.

Life changing.

I feel heavy, locked to the rocky shoreline. I want to roll over and drain into the ground, but I can't find the strength.

I'm so exhausted. Erik is next to me. His arm is around me, but he doesn't move.

My body can't respond. For the first time in weeks, I want to cry—to pour my sorrows into a puddle of mistakes beneath me. I let my tears come then. Tears for the life I lost in Arras. Memories overcome me. My parents dancing in the kitchen, my sister giggling over the daily gossip, Enora fussing about my outfit. Running, running, running with no need, because I wanted to. Now I can't stop running long enough to catch my breath, and the whole world seems murky in the strange shadow of Alcatraz.

I struggle to my feet, my muscles protesting the movement. Immediately I regret standing. Not only does it hurt, but also, it's cold. My suit flaps at the waist, and I realize Erik must have undone it to save me. I stare down at him. He isn't moving and the shaking starts, rolling through me as powerfully as the waves that snatched me from the raft.

The cold makes the tremors of my body more violent, and I realize my clothing is soaked. I drop back onto the ground as quietly as I can and maneuver into Erik's arms.

"You okay?" he murmurs, his eyes still shut.

"I think so." But as I speak, my teeth chatter, the chill curling into my fingers and into my core.

Erik snaps to and stares at me, his eyes wide with concern. Then a moment later he starts unbuttoning my wet jacket.

"What are you doing?" I demand, trying to find the strength to pull away.

"Stop fighting me," he says as he strips off my jacket and starts on my shirt.

"Erik," I begin, but the shuddering stops my tongue from forming words.

He doesn't speak, just tugs my shirt off. I'm too cold and too tired to feel self-conscious or awkward. And then he starts stripping himself.

"Erik!" It's more of a shriek than a name.

Erik wraps his arms around me, drawing me closer until I'm cocooned in the heat of his body. My skin wakes and warms to his, and we stare at each other until I feel heat rising everywhere.

"I thought I lost you," he murmurs.

"You didn't," I say.

"Adelice, I—"

"I know," I stop him.

His lips are on mine, full but gentle, and I feel liberated by his kiss. The want of it. The need of it. We crush against each other. I explore every bit of his mouth—the subtle bow in his top lip, the softness of his bottom lip, where the two crease. When we pull apart, he's breathless and wide-eyed, and I see myself, equally excited, reflected back in his irises.

After a few awkward pants, I laugh, and his mouth splits into a wide grin.

"We have horrible timing," I say.

"No," he says, showering me with dozens of tiny kisses. "Better late than never."

He hovers over me, and I know we have to go. We have to find the others.

"We'll have our time, Ad," he promises me.

I reach up and brush his hair behind his ears, noticing that my fingers still tremble even though I'm no longer cold. I want to believe him.

* * *

The terrain onshore is difficult to navigate. The wild grass can't be counted on for help. One handful might give me enough leverage to hike up higher, but the next betrays me. Erik pauses for a moment, farther up the hill than me.

"You know, Ad," he calls over the bursts of wind off the water, "I could carry you up."

"Like a sack of flour?" I ask in mock interest.

"Nah, like a newlywed," he yells. "Over the threshold into a prison of lies."

"What every girl dreams of," I shout back. I don't stop climbing, although a good part of me would like to see Erik trying to carry me up, and the wicked part of me has other reasons for wanting to be in his arms.

Erik loses his grip and slides back several feet, but I keep going. My effort is rewarded when my hand finds flat, solid ground, and hoisting myself up, I discover a road. Scrambling over the side, I sit and wait for Erik, feet dangling over the precipice I've surmounted.

He takes one look at me and groans. "You're looking smug, Miss Lewys."

"I'm feeling it," I admit, kicking my feet back and forth.

"Mind taking a moment from your superiority and giving me a hand?"

I pull myself to my feet and lean over, arm out wide. "Benevolence is one of my many superior attributes."

Erik uses me to balance, but I sense he's trying not to put too much force on me.

"For Arras's sake," I swear, latching on to his hand more tightly and pulling against his weight, but then he pulls back and I stumble forward under his weight. A small cry escapes my lips before I realize he's already on the road. He's merely pulled me into his arms.

He radiates heat against me, his hair clustered in thick waves from the moisture in the air. In the night, his eyes are silver-gray and wild as the ocean below us.

"I know," he says before I can protest, leaning closer to me, "we don't have time."

I'm caught in the moment. The waves thundering against the rocks, the piercing cries of seagulls, the thick darkness that wraps us in a haze of fog.

"I could make the time. It's another perk of my superiority," I remind him. But before I close the gap between his mouth and mine, light blinds us.

"Ad, this is your father," I hear Dante yell from a distance. "Let go of that boy before you make me vomit."

"I need to speak with him about invoking his parental claims," I mutter, but Erik chuckles.

The rest of the group is on the next bend of the road winding up the side of the island, so Erik and I race toward them. When we reach them, Dante gives me a hug, catching me by surprise. I'm transported back to the night of my retrieval— the last time I felt a parent's arms around me. When he drops his arms, he backs away, not meeting my eyes.

"We thought you both drowned," Valery whispers, looping her arm through mine. "But Jost and Dante wouldn't stop looking."

Wistfulness flashes across her face, but can't settle onto her drawn, tired countenance. I hook an arm around her waist and her head sinks onto my shoulder.

My eyes fall to Jost, but he turns away, not even offering a hello. If he'd had doubts about where my relationship with Erik was heading, he doesn't anymore. I don't blame him for not looking at me. I can't change any of it though, so I trudge forward. Dante nods awkwardly at me. He might be able to pull out his parental feelings in jest, but he can't express them now.

"Have you found the entrance to the prison yet?" Erik asks.

"We've been looking for you," Jost says. His voice, though weary, lacks recrimination.

"You've found us. Let's go," I say, finding myself energized by proximity to our destination.

"Ad." Jost catches my arm and draws me to the side. "I'm glad you're safe. Both of you."

We shift awkwardly and I think he might hug me, but he doesn't. Instead he gives me a small smile before he turns back to our mission.

The island is dark, no light shining from the wind-beaten watchtower. Without the sun, the only light comes from the stars and a crescent moon perched in the dusky sky. The silhouette of the fortress grows larger as we draw nearer. It should intimidate, but all I feel is the tug of familiarity. Stone walls that reach to the sky, a well-placed turret. It's not so different from the Coventry, except this prison has windows—something the Guild didn't permit us. But even with windows, it looks impossible to escape this place.

A variety of buildings dot the perimeter, but they are as silent as death. Save for the occasional dancing light that disappears as soon as I turn to follow it, there's no sign of life.

"What if no one's here?" I ask Dante.

"Then we keep looking," he assures me, but there's doubt seeping into his words. Perhaps he's starting to understand the role of a father after all. He's trying to offer me comfort and assurance even if it's a lie.

If Alcatraz is abandoned, where we will start? I know it will come to a decision: keep looking or reenter Arras through the loophole to save our families. For the first time, standing on the brink of discovery, I face the possibility of returning. I know I can't—won't—go back. I can't choose Amie over an entire world, and I buoy myself against the ache of that realization, because if I let myself feel it, I'll shatter on the spot.

The yard is enclosed by a concrete wall and foreboding-looking wire loops across the top. We circle the perimeter for a long time before we find a loading dock that leads us to an entrance.

"I thought there would be more security," Jost notes. He takes a few steps forward so the handlight's beam travels to the front of the prison.

"Yeah, this place looks dead," Valery says in a small voice. "Maybe we should turn back."

"No," I say firmly. "This place is huge. We won't know anything until we get inside."

Valery whimpers her acquiescence. Dante draws a gun from its holster and hands it to Erik. Jost already has one.

"If something happens, the best thing you can do is warp us some safety," Dante tells me.

The thought stops me cold. Even with practice, I've barely been able to control my grasp on Earth's wild strands. If I choose the wrong one, I could sever one of them. I could bring Alcatraz tumbling down on us.

Dante stops and places a hand on my shoulder. "You can do it, Adelice. You'll have to."

We snake through the entrance, looking for a way inside the prison. We're about to give up when a creak puts us on high alert. No one moves in the group, but as the seconds tick by it seems more likely that we're dealing with the wind and nothing more. The entrance empties into a small sally port like the ones used in the Icebox safe house. The door on the other side is unlocked. If the Whorl was here, they wouldn't allow such lax conditions. My heart sinks right as a gunshot whistles by and buffets along the walls behind me. I'm so taken aback that I don't react until Dante shoves me to the ground, his other arm swinging his gun into position in front of him. The crack of bullets bounces around the large concrete enclosure and I snap to, willing myself to see the wild fabric of the universe. To my surprise it comes into focus easily and I realize we're not dealing with a vacant, decrepit building. The prison has been reinforced against both nature and time.

The strands of time don't flash with the inconsistency I've grown accustomed to. They aren't wild, but rigid and set, making them easier to see and harder to manipulate. But it's amazing what adrenaline can do and I wrench a long, thick strand from its locked position and ruffle it in my hand. The effect is instantaneous, the warp blocking a shot just in time. The bullet ricochets off the strands, skittering across the floor. From a distance I see the guard who's shooting at us peek out from behind a concrete pillar, confused by what's happened. It's the opening we need, and Dante fires around the warped spot, hitting him in the shoulder. The guard's gun clatters to the floor and he falls back. Alive, but stunned.

Scrambling to our feet, we rush at him. Erik grabs his gun, tucking it into the waistband of his pants.

"Where are the others?" Dante demands, pressing the muzzle of his gun to the wounded man's temple.

"There are none," the guard splutters. "Only me."

"We'll find them," Dante threatens.

"Only my family. Please don't hurt them," he begs, clutching his bloody shoulder.

"We won't hurt your family," I say softly. "I promise. We need to know if there are other guards."

"No one else is here but the scientist," he says quickly.

"The scientist?" Dante repeats, daring a glance at me.

"Are you going to kill him?" the guard asks in a tremulous voice.

"We're going to save him," I say.

The guard's eyes dart to each of us, trying to make sense of who we are and why we've come. "They don't keep him here." He nods to the silent cell block behind him. "He lives in the old warden's house."

I'd expected to steal a machine, not stumble upon a scientist tucked away on a prison island.

"If you're smart," Dante says, his gun still on the guard, "you'll get your wife to tend to that wound and then you'll get off this island. If you come back for us, she'll be burying you. Do you understand?"

The man groans a yes, clearly torn between his duty and his life.

"I can't promise they won't hurt your family if you attack us again, Lucas," I say, reading the name tag on the guard's antiquated uniform.

Dante doesn't lower his gun as the man shuffles toward the exit and I wait, dread pulsing through me, to see if he'll shoot him. As soon as he gets to the door, Dante calls out and I freeze expectantly. "Lucas, I wouldn't bother contacting your superiors—not if you want to protect your family. I'd hide if I were you."

"Where?" Lucas asks in a hopeless tone. "There's nowhere to hide from them."

"The Icebox," Dante answers.

"That's four hours from here."

"You better get moving then," Dante says. "And don't look back."

He nods once at us, revulsion and shame mingling in his features.

"Why would they keep a scientist on the island but outside the prison?" I ask. "They have all these cells."

"Prisoners are happier when they forget they're in a cage," Erik reminds me.

"But if he's not locked up, why doesn't he leave?" Valery asks in a shaking voice. Her features are pale with fear.

"Look at this rock," I tell her. "There's no escaping." I keep my thoughts about the composition of the prison to myself. If the Guild has artificially altered it, I need to study it more to understand how and why they've used such resources, although I have a pretty good idea already. Whatever secrets the Guild keeps here are locked not only on this island but also in time, like the moments I warped to guard my rendezvouses with Jost at the Coventry.

"Actually, it's a good thing that he's not locked up," Dante assures Valery.

She gives him a blank look. I'm not sure I know what he's getting at either.

"The scientist will have food," Dante says, making for the exit. "I'm hungry."

THIRTY-EIGHT

THE WARDEN'S HOUSE LIES BEYOND THE PRISON—far enough to be both convenient to it and secluded from it. Its stone façade sweeps into elegant lines and a tiled roof. Light glows from several of the oversized windows as we make our way to the door. The boys keep their guns raised, and I catch Dante looking back over his shoulder.

We congregate on a worn porch, and I rap on the door. Then we wait, barely breathing, for an answer.

When the door swings open, I can't stifle my surprise. I know the scientist. He's the man from the news clipping in the Old Curiosity Shop and from the propaganda film I watched at Kincaid's estate. *Kairos.* He's no older now than he was then. He has the same aging skin and shock of unkempt white hair. His eyes are ancient and tired.

"Company," he says. His tone is friendly but his voice peaks strangely on the word, highlighting the vowels and making them sound exotic on his tongue. He ignores the guns leveled at his head. "I was making tea. I'll have to put more water on."

"Hold it right there," Dante says.

"My boy," the scientist says, and I hear the slight shift in his tone—not to anger but rather annoyance—"I'm a man of science, not violence. Keep your guns if you must, but I promise I'm not going to attack you with boiling water."

I bite against the smile tugging at my lips. No one makes a move to go inside, so I step forward, following him as he shuffles off. Erik is at my side in an instant. He's lowered his gun, but it's still in his hand.

"Your friend does not trust me," the scientist notes.

I blush a little, oddly embarrassed to feel we've insulted him with our wariness. It's a strange reaction given that I know I'm in the presence of the man who's responsible for creating the first looms and Arras itself.

"He's a little protective," I say apologetically.

"Ah, a beau then?" the old man asks with a wink, and I flush more.

"I won't let them shoot you," I say.

The man's head falls back and he laughs, deep and bellowing, ignoring the kettle he's filling. "I like you. I will pretend that was a joke and that we are friends. Yes?"

"Yes," I confirm with a smile.

"What are your names?" he asks, setting the kettle to heat on the stove. He ambles to the cupboard and riffles through its contents. Next to me Erik cracks his knuckles until I push his hands apart.

"I'm Adelice Lewys," I say.

"And you are here to destroy the Guild of Twelve Nations?" He says the last words with mock ferocity, but I hear it in his voice: he's not mocking our desire, he's dismissing it. He must have seen his fair share of failed attempts to destroy the Guild over the years.

"I suppose," I say. "I want to separate the worlds. Not destroy them per se."

"A worthy ambition," he notes. "If a foolish one."

I blink against his honesty. He offers me a mug with a tea bag perched and waiting inside. "You bear my mark."

I look at my outstretched hand, at my techprint, and nod. "Kairos. Your name."

"Not my name, but I'm flattered. They called me Dr. Albert Einstein before they called me a traitor and stuck me in here," he says.

"Dr. Einstein, I'm Adelice," I say, this time offering my right hand to shake his. It feels awkward given my own preference for the left hand, but we manage it.

"Albert," he says firmly. "Call me Albert. I have not been called Dr. Einstein in so long it feels I have lost the privilege."

"We have a lot of questions," Erik says. He's juggling the gun and a chipped teacup and it makes me laugh.

"I think you can put that away," I say, motioning to his weapon.

Erik takes a long look at Albert and then looks back at me. I nod encouragingly and he slips the gun into his waistband.

"Yes, but it will not do to answer them here," Albert says as the teakettle shrieks its readiness on the stove. "And the tea is ready."

Albert carefully pours the boiling water into the waiting cups, trying not to spill and apologizing repeatedly for the few drops that splash onto our hands. He's no threat, but that might mean he's no help either. I help him with the mugs and we take them into the other room and disburse them to Jost, Dante, and Valery. The three linger, uncomfortably, in the sitting room and Albert gestures for them to sit down while he goes to shut the front door.

When he returns he introduces himself and waits patiently while the others give their names. He repeats each as if consigning it to memory.

"We have a lot of questions, Albert," Dante says. "Not the least of which is why you're living here."

"Instead of the cold prison?" Albert guesses. "A concession for good behavior. The Guild of Twelve Nations views me as a threat intellectually not physically. As long as people are kept away from me, I'm not a risk."

"And your guard and his family?" Jost asks.

"Lucas and his family are simple people. Lovely supper guests, but not terribly interested in physics and my scientific mumbo jumbo." Albert pauses, his cup hovering near his lips. His whiskers tickling its rim. "I do hope you have not hurt them."

"We sent them away," I assure him. "We're not here to hurt anyone."

"A curious method of revolution."

"We're not here to hurt anyone who is innocent," Dante corrects.

"But what is innocence?" Albert muses. *"Ignorance?"*

"Maybe," Dante says, shifting in his chair.

"Or good intentions?" Albert adds.

I look across the room at my companions. Only Erik seems at ease, blowing steam off his tea and taking shallow sips. The rest roost with their shoulders hunched, hanging on Albert's every word.

344

"Maybe a gut reaction," I offer. "Lucas was acting on orders. Something we can *all* forgive."

"You have acted under orders then?" he asks.

I remember the thick, coarse strand I removed from the loom under Loricel's watchful eye. I had acted under orders with good intentions, but under Albert's piercing gaze, I don't feel absolved.

"I have," I admit, "but not anymore."

"And that is how you became a rebel," he says. "Did you flee from Arras or were you born of Earth?"

"We're refugees," I tell him.

"So many of you and so young. How did you discover the truth?"

"I was taken into service," I begin.

"A renegade Spinster? Delightful."

"Adelice was set to be the new Creweler, and she can alter." Erik jumps in. I flash him a look for interrupting me, but it's clear he thought I should cut to the chase.

"Then you are the one I've waited for." Albert's words are so soft that I'm not sure anyone else heard them, as though they were meant only for me. "Do you each bear the mark of Kairos?"

"No," Dante says. "Only Adelice and I do. The true rebellion died out years ago, but we are rebuilding. Although another man pretends to have the same agenda as our predecessors."

"There is a *false* rebellion now?" Albert asks questions with the interest of a man awoken from a long sleep. He has no idea what's happened in the outside world since he was left here.

"A man named Kincaid wants to find the Whorl," I tell him.

"I know Kincaid," Albert says darkly. "If he's fallen from the Guild's favor, he's no one to trifle with."

"Unfortunately we learned that the hard way," I say.

"So this is it?" Albert asks. "The final withering offspring of rebellion."

"No, there are more of us, but not enough to stand up to the Guild." Dante has told me of the expectations he had when he came to Earth, of the stories his mother—my grandmother—whispered to him of a powerful legion of men who could free Arras. But they were only stories, and the rebellion was once a fledgling barely able to stand on its own legs.

"When they locked me away, armies were mounting," Albert says, slipping into nostalgia. "They weren't my armies though. No matter what they claimed."

"Why not?" I ask, surprised.

"Because I wasn't interested in starting another war. I didn't believe it was my place to end the Guild or their politics. I merely wanted to stop their destruction of those that remained on this planet. The best way to do this was to separate the worlds and end Arras's dependence on Earth." His tea sloshes dangerously as he waves his arms.

"But you must have known what the Guild was capable of," I say.

"The Guild is not so different from the governments of Earth. Civil war, world war, these are the inventions of men," he says. "Terrible inventions, but part of the span of human history. Perhaps someday we may as a species evolve past violence."

"And you think the Guild is capable of that kind of growth?" Jost asks in a mocking tone full of resentment. "I've seen what the Guild can do. There's been no evolution."

"Evolution is dependent on change. The change of generations. Children learn from the mistakes of their parents. Even small shifts can create a ripple effect, moving people forward, bringing progress. But how can such change occur if the generations are stymied?" he asks, letting the question linger in the air above us.

"You're referring to the race of immortals running this party," Dante says, leaning forward. His tea is abandoned on the table next to him. "Immortals you created."

"A most regrettable side effect," Albert admits. "We were working on a tight deadline against our enemies. The weapon the Axis powers were perfecting could have destroyed everyone. It was a bomb unlike anything the Earth had ever seen. I warned the Allied powers, and when they presented an alternate solution meant to preserve life—"

"The Cypress Project?" I guess.

Albert nods. "I was the one who introduced the idea of splicing strands into threads. It was meant to prevent illness and strengthen the population. We could not foresee the effect this new world would have on the immune system, but our technology could circumvent unexpected diseases. Renewal patching was meant to safeguard the fledgling population."

"But the Guild abused the technology you created."

"It is every scientist's dream to better the human condition. But, as you surmised, the officials realized they could use the technology to prevent aging. It allowed them to stay in power."

"It gave them absolute power," I say.

"A very dangerous thing," Albert says with a sigh. "In retrospect I should have anticipated this issue, but the government didn't give us time to think outside of creating the looms and starting the project. I didn't stop to consider how the looms could be misused. I was merely concerned with making Arras functional and safe for the population. I have often regretted my participation, but I do accept my role in what was done."

Shame falls over his face, but I see the value behind his motives. Unlike Cormac, who tried to sell me on the good of the many, Albert actually acted in such parameters. He had done what seemed best, only to realize too late the dreadful repercussions his actions would cause.

"Why not bomb Arras? Take them down?" Erik asks, and I frown at his callous suggestion.

Albert's answer mirrors my thoughts. "I wanted to save lives, not destroy them."

"How did that work out for you?" Dante challenges.

"Intentions again. I accept my role, and if you could do the same, we could move on," Albert replies.

The reprimand settles over the room. Everyone reacts differently. Dante sits up straighter. Jost and Erik look at each other. Valery slouches, turning her attention to the window.

"You said you didn't anticipate the Guild misusing the looms," I say, prompting him to return to more fruitful topics.

"I did not," he admits. "I should have. You must understand, the government pushed forward with the project, but they weren't the ones who would form the Twelve Nations. Not as you understand them today."

"If the Guild isn't comprised of the governments of the nations, who are these men? Who is Cormac Patton?" I ask.

"Ah, Patton, nasty piece of work but a very rich man. They all were. War had stretched America's funds to the brink.

Families were living on rations and going without. Everyone was doing their bit to help, and many of the other nations in the Cypress Project were doing the same."

"Funny that they never bothered to get rid of those provisions once Arras was a reality," Jost mutters.

"There is security in knowing your people are totally dependent on you to survive," Albert says. "That was one of the first indications that something had rotted at the core of the Cypress Project. I'd had qualms about allowing the financial backers of the project to take positions of authority, but I was merely a scientist. No one would listen to me."

"No one listens to the man who creates the solution," Erik says with an empty laugh. "No wonder things didn't work out."

Albert raises his cup to this as if toasting the lunacy of the predicament. "The officials were heavily involved with the project. These were powerful men—men of immense wealth— and they seemed obsessed with a positive outcome as long as it guaranteed a world where their own standing would not be diminished."

"Warning sign number two," I say.

"Indeed. But they were invested in how the science of the looms could benefit their businesses. They sold us on their concern about the world, the people, their customers. I recognized the greed in them."

"But you missed their ambition to use the looms as a fountain of youth," Dante points out.

"Having never been obsessed with such a ludicrous notion, I did. I fancied myself a man of science, not a man looking for glory and immortality. It never occurred to me," Albert says.

"But how did they do it then? If you didn't help?" I ask.

"Not every one of the scientists shared my ideals, but many of them shared my intelligence. Men like Cormac and Kincaid hung around asking questions—not to explore how the looms could be used to their advantage, but to ascertain who among the scientists could help them achieve these possible benefits."

"So one of your men turned on you." It's Valery who points this out.

"Yes, my lady. The officials established who would help them in their grand plans and set it in motion in secret laboratories in Arras."

"And they made themselves immortal," I say.

"That is not entirely correct." Albert stops me. "To truly be immortal, you would have to be nearly untouchable. They are still vulnerable to disease and injury."

"But they have those who can alter and patch them into health."

"Yes, but their so-called immortality skirts a fine line. It can be taken in an instant."

"So Cormac can be killed," I say.

"He can," Albert confirms. "Do you feel it necessary?"

"How else can we liberate the people? Separate Earth from Arras?" Dante cries, the words a fervent verdict of Cormac's fate. "The Guild's time is up."

Albert holds my gaze. He's not asking us a practical question, he's asking me an ethical one. He's asking me to look inside myself and see how far I'm willing to go.

"If we separated the worlds, Arras would have to learn to

depend on its own resources. There would be upheaval. Change," I say softly.

"The course of evolution would begin again," Albert replies.

"Does anyone have any clue what we're talking about?" Erik asks, but Dante tells him to shut up. If the others are having trouble following, they aren't about to interrupt.

"Where do we begin?" I ask.

"I can guide you," Albert says, a sad smile peeking from beneath his mustache, "but it will be difficult. Arras is a parasitic universe syphoning Earth's time and resources, but if the edges of Arras were bound and released, the composition of Earth would achieve critical mass, creating a rift in space-time that Arras could occupy, separate from Earth. It could heal. The looms would be useless then, but Arras would be self-sustaining."

"And the Whorl can do this?" I ask in a breathless voice, trying to wrap my head around what Albert is telling us. If Arras was separated from Earth, both could survive. I wouldn't have to choose which world to save, and I could prevent the growing threat of all-out war between them.

"The Whorl can tie the edges of Arras together, separating them from the looms and knitting Arras's time into an infinite weave." Albert knits his fingers together into a circle and holds it to his eyes. "Time will flow from beginning to end in a ceaseless circle of life."

"That's why we need you. We need the Whorl," Dante says.

"Ah, dear boy, I do not have the Whorl."

"Then where is it?" Jost demands. He's risen from his seat

and he grips the mantel. His desperation to get back to Arras and save Sebrina is written in anguished lines over his face.

"The Whorl is not a thing. It is a person," Albert says.

"You're the Whorl," Dante guesses.

"No," Albert says with a shake of his head. "She is."

His finger points directly at me.

THIRTY-NINE

THE BURDEN OF HIS WORDS SETTLES DOWN on me, weighing across my chest. I don't hear how the others react. They blur out of focus as I'm forced once again to confront responsibility and purpose. I should be accustomed to this tangled dance of power and obligation, but I feel the constriction of it. I tried to let go of the idea of saving myself, of saving Amie, but the idea of saving the world on my own—of wielding such terrible and awesome power—is nearly more than I can bear.

"Adelice." Erik is beside me, coaxing me back to the present. His hands are wrapped, hot, around my wrists. "You okay?"

I anchor myself in his presence. Erik pushes me and accepts me when I'm still only human. If I can latch on to him and syphon his strength, maybe I can face what's coming next.

"How can you know that?" Dante is demanding of Albert. I focus on his words, willing my mind to participate in the exchange of information.

"You said she was the Creweler," Albert says, but he's holding something back. I can see that.

"I was supposed to be the Creweler," I correct. "I never finished my training."

"So you can catch the elements and command them," he says. "What else? There is more."

I nod, pushing the information out of my torpid mind. "I can alter like a Tailor."

"So genetically you have both powers," he says.

"Yes, I must have gotten them from my parents," I say, filling him in on the strange relationship between Dante and me. On how the time dilation has affected our lives' courses as we lived on the disparate timelines of two worlds.

"Has your mother been tested? It would be interesting to analyze her genetic makeup, along with his—"

I stop him before the lump in my throat swells and dams my voice. "My mother is a Remnant. I doubt she'd cooperate."

"Her mother's genetics and mine," Dante jumps in, "created something special, unique, like a mutation."

"Not exactly, dear boy," Albert says, and then pauses. "I feel especially strange calling you that now, given that you have a nearly grown daughter."

"It's weird for the rest of us, too," Erik says.

"Genetic abilities skip around, appearing in seemingly strange fashion, but they're not random. Once it became clear that I had a method of separating the worlds, the Guild worked feverishly to prevent that from happening," Albert says.

"Why? Why would they want to remain dependent on Earth?" Jost asks. "Earth was a threat to them."

"And an opportunity. You must not forget these were

354

businessmen," Albert tells him. "Earth had resources, and the Guild was uncertain we wouldn't require more of them. But I think, truly, they were unable to divorce themselves from the possibility of this world. What if they could discover ways of using it to their own advantage later? And then there was the real need of a hiding spot should their schemes be discovered."

"In case anyone found out the same men were running the show," I say.

"But they had Tailors to keep that a secret," Dante says.

"Yes, but men are fickle. Uprisings occur no matter how tightly you grip the masses in your hands. Earth was an insurance plan, but more important, tying Arras off from Earth would take away their looms. It would take away their control.

"Your story about your unusual parentage answers a lot of my questions," Albert continues. "The Guild tried very hard to prevent you from existing."

"And they've always seemed overeager to have me." None of this was news. Dante had told me this before, but Albert had insights Dante could only guess at.

"Marriage laws, segregation, courtship appointments. It is a strange way to run a world, no?" Albert asks.

"They told us we had to be pure."

"An antiquated means of control, but unfortunately many well-meaning parents and authorities bought into it. Those laws enabled the Guild to hide the true motivation behind their actions."

"Which was?" Dante asks.

"Controlling the genetics of those who came into the weave," he says. "We engineered Spinsters, cultivated the creative, life-giving nature of women, but Tailors were an unanticipated side effect."

"How did it happen?" I ask.

"We studied boys, too. We needed to see how the experiments would affect male offspring. They did not seem to possess the necessary abilities, so we felt assured we could measure and control the populace. We could easily guess which girls might be born with the ability. Marriages were arranged, children were watched, we waited for signs."

I recall Loricel telling me how she watched me, covered up for me. No one would second-guess her motives. It was clear she had wanted to be done with the system after decades of choosing sacrifice over self, but how had they not known I could be the thing they dreaded the most?

"So you tagged us?" Dante says with a note of disgust.

"I'm afraid so. When we realized we had misunderstood the nature of the genetic ability in boys, I saw my opportunity. A child born with both sets of the genetic makeup to weave and to alter could bind Earth off. Everything centered on that child."

"It couldn't have been a boy then?" I ask.

"No, only a girl could possess both genetic traits. The weaving trait refused to manifest in male children, but alteration could pass to a female. The Guild worked hard to prevent that through monitoring the population," Albert explains.

"But I don't understand," Jost interrupts. "How can she have both if the abilities are both born of the same engineering?"

"The genes evolved, much in the way that genes have evolved to make us smarter, more resilient. Think of it as lines in a book." Albert lifts a volume from the table near him and opens to a page. "We cannot have two line ones in the same book. Weaving is line one, and Tailoring, or altering, is line two. They are different lines of the genetic code. Adelice possesses both genetic lines from her parents. They are separate and unique abilities, even though on a fundamental level their structure and composition are strikingly similar."

"And because I have both I can capture the elements needed to ensure Arras is whole—"

"While being able to tie it off, altering its fundamental makeup in the most profound way," Albert says, his words more an intonation to the universe than fact.

"Good," I say, blinking. "I wouldn't want this to be easy."

"I know it is a lot to take in," Albert says.

"Yes, and we're on a timetable," Dante butts in. "We're going to have to sort out this tangled web elsewhere."

Albert gives him a curious look. "You assume Lucas will betray you?"

"Remember how we said we fell in with Kincaid," I say quietly. "We gave him the slip, but it won't take him long to track us."

"I see," Albert says. "If you have the abilities you claim, you know it will be difficult for me to leave this island. I will need your assistance."

I pause and stare at him, not understanding.

"You must see it," he prompts. "Use your sight, Adelice."

Everything around me fades to the background, softening into a weave. The room comes to life in a snarl of colors and light. The time threads are frozen into place. I stare harder at Albert, willing myself to see his composition. It's still difficult for me and I slow my breath and let go until he shifts into strands of the universe—strands tied to the time of this room.

"That's why you're allowed to live here," I say. "They've bound you to this moment. This house." Albert couldn't leave if he wanted to, not without help from someone who had the skill to disentangle him from the weave of the house's place and time. He was frozen in a prison of space and time.

"Say what?" Jost asks.

"He's been altered. They've wound Albert's strands into the time and matter here." I turn pleading eyes to Erik, knowing he can see it as clearly as I can, but he gives me the barest shake of his head. He won't reveal his secret, and I feel the burning promise I made to him in my very flesh.

"So he's a part of the house," Erik says slowly, obviously playing dumb.

"More or less," I confirm for the benefit of the others.

"Can you, I don't know, extract him?" Erik asks.

"I think I can."

"I was hoping for a bit more assurance," Erik says.

"I can," I say more confidently, "with *Dante's* help." I want Erik to volunteer, but he's made it clear that he won't admit his alteration skills to his brother.

Dante nods, surveying Albert and the objects in the room.

"Why don't you guys wait outside?" Dante suggests.

As soon as the others leave, Dante comes to my side and I see the same look of concentration cross his face. I know he can see the composition of Albert and the objects in the room, which should be enough.

"Can you see it?" I ask.

"I think so, but, Ad, I'm not as gifted as you are," he says, squeezing my hand. "I can see Albert's strands, but it's obvious this is more advanced than simple alteration. You need someone with real training. Someone who knows the Guild's handiwork better than I." The statement peaks on the final word, and he leaves it hanging there. He knows Erik can alter, but he leaves the suggestion open.

"I know, but that's why I need *you*," I say with emphasis. "I can see the big picture. I can see how they've manipulated the time in here, and once I release it, he'll need you to bind it off."

"Tie it off?" Dante says, unsure.

"You'll see. Watch his strands, once he's released from the time of the room, he'll be leaching time, sort of like bleeding, I guess. You have to stop the bleeding. That's all."

Albert in the meantime has remained in his seat, watching us with fascination.

"Are you ready for us to try, Doctor?" I ask.

"Yes," he says.

"I can't guarantee anything," I warn him.

"I understand and accept that. The mortal man in me is—admittedly—a bit afraid. Not so much of death but of pain. It was not pleasant when they did this to me in the first place. But the scientist in me is eager for the adventure. Your abilities fascinate me."

"You say that now," Dante mutters.

I take a deep breath and focus on the room. There are many strands at play in the composition of it, but perhaps because it's more reminiscent of the artificial weave of Arras, I feel oddly at ease. I understand how this room exists and how Albert exists within it. He is part of the larger tapestry of the house, connected to the sluggish time strands that lie within its permanent architecture—objects locked into place and time. In short, a house. The trick will be to rend him of them quickly and with as little pain as possible. I focus harder until I see Albert, his natural time allotment interlaced with the permanent time of the house, locking him into place. I have to separate his strands and sever those of the room. If I fail, if I accidentally sever one of his natural time strands, the results could be disastrous, but I try not to think about that.

"I wish I had a hook or something," I mutter.

"Why?" Dante asks in a shaky voice.

"I need to rip something. It would be easier."

"How did you rip through Arras?" Dante asks.

"I was *really* pissed off," I admit.

"Can you channel that, but maybe over at the wall?" Dante suggests. "If you severed the time over there, we could pull it through his strands."

This is why I asked for Dante's help. His second set of eyes proves invaluable. I'd been planning on severing the time of the room within Albert, which might have gotten messy.

"It would help if I was pissed off," I point out.

"You need help getting there? Let's see. Kincaid betrayed you. Planned to alter you. Your sister is in the Coventry, and Arras knows what they've done to her. They've murdered your f-father." Dante stumbles on the word. "Your whole world is built on lies. Am I helping?"

I feel the familiar ache of rage rising in my chest.

"And if you don't do this, we'll die at the Guild's hands," Dante adds softly. "They'll kill me and him. They'll kill Jost, Erik. If they don't turn them into monsters first."

Something snaps inside, something I'm unwilling to reason with or fight, and I reach out and rend the weave of the room. It splits down the middle in a jagged line. As it hangs open, the room around us starts to change. Furniture cracks and the walls crumble down. The room is unwinding on itself.

"I should have seen that coming," I say.

"Albert!" Dante shouts. Before us he trembles, aging slowly before our eyes, withering as we stare in horror.

"We have to extract him now. He's decaying with the room."

Dante and I set to work, gripping the severed time strands and sliding them out of Albert, extricating him quickly from the fractured web of time in the room. With each strand that's pulled through him, he spasms, but the aging slows and his breathing returns to normal. He still bears the marks of age from the accelerated entropy, but he's free.

Around us the room continues to crumble, falling in at the corners, and turning to dust. If I hadn't had Dante to help me there was no way I could have extracted him in time. Dante pulls Albert up, and the old scientist rests against our shoulders as we dash toward the front door.

Amid the crumbling of wood and walls, Albert leans into me and whispers something in my ear. With time crashing in on us, the words barely process in my distracted mind, but they lodge there. I don't have time to contemplate their meaning now.

Outside, the others wait. Jost paces the porch and Erik leans against the frame of the house, but Valery grips the railing, looking out on the choppy waters of the bay.

"It worked?" Jost says, jumping to help Dante bring Albert into the night air.

"Yes, but we've got to get out of here. The house isn't stable," I say.

"My papers," Albert says with a moan.

"Where are they?" Dante asks. "I'll go for them."

"My study. The third door on the second level." Albert's voice is small and tired.

Dante and I exchange a look. Going back in will be dangerous, but he rushes into the house before I can say anything to stop him.

"We should go now," Valery calls.

"Let's give him a minute to catch his breath," Jost suggests.

"No!" Valery's refusal startles me, and I turn to her. Her shape is small against the blank night sky, but I see why she's pushing us. In the distance, an aeroship is hovering over the water, coming closer to the island by the second.

"We've got company," I yell.

"Who?" Erik asks, coming to my side. "Kincaid?"

"I can't tell," I say.

Valery turns to us, and even in the dark I see her face is hollow. "The Guild."

"How can you know that?" I ask.

She pauses, and I already dread her answer.

"Because I told them we would be here."

FORTY

"WHAT?" I ASK, MY MIND TRYING TO process the rapidly decaying house behind me, the sight of the hovering aeroship in the distance, and Valery's betrayal at the same time.

It's a bit too much to take in at once.

But Erik has his gun drawn. "I thought you landing in our party was a little suspicious. What did it take, Valery?"

She cowers back and he moves forward, edging closer to her, but she doesn't run from him. "They did things to me. You saw the labs, Erik. Don't you remember?"

"And now you've conveniently had a change of heart?" he snarls.

"Erik!" I call in a sharp voice.

"It wasn't like that," Valery says. She points to me as tears begin to stream down her face. "They told me it was your fault. That if I helped them, I could have Enora back, but . . ."

"But?" I prompt.

"They tried to make me forget her. Make me want other things. Cormac said they made me normal, and that when I returned to Arras, I would be happy," she says, choking as she speaks, "because I had served the Guild."

"They sent you here to spy on us," Erik accuses.

"I hated you," Valery says to me. Her words implore me to understand, and part of me does. The part of me that blames myself for Enora's death. "That hate became stronger until it was the only feeling I was sure was true. It consumed me. When I saw you that day in the grey market, I wanted to lure you into an alley and do what the Guild wouldn't do."

Icicles crawl down my spine, branching out in chills through my body. So I hadn't imagined seeing Valery that day, but I didn't know she had seen me, too.

"But you didn't," I say. "You didn't do that, Valery. You're better than they would let you be."

"No, I followed orders. I led you to the shop, so that you would find the truth. Seek Kincaid and walk into their arms. They knew you would come here eventually, but only after you led Kincaid to the same place."

Every moment has been engineered since we got here, carefully executed to ensure we would be standing here right now. Have all our decisions been so carefully directed by Valery? I consider how she warmed to us at the estate after being cold and unfriendly and then shifted back to coldness. Her connection with Deniel, the Tailor who attacked me. The rest is murky.

"You sent Deniel," I accuse her, "so I would distrust Kincaid."

"Cormac's idea," Valery admits. "He knew you would turn against him after you went snooping. We only had to get you to snoop."

"Bit of a gamble," Erik says.

"That's the thing. The reason I've hated Adelice the most. She tries to do what's right even at the cost of alliances and power."

"And you hate me for that?"

"I hated you because it's not that simple," she cries. "Don't you see what you're sacrificing? Who you're sacrificing?"

This time I advance on her, my fists balled, my body shaking. "I never wanted this. I've done the best I can. Do you want me to become another Creweler locked in a room doing the best I can? Or worse—Cormac?"

"I'm starting to understand." Valery holds her hands out, stopping my advance and my words. "I tried to keep hating you, but I can't anymore."

"How is that even possible?" Jost asks, and it's clear he doesn't believe her.

"Emotional and psychological alteration is tricky," Dante says, and I turn to see he's been here listening to her confession. "It takes the most talented of Tailors. Don't do it properly and it never fully takes, but alter too much and you wind up with a void, someone who seems half human, half there. Altering a person's psychology can have drastic effects, turning a person into a blank slate."

Beth, the girl next door when I was a child, a variant in her own little world. The citizens of Cypress watching with apathy as I cut the ribbon on their new school. Enora blankly reciting the Guild's plan to map me. I've seen it myself throughout my life in Arras, never knowing how deep the Guild's fingers were in the minds of those around me.

"But Enora was like Valery," I say, pointing to her. "Except more . . ."

"Cunning?" he asks. "It should have been a warning sign, but it's easy enough to overlook on Earth. They couldn't remove her memories of you entirely, not if they wanted her to find you. But if she was your friend's lover, they removed that. Spliced what they considered to be normal feelings into her."

"I wanted her back," Valery says, a break in her voice. "I remember that. Enough to do anything they asked."

"They couldn't give her back to you. Enora slipped past their fingers," I tell her.

"I know. I *knew*, but it didn't matter."

Grief is a funny thing, I think. It can make you see things that aren't there and ignore what's in front of your face. Bitterness channels itself into anger and stupid backtalk and a million other destructive impulses. I knew that better than anyone.

"But why now?" Jost asks.

"Because it's too late," Erik says.

"No, it isn't," Valery says. "We can leave off the far side of the island."

"That won't buy us enough time," Dante says to her. "You told us now because the alteration didn't take. You may have hated Adelice, but emotional altering doesn't work if a person changes her mind. Am I right in guessing you no longer harbor a grudge against her?"

"I tried. I wanted to keep hating her, because then it was easier," she says.

Albert lifts his head and in a faint voice addresses us. "Nothing can remove free will. Our self-determination is bound to our very souls. It is the thing that defines our humanity."

"You really want us to get away?" I ask in a low voice that only Valery can hear.

"Yes," she says. "I'll stay. I'll misdirect them, but go."

I know what they'll do to Valery if we leave her behind, and part of me wants to go. The part that reels from her betrayal, that feels led around for months. But she's made the same sacrifice that Enora would have made. That's why they loved each other. I can't blame her for being angry and lashing out. Haven't I done the same? Haven't I risked lives in the Coventry with my smart, unthinking mouth?

"No one gets left behind," I say. "Jost, where's the boat?"

"We circled the island looking for you. It's on the northern side," he says.

"The ship is sailing from the south, so she's right. If we go now there might be enough time to get away," I say. "Get it ready."

"Ad," Erik says in a deep voice, "there's no way we can outrun that ship. Someone should stay behind. If you won't let her, then I'll do it."

"I know you think you have debts to pay, but stop trying to prove yourself," I snap. "I'm not letting any of you stay behind, especially not you."

Behind us the warden's house creaks, and a wall caves in, forcing Dante to drag Albert away from it. Dust from the plaster billows out around us.

"This is the first place they'll come," I say. "We shouldn't wait here."

Everyone scurries across the large concrete yard toward the prison, and the road that will lead us to the boat, but before I reach it, Erik's hand grabs my wrist, stopping me.

"You have to get away, Adelice. They're coming for you and Albert. I can't let them take you," he says.

"Why are you telling me this now? We can all go," I say.

"No, we can't," he says. "Not if there's a chance for you to escape. I can confuse them, lead them into the prison. We'll play hide-and-seek. It'll be fun." He tries to shrug nonchalantly, to look charming and casual and carefree, but his shoulders pitch too high and there's no sparkle in his eyes.

"I can't let you do that," I whisper, turning in to him.

"Yes, you can."

"What makes you so sure?"

"Because we love each other," he murmurs. "And we always knew this day would come."

My lips close over his, sealing the truth of his statement. I linger in the kiss, knowing what I have to do and dreading it. His lips stay firm against mine and his hand stays clasped tight in mine. Our bodies aren't fighting to press closer together. This kiss is gentle and full of promises that can never be fulfilled, and it leaves an ache consuming me. It's the kiss we should have shared long ago but never made the time for, and now it's too late. It's more than goodbye—it's regret.

Now. Only now, a tiny voice urges me.

So I kiss Erik. I kiss him goodbye. I kiss him for all the moments we will never have, and because I know I love him.

Because I know I'm leaving him.

FORTY-ONE

THE BREEZE OFF THE OCEAN GHOSTS THROUGH US. Its chill makes me shiver and Erik pulls away, rubbing my shoulders to warm me, both of us dazed enough to forget where we are for a moment.

Unfortunately, a moment is too long to waste.

"Ahh, young love," purrs a voice. "Isn't that sweet?"

We whirl toward the voice. Ahead of us, the others are frozen to the spot. No one tries to run. We're all trying to figure out what the next move is.

"Not expecting us?" Kincaid asks. "We RSVP'd."

"This is so embarrassing," I say, twisting from Erik's arms. "But we have a previous engagement."

"Yes? That is a pity," Kincaid says, snapping the fingers of his gloves and removing each in delicate order.

Approaching footsteps—many, many footsteps—draw my attention away. Even Kincaid turns, but his face doesn't fall when he sees Cormac Patton approaching. My own sags in frustration. We're seriously outnumbered.

"I've tried to help her with her manners," Cormac's voice calls above the wind. He crunches across the pavement, a small army in tow. "But she's resistant to change."

"I like that," I say to him, pushing against the roar of my pulse in my ears. It's been nearly two months since I faced Cormac, years for him. "I'm 'resistant to change.' I think that's a compliment coming from a would-be immortal."

"Would-be?" Cormac cocks an eyebrow. "Don't under-sell me."

"I'll leave that up to you," I assure him. "And, might I say, Cormac, that you haven't aged a day."

Cormac's smirk deepens. "I'm glad we don't have secrets anymore. Now you know what I can offer you. Erik," he says, turning his attention to him, "I guess I know why you didn't come back. It's impolite to go after your boss's wife."

"Adelice isn't your wife," Erik says, stepping closer to me.

"She will be," Cormac says. "You were supposed to watch her, not help her escape."

"What's he talking about?" Jost demands.

"You know how adept your brother is at keeping secrets, Jost. I suppose he never told you—" Dante begins.

"I see where she gets her smart tongue from," Cormac butts in. "Don't look so surprised, Adelice. Valery has kept us well informed of the many sordid developments from the surface."

"That was low, you old dog," Kincaid says, wagging a finger at Cormac. "You knew she was my style."

"It takes an old dog to know one," Cormac says. "And you know we can't be taught new tricks."

The exchange is cordial, even amused, like old friends bantering.

"That's it!" I yell, stamping my foot. "Don't you want to kill each other?" Because I wouldn't mind killing both of them.

"Of course," Cormac says.

"But we can be gentlemanly about it," Kincaid says.

I storm forward against the protests of Erik.

"You hate him," I say, pointing from Kincaid to Cormac, "and I assume he hates you. Why the charade?"

"I don't hate him," Cormac says. "I pity him."

Kincaid makes a choking noise and flips his gloves in his hands. "I don't need your pity, Cormac. I've found the Whorl. The girl has done her part and extricated him, and now your blessed world will unravel into the universe. My only regret is that you won't be there to fade into the stars with it. But you can watch. Imagine everything you worked for, lied for, killed for—gone."

"Sour grapes," Cormac says with a false laugh. He waves off Kincaid's threat. "Come back to Arras. I'm prime minister. Everything will be running smoothly once we tie up this loose end."

I'm surprised when he gestures to me. "You need me," I remind him.

"Need? Perhaps *want* is a better term. Wait, I have an offer you can't refuse, my love, but right now the men are talking," Cormac says, wagging a finger.

"I don't see any men here," I say, but they ignore me.

"An intriguing proposition," Kincaid says, "but I'm afraid I've grown fond of Earth. My estate is lovely, I took the liberty of claiming it from the man with the newspapers. The one we ripped early on."

"Hearst? I remember him. Troublemaker," Cormac says.

"Arrogant, too."

I can't keep my mouth from falling open at the bizarre exchange. Their eyes shift, feet tap—they're buying time. Each trying to determine the best way to destroy the other.

"The thing is, Arras is monotonous," Kincaid says in a bored voice. "You employ the same standards. You add new tech to control the masses. There's nothing *challenging* there, but you've created a virtual playground on Earth and I'm king of the hill."

"So you'd unravel it?" Cormac says, and his eyes flicker to mine. He wants me to hear this.

"Yes," Kincaid snarls, losing his composure. "I want to watch it fade away like I watched her fade before me. I want to see you burn into the sun, and I want to feel that sun on my skin every day and know that *I put it there* and that I took it from you."

"Destroying it won't bring her back," Cormac says. "And without your petty dreams of revenge, how will you fill that loss?"

"There are other realms to reach for," Kincaid says. "Space, perhaps. Maybe even death someday. This is my world, full of liars and cheats and the unwanted wastrels of Arras—my kind of people. Each more honest than a single official left in Arras."

"And when they rise up and start a war?" Cormac challenges. "How will you control them?"

"Why control them? Kill them. It will be no waste. I have my men. They have skills, as you know. I'll start over if I care to."

"Caring isn't in your vocabulary," Cormac says. "Your ability to care died with her."

"Is that why you exiled me?" Kincaid demands. "So I couldn't force you to pay for what you did to her?"

"I did nothing to her." Cormac's voice stays gentle, catching me off guard.

"You told her lies. You turned her against me," Kincaid says. "Why, Cormac? Why did you want her to hate me?"

"I wanted her to help you. The experiments you were doing were against Guild law."

"What kind of experiments?" I ask, thinking of the X-rays and measurements hidden in the labs of the estate.

"Kincaid dreams not only of controlling Tailors but also of being one himself," Cormac tells me.

"It's the natural step in evolution," Kincaid snarls, "and I was close until you ruined everything."

"I warned her. That's all. What you did to her—that was the result of your madness."

"I'm perfectly sane," Kincaid says. "But you awake the sleeping sword of war."

"Poetic," I mutter.

"Whatever you paid those scientists to do to you, it didn't make you into a Tailor, Kincaid. It stripped you of your humanity. That's why you killed Josin." Cormac doesn't look triumphant as he says it. He looks sad.

And I realize he's right. Kincaid doesn't hunger for power and control like Cormac does, and for the first time, I realize he wants something far more dangerous. Destruction. Total and pure nihilism. This isn't about a lost power play. Whatever transpired between Cormac and Kincaid runs deeper and closer to Kincaid's heart than I realized. He guarded the information from me so I wouldn't see that his perverse fascination with change and control had twisted his very soul into something irrevocably malignant.

"What about me?" I ask, drawing their attention from each other. "What's my offer? What will you give me?"

"You can watch it burn," Kincaid seethes. "Everything they took from you. Everything they controlled. You'll have a front-row seat to the dawn of a new age outside the Guild's control."

"A dawn of your control," I clarify.

"I'll share," he says simply.

"Fair offer, but I think I have a more enticing one," Cormac says, snapping his fingers.

The army of guards behind him shifts and out of the dark sea of black uniforms a girl emerges. She's fair-haired and wearing combat gear like Cormac, but her features are painted in lovely contrast to her fair skin, her eyes framed by dark lashes, and although her hair is pinned in perfect curls that frame her delicate face, a few tendrils have escaped, leaving curls behind her ears.

She's my age now, or close to it, and I see the startling evidence of the time dilation we've been fighting against. I told myself a few months wouldn't matter. How old would Amie be? Fifteen. Still a girl. But as she stands before me, I see a young woman. My equal. Her bright eyes recognize me. The last time I saw her, amid a crowd in Cypress, she believed she was someone else—Riya. A result of her being rewoven after my retrieval night. Cormac has been busy preparing for this moment by creating the perfect bait. He's dangling my sister in front of my eyes, knowing I'm too weak to resist.

"Amie," I whisper. I step forward tentatively, and my eyes meet Cormac's. He nods slightly to indicate it's okay, and the part of me that wants to embrace her accepts this, pushing against the smaller voice that reminds me that nothing with Cormac is free.

My arms find her, and she hugs me back. My heart swells, knowing she recognizes me, and for an instant I'm transported to the dark cellar a lifetime ago. She was shorter then, her head rested on my chest, and now it falls on my shoulder and I smell her soap-clean scent and I remember why I fought for her. Why I needed to cling to the hope of getting my sister back. Her bright chatter and mindless gossip. The way Amie's enthusiasm could be catching. She was the sun in my world. On Earth, she could be the sun for everyone. I'd give anything for that.

We stay like this for a long moment and no one speaks, no one breaks the spell, and I don't let myself think of Cormac or his devious intentions.

I pull back and study her face, looking for signs of fear, but I see happiness.

Joy.

"Have they hurt you?" I ask.

"No," she says with a laugh. "I'm training. It's marvelous. A Spinster. Me! Wouldn't Mom and Dad be surprised?"

I bite my tongue. I want to ask her what she thinks happened to our parents, but I know better. Cormac might let her remember me, but he'll have altered her memory.

"Do you remember anything?" I ask her, my eyes traveling from her to Cormac. I don't want to overstep this moment and have her ripped from me again. "Where have you been?"

Her eyelids flutter and she stares at me, like she's trying to dredge up a memory but cannot.

"She's been at the Coventry," Cormac says, prompting her and letting me in on the lie I need to embrace if I want to spare my sister the devastation of the truth about what happened to her and my parents after my retrieval.

"You've been happy there." My voice breaks on the words, my throat swelling over the lie, but I push it through. It's better if Amie doesn't remember Riya and the men who dragged her from the tunnel under our house. Someday I can tell her the truth, when she can understand it.

"I'm not without a heart," Cormac says.

"I never said you were," I respond coolly. "It's just a small one."

"Enough of this," Kincaid says, walking from his entourage toward me and my sister. "Take her with you. My men can handle the rest."

"Why would you think I would leave with you?" I ask him, pushing Amie behind me to keep her a safe distance from him.

"You want to go back with Cormac? Playing dress-up and weaving the world in a tower?" Kincaid asks.

"'Fetter strong madness in a silken thread,'" Cormac says.

"Well done, Cormac," Kincaid says. "But this thread of life is spun."

"Shakespeare suits any occasion," Cormac says, his eyes on me. "'His thread of life had not so soon decay'd.'"

Cormac's message is clear to me. Kincaid is rotten, and I know then what I have to do. I feel my consciousness fading down, focusing in on the basic world around me. The strands of Alcatraz are dark and the time here moves slowly. It's not frozen like in the buildings, but it's still otherworldly. Unnatural. The sooner I get off this island the better. But I'm not interested in the island, I'm interested in the man advancing on me. His composition reminds me of Albert's, and I'm sure if I looked at Cormac now with my newfound ability, I would see something similar—a mass of artificial threads neatly patched into place around the stagnant, staid individual time thread. Kincaid's time thread is worn, mixed with newer threads into a macabre patchwork. Away from the Guild's technology and labs, he would have used any means to survive. How many have died so he could live?

I step forward. I've seen it done. I can replicate it now, but to do so means I have to count on Cormac's army to back me up against Kincaid's entourage, but I know that's why Cormac has drawn us here together. Why he sent Valery to lead us to Kincaid. He's been planning this moment, orchestrating it from offstage. He knows I have a choice: destroy him or Kincaid. I can't have it both ways, but now I understand my choice, what's truly at risk. I could watch Arras fade into the sky, but I'm not jaded enough not to see the thousands of laughing schoolgirls, the mothers fawning over their infants, the couples learning to fall in love. I can't destroy them to destroy one man or the Guild. There's another way, and now I'm playing with a full deck.

I won't turn back.

The realization bursts inside me, flooding me with strength, and I lash out with the ferocity I felt the night I was attacked at the estate, my fingers grazing into Kincaid's very being and latching on to his time strands. I have to pull hard against its efforts to stay in place, but everything rides on this and it gives me a strength I didn't know I had. With a *pop*, it uncoils, pulling through him.

I ignore his agonized shriek and I watch the unwinding in its purest form. I don't see flesh or bone, merely the threads falling apart. The thin silver strand of his soul dissipating into the night sky along with the rest of him, until the golden strand of his life—his unnatural time in existence—fades from my fingers. By the time I regain full awareness, there's chaos around me and dust scattering at my feet.

Dust to dust, Kincaid.

FORTY-TWO

CORMAC'S MEN REACT AS I EXPECT THEM to, engaging in cross fire with the few Tailors that dare to take them on. Most of them are smart enough to make a run for it, and a few even escape the range of fire.

"Leave them," Cormac says flippantly. He has a smug look on his face, and I hate him for it. "I knew I could count on you to make the right decision, Adelice."

"What is right?" I muse out loud. I turn to Amie, but she's backed away from me, her face ashen. I'm a monster to her, but it doesn't matter. I knew that would happen. Better now than later.

"What did you do?" she gasps, one hand reaching to her throat.

"I made a decision," I say in a calm voice. Amie thinks she wants this life, but she needs to know what it really entails. She needs to see the dirty work—the horror behind the looms, the capability of the Guild, the choices she'll have to make.

"And now you have another one to make," Cormac says. "I can't leave you here, Adelice. You're dangerous."

"And you expect me to go with you? To turn my back on my friends and lie down in your clinic, so you can make me into the perfect wife?" I ask.

"Wife?" Amie mumbles, peeking from behind Cormac.

"Cormac and I are engaged, or didn't he tell you? Like he didn't tell you what he did to our mother? Our father?" I ask, but my voice is too cold and I regret speaking so cruelly to her. Amie's as much a victim of Cormac as any of us.

"Come, come, darling," Cormac says. "I have a proposal that will be more to your liking. Your life for hers. If you come with me, she can stay with your friends."

Amie stares at him, confused and hurt, but nothing about his proposition surprises me. Using Amie was always part of his endgame.

"And them?" I ask, gesturing to my friends. "They can go?"

"All of them, even your pitiful scientist. He's no good without you," Cormac says. So he knows. "Good move not telling Kincaid the truth that Einstein is incapable of completing the binding without you—that you were the true Whorl the whole time."

"I am getting smarter," I say absently. I don't trust Cormac to release them, but this isn't just about my choice anymore.

"I'll let her go, too, and you'll return with me. I've seen the light, Adelice," Cormac says. "I'm a changed man. Maybe becoming prime minister has done that. We'll sever the worlds. We have his notes. I'm not unreasonable. You come back to my world and I'll give them their own. We need you there, Adelice.

None of them can do this, and in exchange, I won't touch you."

It's a honeyed promise, coated in something sweet to make it palatable, but I taste its bitterness, the venom he's trying to hide. I merely nod in agreement.

"Adelice!" Erik calls from behind me, and I turn to look at him. He's watched this without a word until now, and his brother stands beside him looking set and determined. "You don't have to do this."

"Take her," I cry, pushing Amie toward him. She's sobbing, and I want to reassure her, but how can I after what she's seen?

Erik's face sinks and he nods. One last promise he'll make to me for a lifetime of promises we'll never keep.

"I'll come with you, Cormac, and if you so much as try to alter my hair, I will rip you in half," I warn him in a low voice.

Cormac's face contorts. He knows I can do it. He's seen it with his own eyes. It doesn't ensure my safety. It merely raises the stakes of our cat-and-mouse game. And I know something he doesn't. Something that could change everything. If it's true and Amie has been training, our small resistance will have everything it needs, save one thing. One thing I can give them: time.

Cormac offers his arm and I take it tentatively, not daring to cast one more look over my shoulder at what I'm leaving behind—a life I'll lose forever.

A bullet whistles overhead, cracking through the solemn moment, and I realize with horror it's come from behind me. I'm simultaneously furious and terrified. Enough blood has been spilled here today.

"Fool!" Cormac yells as his guards rush toward us. "She already lost one father to inane valor."

Dante. The wild card, who never quite wanted me, didn't know what to do with me, is fighting for me now. I whip toward them and see guns raised, but they can't take on all these men. Valery is helping Albert to safety, but Amie is nowhere to be seen. I twirl, trying to find her, but she's hidden from my sight, lost in the chaos of drawn weapons and gunfire. I choose to believe she has fled with Albert and Valery, disappeared into the night, beyond my vision—because I have one last thing to do.

I think of the house crumbling behind them, the severed time strands. Albert wanted me to remember, to look at this world for what it was, and I had. I unwound Kincaid but I studied everything first and I'm able to call it forth now as rifles click into place and fingers press down on triggers, and with a great and sudden fury, I pull against the world around me. This conflict won't be solved with guns, and I'd rather go with Cormac than watch the life seep from another friend, the only family I have left. I can stop the bloodshed with a single choice. My fingers find the right strand, long and wild, a lifetime of possibilities and it cracks against Earth, mutilating what lies in its wake, forming a long barrier of protection. I turn and instantly warp another spot and another, until I've surrounded us in protection. They can't reach me, but Cormac's men can't shoot them.

Their cries are muffled, and I see the look on Dante's face. Grim, but determined, and he waves for the rest of them to flee as I build my own cage. The only way to protect those I love is to cage myself with the Guild. I'm as dangerous to them as these men with guns.

Erik doesn't run with the others, he walks forward and places his hand on the rift between us. He can't reach through, and I can't touch him, but I let my hand rest there for a moment. One final goodbye.

"Go!" I choke at the words, and even if he can't hear them, I know he understands. He doesn't move, not even to breathe.

"I can't." The words are lost in the wind or muffled by the rift, but I see them.

And so I whisper back, carefully articulating each word, so that he understands: "'Love is not love which alters when it alteration finds.'"

He bites his lip and I see the desperation in his eyes, but then Jost comes and pulls Erik away. Jost pushes Erik away from the cage of light and time I've created.

Jost turns toward me, and although his words are lost to the warp between us, I understand them. "Find her."

I give him a determined nod. Somehow I will protect Sebrina for him.

He raises his hand and places his fist over his heart before he turns away from me—perhaps forever.

"I have missed your flair for the dramatic," Cormac says. "A little unnecessary, but if you can't control your men—"

"I'm not interested in controlling anyone," I spit at him.

"You have a world to control, so I'd reevaluate that," he says.

So this is how it will be—the niceties abandoned. A group of men cuff me and lead me toward the waiting aeroship.

"I could still kill them, you know," Cormac calls, pulling a flask from his vest. "But I won't, and then you will see that I can be merciful."

I twist my mouth, weighing my words, searching for the right thing to say, and in the end it's simply, "Thank you."

"Better manners every day," he murmurs. "Take her to my quarters, and put her hands in gages. We don't want her wandering off."

The inside of the aeroship is voluminous and austere. Great metal ribs arch overhead, and my footsteps echo across the metal flooring as the guards lead me. My hands are secured with gages, inflexible gloves that prevent the use of my hands. It occurs to me as my gaze sweeps over the thin metal walls and pressed-glass windows that I could try to escape, that I should try to escape. I'm not interested though. Cormac has no idea he's taking me exactly where I need to go.

The final words Einstein whispered to me as the house crumbled echo through my mind: *Destroy the looms. If you choose this path, others will follow you as Whorl. Embrace and trust them, but know their hearts. As you must know your own.*

I've made my choice. My destiny is one of my own choosing.

Standing, I wander to the small round window and peer out. The aeroship glides along a thin series of strands from the Interface. The world beneath us is made of blocks, gray and black in the lack of light. I imagine the boat, fighting the waves, pushing forward against the tide, and peace settles over me.

"It's lovely."

Cormac's voice startles me, and I turn to find him in the doorway.

"Lovely," I repeat in a flat voice.

"You must enjoy it. The Interface," he says. He crosses to a chair and pours himself a drink. The scene is familiar, but I'm not the girl Cormac used to order around anymore.

"I'm not very interested in it," I say to him.

"The energy doesn't call to you? The pure, brutal force of the universe?" Cormac takes a long swig, studying me over the rim of his glass. "I doubt that. Not up here, this close to it."

I look back out the window at the tangle of threads the ship gathers as it moves across the sky as though it's a fly caught in a spiderweb.

"So what now?" I ask. "A remap? An alteration? A wedding?"

"We will work together for a mutually beneficial solution," Cormac says. "I'm a man of my word, Adelice."

"Since when?"

"I'm not Kincaid. I have no interest in destruction," he snarls. "We can work together. I'll make you immortal."

I nod, but I know we're both lying to ourselves as much as to each other. I'm unwilling to turn a blind eye to how the Guild wants to control the world. "I will help you sever and bind Arras and Earth, but I have no interest in immortality."

"That's your foolish youth talking." He sets down the glass, abandoning it in favor of lecturing me. "Talk to me in your thirties, when time's winged chariot draws near."

"My answer will be the same," I say.

"I doubt that."

"I only have one goal in life."

Cormac's head cocks to the side, inviting me to share it.

"To never be like you," I say.

His smile doesn't slip, but he pushes up from his chair. "You are powerful, Adelice. It's time to accept that. Arras needs you more than ever. Things are happening there and I need you to help me achieve peace."

"Peace," I echo, wondering if he knows what that means. I'm not sure I even know.

"Think about it," Cormac says. "For now, please excuse me."

"Need a trip to the little boys' room?" I ask.

"I have missed your wit." He chuckles and opens the door.

She's standing in the hall, waiting, her arms crossed protectively against her small chest. She bites her lip when she sees me, her eyes finding the floor rather than facing me. My fingers flex against the gages that imprison them.

"This is what you call being a man of your word?" I roar as he takes Amie's arm.

"I said she could go," Cormac says, "but *she* chose to stay."

"You promised." My words are as weak as the final thread holding together a seam.

"You can't have it both ways," he says. Amie won't meet my eyes. "You can't claim your own free will and strip someone else of it."

"You do it all the time," I point out. I walk as calmly as I can toward the door.

Amie steps behind Cormac and my heart sinks.

"Ames," I say softly. "You have a choice. You always will. But this life is the wrong one."

"I made my choice," she says.

I swallow back the words that I want to unleash. *It's the wrong choice.*

"I'll be here if you change your mind," I offer instead.

"I won't." Her tone is set. Determined. "You're a freak."

Cormac's black eyes meet mine as she turns to him. He pats

her shoulder and leads her away, and I watch as my sister chooses the monster of my nightmares.

Outside the window, the Interface grows thicker. Light flashes and sizzles across the pane as the sky shifts to blinding white. On the other side lies a darkness I can finally face and a destiny I will control even as the web consumes me, taking me back to the Coventry.

Acknowledgments

So many people helped and supported me in writing this book, and I am and will continue to be grateful for their insights, advice, and encouragement.

Special thanks to the spectacular team at Macmillan Children's Publishing Group and Farrar Straus Giroux for their enthusiasm and passion for this project. I am so lucky to have an editor that knows her stuff. Thank you, Janine O'Malley. I'm extra lucky to have a fantastic publisher in Simon Boughton. Thank you to my publicist, Allison Verost, who never ceases to amaze me and who is the best traveling companion a girl could ask for. A big thanks to Ksenia Winnicki, Caitlin Sweeny, Kate Lied, Joy Peskin, Molly Brouillette, Angus Killick, and Elizabeth Fithian for all their hard work on this book.

I wouldn't be here today without the guidance of my agent, Mollie Glick, and the team at Foundry Literary, especially Rachel Hecht and Stephanie Abou. Thanks to Katie Hamblin for her amazing notes and mad editorial skills.

Thank you to the fine folks at the Office of Letters and

Light, especially Grant Faulkner and Chris Baty, for teaching me that I can write an entire book start to finish. And to Rainy Day Books, Mysterycape, and all the other booksellers and librarians who have made a home for me in their store and libraries. Thank you to Arielle Eckstut and David Sterry for being endless sources of wit and wisdom.

A lot of fellow authors helped me through my debut year and with writing this book. I am so blessed to be part of such a warm and welcoming community. Thank you to: Sarah Maas, Jessica Brody, Jay Kristoff, and Josin McQuein, as well as to the League of Extraordinary Writers, especially our fearless (unofficial) leader Beth Revis. To my Fierce companions— Leigh Bardugo, Marie Rutkoski, and Caragh O'Brien—thanks for the escalator help and so much more.

I could not have written this book without Bethany Hagen, Laura Barnes, Robin Lucas, Kalen O'Donnell, and Michelle Hodkin. Thanks for the phone calls, the cheering, and the late night writing dates. To all of my WrAHMS, you are more dear to me than you know.

And to my family, who pulled together this year to make my dream a reality: thank you for being there for me on this unexpected journey. James and Sydney, I hope I didn't maim you in the process of writing this book, but I promise to put aside some of the profit for your future therapy bills. And to Josh: you are the light that guides me out of dark places. Thank you.

KEEP READING FOR

ALTERED

BONUS MATERIALS

GOFISH

GENNIFER ALBIN

What did you want to be when you grew up?

I saw a production of *Swan Lake* when I was five and decided I was going to be a ballerina. But my family couldn't afford lessons. Then I was going to be a figure skater, which turned out was also a very expensive profession. So I settled on actress. The funny thing is that all through my childhood, I was writing books while I dreamt about these exotic vocations.

When did you realize you wanted to be a writer?

I think I always wanted to be a writer, but I didn't know it until college. I decided to go to grad school so I would have the flexibility to write books in my free time (insert high-pitched, maniacal cackle). There is no free time in grad school. Although, I did write a few first chapters that I abandoned.

What's your most embarrassing childhood memory?

Because I was quite convinced I could be an actress, I decided I was capable of all sorts of interesting feats: karate, dance, saving the world. As such, I was given the name Hotshot by a group of older girls.

What was your first job, and what was your "worst" job?
My first job was working at the mall's 5-7-9. I followed that up by working at Camelot Music (also at the mall), and that was my worst job. The manager was ten shades of crazy. Both my best friend and I walked out on the job after a month!

What book is on your nightstand now?
I just finished *Ruby Red* by Kerstin Gier, and now I'm starting a few books that haven't been published yet.

How did you celebrate publishing your first book?
A bunch of my friends and family flew in and we had a big book signing with Rainy Day Books. It reminded me a lot of getting married, right down to the very fancy dress I wore for the event. Then I took off for a book tour the next morning!

Where do you write your books?
Wherever I can! I have a pretty sweet home office, but sometimes I need to go up to the coffee shop. A fair amount of book two and three in the Crewel World trilogy were written on airplanes, which is always interesting. There's really not enough elbow room to type and I end up looking like a T. rex while I'm doing it.

What sparked your imagination for the Crewel World series?
There's an amazing painting called *Embroidering the Earth's Mantle* by Remedios Varo in which girls in a tower are sewing a tapestry that flows out and becomes the world. I've loved that painting since college, so I started writing about one of the girls, except one girl doesn't like her job and wants to escape.

How do you relate to Adelice?
I think Adelice and I have some things in common. We both have smart mouths that can get us into trouble and we can both rock red hair, but Ad is more stoic than I am. She tends to bottle up her

emotions rather than feel them. I can't blame her. She was taught by her parents to hide things, and I think for her, sometimes she hides her own feelings to protect herself.

If you were in Adelice's world, how might you fit in?
I'm guessing I would be a lot like Meria, Ad's mom. On one hand, I think I would be aware of the corruption in my world. On the other, and as a mom myself, I would be pretty concerned with protecting my kids even while struggling with those injustices around me.

Do you know how to knit or sew?
I sew pretty well, but I don't knit. I actually have sewn throughout the drafting process for all three books.

I tried to crochet a baby hat once for my newborn daughter, but it popped right off her head. Since then I've stuck with a needle and thread.

What challenges did you face while writing a follow-up to _Crewel_?
At the end of _Crewel_, Adelice has a lot of choices in front of her. So while that meant that I had a lot of ideas, it also meant that _I_ had a lot of choices. While writing _Altered_, I sometimes took the story in a direction that didn't work and I had to go back and rewrite.

Then there's the fact that _Altered_ is maybe even more ambitious than _Crewel_ in terms of the world and how it functions. There was a lot of research and brainstorming and fine-tuning to get that to work.

What was the world-building process like when writing the Crewel World series? What inspired the world of the series?
Creating the Crewel World really meant adding in layers and layers of details: descriptions of their buildings, how the women and men dressed, turns of phrase. That aspect of writing the series required the most fine-tuning. I ended up putting lots of things I

loved into the series for aesthetic reasons. I love the glamour of old-style Hollywood, so I mixed it with a touch of noir to heighten the feeling of danger. Of course, the science fiction aspects of the world played a huge part in building the world, too. It's fun to create new technology, but you have to invent technology that fits within the perimeters of your world.

You mentioned that the painting *Embroidering the Earth's Mantel* by Remedios Varo inspired *Crewel*. Were there any other mythological or artistic sources that inspired the world of this series?
Most of my inspirations were historical. I had a kernel of an idea and I started asking a lot of what-if questions.

I do have a Pinterest board that is my best friend! I often collect images that I draw on for inspiration in descriptions.

What was your favorite part about writing the Crewel World series? What was the most challenging aspect of writing it?
I'm going to answer these two together because it's the same thing. I was so fortunate to get to write three books. Because of that, I got to know my characters and develop my world. It was the most challenging thing I've ever done and the most rewarding. I learned a lot about myself doing it.

The characters became very real to me and so did the world. I'm so thankful that I got to spend so much time with them.

What challenges do you face in the writing process, and how do you overcome them?
Some days I don't feel like writing. Those are the hardest days, but I have to force myself to work and things get better. Most of my other big challenges, like plot issues, I discuss with my writing friends, my agent, and my editor. Talking through problems is the best way for me to see how to fix them.

Which of your characters is most like you?
Admittedly, Adelice. I had a bad tendency to talk back to my teachers. She totally gets that from me.

What was your favorite book when you were a kid? Do you have a favorite book now?
When I was a kid, I adored *Anne of Green Gables*. It's not a coincidence that my heroine has red hair and an A-name that ends with E! My favorite books will always be Harry Potter.

What's your favorite TV show or movie?
My heart will always belong to *Gilmore Girls*, but lately I've become deeply smitten with *Doctor Who*. It's the only show I bother to watch anymore.

If you could travel in time, where would you go and what would you do?
Can I travel throughout space and time? Is there a TARDIS involved? That's my idea of fantasy travel.

What's the best advice you have ever received about writing?
Sit on your butt and do it. There's a lot of great craft advice out there, but that advice is always relevant to every project.

What advice do you wish someone had given you when you were younger?
Don't listen to advice.

What do you consider to be your greatest accomplishment?
My kids. I think all moms say that, but my kids are going to change the world. I just know it.

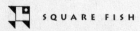

THINGS HAVE CHANGED behind the walls of
the Coventry. When Adelice returns to Arras, she must
choose between an unimaginable alliance and a deadly
war that could destroy everyone she loves.

Keep reading for a sneak peak of *Unraveled*,
the final book in the Crewel World series.

THE BLACKNESS YAWNS ACROSS THE SKY, extending like a floating abyss above us. I thought I knew darkness on Earth, but this is all-encompassing. Allia, the capital of the Eastern Sector, is rendered skeletal in the glow of emergency lights. It's a sketch of a metro that can't be real. If I reached out now to touch it, I'm sure my hands would meet with paper. Only the flicker of emergency lanterns gives the metro depth and dimension. I stop in the rivet, hesitant to enter this place, but Cormac grabs my arm and pulls me through.

"The power grids are offline, sir," an officer informs Cormac as he hands him a pair of goggles. "These are night optical devices that will allow you to see as we travel. They are equipped with infrared technology and will display heat signatures in orange."

"Heat signatures?" a young officer pipes up.

"Humans. Animals. Anything that's alive," his superior explains.

I take a deep breath, wondering what we'll find in the streets.

The officer passes out goggles to each of us. I'm fastening mine over my forehead when Hannox snatches them off me.

"Sir," he barks at Cormac. "I think Miss Lewys should stay behind with the guard."

"I should come along," I butt in, even though I'm not sure why I'm arguing. I'm not exactly eager to explore the dark corridors of the Eastern Sector. Maybe it's that I don't like being told what to do.

"That sounds like an excellent idea," Hannox mocks. He moves toward me and jabs a finger at my chest. "Let's take the *rebel* Creweler in to meet the *rebel* Spinsters."

"I didn't bring my *rebel* handbook to distribute, so I think it will be okay." I cross my arms over my chest, and we both turn to Cormac for his opinion on the matter.

"She won't be running around unsupervised," Cormac says, and I smirk at Hannox. He might have known Cormac for two hundred years, but I'm the one Cormac wants to keep happy.

"It's a precarious enough situation without dragging her into it," Hannox reminds him.

"Then veil her," Cormac orders. Hannox opens his mouth, but Cormac holds up his hand. "I'm not interested in debating this. The looms in the Eastern Sector have been disabled, but if you think her presence in the weave is a threat and you want to veil her, do it. Otherwise, get her in tactical gear."

"I'm not much of a shot," I tell him. In truth, I hate guns.

"I don't want you in tactical gear to use you as a sniper," Cormac says with a huff. "I only thought it would be nice if you survived until our wedding day."

Hannox mutters something under his breath.

Part of me wants to flash him my ring. The part of me that's feeling smug about winning out over the bossy Hannox. But since my engagement to Cormac is something I'm neither proud of nor looking forward to, I keep my fingers to myself.

"And her hands?" Hannox asks.

"Gages won't be necessary. Will they, Adelice?" Cormac says. "We've come to an arrangement."

The weight of the ring is heavy on my left hand as he says it. I've agreed to this, which means small mercies like unbound hands and trips into rioting sectors. I'm not sure if I'm coming out on the better end of this bargain.

"It's a bad idea," Hannox says one final time, but Cormac's angry look silences him.

When Cormac walks away, Hannox hands me tactical gear without offering to help me put it on. I struggle into the thick black vest and scratchy nylon pants, hooking and strapping while officers rush around me. The goggles pinch my nose, so I leave them perched on my forehead. It isn't long before the tactical teams in the sector meet us at the mouth of the rivet. Cormac speaks to them in a hushed voice, and I can't hear the explanation of what's going on within the sector.

When we finally set out to view the area, the streets are empty. Given the near panic of the ship's crew during our flight, I expected looting or mobs of angry people. But the capital is as still as death.

"I thought you said there was rioting," I say to Cormac as we ride through in a large motocade. I see no one, even though our van shines floodlights onto our path.

"There will be rioting soon," Cormac says.

"How do you know that?" I ask him.

"Experience." His mouth twists into a rueful smile.

"Oh." Had there been other riots? How had they started? What had he done in those metros? I want to ask him these questions, but I keep quiet, listening to the terse conversations between the officers in the truck and paying attention to Cormac's reaction to the empty streets.

A blackout happened once in Romen when I was a little girl. There was no warning. No way to anticipate what was about to happen. Amie was only a toddler, and we were both outside playing in the yard while our mother finished the dinner dishes. I picked blades of grass and held them to my lips, blowing a stream of air across them to create a high-pitched whistle. Amie laughed and clapped her hands while our mother watched us from the kitchen window. And then there was no sky.

It was as simple as that. In one moment I sat under the rose-tinged hues of sunset, entertaining my sister, and in the next, the world was black, blanketed in a sudden and absolute night. I remember the sounds of screaming, the wails of terror echoing through the darkness, but it wasn't until my mother lifted me onto her hip, Amie perched on the other side of her, that she shushed me with a gentle: "Quiet now. It will be okay, darlings."

I'd lost my screams in the dark, unaware that the sounds I heard came from my own throat. Dad met us at the stairs, and mercifully, there was still power in the house. But none of us could tear our eyes from the missing sky. It was the absence of it—how half of our reality had vanished—that made it hard to swallow. Dad ushered us into the basement and headed back upstairs as we huddled in our mother's arms against the wall.

I ran my fingers along the bricks behind her back. They were solid. They were real. They wouldn't disappear.

I had never touched the sky. It was too far from the ground, even on my tiptoes, even when the programmed clouds floated so close that they seemed within reach.

"Are the clouds real?" I asked my mother.

She blinked at the question. "Of course, Ad."

"But we can't touch them," I pointed out. I could touch this wall. I could touch her and Amie. I knew they were flesh and blood and stone, but I didn't know what a cloud was or why the sky was sometimes brilliant blue and other times dull gray.

Now I realize my mother could have explained more about the looms and why this was happening. Instead she simply said, "No, *we* cannot."

It wasn't an answer, even then. It was a clue. It was a different way to look at my world. *We* could not, according to my mother, but someone else could. It was the answer that stilled my breath as a girl. It stills my breath now.

Right now, in this metro, families wait behind drawn curtains or in cramped basements, and parents offer words of reassurance. But they repeat the practiced lies of generations: *This is normal. It will pass quickly. Don't be afraid.* And I know they say those things not merely to calm their children and stop the onslaught of innocent questions, but also to calm themselves. The population of the Eastern Sector has every right to believe this is a blip, a temporary issue that will resolve itself soon. But it's been hours since we received the news of the blackout and *soon* must feel like a lie even to those saying it now.

"Halt!" an officer yells, and the van squeals to a stop. In the middle of the road stands a man. He doesn't blink as our bright lights wash over him. It's as though he's daring us to drive forward and crush him.

A group of officers scramble out of the transport with their weapons drawn.

"PC!" an officer orders, but the man doesn't reach for anything.

"What's happening?" the man calls out instead.

"We need to see your privilege card," the officer says, ignoring the man's question.

The man steps forward, trying to see into the transport, but he's stopped with the butt of a rifle.

"My wife and children are scared. The sky has been dark for hours," he says.

"Return to your home," the officer says.

I catch my breath, silently willing the man to listen.

To stop asking questions.

"Your job is to protect us," the man says, shoving a finger in the officer's face. "I want answers."

"Sir, step back." His warning is ripe with violence.

"My daughter is four years old," the man says. "She wants to know where the sky has gone."

Nothing about the man seems dangerous. He's young but starting to bald and a sheen of nervous sweat glimmers on his skin. His questions come from a place of confusion, not rebellion. He's simply scared, and I can't blame him.

Cormac steps in front of the van, and I blink. He'd been beside me a moment ago.

"Tell her the sky will return soon," Cormac says. His back is to me, but I can imagine his practiced smile.

"Prime Minister," the man says, and I hear the shock in his voice.

"Go home," the officer next to the man orders again. The command is more insistent, almost nervous.

"No!" he refuses, and my pulse jumps up a notch. More rifles train on the man.

Go home, I beg him silently.

"I'm a citizen of Arras and I deserve to know what's going on," the man says.

A burst of laughter slices through the air, but it doesn't break the tense mood. Cormac is laughing. He finds this funny. A warning bell goes off in my mind.

"I'm not sure what's funny," the man says, but it's not confusion coloring his voice anymore. Now he's angry.

"I deserve to know what's going on," Cormac repeats mockingly. He strides up to the man and places his hands on his shoulders. "You really want to know?"

I don't hear the man say yes, but I dread where this is going. Before I realize it, I'm out of the van and moving toward them. An officer grabs me by the waist and my hands lash out toward his strands, but I pull them back before I hurt him.

"Your entire world is a lie," Cormac tells the man. "The Spinsters have abandoned you, and you're all going to die."

The man steps back and stares at him and so do I. Doesn't he know his men will talk about this?

Before I can process Cormac's reckless indifference, the man lunges toward Cormac, who sidesteps him. A split second later a shot shatters the air, hitting the man squarely in the chest.

"No!" I scream, pulling loose from the officer's arms and running toward the man.

He stumbles back, a fleeting look of surprise crossing his face. By the time I reach him, there's a pool of blood under his body. I press my hands to the wound and he covers them with his own.

"My daughter." His words are punctuated by gasps as airy as oxygen leaking from a balloon.

"I'll protect her," I promise him, but he doesn't hear me. He stares at me with unseeing eyes, glassy as the still ocean.

"Get rid of that," Cormac orders as he heads back toward the motocade. "I want us at the capitol building in five minutes."

He doesn't look at me when I follow him, but he waits for me to climb into the transport. Instead I stand in front of the van and plant my hands on my hips.

"That was unnecessary," I say. My voice is shaky, betraying my rage.

"You have blood on your hands," he says, gesturing for someone to bring me a rag.

"Someone should have blood on their hands tonight," I say in a low voice. "It should be you."

"That's what I do to traitors," Cormac says. "You'd do well to remember that."

"Then do it to me," I dare him, smacking my chest with my fist so he knows where to aim. "Because that man asked a question, and you killed him. *I ripped apart your world, Cormac.* It's only fair."

"Don't tempt me," he snarls. But it's an empty threat. Instead he pushes me aside and climbs into the transport. Cormac needs me to cooperate with his wedding plan to distract Arras and prevent future episodes like this in the other sectors.

Of course, he's after more than a bride. He's hoping for a powerful ally. But it will take more than threats to control me.

I don't follow him. Instead I watch as they drag the man's body to the side of the street. They don't bother to bag him like they did my father. In a few hours, his wife will come looking for him. She'll bring their daughter, because no mother would leave her young child alone in a blackout. Maybe she'll find him dead in the street, with no clue what happened to him. And then she'll turn to the Guild for security and hope. Never knowing it was they who betrayed her.

I've seen my father's blood pooling on the floor. I dream of it. The sticky blood, black like tar, that can't ever be erased. I'll live the rest of my life with that memory—burned into my mind at sixteen.

His daughter will live with death, too. She won't even have a childhood.

But as we move through the Eastern Sector another thought sends a chill down my spine.

The girl probably won't have to live with the memory for long.